EVERY
WAKING
HOUR

Also by Joanna Schaffhausen:

The Vanishing Season
No Mercy
All the Best Lies

EVERY WAKING HOUR

Joanna Schaffhausen

MINOTAUR
BOOKS

NEW YORK

First published in the United States by Minotaur Books, an imprint of St. Martin's Publishing Group

EVERY WAKING HOUR. Copyright © 2020 by Joanna Schaffhausen. All rights reserved. Printed in the United States of America. For information, address St. Martin's Publishing Group, 120 Broadway, New York, NY 10271.

www.minotaurbooks.com

Library of Congress Cataloging-in-Publication Data

Names: Schaffhausen, Joanna, author.
Title: Every waking hour / Joanna Schaffhausen.
Description: First edition. | New York : Minotaur Books, 2021. | Series: Ellery Hathaway; 4
Identifiers: LCCN 2020035310 | ISBN 9781250249654 (hardcover) | ISBN 9781250249661 (ebook)
Subjects: GSAFD: Mystery fiction.
Classification: LCC PS3619.C3253 E94 2021 | DDC 813/.6—dc23
LC record available at https://lccn.loc.gov/2020035310

Our books may be purchased in bulk for promotional, educational, or business use. Please contact your local bookseller or the Macmillan Corporate and Premium Sales Department at 1-800-221-7945, extension 5442, or by email at MacmillanSpecialMarkets@macmillan.com.

First Edition: 2020

10 9 8 7 6 5 4 3 2 1

For Eleanor.
You are never so lost that I won't find you.

EVERY
WAKING
HOUR

1

"Wait, you're just going to leave us here? Alone?" Ellery Hathaway had faced down serial killers and lived to tell about it, but she felt a cold trickle of fear as she glanced at the lone child playing nearby on the grass. "I believe your ex-wife specifically forbade this proposition. In writing. With her attorney."

Reed laid a comforting hand on her arm. "You're not alone. There are fifty thousand people here," he replied, gesturing at the noisy street fair around them. "And not one of them is my ex-wife, so I don't think you have to worry. Also, I'm getting lunch, not jetting off to Guam. It'll be ten minutes at the most." He nodded down the road in the direction of the taco stand they had passed earlier.

"But I don't know anything about kids."

"Think of Tula as having more or less the same needs as your dog, only with less fur."

Reed's seven-year-old daughter, Tula, frolicked with Ellery's basset hound, Speed Bump. Bump had cheerfully gone belly-up, tail thumping in lazy fashion as Tula sung nonsense to him and scratched his barrel chest. Ellery furrowed her brow. "Do you have a leash for her?"

Reed laughed, but she was only half-joking. She'd met Tula only once before and had no idea how to talk to her or any other person under the age of ten. She'd barely had a childhood herself. She'd agreed to this outing because Reed plainly hungered for family and she had to figure out if she fit into it. One thing she was learning fast was that Tula paid attention to conversations even when it appeared she wasn't listening. She turned guileless brown eyes up at them. "She's right, Daddy. Mama said I shouldn't be alone with Ellery on account that she's got emotional problems."

Ellery put a hand on her hip. "Your mother," she began tartly, but Reed cut her off with a look. "Your mother is a wise woman," she muttered instead.

Reed rewarded her with a smile and reached out to squeeze Ellery's clammy hand. "Mama hasn't met Ellery," he said to Tula. "She doesn't know her like Daddy does." He stepped closer into Ellery's personal space, an intimacy she still couldn't quite believe she permitted. They had been seeing each other since their adventure in Las Vegas six months ago, but Ellery couldn't even use the word "boyfriend" yet. Reed, meanwhile, had started adding family members to the mix. "If this is going to work," he murmured, "you'll have to be alone with her sometime. I promise she doesn't bite."

"Yeah, well, maybe I do." Ellery turned her face away. If this was going to work, she'd have to become a different person. One who didn't wake up breathless from a nightmare about being nailed into a closet. One who didn't freeze up the minute someone touched her. One who was comfortable carrying the little pink sparkly purse that Reed thrust into her hands.

"Hold this. I'll be back with tacos before you know it," he said, pecking her cheek before disappearing into the crowd.

Ellery held the offending purse away from her body. It was surprisingly heavy. "What does a second grader need a purse for, anyway?" she asked Tula.

"For my ponies," Tula replied as though this were an obvious answer.

Ellery risked a look inside and found a dozen plastic horses in various riotous colors staring back up at her. She snapped the thing shut again with a shudder. "So, what else does your mother say about me?"

Tula giggled as Bump's enormous tongue licked her entire forearm. "She says Daddy's only with you because of his God complex. On account of he saved you when you were a kid." She tilted her head at Ellery. "What's a God complex?"

"I, uh . . ." Ellery looked frantically through the crowd for Reed, but he'd only been gone for two minutes. There were so many people on Boston's Common that they seemed to inch along as one giant organism, digesting all the air around them. Claustrophobia threatened to overwhelm her and she closed her eyes to block out the sea of slowly moving bodies. She took several deep breaths and reminded herself she was doing this for Reed. She had to pretend to be socially normal for at least a few hours. Smile at strangers. Not go for her gun at the sharp pop of a child's balloon. Her heartbeat still skittered, but she pasted a smile on her face and resolved to make small talk with Reed's daughter. When she turned around, she found a herd of redheaded children had descended upon her dog. Bump leaped to his feet, woofing and jumping between the kids. She could barely see him amid the chaos. "Hey, wait a second." She tried to grab for the leash as the swarm of children seemed to grow around her.

"His ears are so long!"

"I want a puppy like this."

"Hey, he ate my ice-cream cone. Dad! This dog stole my ice cream!"

A man came huffing over the hill, his round face red like a lobster. "Kieran, Solange! Get away from that dog. Boyd, you know you have allergies." The small one with the freckles increased his carping about the ice-cream cone.

"He ate it! He ate it in one gulp."

The man confronted Ellery. "Did your mutt steal my son's ice-cream cone?"

Ellery eyed Bump, who sat amid the children grinning with his tongue hanging out, a satisfied gleam in his eyes. "I'm going to go with 'yes.'"

"You shouldn't bring him around people if he isn't better trained."

"I could say the same thing about your kids." One of them had placed Bump in a headlock. Before the man could wind up his outrage even further, Ellery put up her hands. "Look, I'll give you the money for another cone, okay?" Anything to make the noise and grabby hands go away.

The man took in the pink sequined bag Ellery had slung over her shoulder. "Fine. It was five dollars."

"Five dollars. For a kiddie cone?" Ellery followed his gaze to the purse as she groped in her back pocket for her wallet, which she stopped doing the moment she realized she'd lost sight of Tula. She called the girl's name, but no brown head popped up amid the sea of red. "Tula," she said more sharply. She started sifting the children bodily as she searched out Reed's daughter. "Tula!"

"Hey, what about my money?" the man demanded as Ellery jogged off, Bump hot on her heels. The street fair filled up all areas of the Boston Common, booths jammed together and throngs of people in front of each one. Ellery threaded her way through the crowds, peering at each child for any sign of recognition. Tula had worn a bright orange T-shirt, and Ellery searched for any flash of it as she pushed onward. Her panic rose with each passing second.

She yelled Tula's name as loud as she could, the rising fear in her throat making her voice turn shrill. People turned to stare. Her heart seemed to go liquid inside her chest, it was beating so fast. She doubled back in case Tula had reappeared by the trees where they'd been waiting, but there was no sign of her. Ellery felt dizzy as she tried to think of what to do next. Go find Reed? Alert the police? She was the police. "He's going to kill me," she said to Bump, who whined and sat on her feet. Desperate now, Ellery nudged him off and went to stand on the nearest bench to get a better view. The crowd looked like a slow-moving river. Tula was small, only about four feet high. Ellery would never be able to see her like this.

Bump barked up at her with enthusiasm, as if asking why she had grown so tall. "Tula," she told him. "We're trying to find Tula."

He woofed again and wagged his tail. His considerable nose dropped to the ground and he began to snuffle. Watching him, Ellery seized on a slim hope. Bump was no trained working dog, but he'd been born with a nose that wouldn't quit. "Tula," she told him again, jumping down from the bench and shoving the purse under his nose. "Find Tula."

She grabbed his leash and her arm jerked as he set off resolutely in a northward direction. He took a meandering route directly through the crowds. She hoped like hell that he was on the scent of the little girl and not a hot dog. He veered behind some garbage cans, past a water fountain, and into some bushes. He crashed his large front paws right through the branches, leaping up and barking. "Ha, ha! You found me! Good boy." Tula sprang up with delight, accepting the dog kisses on the side of her face, and Ellery sagged with relief.

"Yes, good boy. You, however . . ." Ellery grabbed the girl's arm and dragged her out of the brush. "You scared the crap out of me. What are you doing running off like that?"

"We're playing hide-and-seek, him and me," she said as she patted Bump's head.

"Not without telling me first, you're not. Come on, let's go find your father before he literally does call in the rest of the FBI."

Tula stood firm. "You're not the boss of me."

"Listen, bad things can happen to kids who go off without their grown-ups. You have to stay with me, at least until your father comes back."

Tula tilted her head with interest. "Is that what happened to you? How you got those marks on your arm?"

Ellery regretted wearing the T-shirt that showed off her scars. She was trying not to hide them as much, trying not to care. Wearing her violent history on her body gave the rest of the world license to look and ask questions she'd rather not answer. She sure as hell didn't want to be having this conversation with a seven-year-old.

"There you are!" Reed appeared, tall and lanky, no sweat visible on him. The man defied the laws of physics. He held a paper sack of food and a cardboard tray of drinks.

"Daddy!" Tula ran up and hugged him. "Ellery and I played hide-and-seek."

"You did? That's wonderful." Reed grinned and looked so pleased that Ellery pursed her lips and said nothing. Her terror was just starting to fade, evaporating off her like the sheen of perspiration that had covered her body during the frantic search. She had for the first time a taste of what her mother must have felt when Ellery disappeared, and the acid at the back of her throat said this parenting gig was not for her.

Reed set up a picnic for them on a spare patch of grass and Bump eagerly dragged Ellery toward the scent of more food. She took a careful seat some distance from the father-daughter duo, tuning out their chatter as she tried to calm her frazzled nerves enough to choke down a taco. "Ellery?" Reed furrowed his brow at her. "Are you okay?"

She opened her mouth, not sure of what might come out, but before she could say anything, a woman came running past them, screeching at top volume. "Help! She's gone! Someone, please help me!"

Reed leaped up like some superhero and dashed after her. Ellery saw him catch up to her, show off his FBI credentials, and begin walking her back to where she and Tula sat with the lunch. "If that lady lost her daughter, my daddy'll find her," Tula said to Ellery. "He can find anyone."

"I know he can." The entire city of Chicago had turned out to look for Ellery, but Reed was the one who found her, three days gone and half-dead on the floor of Coben's closet.

"Her name is Chloe. Chloe Lockhart," the woman was saying. Her face was streaked with tears and her chin wobbled as she spoke. "I'm her nanny—my name is Margery—but she calls me 'Mimi' just like my grandbabies do. Oh, I don't know how I'm supposed to tell her parents about this."

Ellery rose to join Reed.

"Where and when did you last see Chloe?" he asked Margery.

"Almost an hour ago, way over on that side of the Common," she replied, pointing. "She wanted to buy a pretzel and it was just a few trucks down from where I was sitting on the bench. I said I'd go with her, but she begged me to let her go alone and I didn't want to give up our spot. She said she's not a baby, and I didn't see the harm so I said okay. Why, why, why didn't I just go with her?"

"Probably she's just wandered off to watch the acrobats or listen to the band," Reed said. "But we can organize a search."

"No, I don't think so. I think something's happened to her." Margery waved her cell phone at him. "I've been calling and texting, and she hasn't answered. That girl's phone lives in her left hand like it was born attached. Plus, she knows better than to ignore me."

"Some areas are awful loud right now," Ellery said, her own voice raised over the din. "She may not hear the phone. What is Chloe wearing today?"

Margery sniffed. "Here, I can show you." She called up a picture of a blond girl wearing jean shorts with silver stars studded on them, a pale pink T-shirt, and Teva sandals. A beaded bracelet encircled her left wrist. "Please, I'll do anything. Just help me find her."

Reed looked to Ellery. "Will you stay with Tula while I make some calls?"

This was her territory, not his. "How about you stay with Tula and Bump while I make some calls?" She handed him the leash and took out her shield to show Margery. "Detective Hathaway, Boston PD. This is a local matter right now, and our officers are best equipped to handle it. Agent Markham is just visiting from Virginia." Reed frowned at her but didn't argue as she began leading Margery away.

"Tell me more about Chloe. If she were to run off, where would she go?"

Margery looked perplexed. "She wouldn't run off. She's only twelve. Besides, Chloe's a good girl."

"I'm sure she is. I just want to know what her interests are—favorite foods, music, that sort of thing?" Boston at that moment was a veritable buffet of sights, smells, and sounds. Ellery wanted to narrow her search.

"I—I don't know. Normal girl stuff. She loves her dog, Snuffles. Video games. Makeup that she's not supposed to wear. She'll eat any kind of junk food." The woman turned helplessly in a circle at all the vendors with their ice cream, candy, and deep-fried meat on a stick. Nearby, a toddler began wailing as his red balloon escaped into the sky. "I'm gonna call her again," Margery said, pulling out her phone.

"Wait, take my number first. Text me her photo. If you make contact with her, let me know. I'm going to alert the officers on duty here to be on the lookout for her, okay?"

"Thank you. Thank you so much."

Ellery found the nearest unit and the two guys standing by. She knew one of them by sight and the other not at all. When she explained the problem, they agreed to put word out on the radio and to assist her in tracking down Chloe Lockhart. "I'm going to head to the west perimeter by the Public Garden," Ellery said. Over by Newbury Street, with its allure of fancy shops and eateries. Just the place a twelve-year-old on her own might go.

Ellery searched the faces of passersby as she went. She didn't feel the same abject terror as she had earlier when Tula disappeared on her watch, but there was a tense knot in her gut nonetheless. Most missing kids, she knew, turned up within a few hours. Most of them just lost track of time and forgot to call home. Or they deliberately orchestrated a scheme for freedom, returning when they ran out of money or got hungry. But Francis Michael Coben had stolen sixteen girls and butchered them all before he got to Ellery, so her mind went to him first, last, and always. She picked up her pace as she reached the Public Garden, jogging past the beds of purple and white flowers, the idling swan boats, and the waving willows.

At the intersection to cross to Newbury Street, she waited impatiently for the light to change, bouncing on the balls of her feet like the runner she was. The WALK sign flashed, but a strange sound—a kind of stuttering laugh—drew her up short. She waited and heard it again. She zeroed in on the sound and traced it to the nearest trash can. Inside on top of a pile of garbage lay a cell phone making the Porky Pig signature trill "That's all, folks!" instead of a regular ring. Ellery's cold fear returned in force when she saw the caller ID.

"Mimi."

2

Normally when there was a missing child, people sent for Reed Markham with the singular blazing focus and desperation of Gotham City with its Bat signal. As a young agent, Reed had found the most infamous missing girl of all, Ellery herself, and then many others since then. His pedigree in this area was unrivaled, which was why he hung around Boston PD waiting for them to realize it. He lingered like a wallflower in the precinct hallway, dodging file cabinets, shuffling backward periodically to peek at Tula in the break room. She sat at the table coloring, her short legs not quite touching the floor where Speed Bump lay snoozing. Reed's ex-wife, Sarit, would have him thrown in the basement jail if she could see them now. They only fought about two issues, both of them Reed's shortcomings, according to Sarit: his obsession with his work and his relationship with Ellery, and here he was mixing both together.

He knew he should take Tula back to the hotel. The longer she remained at the police station, the more likely she was to relay the adventure to Sarit, complete with the part where Ellery was down the hall, which would be the narrative equivalent to setting the story on fire. *Is this some sort of midlife crisis? A temporary insanity?*

Sarit had asked when she learned he was seeing Ellery. *Your manic pixie dream girl dances with death more than she tangos with you. Half the time you're with her, you wind up nearly shot to death.* Reed didn't have a satisfactory answer to this jab because he knew it to be true.

He crept forward again to eavesdrop on the investigation into Chloe Lockhart's disappearance. The room vibrated with a tense energy he recognized as the mobilizing fear that accompanied a missing child. Phones rang, seemingly without end. Chloe's unsmiling face beamed out from all the computer monitors. Reed studied the photo, remembering the moodiness that had gripped his older sisters when they were on the cusp of puberty. Mama would compliment a hairstyle or outfit choice, and the wearer would stomp back to her room and change immediately. Chloe's refusal to light up for the camera—or whoever was behind it—could be mere adolescent pique or a sign of something more troubling.

Ellery stood across the room, deep in conversation with a man who Reed deduced must be her captain. The man had a roll of antacids in his hand, and he was chewing through them like they were candy. Reed wondered whether this was an old habit or a new one acquired when he began to supervise Ellery this past summer. She'd survived her suspension from active duty, and now Boston was giving her a tryout as a detective. No one could argue that she didn't get results. But her track record of dead bodies and near misses, coupled with her infamy from the Coben case, rendered her radioactive within the department.

As though she felt him staring, Ellery looked up at Reed and waved him over to her. Reed tried not to appear too eager to join the loop as he strode over to stand near Ellery's side. She angled her body away from him. "Captain, this is Special Agent Reed Markham."

The captain stuck out one beefy hand. "James Conroy," he said as he gave Reed a firm shake. "Hathaway told me you happened to be at the fair today when the Lockhart girl went missing. How about our good fortune that the FBI's number-one child finder is vacation-ing here in Boston. I hope you can help us out."

Reed looked sideways at Ellery, whose face, as usual, betrayed nothing of her thoughts. "I'm happy to help if I can," Reed said mildly.

"Good. Great, even. The Lockhart girl has been gone almost five hours now. What do you think about putting out an Amber Alert on her?"

Amber Alerts went out to the general public in cases of child abduction or endangerment. In Reed's opinion, they did not have enough information yet to know whether Chloe was in danger. More than 90 percent of missing kids were runaways, and most returned home within a day or two. "It's the cell phone in the trash can that concerns me," Reed said, glancing at the clock on the wall. "Most kids Chloe's age would need surgical amputation to remove their phone from their hands, let alone willingly toss it in the trash. But I would wait to put out the alert until you've interviewed the parents."

"We're working on that. Her mother's a surgeon at Mass General, and she's in the O.R., apparently. We have an officer waiting to pick her up as soon as she's free. The father is some bigwig at Fidelity. Chloe's nanny, Margery Brimwood, reached him on the golf course. He's on his way down here now."

"What about Chloe's friends?"

"According to Margery, her best friend is a kid named McKenna MacIntyre," Ellery said glancing at her notes. "Margery contacted McKenna's nanny, who explained about Chloe's disappearance to McKenna's parents. They're bringing her down for an interview."

"I know Judge MacIntyre," Captain Conroy said. "He'll appreci-ate the gravity of the situation."

Ellery twitched with obvious impatience. "If we wait on the alert, aren't we killing valuable time?" Reed knew it had taken more than a day before law enforcement accepted that Ellery was abducted and not a runaway. Her family was poor, her home life chaotic, and

Ellery's time hadn't been closely supervised or monitored. She'd been out alone on the streets of Chicago the night she went missing, and her mother had admitted, shamefaced, that this situation was not unusual.

"The BOLO went out as soon as we received the report. We've put out a description of her to every officer in the city." Conroy looked to Reed. "More eyeballs couldn't hurt, though. Push all the buttons you got, yeah?"

"It's your call. Eyeballs help, yes, but they are most useful when trained in the right direction. Knowing more about Chloe's habits is crucial at this stage."

He didn't have to guess the roots of Conroy's indecision. The named players in this drama so far included two nannies, a judge, a surgeon, and some financial poo-bah. All this added up to the fact that Chloe came from money, and money knew how to make noise. A misstep either way would be bad for the Boston PD. Sound the national alert for a kid who'd just run off to make trouble for one afternoon and they could be airing a wealthy family's dirty laundry for all to see. Keep quiet about a girl who'd been abducted and the fallout could bring all the local parents down to headquarters, demanding answers and impeding any further investigation.

A commotion near the front doors halted their conversation and a silver-haired man in khaki shorts came striding into the precinct. "Where's my daughter? Who's in charge here?"

"Mr. Lockhart?" Conroy asked.

"I'm Martin Lockhart, yes. Where is Chloe?"

"That's what we're trying to determine, sir. It would help us if you could—"

"Where's Margery? Margery was supposed to be watching her."

"We're interviewing Mrs. Brimwood now, sir."

"I want to talk to her. She's paid fifty thousand dollars a year to watch one little girl. How the hell does something like this happen?"

"Martin, let's hear what he has to say, okay?" Another man,

slightly younger, with black shorts and expensive running shoes, stepped forward to put his hand on Lockhart's shoulder. He flashed a set of white veneers at the officers. "We all want the same thing here."

"I didn't get your name," Conroy said.

"Stephen Wintour."

"He's my attorney," Lockhart said, and Reed and Ellery exchanged a look that asked what kind of father stops to bring a lawyer along when his daughter's gone missing. Lockhart must have sensed the question in the awkward pause. "Stephen was also my golf partner for the afternoon. He was with me when I got the call."

"I've known Chloe almost since birth," Wintour added. "Anything I can do to help, just let me know."

"Jeffries, could you show them to interview room two, please? I'll be right with you." As Lockhart and Wintour were led away, Conroy turned to Reed. "Look, it isn't every day we get the FBI to weigh in without going through the official rigmarole. Would you mind taking a listen while I talk to this guy and giving us your opinion?"

"Of course not."

Boston's setup was old enough that they still utilized a one-way mirror. Reed stood with Ellery outside the interview room while Conroy sat with Lockhart and his buddy at a metal table that had been bolted to the floor. Conroy had a legal pad on which to take notes, and Reed was intrigued to see the lawyer pull out a pad of his own. Conroy had an officer round them up bottles of water, and while this was happening Reed looked to Ellery.

"Your captain doesn't know about us," he murmured.

Her lips curled in an ironic smile, but she did not look at him. "The whole world knows about us, Agent Markham. I think the USA channel just ran a new movie last week."

"I don't mean the Coben case."

He waited. "Do you always tell your boss who you're sleeping with?" she asked.

"I think all my trips up to Boston speak for themselves on that point." He'd made the journey at least once a month, but Ellery had yet to come stay with him in Virginia since they had consummated their relationship. He'd envisioned her at his family holidays or playing board games at the kitchen table with Tula. He wanted to play the piano for her and show her around D.C. He'd even sent her links to a dog park near his condo. *Bring the hound,* he'd texted her. *He can size up the local squirrel population.* Ellery always demurred: *Maybe someday.* As the months flew past and he lived his half of their relationship out of a roller bag, Reed felt more keenly the pieces of himself he left behind to be with her and wondered whether Ellery would ever want to see them.

"You don't need to stay here on my account," she said steadily, her gaze fixed on the men inside the interview room.

"At the moment, I'm here for Chloe." He leaned over and turned up the volume to hear the conversation more clearly.

"How old is Chloe?" Conroy was asking, even though they knew the answer to this. Reed approved of the technique: when facing a distraught or combative witness, start with easy questions with concrete answers.

"She'll be thirteen in two weeks. The end of August." Lockhart swallowed visibly. "The day she came into the world was the happiest of my life."

"I feel the same way about my kids," Conroy replied. "What about Chloe—any brothers or sisters?"

An odd pause. "No, it's just Chloe. Her mother and I had her later in life."

"I see. Where does Chloe go to school?"

He looked confused. "It's summer. School's out."

"But when it resumes, where will she go?" He named a school Reed was not familiar with and indicated Chloe would be starting eighth grade in the fall. "A tough age," Conroy allowed. "Kids want more independence, start keeping some parts of their life secret."

"Not Chloe."

Ellery gave a small snort of disbelief. At thirteen, Reed knew, she'd been roaming the streets of Chicago, begging for pocket change. Reed thought of Tula singing to herself, legs swinging under the table as she colored a rainbow pony, and he feared for his future. "Did you ever think about running away?" he asked Ellery.

She folded her arms. "Every damn day of my life."

Inside, Conroy marched Lockhart through a series of questions that did not help Reed feel more comfortable in his role as an absentee father. Who were Chloe's friends? *Not sure. Maybe he's heard the name Jenna a few times.* What were her favorite stores to shop in? "Ask Margery. She knows." The name of Chloe's doctor? They would like access to her medical records, if permitted. *Teresa makes those appointments, not him.* With obvious pride, Chloe's father could name his daughter's accomplishments—first place in a piano concerto competition, straight A's, a talented forward on her soccer team—but he had no idea what her typical day was like.

"I don't get home until almost eight. Her mother sometimes much later. Chloe is often in bed by then and we don't want to disturb her. Children need sleep, right?" He seemed to be looking to Conroy for validation, and Conroy gave it.

"My teenagers couldn't get enough of it, but they wanted to do it all in the daylight hours. They'd sleep past noon if we let 'em. Chloe's not a night owl?"

Martin seemed to be searching for answers. "She has a television in her room. Video games. Sometimes I see the light flickering under her door at night. I'm sorry, I don't see what these questions have to do with finding my daughter."

"We have every available officer out looking for her."

"How many abducted-kid cases have you worked?" Ellery asked Reed, still not looking at him.

Inside the room, Lockhart had his head in his hands. "Twenty-four." Reed didn't have to do the math. The children he always remembered.

She nodded to herself. "How many did you bring home?"

He hesitated. "Nineteen." A high average, but the gap gnawed at him on the nights when his own sleep proved elusive.

"Alive?"

He didn't want to say. Not to her.

Ellery persisted, turning and pinning him with her stare. "How many came back alive?"

He hesitated another beat. "Three."

Ellery turned around again, her mouth set in a grim line. "I know this is difficult," Conroy was saying. "We're just trying to cover every angle. Is there anyone at all you can think of who might have wanted to hurt Chloe?"

"H—hurt her?" Lockhart's face twisted. His mouth opened and a wheezing sound emerged, like a deflating balloon.

The lawyer, Wintour, spoke for the first time since the interview began. "You mean like someone with a grudge? She's a little girl." He laid a hand on Lockhart's arm. Wintour might have made the gesture to comfort him, but to Reed, it looked like a caution: *Don't say anything. Let me handle it.*

"You might be surprised at the complexity of a middle schooler's life these days," Conroy replied. "What about it, Mr. Lockhart? Anyone who might have wanted to help Chloe disappear, even if only for a few hours?"

"Disappear?" His chin quivered. His voice was hoarse when he answered. "No. There's no one. Are we done yet? Shouldn't you be out looking for Chloe rather than asking me all these questions?"

"He's lying," Ellery remarked to Reed. "Or at least there's something he's not telling us. His kid is missing—why hold back information now?"

Wealthy families, he knew, weren't used to answering questions they didn't care to answer. Reed had lived for decades with an explosive secret right within his DNA. However, he'd seen enough of his father's infidelity over the years to have a guess as to what Martin Lockhart might be hiding.

"Detective Hathaway?" A uniformed officer poked her head around the corner. "The mother just arrived. What do you want me to do with her?"

"I'll handle it. Thanks."

Curious about Chloe's other parent, Reed trailed Ellery out to the bullpen to get a glimpse of Teresa Lockhart, who stood trembling amid the chaos. She was tall, with close-cropped blond hair worn in a trendy, almost spiky 'do that Reed was surprised to see on a married, fifty-something surgeon. Her blue eyes were darker than her daughter's striking aquamarine hue, and they were wet with tears. Ellery introduced herself and the woman collapsed into the nearest chair.

"You haven't found her? I prayed the whole way here it wasn't true."

"We're looking everywhere. I promise you."

Teresa Lockhart didn't seem to hear her. She accepted the box of tissues that Ellery passed to her and took a fistful as the tears welled up inside her once more. "Not again," she said. "This can't be happening again."

3

Happening again. The words vibrated like a live wire inside Ellery, the one Coben had installed as surely as if he'd cut her open and strung it taut through her ribs. Her skin rippled under her clothes and a buzzing started in her ears. *Focus,* she ordered herself. *Find Chloe.* Aloud, she asked, "Do you mean that Chloe has disappeared before?"

"Not Chloe. Trevor. He didn't disappear." Teresa Lockhart broke off with a sob and covered her mouth with one hand. "He—he was murdered."

"I'm so sorry." Ellery searched her memory banks for any trace of the name Trevor but came up empty. "Who was Trevor?"

"My son."

"Your son?" she echoed, confused. They had verified with the nanny that the Lockhart family consisted of three members: Martin, Teresa, and Chloe. Ellery cut her gaze to Reed, but he looked as startled by this development as she was. She also noted the gawking eyes of the officers around them. "Mrs. Lockhart, would you mind coming with me to a quieter space where we can discuss this further?"

Teresa shredded the tissues in her hands with nervous fingers. "I don't understand. Shouldn't you be out looking for Chloe?"

"We have a hundred people on the street right now doing just that. You can help us most by giving us a detailed account of your day and how you interacted with Chloe. Come this way, please." She shepherded Teresa toward a windowless interview room with a cheap table and several folding chairs. Trailing behind them, Reed made a gesture at himself—*Should I join?*—and Ellery hesitated just a moment before nodding. This case was rising like quicksand around her and she wanted someone on the outside with a rope. "Can we get you anything? Coffee, water, soda?" Ellery asked as they entered the room.

"No, thank you." Teresa paced the narrow confines while Ellery and Reed took their seats. She twisted her hands together and muttered something to herself that Ellery couldn't decipher. The nervous energy radiating off the woman was contagious and Ellery had to take a steadying breath to keep herself calm.

"Won't you please sit down a moment so we can talk?"

Teresa stopped in her tracks and looked hard at Ellery. "Hathaway. That's your name, right? I read about you. You're that girl, the one who—"

"Yes." She could choose any fill-in and it would be correct. *The girl who got away. The one who lived. Who shot a murderer and refused to apologize for it. The girl, now a woman, who had one last chance to keep this new job and carve out a slice of life that belonged to her and no one else.*

They stared at each other some more as Teresa seemed to weigh whether or not to trust her. At last, Teresa pulled out a chair and perched on the edge like a bird. "And you're him, then." She glanced at Reed. "The one who found her."

"Reed Markham, ma'am. Yes, I'm a special agent with the FBI."

"The FBI is involved already?" With the strain in her voice, Ellery couldn't tell if Teresa found this prospect reassuring or alarming.

"Not officially. I was at the fair today when Chloe went missing."

"When did you last see Chloe?" Ellery asked her.

Teresa's restless hands skimmed the plastic edge of the table. "I've been trying to think. It was Thursday . . . no, Wednesday night. I stopped in her room when we got in from dinner. She was listening to music and texting on her phone."

Three days ago. Ellery made a note of it. "I see. Have you been traveling?"

"No." There was an edge to Teresa's reply. "I have a demanding but somewhat unpredictable surgical schedule as well as other work obligations. This week we had a benefit dinner for the Children's Cancer Fund. Chloe is busy with school, dance, and music lessons. We don't always see each other face-to-face, but we keep in touch all the time. See?" She reached down into her Coach handbag and pulled out a sleek silver phone. She called up her most recent text to Chloe: *Have a great time, but don't eat too much junk! Win a bear for me & your dad. Love you!* Ellery saw the text had been marked as read by Chloe at 10:08 A.M., but there was no reply. "Do you mind if I have a look?" Ellery asked, extending her hand for the phone.

Teresa pulled back. "There's nothing here to say where she went. Just mother-daughter chitchat."

"You never know what might spark an idea."

Teresa looked at the phone, bit her lip, and thrust it at Ellery. "Do you have kids?"

"No." Coben had ruined that chance, according to the doctors. They'd repaired the damage and cured the infections, but the scar tissue remained.

"I do. One daughter." Reed smiled and inclined his head. "She's seven going on seventeen, I think." Teresa flashed a brief, relieved smile, so Ellery let him take the lead in questioning as she paged through the texts between Teresa and Chloe.

Hi, sweetie. How did your math test go?

Fine.

Fine . . . is there a numerical value attached to that assessment?

3.1415926 . . . you want me to keep going?

Pi, Teresa wrote back. Very funny.

Ellery hid her smile. She would've punked her mother with some similar non-answer at Chloe's age.

"They teach you the facts of life in school and warn you not to get pregnant," Teresa said to Reed. "They make it sound like if a boy even looks at you wrong, you'll get knocked up. I used to break out in a cold sweat when my date tried to hold my hand. Then I took a serious biology course in college and found out how supremely difficult the whole thing is. It's such a narrow window of conception each month. The egg can get lost. The sperm basically start dying the minute they're released. Then, even if it takes, that cell has to divide and divide, each new cell knowing where to go and how to form a body with hands and feet and lungs and a brain." She shook her head. "It's a wonder it ever works at all. A miracle, really. With Trevor, we weren't trying. I was in med school. Not a convenient time to be pregnant. Later, with Chloe, I was older. It wasn't so easy then. She was high-risk, even from the start." A tremor crept into her voice at those last words.

Look. Snuffles is going to be a social media influencer. Chloe had sent a picture of a white froufrou dog posing for the camera in a pink scarf and sunglasses.

Are those my sunglasses? Teresa had texted back.

She has 111 followers already. How many do you have?

No social media for you OR the dog. Not until you're thirteen.

Snuffles is 55 in dog years. Practically a grandma.

Do you know how old I am?

Chloe had texted an emoji batting its eyelashes. *No. We haven't studied how to date fossils yet.*

"She's a good kid," Teresa said, her voice cracking. "Smart. Funny. Oh, she was a beautiful baby. Strangers would bend over the carriage and gasp out loud when they saw her huge blue-green eyes and tiny dimples. She had smiles for everyone back then. I could hardly believe she was mine, that I got this lucky after . . . after what happened before."

"To Trevor," Reed said, his voice gentle.

She answered with a tight nod. "He wasn't supposed to be home alone," she replied, just above a whisper. "I got called in on an emergency cabbage."

"I'm sorry, what?" Ellery slid the phone back to her and returned to taking notes.

"Sorry. It's a coronary artery bypass graft procedure—CABG. Trevor would be home alone after school, which wasn't usual but also wasn't something we thought would be a problem. He was in the seventh grade, like Chloe. He never got into trouble. He'd do his homework and then play video games or watch TV. We'd left him on his own for a few hours many times before this and nothing ever happened. We lived in Spring Garden, one of the safest areas of the city."

She stressed this last part, her palm flat against the table. "Go on," Ellery said.

"The police, afterward, kept pressing us on what was unusual about that day, but it was all minor stuff. I got called to the hospital because there was a flu going through the unit and they were short staffed. Not normal, but not out of the ordinary, either. Our housekeeper, Carol, came by that afternoon when usually she didn't come on Tuesdays. She'd been with us for years—not live-in, but helping out a couple of times per week. Ethan, my husband at the time, was teaching at Penn as he typically did."

"So, Martin Lockhart wasn't Trevor's father?" Ellery asked, taking notes.

"No. My marriage to Ethan . . . well, it didn't survive. I met Martin later."

"Where is Ethan now?" Reed asked.

"Still at Penn, the last I heard. We don't keep in touch."

"Understandably," Reed replied. "Please tell us more about what happened to Trevor."

"Well, that's the worst part," she said, blinking rapidly as tears threatened again. "No one knows for sure. They tell me he was suffocated in his bedroom with a plastic bag. The back door was unlocked, but it usually was. Nothing was stolen that we could see. It's like the person came to the house that day specifically to hurt Trevor. Whoever it was, Carol tried to fight him off. He threw her over the stairway railing in his effort to get to Trevor's room. She was still breathing when Ethan came home and found them, but she died before regaining consciousness. We hoped she might be able to tell us who . . . or why."

Reed pushed a box of tissues toward her. "I'm so sorry for your loss."

She took another fistful but didn't use them, merely clutching them into a ball. "Thank you. When I got the message that Chloe's missing, I felt like I traveled back in time right to that moment. You have to find her. You have to."

"That's what we're trying to do," Ellery said. "The police must have investigated Trevor's death."

"They tried, yes. They looked for sex predators and grieving families of patients who died on my table. They even interviewed students dissatisfied with the grade Ethan gave them. Can you imagine? Murdering a little boy because you failed an economics class?"

Ellery had nearly died for the sin of being out alone on the street at night. "They had no leads at all?"

"Nothing that they told us."

"We'll look into it." The cops often withheld theories and developments from the family prior to an arrest. Philly PD would be able to give them the background on the case. Rich white family, murdered kid. Ellery would bet they'd need a truck to bring in the case files.

"Whoever did it, they're still out there." Teresa's voice took on a renewed desperation. "That's why we've been so careful with Chloe, why we told Margery never to let her out of her sight, not even for a moment."

"Maybe Chloe gave her the slip," Reed suggested.

"No, never. She knew what happened to Trevor. She knew to be careful."

"Kids don't think the way we do," he countered. "The risk of something remote, which they have no personal experience of, may seem trivial compared to daily concerns like a schoolyard bully or not making the soccer team."

"Chloe was on the soccer team and she wasn't bullied."

"Still, it would be helpful to think of where she might go if given the opportunity. Most often in these cases, kids just aren't considering how worried their parents might be. They head out for some fun and then maybe get into a sticky situation if they can't figure out how to get home again."

"Where would she go? She can't drive. She doesn't even have a bicycle."

"There's the T," Ellery pointed out. "Her phone was recovered near one of the stops."

"She doesn't take the T. We pay for a car service to take her and Margery anywhere they want to go. Please, I'm telling you. I know my daughter. She makes straight A's and has never given us an ounce of real trouble. She's a good kid who wouldn't disappear like this without telling us or Margery where she was going. Someone must have taken her or lured her away."

"We're interviewing possible witnesses near the intersection where we found Chloe's phone. We're also asking nearby shops to share any security video they might have from this afternoon, so we'll hopefully have an idea soon of where Chloe went. In the meantime, it would be helpful if you could take this paper and write down a list of all of her friends, relatives, teachers, tutors—anyone she has contact with—so we can start running them down."

Teresa wiped her eyes with her fistful of tissues and took the paper Ellery offered her. "None of the people we know would hurt Chloe. We ran background checks on all of them."

Reed gave her an encouraging nod. "That's exactly why we're hoping she's with one of them. Thank you for helping us quicken our search."

"We'll be back in a second, okay?" Ellery rose to leave and Reed followed suit.

"Wait," Teresa blurted. Ellery turned around. "The man who . . . who took you." She broke off and swallowed. "You weren't the first one. The others . . . they didn't get away."

"No."

"But you survived," Teresa persisted steadily. "How?"

The woman's searching, anguished stare held Ellery prisoner again, trapped by the question she could never answer. The world demanded a reason, she knew. Why did this one live and not the others? She'd survived in Coben's closet longer than the girls before her. Coben had been decompensating, becoming erratic as the net closed in; her body's immune system fought the blood loss and the infections just long enough for help to arrive; her sheer refusal to die when her mother was already poised to lose Ellery's brother to cancer may have helped, even if it was hard to say how. Finally, of course, there was Reed. For most people, his arrival in the nick of time was a thrilling, satisfying end to the story. For Teresa Lockhart, Ellery could see it would not be enough.

"I wanted to see my mother again."

She could see it was the reply Teresa needed when she sagged with relief in her chair. She took up the pen to begin writing, and

Ellery made her escape. Outside in the hall, Reed looked her over, his brown eyes shrewdly assessing. "Politic move there, not telling her the postscript about how you and your mother barely speak now."

"Teresa's writing out the list for us, isn't she?" Ellery would do or say whatever it took to find this girl. "What do you make of that story about Trevor?"

Reed pinched the bridge of his nose. "It's horrific. It's hard to speculate too much without knowing more of the details, but I'd say we're talking about either a deranged psychopath, someone who targeted the boy for reasons that made sense only in their own mind, or a revenge killing for something the adults in his life had done."

"Like she said—relatives of people who died on her operating table."

"Exactly."

Ellery considered. "Doesn't the fact that they haven't solved it yet make the stranger angle more likely?"

"I'd be concerned so, yes."

She didn't want to say the next part aloud. "And if Trevor's killer had their own motives, reasons no one else could understand, couldn't they also have tracked down Teresa and taken Chloe as well?"

Reed's mouth thinned to a grim line. "Let's hope not." He checked his watch. "Listen, I've got to get Tula out of here. If you like, I can pull information on the earlier case and give it a close read."

"That would be great."

"I can also take Bump with us to get some dinner."

"Even better."

He looked at her. "This means you'd have to give me your keys."

Her hand went protectively to her pocket. He'd stayed at her apartment a few times now, and given the upgrade in their social relationship, it would make sense for her to give him his own keys. She just couldn't bring herself to do it.

Reed read her hesitation. "Don't you trust me?"

More than anyone in the world. This was part of the problem. Reed was enormous on her landscape, even before she'd started sleeping with him. He came accompanied with a daughter, an ex-wife, three loud sisters, two mothers, and an opinionated ass of a father. Ellery had a one-bedroom loft and a basset hound, a small life that could easily be swallowed up inside his larger one. Behind her apartment walls, she had no one to judge her or ask her questions about her past. No one to stare at her scars. Reed treated her as normal, so she'd let him inside her sanctum. But whenever they ventured out, she was reminded that, to the rest of the universe, she was the victim and he was the hero.

She looked at his outstretched hand a moment longer before thrusting her keys into his palm. "Thanks," she muttered.

His warm fingers closed over her clammy ones before she could pull away. "Call me if you need anything. And Ellery . . ." He waited until she looked at him. "You don't owe Teresa Lockhart anything more than the other detectives here. Don't let her convince you otherwise."

She nodded, mute, and he squeezed her hand before making his departure. She leaned against the cold, hard wall and shut her eyes for a long moment, trying to think. Her first move should be to loop Conroy in on the Trevor development, maybe even pulling him out of his interview with Martin Lockhart. She pushed off from the wall and wondered whether she could spare the time to grab a soda. Traipsing all over Boston Common in the hot sun had left her scorched and depleted, a sticky residue of dried sweat all down her back.

All thoughts of a caffeine hit disappeared when she reentered the bullpen area and saw Conroy had emerged from his interview and was in conversation with a silver-haired man with round glasses. Standing nearby was a girl of about thirteen dressed in jean shorts, a pink T-shirt, and glittery sandals. She had her phone out and was poking at it while the men talked. Ellery guessed this had to be McKenna McIntyre, Chloe's friend.

Ellery approached the group, and Conroy moved to make room

for her. "Hathaway, come meet Judge Aaron McIntyre. His daughter McKenna goes to school with Chloe."

Ellery shook the judge's large hand. "Thanks for coming in."

"Of course. We're all terribly worried about Chloe."

"Detective Hathaway is the one who recovered Chloe's cell phone," Conroy explained.

At this, McKenna looked up. "Which one?"

"Which one what?" Conroy replied.

"Which phone did you find?"

Conroy looked at Ellery. "It's with the tech guys," she said. "It had a pink case with the letter C on it."

"That's her regular one," McKenna said. "She's got another. It's black and kinda cheap looking."

"Where did she get this other phone?" Ellery asked her.

McKenna shrugged one thin shoulder. "She said someone gave it to her. I asked who and she wouldn't tell me. I teased her that she had a secret boyfriend and she turned all red and stopped talking to me for the rest of the day. I didn't bother asking her after that, but I could see her sometimes at school, texting on it."

Conroy leaned down. "McKenna, this is very important. Do you know how long Chloe has had this phone?"

"Not for sure. But at least four months."

He straightened up and looked at Ellery, and she could read the fear in his eyes. Chloe's abductor, if there was one, didn't have an afternoon's head start on the investigation. They had months. "I'm going to put out that alert now," he said softly, his worried gaze drifting toward the main doors. "We're going to need to contact the media right away."

"You don't need to," McKenna said, matter-of-fact. She held out her phone to show him a live shot of headquarters where at least one reporter has already set up camp on the steps. "They're already here."

4

Popular wisdom said everyone had a twin somewhere, but Chloe Lockhart might as well as have come from a tween blond girl factory pumping out clones of her according to the voluminous tips that came flooding into BPD. Ellery got the thankless job of sorting and prioritizing them as they rolled up to her from the officers manning the phones, email, and social media. A girl playing in the Frog Pond on the Boston Common could be Chloe—except it wasn't. It also wasn't her at a gas station in Allston, a video arcade in Watertown, or on a ferry to the Harbor Islands. Chloe Lockhart, it seemed, was everywhere and nowhere all at the same time. Ellery held a cold can of soda to the back of her neck and slumped in her chair.

"You look like hell."

Ellery snapped to attention at the sound of Dorie Bennett's voice behind her. "Hello to you, too," she replied. Dorie was the senior detective who served as her partner in most cases. *So, you're the one who's supposed to keep me away from trouble,* Ellery had remarked when they'd first been paired up.

I'm supposed to teach you not to go chasing it in the first place, Dorie had replied. Thus far, the training had stuck. Ellery had kept her nose clean for five months, with just thirty days remaining on her probationary period. Dorie liked to give her a cheerful slap on the back at the end of each day. *We survived another one,* she'd say, and Ellery wasn't sure whether she meant they'd survived the job or each other.

The only Dory I know is that forgetful blue fish from the movies, Reed had said when Ellery told him of her new assignment.

Well, she's just like that except imagine that the fish is a middle-aged lesbian with a wife and three Labrador retrievers, Ellery had replied. *She can't remember where she put her coffee cup, her pen, or her glasses, but I swear she knows the name of everyone we pass on the street. Even the guy at the hot dog stand smiles and jokes with her, and he's a first-rate grouch.*

This seemed to be Dorie's essential trait in landing the dubious pairing with Ellery. When Conroy put them together, he'd told Ellery, *I'm sure you'll get along great. Dorie likes everybody,* and Ellery heard the unspoken part: *She'll even like you.*

"Sorry about your vacation," Ellery said as Dorie pulled up a seat next to her. "Was the Cape nice, at least?"

"Sun, sand, and ocean breezes. It's about ten degrees cooler than this hellhole. Of course, it dropped to near Arctic temperatures when I told Michelle I had to come in."

"We've got a missing kid. What are you going to do?"

"It's our anniversary." Dorie held up her left hand to show off her wedding band. "Ten years tomorrow."

"Congrats."

"Yeah, maybe hold off on the kudos until we see if there will be an eleventh year."

"That bad?"

"Nah, she'll come around." Dorie looked at her ring. "I hope. What about you? Conroy says you're working the tips."

"More than seven hundred of them logged so far. Not a genuine lead to be found," Ellery replied with disgust. "Our guys estimate there were a hundred thousand people on the Common at some point today. You'd think one of them would've seen something useful."

"Maybe they did. It takes time to interview that many potential witnesses. About all you can say is that she probably wasn't dragged kicking and screaming into the back of some van—someone would've put that up on YouTube by now." She glanced at the clock on the wall. "She's been gone more than seven hours. What's your gut say?"

"You're asking my gut?" Her instincts had been broken years ago; at least that's how the brass explained it to her during the shooting investigation. Too damaged. Unstable. Sees the Bogeyman in every shadow. As such, Ellery hesitated to give voice to the tension coiled in her midsection. "I think it's bad," she said reluctantly.

Dorie digested the confession in silence for a moment. "I heard there was already a dead kid in the family."

"Chloe's half brother, Trevor. We're pulling the available files."

"We?"

Heat flooded her face. "Reed Markham was here visiting when Chloe disappeared. He's agreed to help with the case—unofficially for now, until we have any confirmation of an abduction."

The door to the small room swung open and Officer Owens stuck his head in the room for what felt like the hundredth time that day. "Here's the latest," he said, handing Ellery a stack of notes. "The one on top just came in right now. Thought you'd want to see it first."

"Thanks." Ellery scanned the message and her breath caught in her chest.

"What is it?" Dorie asked, leaning forward.

"A dry cleaner in Roslindale just had a customer come in for help in getting stains out of a dress shirt. The cleaner says it's blood."

"Okay," replied Dorie in a tone that suggested she didn't think much of the tip.

"The customer's name is Frank Brimwood. Brimwood is the last name of Chloe's nanny, the one who was with her when Chloe went missing."

"Related how to this Frank Brimwood?"

Ellery stood and headed for the door. "I don't know, but let's find out."

Frank Brimwood turned out to be Margery's husband, age fifty-six, no wants, no warrants. They had three grown kids and he worked as a loan officer at a bank in the city. The dry cleaner, Carol Rosales, kept the store open late so Ellery and Dorie could survey her findings. "Tell me that's not blood," she said, pushing the shirt across the counter to Ellery.

Ellery snapped on gloves and examined the dark red smears across the front of the white shirt. "It looks like blood," she agreed.

Mrs. Rosales folded her arms. "That's because it is. I've been doing this thirty-two years now. I know blood when I see it."

"What about Frank Brimwood?" Dorie asked. "Do you know him?"

"Never seen him before today." She watched as Ellery withdrew a Kastle-Meyer kit, took a cotton swab, and ran it over one of the red stains.

"How did he seem to you when he dropped off the shirt?"

"Sweaty. In a rush. He wanted the shirt back tomorrow, but we're not open on Sundays."

It was dark outside and still over eighty degrees. The entire city was sweaty. Ellery added a drop of the reagent to the tip of the swab and the cotton turned pink. "It's blood," she announced.

Mrs. Rosales gave a short, authoritative nod. "Told you. He did it, didn't he? He took that girl."

"That's getting ahead of things," Dorie said. "Did he mention how he got the stains?"

"No, just gave me orders on the shirt. I saw he had a big scratch on his arm, right here." She indicated her forearm. Ellery wondered if that meant the blood could be his, but the stains seemed too large to have come from a scratch.

"Thank you for calling us," she said to Mrs. Rosales. "We'll take it from here." She bagged the shirt and prepared to go.

"What if he comes back here looking for it?" The woman's dark brows knit together in concern.

"I wouldn't worry about that. We'll be keeping him company for the next while. You have a good night."

Outside, they gave the shirt to the waiting Officer Owens, who had tagged along in a squad car. "Take it to the lab for processing," Ellery said. "Tell them it's a rush."

She climbed behind the wheel of her SUV while Dorie took the passenger side as usual. This was one aspect to their partnership that fired on all cylinders, so to speak—Ellery liked control and Dorie loathed driving in Boston traffic. *It's the only city where the driver's manual shows you how to give the finger,* she liked to say. To prove her point, a blond driver in a BMW (license plate "BEEMAH") cut off Ellery as she tried to merge into an open slot. Ellery might have replied with double-barreled fingers except Dorie was sitting right there and Dorie was the one who'd be evaluating Ellery's temperament in next month's report to Conroy. When she glanced over, though, Dorie wasn't watching her. She had her phone out and was scrolling through it.

"We've got something back on Frank Brimwood. He's clean in Massachusetts, but there's an old record for assault in Providence. Old as in 1988." She looked at Ellery. "Before your time."

"I was born in 1988." Barely.

Dorie laughed in reply. "Yeah, sure, kid. Check it out, though— the victim was a female minor."

Ellery pressed the pedal closer to the floorboards. "What kind of assault?"

"Doesn't say here. But there's no good kind when we're talking about a grown man and a little girl. Turn right up here; it's faster."

Dorie may have hated to drive, but she was a Boston native who knew every back road better than Ellery's GPS. The car swayed as Ellery took the turn harder than she should. "Margery's worked for the Lockharts for eight years," she said. "That's like three thousand days where Frank could've grabbed Chloe and didn't. Why snatch her in broad daylight in the middle of a street fair after all this time?"

"Some of these guys who like to diddle kids can go years without acting on their impulses. They get by with fantasy and black-market porn until one day it isn't enough to just think about being with a kid. They need the real thing."

"I keep thinking about the blood. There was a lot of it on his shirt."

"That's the other thing about these guys. When they do grab a kid, it's usually over with quick."

"How quick?" Ellery had lived three days.

"Hours. Sometimes before anyone even knows they're gone." She stretched toward the windshield and squinted out at a Cape-style house on the right. "That's the place."

At twilight, the house looked like a paper lantern, aglow with light from within. It sat next to a line of homes exactly like it, all of them wood-frame one-story houses with a pitched roof, little space between windows and the gutter, and no overhang. The central front door was painted red, with two symmetric windows on each side, like big eyes peering out into the night. Ellery and Dorie walked up the cement path that cut through the patch of front grass. Ellery heard the television playing inside, but it went mute at her loud knock. A tall, balding man with a long face and broad forehead answered. He reminded her of the stone statues on Easter Island. "Yes?" he said, frowning down at them.

They showed off their shields. "Are you Frank Brimwood?" Ellery asked.

"Yes." His imposing frame blocked the entryway entirely.

"We're investigating the disappearance of Chloe Lockhart. Can we please come in to talk to you for a few minutes?"

He turned where he stood and hollered behind him, "Margery! There're two detectives here to see you." He moved aside to let them enter.

"Actually, sir, we'd like to speak with you," Ellery explained as Margery appeared, wiping her hands on a dishrag.

"Is there news?" Margery asked, her eyes anxious. "Did you find Chloe?"

"No, ma'am, not yet." Ellery replied to Margery Brimwood, but her eyes were busy cataloging the room for any signs of trouble. She found only a brown sofa, a coffee table with a beer can sweating on it, and a wall jam-packed with family photos. "We just have a few questions for you. First, though, do you have a gun on the property?"

"I have a Walther PK380," Frank answered. "Why?"

"Could I see it, please?"

The Brimwoods looked at each other for a beat, but Frank went to retrieve the weapon. He returned with an opened lockbox and handed it to Ellery, who made a perfunctory check of the contents. "Thank you." As he took his seat, she noted the fiery red scratch on his arm, the one Mrs. Rosales had mentioned.

"I don't understand. What does my gun have to do with Chloe Lockhart?"

"Did you know Chloe?" Dorie asked.

He looked befuddled. "Not really. I've met her a few times here and there. Margery's like a second mother to her, though. Maybe even a first mother if you want to be honest about it."

Margery slapped his arm. "Oh, hush now."

"When is the last time you saw Chloe?" Dorie asked him.

"Jeez, I don't know. Last winter, I guess. She had some kind of Christmas concert and Margery dragged me along to see it. We ate sugar cookies and drank warm punch." He sounded bored as he re-layed the story, not like a pedophile eager to get close to his prey.

"Mr. Brimwood, you have an old arrest on your record," Ellery said, laying out her cards. "You assaulted a female minor."

His cheeks darkened as he caught on to why they were at his home. "Now look here, I didn't touch that girl."

"Do you mean Chloe or the one from 1988?" Ellery asked him.

"Both. Neither. That girl from before, her name was Melody Marshall. She was bullying our daughter, Cindy. Roughing her up on the bus and taking her money. The school wouldn't do anything about it, so I paid Melody a visit one evening. I told her to leave Cindy alone or she'd have me to deal with. She wasn't impressed, said my kid was a crybaby liar. I said I'd wait to talk to her parents, and she said good luck because her dad went to buy milk fifteen years ago and never came back. Then she, uh . . ." He broke off with a cough. "She hit on me."

Pedos always made this claim: the kid started it. "Go on," Ellery said as neutrally as possible.

"She grabbed my crotch and said she had some ideas about what we could do while we waited for her mother. I shoved her backward away from me, and she fell and cut her arm. She wasn't crying about it, neither. She thought the whole thing was hilarious. I told her again to leave Cindy the hell alone and I left. Later, I guess her mom came home and filed the complaint."

"The judge saw Melody had a record for drug use," Margery said. "So he believed Frank."

"Uh-huh." Pedophiles often picked victims no one would believe. "You mind if we look around?"

"You think I have Chloe stashed here?" Frank leaped to his feet. "You think I'm some kind of pervert, is that it?"

"We're looking everywhere, Mr. Brimwood," Dorie said, her voice soothing. "We'd go door-to-door if we could."

"We have nothing to hide," interjected Margery. "Do we, Frank?"

"You're wasting your damn time here," he said, his color still high. He rammed his hands into his pockets. "Look all you want. I don't care."

Ellery and Dorie went room by room, opening closets and peering under beds. Ellery checked the laundry hamper for any signs of more bloody clothing but found none. The only photos of children she observed were the old family portraits on the wall and one snapshot of Margery and a younger Chloe that sat in a handmade frame decorated with glue and glitter. Dorie came up from the basement and shook her head. "Nothing down there."

"Let's hit him with the shirt."

They rejoined the Brimwoods in the living room. Frank had poured himself a bourbon. His eyes were on the television, where the Red Sox played the Blue Jays, but the angry set of his mouth said his mind wasn't on the game. "Well? Do we pass?"

"You took a shirt to the cleaners today," Ellery said. "The front was stained with blood."

Margery turned to him, aghast. "Frank?"

"It wasn't what you think. I was driving home, and I saw this hurt dog by the side of the road. A small poodle-like thing. I think it got hit by a car. Anyway, there was another bigger dog snapping at it, like it wanted to attack. I stopped the car and put myself between the two dogs. The big one reared up and lunged at me. His paws caught my arm, right here. I growled back at him and eventually he backed off. Then I took the hurt dog out of the street and onto the sidewalk. That's when I got the blood on my shirt. I called the cops and they sent Animal Control to come take the dog to the hospital. I went to the nearest cleaners."

If it was true, there'd be an incident report to back it up. "Where was this?" Ellery asked.

"Down by the Arborway."

At his words, her phone buzzed and she fished it out for a look. A message from Owens came through: *The lab reports the blood on the shirt is not human.* She tucked the phone away, relieved and frustrated at the same time. The blood wasn't Chloe's, which was good. But if Frank Brimwood hadn't snatched her, where did she go? "The lab tests came back on your shirt," she told him. "It supports your story."

"It's not a story," he snapped. "It's the truth."

Margery tried to rub his arm, but he brushed her off. "Honey, they're just doing their jobs. They're trying to find Chloe."

"Maybe she doesn't want to be found."

He sounded so certain that the little hairs on Ellery's neck rose up. "What do you mean by that?"

"That girl has bars on her bedroom window. She's never allowed to go anywhere alone. It's a big fancy house, all right, but if you ask me, it's a prison."

Margery looked pained. "And I suppose that makes me the warden, then."

He threw his hands at her. "Your words, not mine. But remember what happened when you stopped to get her an ice-cream cone after soccer practice?"

Margery's face fell and she drew her hands into her lap. When she didn't explain, Ellery pressed her. "What happened when you bought her an ice cream?"

The woman licked her lips in a nervous gesture. "It was my mistake, really. I hadn't been working with the Lockharts long—only a few months. Chloe was cranky and hungry. I thought a small treat wouldn't hurt her and we wouldn't even be late getting home. That's the thing. We weren't even late." She looked to Ellery for understanding. "The Lockharts have a tracker on my phone and I guess it alerted Teresa that we weren't on our normal route. She didn't call me to ask what was up or anything like that. Instead, she called the cops."

"You see?" Frank looked at them with a gleam of vindication in his eyes. "There's crazy in that house, and it starts with the mother. Mark my words—Chloe wasn't snatched up by some nutter. That girl escaped."

5

"Daddy, look. Speed Bump wants to help you cook!" Distracted, Reed turned from watching both the pancakes and the bacon frying on the stove to see the hound had reared up on his hind legs and planted his enormous paws on the counter. The animal was approximately one foot tall but practically human sized when he stood up like this—just one of his many ridiculous qualities.

"Down!" Reed ordered, unnerved by the lolling tongue unfurling in his direction. "I don't need a sous-chef."

Bump wagged and grinned at him before licking his chops and eyeing the bacon.

"Out, now." Reed nudged the dog away and Tula slid off her stool to grab him around the neck in a hug.

"I'll help him find his ball," she said, running off into Ellery's living room with the dog close at her heels. Reed expertly flipped the pancakes and turned the bacon. He'd selected "breakfast for dinner" because it was a meal that would please both Tula and Ellery, if Ellery happened to make it home to eat. This had required a stop at the corner store, where he'd tied up the hound to a metal post outside while he and Tula ducked in for a quick shop. He might have worried for the dog except there were two other mutts also tied up along with him, patiently waiting for their owners to return. City life, as it were. Reed and Tula had emerged to find the smaller dog using Bump as a trampoline while Bump just took it like the good-natured lout that he was.

Reed had considered the degree of trust necessary to leave furry family members unattended, how the system worked because most people were good and not, as Reed sometimes had to remind himself, harboring plans for kidnapping or murder. He'd been asked often over the years by family and friends how they could keep their children safe, and he knew better than to tell them the unvarnished truth. You could put your baby out on a street corner every day for a week and odds were good that no harm would come to her. But if there was someone determined to get to your child, someone willing to risk everything of their life to destroy yours, then no protection would ever be enough. Chloe's parents had a full-time nanny, an on-call car service, and a tracker installed on her phone, but she'd disappeared just the same.

"Supper's on," he called to Tula, and both she and the dog came running. He set two plates of pancakes, bacon, and colorful fruit salad and joined his daughter to eat at the kitchen island. Bump collapsed with a whine near his bowl, which was lamentably free of bacon.

"Daddy?"

His heart never failed to warm at the word. "Yes, my sweet?"

"Is it dangerous here at Ellery's house?"

Reed halted with his fork in midair. "Why do you ask?"

"Because there's three locks on the front door."

At this, his heart sagged. Ellery's keys resembled an old-time jailor's, one for each cell, but her home held a single prisoner. "That just means it's extra safe here, right?" He ruffled Tula's short, baby-fine hair.

"I guess." She shoveled in a few bites of fruit. "But we're sleeping at the hotel tonight, right?"

"That's the plan." The clock on the microwave said it was almost eight, and the city lights flicked on outside the windows. He'd spent half his life chasing missing children, and the nights were always sharpest, when time stretched like a blade across his skin. He knew in his gut that Chloe Lockhart's bed would go empty tonight.

"Daddy?" Tula's voice jolted him from his dark thoughts.

"Yes?"

"You know how you moved out of our house and got a different apartment near us in Virginia?"

Reed and Sarit had split up two years ago when she'd asked him for a separation and suggested he move out. *You're gone so much as it is,* she'd said, and the implication was clear: she and Tula would barely feel the difference. "Yes. I wanted to be close to you."

"When we move to Houston, will you get an apartment there, too? Or will you move up here and live with Ellery?"

Reed's stomach seized. "What? Who said anything about moving to Houston?"

"Mama." Tula popped a raspberry into her mouth. "She was talking about it with Randy because he got a job there."

"She hasn't said anything to me about it."

"That's 'cause she's afraid you'll blow your lid off." She peered up at him, concerned. "You're not going to blow your lid, are you?"

Reed's hand went to his cell phone, tightening his fingers around the hard edges. He had a hundred choice words he'd like to share with Sarit, none of which he could repeat in the company of his daughter. Sarit had primary physical custody, but they shared legal custody fifty-fifty and he didn't believe she could just up and move to Houston without consulting him. The problem was: he wasn't sure she couldn't. "No," he managed at last. He forced himself to let go of the phone. "I'm not going to blow my lid off. And no one is moving to Houston right now—especially since we have that ice cream waiting in the fridge."

Tula cheered and hopped down to dance around, causing the

hound to run in circles while howling his head off. Reed was happy to give him the bacon leftovers just to stop the noise. Later, Tula fell asleep watching television on one end of Ellery's couch with Bump curled up snoring at the other. They shared an afghan covering both of them, and it was so damned adorable that Reed snapped a picture on his phone, not even caring that it could be used as evidence that he'd reneged on his promise to Sarit not to bring Tula to Ellery's house. At least he wasn't talking about moving her here.

He sat in the armchair next to the sofa, the one that faced the door, so he could watch for the moment Ellery would walk through it. His laptop rested atop his thighs unopened. He knew the horrors that awaited within it, the ugliness of a case that involved a dead boy with a bag over his head. He looked instead to Tula, who slumbered as she had as a baby with one fist tucked beneath her chin. Her face had lost some roundness over the past year. She'd grown two inches and started to ask hard questions, like why people with brown skin had been slaves in America and whether that could happen again to her or her mother. Or whether the monsters Reed hunted could ever come for her. Years ago, Reed had spent one agonizing weekend contorted into different painful positions, screwing on outlet covers and safety latches so that Tula could toddle around the house. These plastic protections had disappeared one by one as she grew and now Reed had no shield against the real threats that awaited them. *What an audacious act it is to bring a child into this world,* he thought. Babies were born every minute into uncertain futures. Guns and locks and fences failed; monsters could wear a human face. You had to believe somehow that your child would be different, blessed and safe. He looked again to the couch where Tula sighed, content for now with her dreams.

At quarter to eleven, Reed answered a knock on the door. He flipped the three locks to reveal Ellery, looking drawn and tired, on the other side. Her tight ponytail from this morning was now sloppy and frizzed out and there were shadows under her eyes. He didn't need to ask if there had been any good news. "Stop looking at me like that," she said as she dragged herself over the threshold. "I got enough of it from Dorie."

"When did you last eat?" Reed said as he shut the door behind her. She waited to watch him flip all three locks. "I can make you some pancakes."

"I'm not hungry."

This registered in the red zone on the Ellery Alert Scale. "You have to eat something. I have fruit salad if you'd prefer that."

"I just said I wasn't hungry." She went to the refrigerator and got out a can of Coke. The dog's nails tap-danced across the wood floor as he circled her in greeting. She reached down to rub his ears, and when she rose up she saw Reed still watching her. "Stop it. You're looking like you expect me to crack up or something. I'm just tired."

She popped the top on the soda and drained it in one go. Ellery, he knew, had cracked long ago. She'd put herself back together so tightly that you had to be up close to see the damage, which explained why she didn't usually let anyone get that near. "Let me make you some pancakes," he repeated as she started picking the grapes out of the leftover fruit salad. "You can tell me how the rest of the day went."

"If you saw the news at all then you already know," she said as she took a seat on the stool that Tula had occupied earlier. "It's all over town now."

"I heard there was a suspect."

"For about ten minutes." She told him about Frank Brimwood, his bloody shirt, and his assessment of the Lockhart house as a virtual prison.

"I imagine having someone come in and murder your first child could make you more cautious with the second. Do you think Mr. Brimwood is on to something? Could Chloe have run away?" He tested the griddle and was satisfied by the sizzle.

"It's possible." Ellery stretched across the island to grab another grape. "We have CCTV footage of her from a jewelry store across from the Public Garden. It's just a glimpse because there were so many people downtown today, but it's definitely her. She left the grounds on her own and headed west. Conroy is trying to get more video to see if we can pick her up down the road."

"Can I see it?" Reed asked as he dropped the batter in silver-dollar circles into the hot pan.

"Yeah, sure. Let me get my laptop." Bump accompanied his mistress on even this short errand, pendulous ears swaying with his waddle. She cued up the video and then scratched the dog's head while Reed finished cooking her late supper. He studied the black-and-white footage as she picked at his offerings.

The camera was trained to catch people coming into the store, so pedestrians walking past the glass display windows out front were only incidental. They streamed past like salmon, thick and crowded on the summer city street. A slight girl came into view on the right side. She was blond and her T-shirt and shorts matched the description for Chloe Lockhart. "She's got a cell phone," Reed remarked, noting the small rectangular object in her hand.

"Yes. Her friend McKenna says someone gave Chloe a second phone, but she swears she doesn't know who it is. Chloe wouldn't tell her. The Lockharts had no idea Chloe even had a second phone, and neither did the nanny."

"This could have been planned in advance, then."

"That's Conroy's current thinking. Chloe's gone off to meet whoever gave her that phone."

Reed looked at the girl on the screen. She walked with purpose, her eyes forward. She definitely had a destination in mind. He set the video in motion again and watched her exit to the left side. Four seconds in total. Not much to go on. He watched it several times more. "Do you have any additional footage from this camera?"

"That's all you see of her."

"I know. I mean a longer clip—before and after Chloe shows up."

Ellery swung the laptop around and called up a different video. "Here's all we have. It's a fifteen-minute chunk that chops off just after Chloe goes by." She scraped most of her supper into the dog's dish and cleared the counter while Reed studied the video. "I'm going to shower and change," she said. "Are you taking Tula back to the hotel?"

The late hour and the vulnerable slump of her shoulders bade him to stay. Ellery did not like to admit she needed him, ever, so he tried to glean it from her body language. Only sometimes did he wonder if he was deluding himself. "If it's okay with you, we'll bunk here tonight. She's out cold."

Ellery played it off with a shrug. "Suit yourself."

While she showered, he examined the video with repeating viewings, each time focusing on a different quadrant of the screen. Several vignettes caught his attention. He saw a toddler with a poof-ball ponytail on top of her head take a pratfall and skin her knees on the sidewalk before being scooped up into her mother's arms. Elsewhere, a young couple lingered at the front of the jewelry store, perhaps discussing an engagement ring, since the woman's left hand currently appeared to be empty. A freckled kid bouncing on and off the curb dropped an ice-cream cone; ten seconds later a passing German shepherd hoovered it up. Reed squinted and leaned in to study a shadowed figure in the upper right corner, just visible across the street. It appeared to be a man of indiscriminate age and race—not a kid, not a senior citizen, but he could be anywhere in between. His skin appeared gray due to the black-and-white video, and the camera was too far to make out any facial features. He wore a dark baseball cap and sunglasses. Reed noticed him because he was the only presence in the video not moving, which gave the impression that he waited for someone or something. Reed had difficulty discerning anything further because of the crowd that amassed in front of him every time the streetlight changed. Indeed, the man disappeared behind a mob as Chloe crossed in front of the camera. By the time she was gone again, so was he.

Ellery returned with her usual sleep attire, a T-shirt and soft cotton shorts, which showed off her bare arms and legs. Normally, he didn't even notice the scars Coben had left on her body, but tonight they screamed his name. Reed averted his eyes. "Were you able to find out anything on the earlier incident Teresa mentioned?" she asked as she took a seat next to him. "The one involving the death of her son?"

Reed scrubbed his tired eyes with both hands. "I've contacted Philly for the details, but there is a lot of information available even via web searches if you know to look for it." The local papers had carried 72-point headlines:

YOUNG BOY, HOUSEKEEPER SLAIN
NO SUSPECTS IN MURDER OF TREVOR STONE
CHILD KILLER STILL AT LARGE

"It's late, so let me just tell you the one key fact Teresa didn't mention," he said. "The main suspect was Trevor Stone's half brother, Justin. He's Ethan Stone's son from a previous marriage. He was seventeen at the time and apparently had a serious drug habit. The theory was that he wanted his little brother's birthday money."

Ellery gave a slow blink. "Then couldn't he have just . . . taken it? Murdering your little brother for his birthday money seems like a seriously drastic step."

"Rumor has it the grandparents forked over five hundred dollars for Trevor's recent birthday. But yes, I agree, murdering your brother is a big leap from simple theft. I think the Philadelphia investigators were grasping for any kind of motive. In the end, though, no charges were ever filed."

"Where is Justin Stone now?"

"That will be one of the questions I ask Philly when I talk to them tomorrow." He shut his laptop and looked at his watch. "Which starts in about half an hour. Maybe we should get some rest, hmm?"

The dog was already snoring at her feet. "Sure. Okay."

She took her time brushing her teeth, while he idled beneath the sheets. When at last she reappeared in the bedroom, she moved to lock the door as usual. "For Tula, can we leave it open tonight?" he said, rising up from the bed on one arm. "I don't want her to wake up and not be able to find me."

Ellery's capitulation came slower this time. A short nod. Her shoulders tensed, but she slid beneath the sheets without argument. He took off his watch and set it on the nightstand, all the while trying not to notice the way her eyes kept finding the open door. He wanted to tell her not to worry, that he would keep her safe, but she believed in doors, not people. *I love you,* he'd said to her, after his family had exploded and it had been just the two of them standing in the smoking ruins. He'd spoken the words out loud only once. Now he waited for her to catch up.

When he shut off the bedside light, he expected her to turn away from him and lie rigid through the night, but she rolled to face him in the dark. "Tell me about the children who make it back," she whispered. He took her in his arms, the way he'd longed to do since he'd stepped off the plane with Tula what felt like a million years ago. She had taught him how to hold her—full body, but not too tight. He smoothed his hand over the supple plane of her back and inhaled the fragrant scent of her hair.

"What do you want to know?" he murmured as she worried the hem of his T-shirt between her fingers.

"There are people who take kids because they want to love them, right? They're just mixed up and they want a kid really bad."

"It happens." *Mostly to babies,* he did not say.

"You've seen it?" she asked, raising her head, trying to peer at him to see the truth.

He hedged some more. "Once."

Ellery settled down uneasily, her cheek to his chest. He could feel the tickle of her eyelashes in her rapid blinking, and he fought the urge to pull her deeper into his arms. She did not cuddle under normal circumstances. He was lucky if she slept an entire night in the same bed with him, so he was not surprised when she shifted away after a few minutes and curled into her usual ball, facing the door. "Good night," she murmured, signaling that she was done with him till morning.

He stared at the inky shadows on her ceiling and thought about the case he'd mentioned. His team had tracked a nine-year-old girl taken from her large, religious family by another woman who'd left the religion, claiming it was a cult. Both the family and the kidnapper lived off the grid, and the woman had moved around with the child multiple times over a period of several years. The girl was fourteen by the time they found her. Reed got to travel out to the family's cabin in the woods to share the good news. Her stoic parents had been grateful at last for the law's intrusion into their lives now that their girl was safe and sound. The trouble was, she no longer wanted to go home.

6

The day Ellery got assigned to train with Doreen Bennett, Dorie had shaken her hand, looked her straight in the eyes, and said, "Captain Conroy said someone has to show you how to do this job without you acting like everyone is out to get you all the time. He asked me if I was up to the task."

"And what did you tell him?"

"I said from what I'd read, everyone is out to get you. Leastways, a piece of you."

Ellery's ears had turned hot. People recognized her all the time, but rarely did she ever feel seen. "There's another movie coming out next month," she'd admitted. Hollywood liked to remake the Coben story every few years, and now they had a new chapter to add.

"Uh, yeah? Who's playing you?"

Ellery had feigned indifference. "I don't know."

"Ha, that's bullshit," Dorie snorted with good humor. "Tell me who it is."

"Sophia Bush," Ellery muttered to the floor.

Dorie had let out a low whistle and clapped her hands in

appreciation. "Damn, she's fine." Later, when they drove out with Ellery behind the wheel, Dorie had put on her sunglasses and stared straight ahead. "Listen, Sophia or no Sophia, I won't be watching that movie. I make up my own mind about people."

"What about what Conroy said?"

"James Conroy is a good guy and he's my boss, but I don't work for him. I work for the citizens of Boston, because their money pays my checks. They're the ones trusting me with their lives. As long as you do right by them, you'll be right with me."

Five months on, Ellery clung hard to her good standing. Dorie was watching her with a new intensity, though, as they worked the Lockhart case. "You get much sleep last night?" she asked when Ellery picked her up.

"Did you?"

They had a twelve-year-old girl missing in the city. No one with a badge slept easy last night. Dorie didn't press her, and as Ellery rolled up in front of the Lockhart estate in Brookline, Dorie peered over the edges of her shades. "Wowzers. I guess the rich people have to live somewhere, so why not here?"

Ellery took in the wrought-iron fence, the impeccably trimmed landscaping, and the stately white-brick home set well behind it. As Frank Brimwood mentioned, there were bars on the windows—ornate and bronzed, designed to look ornamental but bars nonetheless. Ellery also spotted three different security cameras. "I can't guess the first numbers in the price, but I guarantee it back-ends with a ton of zeroes." They were there to view Chloe's living situation for any clues to her whereabouts, as well as prod the Lockharts for further information. "Wave for the cameras," Ellery said as they went up the walk.

"Which ones—the news vans outside or the security cameras fixed at the front door?"

"You can't blame them. If I'd had my kid murdered inside my

home, I'd want to post an armed guard twenty-four-seven." She rang the doorbell, and a few moments later the heavy black door opened to reveal Stephen Wintour, Martin Lockhart's attorney who had accompanied him to the station the previous day. "Mr. Wintour," Ellery said with some surprise. "Were you and Mr. Lockhart out on the links again this morning?"

"I'm here to support the family in any way I can. Please, come inside. Martin is expecting you." They walked past the marble entryway with its sweeping staircase into a living room dominated by an L-shaped low-back gray sofa. There was no trace of a child here or even a particular family. No personal photos. The built-in bookshelves held some classics and beautiful knickknacks—a jade vase, a painted tiger on the prowl. To Ellery, the room looked like something out of an expensive catalog, and she wondered how much time the Lockharts actually spent sitting on the pristine sofa.

Martin Lockhart stood by the large windows, maybe staring at the press gathered on the street or perhaps hoping to see Chloe come up the walkway. He turned when his lawyer ushered them in, his face briefly hopeful. "Has there been any news?"

"I'm sorry, no," Ellery replied.

He nodded as though he'd expected as much. Ellery knew from his records that he was sixty-one, on the old side to be the father of a middle schooler. Ellery's own father was only fifty-three even now, although he'd long skipped town by the time Ellery was Chloe's age. Maybe there was something to be said for having a more settled parent.

Martin gestured at them to have a seat and he lowered himself into a high-backed chair, joints creaking like the grandpa he might have been. "When Teresa was pregnant, I would put my hand on her stomach to feel the baby move. We knew her name already, Chloe, and I'd use it when I talked to her. I wondered what she would look like, how her laugh would sound, whether she would love tennis like me or horses like her mother. It felt endless, those months I waited for her to be born, and then when she was finally in my arms, I understood why the wait had been so long. It wasn't just nine months. It was my whole lifetime. Some part of me had known she was coming long before she was conceived, even before I knew Teresa. She was born in my heart, you see. I knew it the moment I saw her face. I know because—" He broke off painfully and swallowed. "It's the part of me that's breaking now. I'm bleeding inside and can't seem to stop it."

Wintour went to Martin and patted his arm. "We'll find her," he said. "Hang in there."

"Is your wife at home?" Dorie asked Martin, noticing Teresa's absence.

"She's upstairs." Martin cast his watery gaze to the door. "I hope she'll be feeling well enough to join us shortly. It was a rough night for her, as you might imagine."

"It must be her worst nightmare come true," Dorie agreed with sympathy.

"You have no idea," he said sharply. He caught himself and softened. "I—I didn't, either."

Ellery saw the lines on his face deepen, almost cracking. Her family had survived the hole left by her father, but it shattered with the loss of her older brother to cancer. Her mother remained as if frozen in amber, still living in the same Chicago apartment among all of Danny's things. "Chloe must have been a blessing," she said. "After what happened to Trevor."

"Yes, of course. Teresa took some convincing at first, but she came around. I think it helped that Chloe was a girl—different from her first experience."

"What is your wife's relationship with Chloe like now?" Dorie asked.

"Fine. Good."

"Yeah? That's great," Dorie replied. "My mom and I fought like a pair of octopuses in a jar when I was twelve. I was embarrassed that she even existed and made sure she knew it on a daily basis."

"How sorry for her."

Ellery took a different tactic. "When you did argue with Chloe, what was it about?"

"Trivia. Nothing serious." His voice took on a note of impatience. "Does it really matter? I didn't take off with Chloe and neither did my wife. She didn't run away from home because we told her not to leave her dirty socks on the floor."

The worst fight Ellery had with her mother at Chloe's age was over money. Ellery had taken twenty dollars from her mother's purse, skipped school, and treated herself to a matinee of *The Matrix*. The family would have eaten for a week with the money Ellery blew in a single afternoon, and her mother's fury upon finding it missing had shook the walls of their little apartment. She'd called Ellery selfish and sneaky. She'd sent her to bed without supper. Daniel was in the hospital fighting for his life while his sister threw herself a little party. *You're the one I'm not supposed to worry about,* her mother had raged. In bed that night, hungry after the sugar high from the movie candy wore off, Ellery had realized why the tears were stinging in her eyes. Just once, she'd wanted to be worthy of worry.

"Right now, we are operating under the theory that Chloe left voluntarily, for a specific reason," Ellery told Martin. "We could find her quicker if we knew what it was."

"If I knew, I'd tell you." He seemed to search himself again for answers. "She didn't like the tracker on her phone. She said it meant we didn't trust her. Her friends, some of them are allowed to take the T on their own—go off to the mall or wherever. We told Chloe she could go, too, as long as there was an adult chaperone. Mimi would've been happy to do it."

Ellery saw on Dorie's face the same thing she was thinking: no middle schooler wants their nanny tagging along on an outing to the mall.

Martin hesitated. "I might have been willing to loosen the reins just a little, but Teresa insisted on close supervision. Of course, I deferred to her. How could I not?"

"We are working on unlocking Chloe's phone," Ellery said. "We'd also like to take a look at the data from the various household accounts."

"Do you have a warrant?" Wintour asked.

Ellery swiveled her head to look right at him. "Do we need one?"

"I, ah, of course you can have Chloe's computer," said Martin. "We'll supply the passwords. But I use email for private communications with my clients, as Teresa does with her patients. Also, Chloe didn't use our laptops or cell phones, so there wouldn't be anything of relevance there."

"With all due respect, Mr. Lockhart," Dorie said, leaning forward, "up until yesterday you didn't know your child had a second phone. We're not sure at this point who she's been communicating with and through what avenues."

Wintour stretched across to whisper something in Martin's ear. Martin nodded. "There are legal considerations here that go beyond the Lockhart family," the lawyer said after a beat. "It's not even clear that they could consent to the privacy breach in the absence of a warrant. If the situation changes such that investigation of Martin's and Teresa's private accounts becomes imperative to finding Chloe, we can explore options at that time."

"We can't know what's relevant if we can't see it," Ellery replied.

"There's nothing. I swear to you."

The doorbell rang and Wintour hopped up to answer it. "It had better not be that asshole from Channel Five again," he said as he strode out of the room.

"The news vans have been here since we got home," Martin said wearily, sinking back in his chair. "Everyone wants an interview, but I don't know what I'd say. I just want Chloe back."

Wintour reappeared with a blond woman about Ellery's age, only dressed like a fashion ad in high boots, a crisp navy dress, and silver hoop earrings. "I'm so sorry to bother you at home, Martin, but we need those papers signed today." She hefted a leather briefcase to show him, and Ellery noted the French manicure.

"Amanda, these are detectives helping us look for Chloe. Detectives, my colleague at Forsythe, Amanda McFarland."

"Has there been any news?"

"Not yet. Let's, ah, let's go to my office, okay? Please excuse me."

Dorie turned to Ellery as Martin left with Amanda. "Are the markets open on Sunday?"

"In Asia they are," Wintour answered. He gave them a tight smile. "Money never sleeps."

Dorie snorted. "Tell that to my savings account."

"I'd like to check out Chloe's bedroom next," Ellery said to her. "What do you think?"

Again, it was Wintour who answered. "I can show you the way." Dorie followed him and Ellery brought up the rear, wondering if her years on the job had made her overly suspicious or whether it was normal for an unrelated adult man to know the path to a tween girl's bedroom.

"You and Chloe are close, then?" Ellery asked as they walked.

"I've known the family for years," he replied, which she found to be a non-answer. He led them up the front staircase, down the gleaming dark hardwood floors of the upper hallway, and past several closed doors to make a sharp turn down a shorter hall to a white door with the name "Chloe" on it in painted letters. "Oh, Teresa, I'm sorry," he said as he opened the door and walked through it. "I didn't realize you were in here."

Teresa Lockhart sat up from where she was lying on Chloe's

bed. "No, it's okay," she said, wiping at her face with both hands. "Please, come in."

Ellery couldn't help feel a twinge of awe at the size of the bedroom. She and Danny had shared a cramped room covered in posters to hide the cracks in the walls. Chloe's bedroom was nearly the size of Ellery's current apartment. At one end, Chloe had a four-poster queen bed draped in white taffeta. At the other end, she had her own sitting room, complete with an overstuffed couch, a shag zebra-patterned rug, and her own large-screen television. Ellery even spotted a mini-fridge.

"I know what you're thinking," Teresa said. "It's all a bit much."

"It's like a princess movie come to life," Dorie said with a smile. "I bet she loves it."

Teresa gave a hesitant answering smile and pointed up. "The ceiling is her favorite." Ellery tilted her head back to see the twinkle lights that had been built in, shining like diamonds against the dark sky. "There's a switch, see?" Teresa flicked it and the crystals lit up in various constellations.

"Amazing," Dorie said with admiration. She walked over to the dresser, which displayed several family photos.

"We knew Chloe would be our only child," Teresa explained as Ellery and Dorie continued to survey the lavish bedroom. "So, we had the wall knocked out between the two bedrooms to make one large room. We wanted it to be special for her." She glanced over to where Wintour stood near the door. "It's fine, Stephen," she said, her voice edging on impatience. "There's no need for you to stay."

He didn't seem to be in any hurry to leave, however. "I don't mind. Martin is busy with someone from work downstairs." He reached out and touched a silver music box that sat on Chloe's lacquered dresser.

"Work? Right now?"

"She said it was urgent."

"She," Teresa repeated, her face blank.

"Amanda McFarland."

"I know the name," Teresa said with obvious displeasure. "Tell Martin to hurry things along, will you? Nothing's more urgent than this." She crossed to smooth the wrinkle she'd put into Chloe's bedspread.

"Okay, I'll relay the message."

Wintour departed and Teresa sat down on the bed, her face in her hands. "I'm going crazy. I keep thinking I hear her footsteps in the hall, but when I run to look, there's no one there. I check my phone every two minutes to see if she's messaged me." She held it up to illustrate. "I just can't believe she'd run off without telling me."

A little white dog came zipping into the room, yipping and dancing around the newcomers. Ellery smiled and knelt to greet the creature.

"Snuffles," Teresa said. "Who let you inside? I'm sorry. We can put her in the yard out back."

"It's no bother," Ellery said as she scratched Snuffles under her tiny chin. "She's Chloe's dog, yes?"

"Yes. They adore each other. Snuffles has had her nose in every corner of this house, looking for Chloe. She whines and looks at me like I've hidden her someplace, and I don't know what to do with her."

"You miss your pal, huh?" Ellery patted the dog, who whimpered and put her delicate paws up on Ellery's leg.

Teresa sniffed. "Sometimes I get jealous about the way she coos over that animal. The dog can do no wrong, not even if she chews up one of Chloe's shoes or favorite stuffed toys. Snuffles just wiggles up to Chloe and all is instantly forgiven."

"Dogs are easier than people," Ellery agreed as Snuffles rolled over and showed off a white fluffy belly. "Chloe gave you trouble, then?"

Her blue eyes looked pained. "Not trouble, no. More like attitude. She doesn't like the rules we have in place nor what she says are our 'unrealistic expectations' for her. She doesn't understand what the world is like. She doesn't see that we're trying to protect her, to arm her."

"Arm her?" With the bars on the windows and the cameras everywhere, it seemed possible they had guns in the house as well.

"To prepare her for what's out there," Teresa corrected, drifting to the window. The gauzy white curtains hid the iron bars on the outside. She peeked once and shuddered as she let the curtain fall back into place. "Chloe sees sunshine and rainbows. She imagines everyone is her friend. She does the bare minimum work for school to maintain her grades and then spends the rest of her time playing video games or dressing up the dog in silly outfits."

"We were under the impression that Chloe does well in school," Ellery said. "That she excels in music—piano, right?"

"Chloe has a gift. To neglect it would be wasteful." When Ellery didn't reply, Teresa gave her a hard look. "You think I'm being too tough on her. On the contrary, I don't think I push her hard enough. She has everything a child could ask for, and it's all she's ever known. Everything comes easy as far as she's concerned, and she thinks it's the only way it could be. I know better. I grew up with hand-me-downs and mac-and-cheese dinners. I had to scrap for everything I got. Took out loans, took chances, pushed myself twice as hard because I knew I had to be twice as good to get into the boys' game. You know how many surgeons are female? Fewer than one in twenty. I've had to fight for every position I've gotten. The payoff for all that work is this life of leisure for my daughter. Best schools. Best clothes. Opportunities I only dreamed of, and she thinks they're like tissues in a box—pull out one, discard it, and there will be another just waiting right behind it."

"I get it," Ellery said. "There aren't a lot of female detectives, either."

Dorie flashed a smile and indicated the pair of them. "That's why we stick together."

"I see that you're very generous with your daughter," Ellery said as she surveyed the lavish bedroom, "but if Chloe wanted freedom . . ."

"She might have run away," Teresa finished for her. "I've thought of the possibility. I even wish I could believe it's true because that would mean she could change her mind and come home again. But I can't believe she would do that. Not after what happened to Trevor."

"Your security measures are impressive," Ellery said, nodding in the direction of the bars.

Teresa gave a tight, humorless smile. "Draconian. That's what Chloe called them once she learned the word. She was six at the time."

"I was wondering if they're in response to a specific threat."

"Something other than my dead son, do you mean?"

Ellery held her gaze, and Teresa let out an irritated breath.

"Trevor's murder is unsolved. I wasn't prepared for that. Of course, who prepares for the death of their child? It's impossible. But once it happened, I thought: The police will find the person who did this. They will pay. But it's been years now, and the only one who's paid is me. Me and Ethan, Trevor's father. I did some reading and found that two-thirds of murders go unsolved. I honestly don't know how you cope with that. If I lost one-third of my patients for unexplained reasons . . ." She blinked slowly in Ellery's direction. "I think I would go mad."

In the ensuing awkward silence, Dorie walked over to Chloe's desk, which held a large computer monitor. "Mr. Lockhart said you might be able to access her computer and social media accounts for us."

"Yes, I can do that," Teresa answered, breaking free from her thoughts. "We require her to let us supervise her accounts, or she doesn't get the Wi-Fi password. It will just take a minute to boot up."

Ellery used the time to inspect the rest of Chloe's room. She found the closet messy, crammed with shoes and clothes, luggage, and what looked like an old box of Barbie dolls. The floor-to-ceiling bookshelf had been painted white to match the room. It held reams and reams of actual books, mostly young adult titles with colorful spines and girls on the cover. The slight wear at the corners and finger smudges on the glossy covers indicated the books were not for show; Chloe clearly read them. Her other main hobby appeared to be video games, judging from the Nintendo console and stack of games sitting by the television. Ellery paused to study a framed photo on the wall. Martin and Teresa, both noticeably younger, sat on a large rock with pine trees at their backs and snow at their feet. Baby Chloe wriggled in Teresa's arms, grinning for the camera as she attempted to stand on her mother's lap. She wore a brown knit hat with bear's ears on it.

Teresa came to stand next to Ellery. "That was taken at our house in New Hampshire. The hat Chloe's wearing . . . it belonged to Trevor. I saved it when he outgrew it thinking I'd give it to my next child, and then after he was gone I didn't think I'd ever have another. I guess there was a reason I held on to it all those years."

Over at the computer, Dorie was paging through the photo stream on Chloe's social media. "This is her main account?"

"The photo one, yes." Teresa and Ellery joined her at the computer.

Chloe featured many selfies taken in the bedroom in which they stood. She sometimes used an app to add clown hair or a moustache. Snuffles featured heavily on the account as well. There was a video of Chloe trying to teach the dog to jump through a Hula-Hoop and Snuffles just trying to lick the camera instead. Ellery recognized Chloe's friend McKenna in some shots, the pair of them trying out different hairstyles or making crazy faces. They'd done a video of a makeup tutorial in which they both put on terrible British accents. Teresa identified several other friends from Chloe's school who appeared in the photos—a dark-eyed boy named Barnaby showed up a few times, as did a Chinese girl named Leah.

"I've seen all of these before," Teresa said. She bit her lip. "Chloe prefers that I not comment, though. I'm not even allowed to click 'like.'"

Dorie left the photo stream and went to the computer's main files. "If she's hooked up her phone to the computer, it may have automatically downloaded other pictures. Ones she didn't choose to show off."

Martin entered the room. "Stephen said you needed me?"

Teresa hugged herself. "Our daughter is missing, Martin. Of course I need you."

"Wow, okay. Looks like we'll be here awhile." Dorie located the images folder, which contained more than four thousand items. Ellery held back a groan as Dorie began the painstaking process of clicking through each one. Many more shots of Snuffles, sometimes dressed in diva clothing. Bad selfies that came out wrong. McKenna doing handstands in what must be someone's backyard. Pool shots. A vacation to the beach somewhere.

"Are you looking for something in particular?" Martin asked.

"Well," Dorie said. "How about him? Who is this guy?"

They all looked at the photo she'd stopped on, which depicted Chloe and an older boy, their arms around each other, tongues out as they mugged for the camera. The wind blew his large Afro into her hair. She made a peace sign, while he chose the old "hang ten" gesture. There was ink across his knuckles—a tattoo, maybe?—and it spelled out *D-E-A-T-H*."

"I—I've never seen that boy." Teresa looked at Martin, a question in her eyes.

"I don't know him, either."

"He's in a couple of other shots," Dorie said. "This one shows part of a mural in the background. See that orange sun?"

"I don't recognize that, either." Fear crept into Teresa's voice. "Maybe Margery knows?"

"We'll ask her," Ellery replied.

Teresa's phone dinged, signaling the arrival of a text. Eagerly, she pulled it out from her pants, only to drop it with a soft cry when she saw the screen.

"What is it?" Ellery asked as she moved to pick up the phone. Her stomach flipped as she read the text:

U WANT 2 SEE CHLOE AGAIN?

GO ON TV & TELL THE WORLD WUT A SHITTY MOM U ARE.

DO IT 2DAY OR U WON'T BE A MOM ANYMORE.

7

To understand a perpetrator in the present, Reed always had to look to the past. He had to interview relatives and talk to the guy's third-grade teacher. He had to visit his previous homes and learn his habits, his hobbies, his obsessions, and his hatred. All of this took time, time the victims didn't have, but there was no short-cut. So, absent any current suspects to investigate, Reed turned to Chloe Lockhart's ugly family history, specifically her murdered brother, Trevor. He kept one eye on his daughter as she performed acrobatics on the playground and the other eye looking about the Boston Common for the stranger he'd arranged to meet. His re-search had revealed that Lisa Frick, the grown daughter of murdered housekeeper Carol Frick, was in graduate school at Northeastern University, so he'd phoned her and asked her to speak with him. Lisa had been about Tula's age when her mother was killed inside the Stones' home. She had a younger brother, Bobby, and an older sister, Elizabeth, who had died in a car accident about a month before their mother's murder. Reed had hesitated to ring Lisa and invite the trag-edy back into her life, but he suspected it had never left her. A loved one's unsolved murder, he knew from experience, was a wound that never healed.

He clapped loudly as Tula nailed the dismount. His phone rang, and he checked the ID, half-expecting Lisa to be canceling on him. She was already fifteen minutes late. Instead, he saw Ellery's name on the screen. She'd slipped out early that morning without a word, her pillow cold by the time he awoke, and he had no idea how long she'd been gone. In the gray silence of her bedroom, he'd lain awake and wondered if this was how Sarit had felt when he disappeared into a case.

Still scanning the horizon for Lisa Frick, he answered Ellery's call. She didn't give him a chance to say more than, "Hi."

"I need your help. Someone sent a threatening text to Teresa Lockhart saying she has to go on television and say she's a terrible mother or she'll never see Chloe again."

"What?" He leaped to his feet from the shock. "No ransom request?"

"No, just this weird demand for a 'bad mom' confession. I'll send you the screenshot." She paused to do just that. "We need some insight here, Reed. Who the hell would do this? Should Teresa go on TV to say what they're asking? We've traced the number and it's a prepaid phone. We're trying to get the provider to pinpoint its physical location now."

Reed turned in a circle, one hand to his head as he tried to think. He'd been with the FBI for twenty years, but he'd never encountered anything like this. "You need to establish proof of life if at all possible. The person texting Teresa may have Chloe or they may be a crank responding to the media reports on Chloe's disappearance and Trevor's murder."

"I thought about that. But I'm wondering how a crank could have gotten Teresa's private cell phone number."

"Good point. Okay, assuming for a moment this person does

have Chloe, it's clearly personal. This is someone known to the family, not a stranger."

"That's good, right? They're less likely to hurt her."

He had a flash of Teresa's son dead on the floor with a plastic bag over his head. Someone close to the family got that kid, too. "Possibly, but there are no guarantees. We had one case where the kidnapper repeatedly engaged the family with notes and phone calls, always promising that he would return the missing girl when she was free of sin. We eventually apprehended him and discovered that she'd been dead the whole time. He had a recording of her voice from the initial hours that he played to string the family along." Reed kept churning through old cases in his mind, looking for any similarities that might give a direction on how to proceed.

"So, do we do this TV thing or not? Conroy wanted me to get your opinion. People here are divided."

Reed looked down at the message again and considered the abbreviated text-speak language. "We know Chloe left the park on her own. We know she's got a second phone. What if she's the one who sent this message to Teresa?"

Ellery made a humming noise, pondering. "Yeah, maybe. I mean, who's more likely to think you're a shitty mom than your own teenage daughter? But that doesn't help us with the immediate question: Does she go on TV and do the mea culpa?"

Ticktock, no pressure. Guess wrong and a little girl could die. The closest approximation to this situation that he could come up with was hostage negotiation, which centered on a give-something, get-something exchange. Make the hostage taker feel heard without giving in to every demand. "She should do the television appearance," Reed said at length. "She should talk about Chloe and how much she loves and misses her, how much she wants her to come home. I recommend she admit generally to making some mistakes, like all parents do and kids included. Make sure to use conciliatory language but stop short of using the exact phraseology of the text.

If Chloe's behind this stunt, she's probably looking for a safe way to come home. Teresa should signal that she won't be punished, that all everyone wants is for Chloe to be safe at home again. Meanwhile, she should answer the text and ask for assurances that Chloe is okay."

"She's done that already. No reply yet."

Reed spotted a dark-haired woman in sunglasses making her way across the green toward him. "Okay, let me know how the TV spot goes or if there is any further contact about Chloe."

"Will do."

He glanced to where Tula had occupied herself by making a young friend by the swings and turned to greet Lisa Frick. Her hair had purple streaks that he could see now that she was closer, and she wore a small stud in her nose. "You must be Ms. Frick," he said, extending a hand. She did not take it.

"No offense," she said, "but could I see some ID?"

"Of course." He supplied his FBI credentials to her, and she studied them closely before handing them back to him.

"Not like I'd know the difference, I suppose," she said with a resigned sigh. She took off the glasses to assess him. "You do look like the picture I saw on the internet."

"I assure you I am who I say. Special Agent Reed Markham—and that's my daughter over there, Tula." He waved and she returned the gesture with typical childish enthusiasm. He indicated the bench behind them. "Thank you for agreeing to talk with me. Shall we sit?"

She still looked unconvinced, whether about him personally or the purpose of this whole venture he couldn't say. "I'm supposed to be writing an anthropology paper," she said as she perched on the edge of the wooden bench, poised as if to flee. "But I've been watching the news all morning to see if there's any update on Chloe."

"Do you know her?"

She seemed surprised by the question. "Why would I?"

"I thought perhaps you'd kept in touch with Teresa Lockhart."

Lisa's jaw hardened and she looked out at the playground for a long moment. "I knew her as Dr. Stone, not Lockhart. We only met once or twice in all the years my mom worked for her family and I was just a kid back then. It's not like we were friends."

"I'm very sorry about what happened to your mother." He'd read enough last night about the case to know the outcome for Carol's children. No father in the picture, two young kids left orphans. Lisa and her brother, Bobby, had ended up in foster care.

Lisa nodded, unmoved by his statement. "Yeah, you're sorry. Okay."

"If you looked me up, you may have seen my background," he offered.

"FBI man. Right."

"I mean the part where I was adopted after my mother's murder. I was five months old at the time. The police couldn't find who did it, and her killer went free for decades." The case made headlines again this year when he and Ellery had finally solved it—a bittersweet ending that had changed everything he knew about his family. "She was a Latina teenager living on the edge of poverty in Las Vegas at the time of her death. There was no one to advocate for her and so the case file just gathered dust."

Lisa unclenched for the first time and she looked at him with a kind of hunger. "Then maybe you do know what it's like," she said, her voice soft. "Growing up, my friends would complain about their moms giving them chores, snooping in their stuff, asking stupid questions, and that sort of thing. My foster mom was okay, but she had seven other kids besides me. I'd hear my friends run down their moms and think how if I got sick in school, I had to wait at the nurse's office, sometimes for hours, before my foster mom could come get me. I'd think how they did sports or clubs and how they ate lunches someone packed for them every day. I ate free lunch. I wanted to tell them to shut up, but I never did because then they'd remember what happened to my mom and feel sorry for me and that was worse."

"And here you are in graduate school. I bet she'd be proud."

"Maybe." Lisa almost smiled. "She cheered like crazy for Beth when she graduated high school."

"Beth . . . that's your sister?"

"She was going to Penn that fall on full scholarship. My mom bought all of us T-shirts. Mine was too big, so I used to sleep in it until it fell apart." She shook her head. "Everything fell apart. Looking back now, it started when Dad died. We just didn't know it at the time."

Reed pulled out his notebook. "Your father was Vincent Frick. You must have been very young when he was killed."

"He died three years before Mom. We were living in Maryland back then. Dad ran a convenience store six blocks from our house, and he'd walk back and forth to work, no matter the time, no matter the weather, so that Mom could have the car for us kids. One night he was covering a late shift at the store and he never came home. There'd been a big thunderstorm that night—I remember crawling into bed with Beth when the thunder rattled our house. I thought we'd blow away like in *The Wizard of Oz*. The storm spared our roof, but it got our father. One of the trees fell over when he was walking home and killed him right there."

"I'm sorry."

"He looked out for us, though." Her chin rose, daring Reed to defy it. "He had good life insurance and Mom used the money to move us to Philadelphia."

"That's when she started working for the Stones."

Lisa watched the kids playing for a long moment. "I guess maybe we should've stayed in Baltimore, huh?"

"Did you know Trevor Stone at all?"

She gave a half shrug. "Days when we had no school, Bobby and I would go with Mom to work. Trevor was there sometimes. He was cool, I guess. He had these remote-controlled fighting robots, and he let us play with them. Once, he wanted to give us a box of toy cars that he didn't use anymore, but Mom wouldn't let us take them. She didn't like it when the Stones tried to unload their stuff on us, even when we could've used it. She'd say, 'They pay me with money, not with old shoes or toys.'"

"She worked for several other families in the area, is that right?"

"Yeah, she had a regular rotation of about five or six places. Sometimes she'd try to squeeze in a few more, like if it was back-to-school time and we needed new clothes. I liked the Stone place best of all, though. They had a roof garden and a library and the floor when you came in was black and white squares, like a chessboard. I used to wish I could slide down the shiny banister. Now when I think of that floor, I see my mother lying on it with her head bashed in." She looked sideways at him. "I don't think this can really be helping you, can it?"

"You never know what might turn out to be important."

She hunched her shoulders. "No one told me anything back then, but when I realized I could look it up at school on the computer, I saw that the police thought Justin Stone might have done it."

"What do you think?"

"Kill his brother over some weed or pills? I can't believe it. But I never met him. Maybe he was crazy or high and didn't know what he was doing." She turned to Reed abruptly. "They didn't come to her funeral, you know."

"I'm sorry?"

"The Stones. They paid for my mother's burial, but they didn't come. It was me, Bobby, and our temporary foster mom—not even one of the ones we ended up staying with. We got split up soon after that. Mom's friends from church and our neighbors came for the services. Plus, a bunch of strangers who were probably curious about the murders. I didn't even want to go. We'd been at the cemetery just a month earlier for Beth, and now we were back to put my mom in there with her. It felt like the ground was taking my whole family, one by one."

"Not your brother," Reed said, although he wasn't sure what had become of Bobby.

"No," she said, her tone turning wry. "But for a while there, I thought Bobby might self-destruct on his own. He drank too much, dropped out of school early. Then a few years ago, I guess he grew up. He got clean, got a GED, and started working. He moved up to this area when I started school because he said we're all the family each other's got left. We have dinner every Sunday." She paused. "I called him when you contacted me and asked if he wanted to come to this meeting. He said no. He said you're just here about Chloe anyway and that you don't care what happened to Mom."

Reed couldn't deny this was partly true. He cared, of course, but Chloe was the pressing concern. "If we find out who killed Trevor, that would avenge your mother as well."

"Bobby sounded jumpy on the phone, almost paranoid. He's been watching the news, too. It brings back memories for all of us." She looked at Reed. "You're not going to try to talk to him, too, are you? I honestly don't think he could handle it. I don't want you pushing him off the rails again when there's nothing he can do to help you anyways."

"I won't bother him." The kid had been six at the time. What could he realistically contribute in any case? "What I'm trying to find out is if there is any connection between what happened to your mother and Chloe's disappearance."

Her lips thinned. "Bobby's right, you know, about how everyone forgot Mom. You're the only one who's even asked about her in years. Once everyone decided Trevor was the target, it was like Mom didn't matter anymore. Even the news stories mostly left her out. She was just 'the housekeeper' and they didn't show her picture or talk to us about her. It was Ethan and Teresa doing the interviews and everyone always crying over Trevor. I'm sorry he's dead. I am.

But my mom died, too, you know? And she was a hero. She tried to stop that guy from getting to Trevor and he killed her for it."

"I know. I'm sorry."

She blinked back tears but failed to hold them, so Reed dug out his handkerchief. She gave a disbelieving, watery laugh as she took it. "You Southern guys are a different breed." She wiped her eyes and nose and held the white square in her lap. "I just don't think I can help you. I was only eight years old when it happened."

"What can you tell me about that day?"

She took a shaky breath. "All I really know is that she wasn't supposed to be there. It wasn't her usual day. The Stones must have asked her to come for a particular reason, which they did sometimes like if they were having a party or something. We weren't home, so I don't know what they said when they called her. She had us stay at the neighbor's house for the afternoon because she was cleaning out Beth's room and she didn't want us underfoot—at least that's what she said. I think it's more that she didn't want us to see her crying. But after Beth's funeral, money was tight, so she took all the work she could find. If the Stones said they needed her for the afternoon, she would've dropped everything to go over there."

"And she never mentioned anyone hanging around the house? No trouble with any other people who might have been nearby, like landscapers or a repairman?" In reinvestigating the murders at the Stone house, he planned to start at zero, including the idea that Carol could have been the target.

She considered. "There was a gardener, not for the Stones but for the family across the street. He used to whistle at her and make rude comments. Guys like that are everywhere, though, and they don't go after twelve-year-old boys."

"You're right. They usually don't."

"Daddy, Daddy, watch me!"

Reed shielded his eyes from the sun to watch Tula flip backward off the monkey bars. He took perverse pleasure in knowing Sarit would have had a heart attack if she'd been watching. "Bravo," he called to Tula. "A perfect ten!"

"She's brave," Lisa said with a trace of wistfulness in her voice. "I was afraid to climb to the top of the jungle gym at that age. In fact, I'm not sure I ever did. Guess it's too late now." She faced him. "Do you really think the same person who killed Trevor and my mom could have Chloe?"

"I think we need to examine that possibility."

"Back then, I missed my mom, but I mostly thought about what happened to him. Trevor. I used to have dreams that someone was coming to put a bag over my head and I'd wake up because I'd literally stopped breathing in my sleep out of fear. If someone could come into his huge house in the nice neighborhood, what was to stop them from coming to mine? Especially now that my mom was gone." She pursed her lips and shook her head. "Now I think about her. How she didn't even worry about herself, just tried to protect him. I wonder what she was thinking when he threw her off the staircase and onto that marble checkerboard floor."

Reed could almost hear the crack of a skull hitting the floor and he tried not to flinch. He struggled to come up with some words of comfort, imagining what someone could have said to him to make him feel better when his mother's murder had been unpunished. Nothing, he realized. There was nothing.

Lisa remained quiet for a few minutes as they watched the children play. "I hope you find Chloe," she said, not looking at him. "I hope she's safe. I hope wherever she is, there's someone like my mom willing to fight for her."

"I hope that, too."

Lisa Frick left shortly thereafter, and Reed felt a twinge of guilt for having bothered her at all. She and her brother, Bobby, had been too young to have real insight into whatever precipitated the attacks at the Stone house all those years ago, and he'd contacted her mainly because she was geographically convenient. To dig deeper, he'd have to go to Philadelphia to talk to the remainder of the Stone family, Ethan and Justin. Fortunately, he'd hit on a potential opportunity to engineer such a trip.

He took out his phone and called his sister, Kimmy. She was the closest in age to him, the baby of the family before the Markhams had adopted Reed. Being bumped from such a favored status might have upset some kids, but Kimmy took her big-sister role so seriously that their parents would often find toddler Reed passed out in her bed at night, where he'd succumbed to her endless bedtime stories. She was his biggest rival and closest confidante and he dearly wanted to hear her voice right now.

"Hey, ugly brother," she said when she picked up the line, her voice full of affection. "Have Tula and Ellery made fast friends yet?"

"Uh, I'm working on it."

Kimmy gave a deep belly laugh. "Oh, honey, you say that like you're the one who gets to decide."

"Fine, then. Do you have any sage advice?" Kimmy had married her college sweetheart twenty years ago and they were still blissfully happy, as far as Reed knew. But she did spend her days as a family lawyer, which gave her a window into all kind of mucked-up relationships.

"Focus on whatever they have in common and go from there."

"Food," he answered without hesitation. Both Ellery and Tula loved to eat.

"There you go. Lots of meals, then. Maybe make them Mama's peach cobbler. That's how I reeled in Beau back in the day."

"I would try that except we haven't had much time together." He explained briefly the situation with Chloe Lockhart, and Kimmy replied with a stretch of silence on her end.

"I'm so sorry for that girl," she said in the Virginia twang that they both shared. "But Reed, every missing child can't be your responsibility."

He chuffed. "Now you sound like Sarit. Besides, it's Ellery's case. I'm just unofficially consulting at this point."

"Uh-huh. Sure. So, let me guess . . . this isn't actually a social call?"

He felt his ears go hot as she called him on his true motivation. "I'd like to swing by Philadelphia tomorrow or Tuesday to talk to a couple of people. I have Tula with me, though, and . . ."

"Save it. You know I can't get enough of that girl. I'll bring my two and we'll all get mani-pedis or something."

"Thank you," Reed said with relief. He looked to Tula, who had ceased playing on the jungle gym and now seemed to be making clover crowns for her new friends. Lisa Frick's parting words rang in his ears. *I hope wherever she is, there's someone like my mom willing to fight for her.* "I, ah, I was calling for another reason, too. I may need your professional advice."

"Oh?"

"Sarit may be moving to Houston, which would mean taking Tula with her. She hasn't said anything to me directly, but Tula indicated Sarit has been house-hunting there recently. I gather her boyfriend has a new job. Can she just do that? Take her so far away from me with no negotiation?"

"I'd have to see the terms of your custody agreement. You have joint legal custody, but she has primary physical custody, yes?"

"Yes."

"And you've been abiding to the terms faithfully, is that correct?"

"Of course," he said automatically. Then doubt crept in. "What do you mean?"

"I mean you've been following the agreement as it's spelled out. Child support, visitation, et cetera, all on time and as scheduled."

"Well, I . . . uh . . ."

"Reed," she said with resignation. He heard the squeak of her leather chair as she leaned backward, could picture her taking off her glasses to pinch her nose.

"I pay on time," he told her. "Always. Visitation is a little more complicated. I travel for work and now there's Ellery . . ." He could

feel a chill come over him as he said the words. If Sarit could use Ellery against him, she would.

"Reed Alexander Markham, you haven't been ditching your
daughter to go bone your girlfriend."

"No. Look, I get dinner with Tula on Tuesdays and then every
other weekend with her, plus some vacation time. The total time I've
seen her hasn't changed a bit—it just doesn't always happen exactly
as scheduled. Ellery's been training in her new job and she doesn't
have much flexibility, so it's been easier to juggle the weekends with
Tula. Plus, I still have to travel for work at times."

"Mmm-hmm," Kimmy replied, not sounding pleased.

"You have to help me." He forced a smile as Tula caught him
looking at her. She grinned in return, showing off the dimple she'd
inherited from him. "I can't lose her."

"You know I will go to the mat for you and Tula. But Sarit's in a
strong position here, so you should think carefully about how hard
you want to fight."

He didn't have to think about it. "As hard as possible."

"Okay. I'll look into your options, but Reed, you have to
remember . . ."

He closed his eyes. He didn't want to hear whatever came after.

"In a fight, someone always gets hurt, and it's not always who
you'd expect."

8

Ellery stood next to Dorie by the wall of the Lockharts' pristine living room, careful not to lean against the wallpaper lest she leave a sweat stain on it. The number of bodies in the room, combined with the camera lights, had raised the temperature on what was already a humid summer day and Ellery regretted her long-sleeve shirt. Teresa Lockhart sat on the gray couch with her husband shoulder to shoulder. Her face was pale and her eyes fixed and unblinking. "I love Chloe with all my heart," she said to the bouquet of microphones in front of her. Her monotone was hard to hear even in the otherwise silent room. "We miss her and we want her to come home. If someone saw her playing in the park and wanted to spend time with her, I understand their motivation. Chloe is a beautiful, loving girl. But she needs to come home now. We won't ask questions. We won't point fingers. We just want Chloe to be safe. Everyone makes mistakes sometimes, even parents. Even children. This mistake is not too late to fix if Chloe can just come home."

Ellery released her breath when Teresa finished. Reporters asked questions, but Wintour shut them down, with an assist from Captain

Conroy. "Is it just me," Dorie muttered to Ellery amid the chaos, "or was that kind of terrible?"

"She's no actress," Ellery murmured back.

"I get more emotion from the teenager giving me my cheeseburger in the drive-thru." She jerked her head in the direction of the back of the room. "Come on, I see the nanny's here. We can ask her about the boy with Chloe in those pictures."

Ellery threaded her way through the bodies in the room, glancing back to see Teresa shrug off Martin's hand from her shoulder. Yes, she'd been robotic in front of the cameras, but Ellery didn't share Dorie's disdain. Dorie hadn't ever been under those bright lights, blinded while the cameras flashed away at your moment of weakness, like jackals closing in for the kill. *We just want your story!* the reporters always shouted. *You need to tell your side!* They persisted until you gave in to their questions. You'd try to set the record straight. Only then, too late, you'd realize your mistake. Once you gave it up, the story was no longer yours.

Margery did not look thrilled to see them headed her way. "I heard about the text," she said, her voice bitter. "You're not here to accuse my husband of sending it, are you??"

"Did he?" Ellery asked, just because.

Margery's mouth fell open. "No."

"Did you?" Ellery didn't believe this possibility, either, but as she said the words it occurred to her that Margery was both the last person seen with Chloe and the only outsider to have an up-close view of Teresa Lockhart's parenting.

"Of course I didn't. I can't believe you would even suggest such a thing."

Ellery nodded. Margery was a fifty-something granny with stretch pants, sensible shoes, and a pristine white cardigan. She did not look the part of a child kidnapper, and Ellery couldn't imagine her using text-speak in any case. "What did you think of Teresa Lockhart's TV appearance?"

Margery glanced over her shoulder before answering. "I pray that works to bring Chloe home," she told the detectives. "Mrs. Lockhart doesn't even like having her picture taken. This must be torture for her."

Ellery wondered if that was part of the point, if the person who texted the request knew Teresa well enough to understand the special agony of forcing her to appear on television. No doubt the woman had endured a hungry press once before when her first child was murdered. "We have a couple of additional questions for you," Ellery told Margery. "Is there someplace quiet we could talk?"

Margery looked around at the houseful of people. "The greenhouse," she said at length. "It's attached at the back." She took them to an enclosed glass room off the kitchen where riotous plants unfurled giant leaves all the way to the ceiling.

"Is that a banana tree?" Dorie asked with incredulity.

"Theoretically, yes. I'm not sure it's ever borne fruit." She eyed the closed door behind them. "What is it you want to ask me?"

"You know that the video we've found so far shows that Chloe left the fair on her own."

"I still can't quite believe it. But yes, that's what her parents told me." Her worried gaze slid to the door again as though she feared who might walk through it and catch them talking. "I don't know that I'll have a job when Chloe comes home. They blame me for her running off."

"Who do you blame?" Ellery asked.

A furrow appeared in her brow. "Do you have kids?" Ellery and Dorie both shook their heads. "Well, I've raised three of them. All good kids, but let me tell you, there were some years in there . . . My oldest once told me she was saying the night at a friend's house, only it turned out they drove to Quebec, got drunk, and had to be fished out of a canal by the local authorities. My son, he went six weeks without saying more than two words to any question I asked him. I know because I counted. Chloe was turning thirteen in a few weeks, which I suppose makes her ripe for this sort of behavior. They drive you up a wall so that you're not sorry when they move out."

"You think she was reacting to her home life," Dorie said.

She found her parents to be too strict. Especially Mrs. Lockhart. Truthfully, so did I, but no one could really blame the woman after what happened the first time." She bit her lip. "Mrs. Lockhart loves that girl, of that I have no doubt. But she was more comfortable giving her rules than affection. Almost like she didn't want to get too close. She'd come into the room, ask Chloe about her day, and then find some reason to leave again. It wasn't as bad when Chloe was younger because she'd just grab her mother's legs or climb into her lap. These days, they seemed to communicate more by text than anything else."

"What about Mr. Lockhart? How does he get along with Chloe?"

"Oh, he dotes on her. They go for bike rides together on the weekends. Whenever he travels for work, he brings her back chocolate or a stuffed toy." She paused. "Of course, the last one she threw in the trash."

"When was that?" Ellery asked.

"About a month ago. He went to Japan and brought her back a Hello Kitty. She said it was for babies and threw it away. I could see on his face that she about broke his heart. He's been working longer hours lately—something about a big new client—and I think Chloe took it kind of personal." She took a deep breath and folded her arms across her chest. "This house gets awful quiet sometimes with only me and Chloe in it. Maybe . . . maybe she went looking for some noise."

"Where would she go?"

"I keep asking myself that same question. I guessed she'd be off with McKenna or one of her other friends, but they all seem accounted for."

Ellery pulled out her phone and called up the picture of Chloe and the unidentified young man. "Do you recognize this boy?"

The creases around Margery's eyes scrunched together as she studied the image. "He looks vaguely familiar, but I can't say I know him. Where was this taken?"

"We were hoping you could tell us."

Margery examined the photo again, taking in his patched-up army jacket, the chain around his neck, and the ink across his hands. "This boy looks like he's high school or older. I don't know how Chloe would've run into him."

"Could he be related to one of her friends? The son of one of her tutors?"

Margery's lips thinned and she handed back the phone with a firm gesture. "No. We don't know anyone who looks like that."

Like what? Ellery wanted to ask her. *Black? Poor? "Street"?* But Dorie had been teaching her that the most important part of being a detective was to keep your mouth shut and your ears open, to remain neutral or even sympathetic when people confessed their worst thoughts and deeds. *People will share their whole story,* she'd counseled Ellery, *but you have to give them the space to do it. You've got to be willing to buy a murderer a donut and cup of coffee, to hold his hand while he explains how he used his neighbor's chain saw to dismember his wife. Tell him he's not such a bad guy after all.*

Dorie had the rep to back it up; her wide blue eyes and friendly, open face had wrung out more confessions than any grizzled male cop with the urge to put the perp's head through a wall. Ellery just found the head-through-the-wall scenario more personally satisfying. "Okay, if you think of where you might have seen him, let us know," she said to Margery. "If we can figure out where she met him, we can identify who he is."

"If you send me the picture, I can ask around. My younger two kids are closer to his age. Maybe they would recognize him."

"Your kids, do they know Chloe?"

"Of course. She used to come over to my place a bunch when she was smaller. She loved to help in my garden, and she was crazy about Miss Piggy, our guinea pig."

"She still visits your place?" Ellery asked.

"Not anymore." She paused. "Mrs. Lockhart asked me to stop bringing her over there a few years ago, and so I did."

"Any idea why she'd ask that?" Dorie wanted to know.

Margery glanced toward the main house. "Chloe asked if she could move in with me. I said no, of course. She has a lovely home here. But she must have repeated the request to the Lockharts, and they didn't take kindly to it."

"How did Chloe take it when you said no?" Ellery asked.

Margery smiled sadly. "She didn't kick up a fuss. She never did. She said, 'Tell the sunflowers that I miss them.' They're blooming now, almost five feet tall. I look out my kitchen window and see them at different times, moving their heads around this way and that. I know in my head they're just following the sunshine, but I can't help feeling like they're looking for Chloe."

"Okay, well, thanks for your time. We'll be in touch if we have any more questions." Margery left them in the greenhouse.

"More questions?" Dorie asked. "I have about a thousand of them."

"Me, too." Ellery's phone buzzed in her pocket, and she drew it out to study the latest message. "Apparently, the tip line got something interesting enough to forward up the chain. Someone who didn't care to leave their name phoned a few hours ago to say that Martin Lockhart is having an affair."

Dorie sighed. "Yet more questions. Did they say who with?"

"Amanda McFarland."

"You mean that cool drink of water from his office who made up some excuse to drop by yesterday?"

"It has to be. How many Amanda McFarlands can he know?"

"We can go in there and hit him with it now. See what he says."

Ellery checked her watch, feeling time slipping away. "Give me a second. I want to consult an expert." She walked off behind the banana plant and dialed Reed's number. He answered straightaway.

"I saw Teresa's plea," he said. "Hopefully whoever has Chloe saw it, too."

"Did she look contrite enough to you?"

"She looked terrified."

Ellery hummed a reply. "Maybe that will be enough. Listen, we've uncovered a new wrinkle. Someone phoned the tip line to say that Martin Lockhart is having an affair with a woman at his office named Amanda McFarland. I'd say it was nothing, but she made up a pretext to drop by the house yesterday to see him. Teresa wasn't pleased."

"You think she knows?"

"What do you think?" Reed's family had spent decades ignoring his father's serial infidelities.

"In my experience, the wife's radar is rarely wrong. What does Martin Lockhart say about it?"

"We haven't asked him yet. We were just on our way to talk to Chloe's best friend again. The nanny couldn't ID the boy from the photo, so we thought McKenna would be our best shot."

"That does seem to be the more pressing lead."

"Yeah, it's hard to see how Martin Lockhart's inability to keep his pants zipped could be related to Chloe's abduction."

"It's probably not. Except . . ."

He didn't finish his thought. She waited and then prodded him. "Except?"

She heard a long exhale. "Where there's one secret, you'll find others. There's something hiding in the middle of that family, something they're not telling us."

Ellery agreed the Lockharts seemed haunted, but she didn't see any mystery to it. "Maybe it's just the ghost of Trevor Stone."

"Maybe. I can talk to Martin Lockhart if you like."

"You would? That would be great." Ellery peeked out from behind the plant and signaled Dorie that they could go. "If Martin Lockhart was boning his younger colleague while his daughter got kidnapped, let me know. At least then he'd have a solid alibi."

"Wasn't he playing golf with the lawyer? Stephen Wintour?"

"Like you said—where there's one lie, you'll find others."

9

Reed regretted his hasty decision when he saw the news vans with their satellite dishes outside the Lockhart home. The shouts of the reporters being held at bay by sawhorses and uniformed officers landed like blows on his back as he ushered Tula up the front walk. "Whose house is this, Daddy?" Tula skipped along beside him, the picture of innocence. "It's big like Grandma and Papa's."

"The girl who is missing, Chloe Lockhart, lives here. Daddy just needs to talk to her father for a few minutes."

"Oh. Does he know where she is?"

Let's hope not, thought Reed. He rang the bell and Margery Brimwood answered. "Agent Markham," she said with a note of surprise as she glanced at Tula. "Bringing along the young recruits today?"

"This is my daughter, Tula. Tula, this is Mrs. Brimwood. I wondered if maybe Tula could have some cookies and milk while I spoke with Mr. Lockhart for a few minutes."

"Sure, we can do that," Margery said as she welcomed them inside. "It would be nice to do something normal for a change. Maybe after the cookies, we could take Snuffles out to the backyard for some exercise. She's missing her little girl, you know."

"Snuffles is Chloe's dog," Reed explained to Tula, who lit up at the prospect.

"I love dogs!"

"And Snuffles will love you, too, I'm sure. Come this way to the kitchen, love." She looked over her shoulder to Reed. "You'll find Martin in his study—through those doors and down the hall on the right. Fair warning, though: he's not alone."

Reed followed the directions to a mahogany paneled door, where he paused to listen. He heard murmured voices on the other side, one male and one female. *Here we go,* he thought, and he pushed open the door without knocking. A blond woman looked up sharply from her place at Martin Lockhart's side. "Who the hell are you?" Lockhart demanded. He sat at his desk with some papers in front of him. The woman had her arm across the back of Lockhart's chair, and her body posture, leaning down over him, put her breasts in direct line with his eyeballs.

"Special Agent Reed Markham," Reed replied. "I'm consulting on your daughter's case." He took in the masculine room with dark wood paneling that smelled like books and leather. The floor-to-ceiling shelves gleamed in the recessed lighting, while the large window gave a prime view of the rosebushes blooming outside. It reminded him of his father's office back at home.

"Oh, right," said Lockhart gruffly. "Captain Conroy mentioned you. What is it? Is there some news?"

"Nothing yet." He looked at the woman, who had not been introduced. "I'm sorry . . . you are?"

"Amanda McFarland," she said as she offered her hand. "I work with Martin."

"Is that what you're doing here? Work?"

"Actually no. Amanda thought it might make sense to offer a reward for information leading to Chloe's return. I agree with her and we're just discussing some possibilities on how to go about it. Her background is in PR, so her knowledge is helpful here."

"I see. Have you talked about this with Teresa?"

Martin's cheeks hollowed out with his frown. "My wife is upstairs resting. The TV appearance did her in, as you might imagine."

"Yes, it would be devastating to have your child abducted and then have the kidnapper suggest the motive is your miserable parenting. Why do you think the text focused solely on Teresa with no mention of you?"

"I have no idea."

"Someone called the tip line today with an idea," Reed said, looking from one to the other. Amanda McFarland's blue eyes appeared cool and speculative. Martin seemed tense and distracted. "The tipster said you're having an affair. The pair of you."

Martin sucked in a quick breath, as if he'd been punched. Amanda laughed. "Since it's not true," she said, "I can tell you exactly who phoned in that tip. Teresa Lockhart."

"You don't know that." Martin turned to her with scorn.

"Come on now, Martin, you know she can't stand me."

"You're saying there is no affair?" Reed watched closely for their denials.

"Of course not," Amanda replied, but Martin didn't meet his gaze.

"No," he said at length. "No affair. Nothing like that."

"Why would someone call in the tip then?" Reed asked.

"I just told you—" Amanda began, but Martin cut her off.

"You get loads of tips that are wrong or go nowhere, right? Conroy told me that earlier when I broached the reward idea with him. He said it would only bring out more cranks."

"He's probably right."

"Yes, well, I don't give a damn how many bottom-feeders come nibbling to the surface. It only takes one real call to get the answer. If I have to pay a thousand people to man the phones, I'll do it. Whatever it takes to bring Chloe home." His fiery delivery seemed convincing, but Reed still believed the man was holding something back.

"I'd like to speak to Mr. Lockhart alone, if I could," he said to Amanda.

"Fine." She uncrossed her arms and stopped glaring at Reed long enough to give Martin's arm a sympathetic squeeze. "I'll add a thousand to the total, whatever it is. Just let me know how I can help, okay?"

He covered her hand with his own. "Thank you."

As she left, Reed noted the crisp linen skirt, the high heels, and a heavy scent of perfume and makeup in her wake. Whatever her relationship to Martin Lockhart, she'd come dressed for a date, not a strategy meeting over reward money. Martin watched her go with a searching expression that Reed couldn't decipher. The heavy quiet was interrupted by a child's happy shout and the noise of barking. Behind Martin's shoulder, Reed could see Tula with Margery in the backyard. His daughter laughed as she ran in circles, presumably with a little white dog yipping at her heels. Martin heard the giggles and turned to look. "Who's that out there?" he demanded, rising from his chair. "I didn't let a child in here."

"She's my daughter. She and I were visiting Boston when Chloe went missing."

Martin turned to him with fresh understanding in his eyes. "You have a daughter."

"She's seven."

Martin nodded dumbly. "I liked seven. Chloe had such an intense curiosity back then. She wanted to know all about my trips. We'd sit in here and look at the atlas together. She was especially fascinated with Egypt. I brought her back a little pyramid with a mummy inside and she slept with it for a week. I think she still has it in her room."

"I take it almost-thirteen is harder."

"She doesn't laugh like that anymore," answered Martin, looking out the window again. "She hasn't for a long time."

"Why do you think that is?"

He turned with a heavy sigh. "Adolescent hormones, maybe. Also, as I mentioned, she wanted more independence, more freedom. I suppose I did, too, when I was her age. I remember thinking my father was like a fossil and he was fifteen years younger at the time than I am now." He gave a ghost of a smile, thinking on it.

"Someone thinks you're having an affair with Ms. McFarland," Reed said. "She seems pretty convinced it's your wife."

Martin snorted and picked up some papers from his desk. "Teresa sees threats that aren't there. It's rather her defining characteristic, if you will."

"So there's nothing there between you and Amanda McFarland," Reed replied, unconvinced. "Nothing at all."

Martin shuffled paper and didn't answer for a long time.

"Mr. Lockhart?"

He frowned at the papers with faint accusation. "I met Teresa two years after Trevor died. It was at a benefit for the hospital and she gave an impassioned speech about the medical profession and 'the duty to care,' about how patients come to the hospital at one of the worst points in their lives and doctors need to be mindful of how utterly terrifying that is. We need to see the person, she said. Not the disease. I remember thinking at the time that she must have been a patient herself at some point and something went wrong. You could see it in her. There was a woundedness in her eyes, like she hadn't properly healed. I wanted to take care of her."

"Did she tell you about Trevor's death?"

"No, someone else did when I started asking around about her. I was appalled. I—I tried to fix it. I offered to pay a private investigator to look into the case, but she refused. She said they had hired one back when the murder happened, but he didn't have any luck. The entire Philadelphia police force couldn't solve it, she told me. What's one more person going to do at this late date? I asked what I could do—something, anything, to help her. She said she wanted to plant some spring bulbs at her home and if I wanted to, I could help her with that. We started seeing a lot of each other after that."

"You fell in love," Reed said.

"I did," he said, lowering himself into his chair like a man much older than he was. "I told myself Teresa did, too. She didn't say the words, but there was tenderness and care in her actions. She would make the coffee strong, the way I liked it, and just add more milk to hers. She would bring along my sweater when we went out because she knew I'd get chilly and wouldn't think to bring it. She kissed my cheek every morning before she left for work, no matter where I was in the house. She would find me and give me that kiss." He touched his cheek, rubbing it absently. "Then Chloe was born and I saw it at last—love, real love. Not just for the baby, but for me, too. She beamed. She laughed. The passion she always had at work spilled over into our home, and it was glorious. It was like she came back to life. Teresa's heart expanded and we all fit inside, snug as a bug in a rug, as my own mother used to say."

"So, what happened?"

His smile faded. "Chloe got older, more mobile, and she wanted to explore the world. Teresa's fears started to grow as she imagined all sorts of terrible fates befalling Chloe. Poisons, predators, accidents on the street. We put up bars on the windows and cameras around the house and we stopped taking Chloe out in public as much, but none of it seemed to calm Teresa's fears. I asked her to see a doctor, someone to help her manage her anxiety, but she snapped at me that she wasn't crazy, that her child had died and I would never understand that." He looked at Reed, his eyes wet. "What can you say to that?"

Reed had no answer. "And Amanda McFarland?" he asked.

"We kissed," Martin admitted, shamefaced. "Once. No, twice. She initiated it, not me, although I didn't push her away as quickly as I might have. She wanted more, but I was clear with her. I would never leave Chloe. I would never betray my family."

Reed's cell phone buzzed from his pocket, an insistent ring. He dug it out and noted the name. Sarit. He declined the call and stuck the phone back in his jeans. "Who besides Amanda McFarland knows about the kisses the two of you shared?"

"No one, or so I thought." He shrugged. "Maybe Teresa has been paying more attention to me than I gave her credit for."

Reed's phone rang again. Sarit would not be denied. He reached into his pocket and silenced it. "You never considered leaving? Moving out or starting over?"

"And risk leaving Chloe alone with Teresa? No." He leaned back in his seat, seeming defeated. "I owe her an apology, it seems. All these years, I thought she was stifling, too overprotective. I thought she'd been broken in a way I could never fix. It turns out she was right all along."

A sharp knock on the door made Martin sit up and Reed turn around. Captain Conroy poked his head into the room, his expression troubled. "Agent Markham, could I grab you for a few minutes? I need your opinion on something."

"What is it?" Martin asked as he got to his feet. "Has something happened?"

Conroy held out a forestalling hand. "You stay put for now, okay? I'll call you if I need you."

"What's up?" Reed asked as they walked through the house. He peeked at his cell phone and saw that Sarit had left a voice mail and also sent a text. He ignored the voice mail for now. The text was a screen grab of a television, some news channel. The slightly blurry image showed him and Tula outside the Lockhart home and the chyron read: *FBI PROFILER JOINS CASE FOR MISSING GIRL.* Sarit had included her own caption as well: *What the ever-loving fuck, Reed??*

"Someone found a large envelope on a bench in the Common. It has Teresa Lockhart's name on it, so they turned it over to the nearest beat officer. He brought it to his precinct, and we are having it couriered over to us."

"What's in it?"

"Don't know yet," Conroy muttered. "My guess is nothing good. Ah, here we go." The front door swung open and a uniformed officer appeared with a paper bag. "Is that the parcel?"

The man nodded. "Press outside is mighty curious."

"Forget them." Conroy jerked a nod at Reed. "Let's check it out down here, away from prying eyes." The two men found an unoccupied room, empty save for a grand piano and some bookshelves. Conroy put on gloves and removed the large envelope from inside the bag. He set it on the piano bench and took a few pictures with his phone. The envelope itself appeared unremarkable, the kind you could purchase from any office store or even a supermarket. The block lettering on the front gave Teresa's name and nothing more. "Here I go," Conroy said with a deep breath. He used a pocketknife to slit the envelope open and then tilted it sideways so the contents fell out onto the bench.

Both men gasped as a pile of silky blond hair spilled out across the black lacquer. A note card fell atop the pile: *NOT GOOD ENOUGH. NEXT TIME, IT'S HER FINGERS.*

"Jesus, what a sick fuck," Conroy whispered. The color had drained completely from his face. He appeared to be swallowing back nausea. "What would make someone do this? What do we do now, give in to him? Set up another TV spot with the mom?"

Reed barely heard him over the buzzing in his ears. He stared at the pile of hair, pictured Chloe's face in his mind, and imagined her being held down as someone took a razor to her. From outside, Tula screamed—a happy noise, but Reed's heart lurched to a stop. "I have to go," he said, feeling the walls closing in around him.

"Wait," Conroy protested. "I need advice here."

"I'll call you," Reed said without slowing down.

Only once in the taxi, with Tula leaning against his arm and making up some tuneless song about Snuffles, did he breathe again.

10

Ellery braced herself for a fight with McKenna's father the judge about whether they would be allowed to question her outside the presence of her parents, but Dorie's soft touch won him over. Head tilted downward in deference, big pleading eyes. Dorie gave him the works. "If it was the other way around and McKenna was the one who was missing, wouldn't you want Chloe to share absolutely everything she knows?"

"Of course you can talk to her," Judge McIntyre said as he let them inside another posh suburban home. "I just don't think she can be of any additional help. McKenna answered your questions yesterday and she's been in bed with a stomachache today. This whole business is quite upsetting for her."

"I feel for the girl. I do," Dorie said. "But you must have seen the news conference this afternoon with Chloe's parents today."

He gave a short nod of assent. "I saw."

"Then you don't have to imagine how upsetting it is for the Lockharts."

He hesitated another beat before relenting. "McKenna is upstairs in her bedroom. I'll show you the way."

Soon Ellery found herself in another teen girl's bedroom, this one smaller than Chloe's but screaming money all the same. McKenna's room featured gleaming white crown moldings set off against chiffon-pink walls. Her bed was as big as Ellery's at home, and above it hung a crystal chandelier. McKenna took out her earbuds and put down her phone as her father and the detectives entered her room. "Sweetheart, these officers have a few more questions for you about Chloe," he explained.

McKenna curled into her overstuffed pillows, hugging a heart-shaped one against her chest. "I said everything I knew already. If I knew where she was right now, I'd tell you. I swear."

"We believe you," Dorie assured her. "We just have a few minor details we think you can help us with."

"Like what?" McKenna asked, still wary.

"Some more information about who Chloe's friends are. Stuff like that."

She shrugged one shoulder. "I guess."

"I'll be downstairs if you need me," her father said. He paused at the door and ran his hand down the edge. "We're all praying for Chloe to come home safely."

He left and McKenna regarded the detectives. "It's true," she said. "We had a special prayer in church for her this morning."

"Does Chloe go to your church?"

"Only sometimes. Her mom works on Sundays."

"What do you think of Mrs. Lockhart?" Dorie asked as Ellery wandered about the room. McKenna apparently collected glass figurines of sea creatures. There was a shelf of them next to her desk.

"She's okay, I guess." McKenna picked at the edge of her bed-spread. "When we were little kids, our families had a picnic at the park and this guy on a motorcycle had an accident right near us. He lost control or something and flipped through the air and landed on his head. Mrs. Lockhart ran over there to give him CPR and other first aid before the ambulance came. My dad told me later she saved that guy's life, which I guess is pretty cool when you think about it. But mostly, she's not around when I'm at their house. Mimi is."

Ellery looked over the truly amazing amount of makeup and jewelry covering the top of McKenna's vanity. She picked up a metallic blue eyeliner, a brand she didn't recognize, and put it back down. Her own mother would've thrown a fit if she'd tried to wear this stuff at age thirteen. McKenna had tacked some photos along the edges of her large mirror, and Ellery scanned each one in turn, looking for Chloe. Where McKenna had featured prominently in Chloe's photo stream, Ellery saw only one picture of Chloe in McKenna's grouping. It showed the girls in pigtails and one-piece swimsuits, obviously taken years ago.

"Did Chloe get along with her mother?" Dorie asked as Ellery continued snooping.

"Not really." McKenna kept her eyes on Ellery. "No offense or anything, but moms can sometimes be a total drag. Mine won't let me wear heels higher than one inch. She's got a ruler to check them and everything. Chloe's parents were even way more strict. They barely let her out of the house."

Ellery pointed at the pictures. "Is that why you've been hanging out with her less?"

McKenna's face turned red. "Yeah, I guess. Like, my sister and her friends drove out to Six Flags earlier this summer, and they said they'd bring me and a friend of mine, too. Chloe couldn't come because of her parents, so I took Brooke instead."

"Was Chloe ever tempted to sneak out?" asked Dorie.

"She tried once last year when Kevin Rohr was having a pool party. But somehow she set off the alarm in her house. Her parents took away all her electronics for a month after that." McKenna gave a small shudder of horror at the thought. "Her phone and computer are, like, her lifeline. They may as well've put her in a dungeon."

"Except Chloe had a second phone," Ellery pointed out.

"Yeah." There was a touch of admiration in McKenna's voice. She held her own phone like a talisman between her hands.

"Still no idea who could've given it to her?"

A shadow crossed the girl's face. Ellery could see Dorie saw it, too. "If you know something," Dorie told her, "now is the time to tell us."

McKenna blew her bangs out of her eyes. "You've got to understand, Chloe was the youngest kid in our class. She wasn't even thirteen yet and a bunch of us are turning fourteen soon. A couple of the guys are shaving." At their look of disbelief, she pulled out a picture on her phone to show them. "It's true! Barnaby's parents redshirted him. He's going to be fifteen in December."

Ellery and Dorie leaned in to squint at a blond kid with no discernible facial hair. "Redshirt?" Ellery asked.

"Held him back when he should've started kindergarten. It's supposed to give you an edge because you're like a year older or something. Chloe's parents could've had a legit reason for keeping her back because her birthday was so close to the cutoff, but, like, that would've been totally insane. She's wicked smart. Mr. Donovan stopped calling on her in math class because everyone else would just wait for her to get the answer first."

Ellery had been the smart kid in her early years. By middle school, she'd stopped caring where X went or how to diagram a complex sentence. Her father had left. Daniel got sick. She'd liked school because her friends had shared their extra food with her—cookies and chips and half a sandwich crammed full with meat. All stuff they never had at home. "So, Chloe's the youngest and she knows lots of answers. How'd that shake out on the playground?"

McKenna made a face that said her classmates wouldn't be caught dead near a playground. "Chloe tried hard. Too hard. You could see her trying to impress people, but they mostly ignored her or made fun of her behind her back. It's not like she could invite friends over. The Lockharts would only allow that if they knew the other parents and had met them first. So, sometimes Chloe made up stories. One time she said Tom Brady—you know, the quarterback!"

Dorie suppressed a grin. "We've heard of him," she said dryly.

"Chloe said her parents had a dinner party and Tom and Gisele came. She said Mrs. Lockhart knew him from the hospital, where he stopped by to visit sick kids. A few kids believed her because she had a signed picture from him, but if Tom Brady comes to your house, you're gonna take a selfie with him, right?"

Ellery thought of the picture of Chloe and the unidentified boy. "Right."

"It turns out the part about the hospital was true. Mrs. Lockhart got Tom to sign a picture over to Chloe, but Chloe didn't meet him. He definitely didn't come to her house for dinner."

"Okay, so she exaggerates sometimes," Dorie said.

McKenna took a deep breath. "Right. So, when she said she suddenly had this mystery friend who gave her the phone, I kinda figured that maybe she bought it for herself."

Now that would be an interesting development, thought Ellery. It would fit with the notion that Chloe orchestrated the disappearance to get back at her parents for their restrictive upbringing. But would a twelve-year-old girl send that vicious text to her mother? Also, Chloe obviously had some sort of destination in mind when she left the park. She had to be somewhere. Ellery pulled out her phone to show McKenna the picture of Chloe and the unknown boy. McKenna's hand flew to her mouth when she saw it.

"Wait, he's real?"

"Who's real? You know this guy?" She tried not to leap on the girl too hard, but she felt the familiar tingle of a developing lead. Finally, they were going to get a name.

"She called him Ty. She said she knew this cool older skater guy and he liked her back, but he didn't go to our school. I figured he was just another one of her stories. Like, where's Chloe going to meet a guy like that? Mimi doesn't let her out of her sight."

"Online, maybe," Dorie offered, and Ellery agreed.

"We really need to get that dump of her computer and cell phone."

McKenna looked horrified. "Wait, you're going to like . . . read all her messages?"

"Don't worry," Ellery told her. "We won't share them around. But if there's anything in there you think we need to know, it's better if you tell us now."

Her shoulders went up around her ears. "No, nothing illegal or anything like that. Just stupid jokes and stuff about boys that I wouldn't want my dad to read, you know?" She got up from the bed and went to her window—the one with the heavy custom drapes that shimmered as she pushed one aside. "I don't like to think about her out there by herself. I can't even believe this is happening. When my dad first told me Chloe was gone, I kept hoping it wasn't real, that it was just a game she made up to trick her parents. Like hide-and-go-seek or something." She turned to look at them and Ellery saw a little girl's frightened gaze pleading under all that eyeliner. "But it's not, is it? It's real."

They didn't have to answer her because she already knew the truth. Ellery took in the large flat-screen television mounted to the wall, the two-hundred-dollar headphones lying on McKenna's bed, and the enormous rack of shoes visible through the open closet door. She'd never liked the admonition that "money can't buy happiness," because in her experience, the people who said it had never had to go hungry or sleep alone in a car at night. If money wasn't going to make you happy, it could at least make you comfortable while you dealt with all your other shit. But she felt some sympathy for McKenna, and for her father and all the other parents feeling vulnerable or bewildered. They were learning what Teresa Lockhart surely knew: Tragedy swept in like fog, seeping through the cracks of even the richest homes. Once it happened, it didn't matter how big or fancy your place was on the outside. Inside, it felt the same.

11

Ellery picked up Bump from the pet sitter and returned to her apartment building to find Reed and Tula hanging out in the lobby. They sat side by side on black armchairs, Reed studying his phone and Tula slumped almost to the floor like something out of a Dalí painting. Reed looked up, expectant at the sight of her. "Anything from the package?" he asked her.

She shook her head. "Several unknown prints. No one saw who left the envelope on the bench."

"But it's her hair?"

"It's human and a color match. That's all we can say right now. There are no roots available for DNA testing. Everyone is still holding on to the idea that Chloe did this herself to get back at her mom. She's obviously smart, she left the park on her own, and the shaved head is the kind of dramatic move an angry teenager might make."

"It's possible," Reed agreed. "Overall, this doesn't fit the pattern of any traditional kidnapping. But she would've required help to pull this off. I don't think a kid that age, especially given her coddled upbringing so far, is surviving on the streets on her own."

She nodded, exhausted. "We're still trying to figure out who gave her the second phone. Conroy made us go home for at least six hours. Night shift is taking over for now."

"Let's go up, then."

She looked him up and down as they waited for the elevator. "Conroy said you ran out on him at the Lockhart place."

"I shouldn't have been there in the first place. Not with Tula." He reached out and hugged his daughter to his side. "I phoned him back later and told him what I could. I think Teresa should do another television appearance. At least it keeps the conversation going. If there's a chance Chloe herself is behind this, she'll be watching to see that her mother cares to engage."

Ellery bit back what she wanted to say, which was that the "conversation" was one-way and now possibly involved severed body parts. She curled her fingers inward and looked at the ceiling of the elevator. She'd been anticipating the cool solitude of her loft apartment and instead she now had to play hostess. They crowded awkwardly in the hallway in front of her door while she went through the elaborate process of unlocking it. Tula fidgeted the entire time and then burst through the open portal like a flash flood.

"Is there any ice cream left? What are we having for dinner?"

Bump, who pursued any creature in motion, tore the leash from Ellery's hand and went galumphing after her. The cacophony of Tula running in circles and the dog barking reverberated off Ellery's hardwood floors and into her bones. She eased into her own home as though she was checking it for intruders—slow, careful, and with her back to the wall. Behind her, Reed's Southern accent took on an amused drawl. "We'll be out of your hair after supper, I assure you. We'll go to the hotel where she can take a swim before we head out to Philadelphia tomorrow."

"You're leaving already?" She felt bereft. She felt relief.

"If I'm to understand the murders at the Stone house, I need to go there myself. Tula will stay with my sister for the day while I poke around to see what I can find out."

She paused from where she was filling the dog's dish with water and looked him over searchingly. "You'd do that for me?"

He lounged against the counter next to her. "Well now, I'm not going there for you. I'm going for Chloe and Teresa Lockhart." He materialized a small cardboard box tied with red-and-white string. "This is for you, though."

"Mike's!" she exclaimed with delight, seizing on the box. Inside sat two fat cannoli. "You do love me."

His expression faltered, just for a moment, and hot shame washed over her as she remembered she had not said the words back to him. She'd tried. She'd practiced in her head a few times, but terror made her throat close up every time she imagined saying them aloud. Everyone she'd ever loved had left her in one way or another. "Maybe not as much as you love food," he said lightly, nudging her hand with one finger. She curled her hand around his, and this minor contact felt so good that she moved closer, into his intimate space. As always, he took his cues from her, waiting until she signaled she wanted more. They embraced and she tucked her nose into his warm neck. How he managed to smell so divine after a day in the sun remained a mystery. His hand took up a slow caress of her back, and she felt some of the tension in her spine loosen and fall away.

"You're too good to me."

"There is no such thing."

"Ah-hem." Tula's loud throat clearing made Ellery jump back from Reed. She turned to find both the girl and the dog staring at them. "What's for supper?" Tula asked. For emphasis, Bump leaned over and nosed his food bowl.

"I'm working on it," Ellery told the hound. He whined and stamped a meaty paw to show she wasn't moving fast enough.

"What about sandwiches from the deli down the street?" Reed suggested.

"Sure, I'll go," Ellery volunteered quickly. Her house had too many people in it. She filled the dog's bowl with kibble and straightened up again, dusting her hands on her jeans.

"Great. Maybe you could take Tula with you while I catch up on email."

She opened her mouth to object, but the hope on Reed's face made her shut it again. She swallowed hard and gave a short nod. "Sure, okay."

Tula looked about as excited as she was by the prospect. "Is it really far?"

Reed tousled her head. "I've seen you do fourteen hours straight at Disney World without a single peep. I think you can manage three blocks to the deli."

Ellery gritted her teeth, fearing she'd be dragging a sullen child with her, but Tula's natural enthusiasm took over as they reached the outdoors. She moved in a bouncy gait that was almost a skip. "Daddy said your apartment used to be part of a factory."

"Yep."

"That's cool. I want to live in a fire station one day. Like with a sliding pole?"

"I don't think firefighters actually live at the station."

"Oh, I don't want to be a fireman. I want to be an acrobat. See?" Damned if the girl didn't turn a cartwheel right there on the cement sidewalk. Ellery's heart lurched at the sight, envisioning Tula with a cracked skull. How the hell did Reed think she could be in charge of a kid?

"Maybe save the tricks for the Big Top, okay?"

They reached an intersection and Tula automatically slid her hand into Ellery's as they crossed. Ellery almost recoiled but managed to tamp down her instinct to shake off the physical contact. Tula twisted her arm as they reached the other side. "Those marks you got are from the bad guy, right?"

More anxiety, filling up her stomach like a balloon. She had no idea what Reed had told the girl about her history. "Um, yeah. A long time ago."

"Were you scared when he got you?" Tula still had her hand in a tight grip, swinging it back and forth as they walked.

"Yes." Ellery glanced down at her. "A lot."

"I would be, too."

"He's in prison now," Ellery felt compelled to add. "He can't hurt you." The feel of Tula's small, soft hand in hers made her weirdly protective.

"Or you." She halted and released Ellery's hand. "I have a scar, too, on my knee right here. See it?"

Ellery could just make out a faint line on Tula's tawny knee. "I see, yes."

"I was climbing on some rocks at the beach and I slipped. Mama and Daddy had to take me for stitches. Daddy says the scar is proof of how brave I was."

"Oh, yeah? He says the same thing to me."

"Do you believe him?" Tula tilted her head, hanging on the answer.

Ellery looked away, not wanting to lie. "I believe he believes it," she said finally.

Tula nodded and reinserted her hand into Ellery's as they began walking. "Yeah, me neither."

As they waited for their food to be assembled, Ellery's cell phone buzzed. She dug it out and saw the message was from Reed. She thought he might be checking to see that she'd kept Tula alive for ten consecutive minutes, but his message turned out to be about the Lockhart case: *I'm doing reconnaissance on Ethan Stone, Teresa's first husband. Turns out he was speaking at an economics conference this week. His talk was on Friday. Care to guess where?*

Boston, she typed back.

Bingo. It was hosted by MIT.

Is he still here? She would love to get a look at him.

Doubtful. Conference wrapped up this AM. He will be my first target in Philly.

He'd shot to the top of Ellery's list, too. She wondered if she could convince Conroy to allow her to accompany Reed to Pennsylvania. She was still lost in thought about this new development as they received their bag of sandwiches and started the walk home. Tula had hold of her hand again and she was humming some tune that Ellery barely registered.

"Ellery! Ellery!"

It took her a moment to hear her name. People recognized her in public all the time, but usually they responded with whispers and furtive attempts to snap her picture, like she was some lioness they spotted on safari.

"Ellery!"

"What?" She looked down at Tula with a trace of impatience. "What is it?"

Tula pointed across the street. "It wasn't me. It was her."

Ellery turned to see an unfamiliar young woman with a large backpack loping across the street. She stopped in front of them with an excited little hop, her cheeks pink from either the effort or the unusually warm evening. "Wow, I was just heading to your place when I happened to see you. I can't believe I found you here!"

"Well, you did." Ellery frowned, trying to figure out who the hell she was. Up close, the girl pinged around her brain, but she couldn't recall her name. "Can I help you with something?"

"It's me," she said, spreading her arms and smiling brightly like a model in a fifties soap commercial. "Ashley."

Ashley. Her stomach dropped and her mouth went dry in sudden recognition before the girl could add her final words.

"Your sister!"

Tula looked up at Ellery and made a noise of dismay at her incompetence. "You don't recognize your own sister?"

"It's okay. I didn't have hair the last time I saw her. It's growing out real fast now, though." Ashley Hathaway sported short black hair worn in a slightly spiky style. She ran a hand through it. "What do you think?"

"I, uh . . . it looks great." Her mind whirled as she tried to find the right words for this situation. Last she knew, Ashley didn't know who she was. Their dad had skipped out on Ellery's family to start a new one, unbeknownst to anyone at the time. He'd only returned when his new daughter needed a bone marrow transplant. Ellery had gone through with the procedure and abided by their father's wish that she not reveal her identity to the teenager. "How are you feeling?" she asked her now.

"Really good." She became shy and gave Ellery a mild shove. "Thanks to you."

"No need to thank me. Really." She hoisted the sandwich bag on her hip. "Uh, what brings you to town?"

"I came to see you. My sperm donor of a father finally confessed everything a couple of days ago. We had this huge fight and now here I am."

"Wait. You're saying your parents didn't bring you?"

"No, Peter Pan did." Off Ellery's look, Ashley rolled her eyes. "You know, the bus?"

"You took the bus all by yourself?" Tula clasped her hands in admiration.

"From Michigan?" Ellery echoed.

Ashley's bravado faltered. "I thought you'd want to meet me. For real this time."

"I did. I do. It's just—you didn't tell your parents where you were going?"

"He said to leave you alone! He said you didn't want anything to do with us. I knew that wasn't true or you wouldn't have agreed to be my donor." She looked hurt, angry, and hopeful all at the same time—a trifecta that only a teenager could pull off.

Well shit, Ellery thought. Now she had a second missing kid to deal with, and this time she'd be booked as the kidnapper if she didn't watch her step. She sighed and took Tula's hand again. "You may as well come home with us for now," she said. Her one-bedroom apartment was starting to resemble a crowded subway car.

12

"She looks healthy," Reed said as he watched Ellery pace the length of her bedroom. They had shut themselves away while Ashley and Tula devoured the sandwiches in Ellery's kitchen. "That's something, right?"

Ellery halted and looked at him, her gray eyes pensive. "It's everything."

"I know you've wondered how she's been doing," The last time Ellery saw Ashley—the only time—had been just before Ellery donated the bone marrow cells to treat Ashley's leukemia, when she lay half-alive in a hospital bed. Ellery's antigens hadn't been a match for her brother, Daniel, years ago, and she'd been afraid to check up on the girl for fear that she had failed a second time. Ashley, it seemed, had no such compunctions.

"I can't believe she just hopped a bus and traveled over eight states without telling anyone. She's only sixteen."

Reed folded his arms. "There must be an impulsive streak in the family."

"Ha, ha. Funny." She resumed her pacing. "I have to get in touch with my father, but I'm kind of enjoying the fact that he doesn't know where his kid is. That's terrible, right? Hell, maybe he doesn't even care. He didn't give a rat's ass where I was for twenty years."

"It's not terrible." John Hathaway had hared off for twenty years, leaving a wife and two devastated children. He hadn't returned when his daughter was abducted by a serial killer. He hadn't returned when his only son died of cancer. He hadn't known about any of it because he hadn't cared to know. "But you'll still have to tell him soon. Or have her do it. Otherwise, we're going to end up on the wrong end of a missing child investigation." He imagined another version of themselves in Michigan, a cop and an FBI agent starting the search for a lost child. "Tula and I can clear out of here and give you two some space."

Ellery looked alarmed. "You can't leave me alone with her. I don't know anything about kids."

The first baby Reed had ever held was his own. "No one does at first," he said with sympathy. "It gets better with practice."

"Easy for you to say. You've been on the job seven years."

"Oh, I never said it was easy." He crossed to take her gently by the arms. "She has parents, yes? She doesn't need that from you. She came here to find her sister. That, as I recall, you do know how to do."

She looked at him for a moment. "So, I should put her in a head-lock and tell her I'll cover her sheets with itching powder if she ever reads my diary again?"

He allowed himself a rueful half smile because her comment underscored how young she'd been when she lost Daniel, first to chemo and later to the cancer itself. "You keep a diary?"

"Don't you go snooping or I'll sic my attack dog on you."

Reed glanced at Bump, who was belly-up on the bed, snoring. "I'm not especially concerned."

Ellery only tolerated physical touch for so long. She extricated herself from his hands and wiped her palms on her jeans. "It would make our lives easier if Chloe kept a diary, huh?"

"I think that's all online now," Reed said, resigned. "No one bothers with private thoughts anymore."

"All the more reason we need her cell phone and computer data. I'm going to check to see if it's come in yet."

Reed nodded toward the other room where her half sister waited. "Don't you have something else to attend to first?"

Ellery already had her phone out to consult her email. "I'll multitask."

Reed bit back any further criticism or prodding. It would only make her retreat further behind her wall. Back in the kitchen, Ashley was painting Tula's fingernails a neon blue while Tula peppered her with questions about her trip. "Did you get to sleep on the bus? Like, all night?"

"Uh-huh."

"What about when you had to go the bathroom?"

"They had one on the bus."

"A bus with a bathroom? How was it?"

Ashley made a face. "Smelly," she said, and Tula giggled.

"Okay, time to wrap it up," Reed said, rubbing his hands together. "Tula and I need to get back to the hotel."

"Aw," Tula replied. "She's only done eight fingers."

"Once you hit ten, it's time to go." He began clearing away the sandwich wrappers while Ellery remained engrossed in her phone.

"You don't live here?" Ashley asked him.

"Nah, we live in Virginia," Tula answered as she admired her fully painted hands. "But maybe we could move here instead of Houston. Right, Daddy?"

Ellery's head jerked up in surprise. "Houston?"

So she wasn't completely checked out of the conversation. "I'll explain later," he said.

"You're moving to Houston?" she said as though he hadn't spoken.

"Ouch, touchy subject," Ashley muttered.

Tula rolled her eyes like she, too, was sixteen years old. "I know.

My mom and Randy whisper about it when they think I can't hear them."

"It's not me moving," Reed said to Ellery sotto voce, although the whole room was in on the secret now. "Sarit, maybe."

"How would that work?"

"I don't know." He rubbed the side of his head, which had started to throb.

Her phone pinged and she looked down at it. "The records are in," she said. "We should have a month's worth of Chloe's data."

"Can you send it to me?"

She gave him a cool glance. "I don't know. Are you officially on this case now, or what?"

Okay, he thought, *you're still mad about the Houston thing. Join the club, darlin'.* "It hasn't been an issue so far."

She shrugged one shoulder. "Granting you access to evidence that requires a warrant might be a good place to start."

He pursed his lips and shook his head slightly. Ellery had never been a stickler for rules, which meant the point of this exchange was just to stick it. To him.

She looked him over, her gaze challenging. "What's it going to be, Reed? Are you in or out?"

Tula jumped down from her stool and flapped around like an excited bat, drying her wet nails. "Wait till I tell Mama about this!"

God help me, Reed thought. "I'm in."

Reed took Tula to the hotel and they enjoyed a brief swim in the pool. He parked her in front of cartoons on the bed opposite his and pulled out his laptop, eager to see if Ellery had forwarded the information from Chloe's mobile phone and computer. When he saw she had sent the files, he propped up the pillows and settled in to read. Most of the exchanges were banal or ridiculous. Chloe and her friends had entire conversations in emojis. *We've come full circle to hieroglyphics*, Reed thought as he scrolled onward.

Did u c the sequin boots Emily wore 2day? McKenna wrote last week. *I need them!!!!*

Kinda extra if u ask me, Chloe wrote back.

Yah, extra AWESOME. That's facts.

Whatever. They r like $1000.

Ok, I'll put them on my b-day list.

Maybe I will get them 4 u. If ur nice enuf.

Ha! U don't have that much 💰 .

Ive been saving up. Plus, someone gave me a late b-day present.

$1000?????

Close enuf, Chloe said.

U lie.

Chloe sent back a picture of a hand (hers?) closed around multiple hundred-dollar bills.

HOLY SHIT, grrrrrl. What U been doing . . . turning tricks lol?

I told u. It was a present.

Don't even tell me it was Ty.

U don't believe he's real, so I won't tell u.

Even if he's real, u said he's what . . . 17? He doesn't have that kind of 💰 .

Ok, he doesn't have it. I do.😈

Ha ha ha. Ok, slut. We'll sneak you out & have sum real fun.

I wish. My warden can't be bought off.

Ask ur mom if you can sleep over this wknd. My dad will b working late and we can do wut we want.

If ur dad isn't home, there's no way my mom says yes.

So we don't tell her.

She always checks.🙀

Reed scanned through a bunch of texts from Barnaby pestering Chloe for math help. He was apparently in summer school. Chloe seemed happy to reply. Each day, there were multiple texts from Teresa:

Hi, sweetheart. Did you find the fruit salad for breakfast?

Yes, sir.✋

Mimi said she'd be happy to take you swimming at the club today. It's gorgeous outside.

If it's nice out, I want to go to the beach. Not the dumb old people's club.

No beach. There was a shark spotted there last week.

You never let me have any fun. 🌀 😤

One particular exchange with Teresa three days before Chloe disappeared caught Reed's attention:

Honey, the Metrowest Symphony Orchestra is holding auditions this fall for a young artist's concerto competition. I think you should try out with the Mozart 21.

I don't know if I feel like it.

You have a gift, Chloe. You should share it with the world.

If it's my gift, I should choose what to do with it, right?

Yes, but your father and I are the ones who pay for the lessons.

I didn't ask for those either.

You did. You begged me for a straight month when you were five.

I'm 12 now. Almost 13.

As the person who gave birth to you, I'm well aware of your age. Just think about the audition, okay? We can talk about it later. It would be a good thing to have on your resume.

My resume??? Mom, I'm not getting a job. Just playing the piano.

Honey, competition for good schools starts early. Many of your peers are juggling twice the extracurricular activities that you are. Remember, we agreed to let you drop French for the summer.

My "peers" are at the movies seeing Avengers right now!! Not me.

We can go this weekend. I have Saturday off.

I don't want to go with you. I want to go WITH THEM. No chaperone. Def. no NANNY!

I know you think we're too protective, but you don't understand the dangers.

I don't care. I wish some "predator" would come and take me. At least then I'd get out of the stupid house!

You don't mean that. The very fact that you could say it shows you're not mature enough to make these decisions. Your brother didn't get to be thirteen and—

I'm sorry he died!! I really am. But I'm alive, Mom. I'M ALIVE . . .

Reed did a search on file for "Ty" and he got a lot of "ty" for "thank you." Chloe did not appear to be conversing with anyone named Ty at any point. His name cropped up a couple of times in other chats, such as when someone named Aimee suggested Ty could give them a ride to Providence to see some YouTube star's appearance:

Get your bf Ty on it! The whole point of dating an older man is bcuz they have wheels!

He's not my bf, Chloe wrote back.

That's bcuz he doesn't exist, McKenna wrote.

One day u will c. I expect 2 c your apology on a cake. Chloe had attached an example—a multilayered professionally decorated cake that had a beautiful bouquet of frosted flowers and an elegant I'm sorry written out in sugar form.

His cell phone buzzed and he glanced at Tula before answering it. She had dozed off with a stuffed pony in her arms. Reed muted the television and took the call from Ellery. "Did you read it yet?" she asked by way of greeting.

"I'm looking at it now."

"Nothing on this Ty kid." She sounded frustrated. "If they were communicating recently, it wasn't through this phone or through her computer. I'm wondering about the gaming system she had in her room. Maybe she met him that way."

"Worth checking out. Did you see the picture of the cash? She must have amassed at least six hundred dollars."

"I saw. It could explain where she got her second phone."

"Except she said someone else gave her the phone."

"Ty, maybe. Or maybe she bought it to escape the Lockharts' monitoring and she just wanted to be mysterious with her friends. Either way, we have to find this kid Ty and find out what he knows."

Reed made a noise of agreement. "Speaking of wayward children . . ."

"I made Ashley call our father. He said he was going to get on a plane to come get her. She told him to fuck off."

Reed smiled in spite of himself. "Bet that felt good."

"She's in the shower now. But Reed, she can't stay here. I can't drop everything with this investigation to look after a kid."

Reed took off his reading glasses and rotated his neck to crack it. *All the lost people are not your personal responsibility,* Sarit used to say to him. He always had the same comeback: *What if it was our daughter who was missing?*

She is missing, Sarit would inform him. *She's missing her father.*

The cutting remark drew blood because he knew it to be true. Tula would love to see him more, as he would her. If he had a regular nine-to-five job that required no travel, he might have scored fifty-fifty physical custody of his daughter. He wouldn't miss a single recital or a soccer game. The FBI could slot another profiler into his job and the search for the missing people would continue. What he was coming to understand, though, was that everyone was lost at some point. Sarit had been lost in their marriage and he had not recognized it until she'd faded from sight. He'd been lost himself last year when he had discovered the truth about his parentage. Tula would be lost one day, too. What he hoped she saw now was his dedication to helping other people, his willingness to listen. He hoped she knew how his heart followed her wherever she went. He hoped she knew he would travel the earth to find her and bring her home, no matter what form that took.

"You don't have to let Ashley stay," Reed said. "But if you don't make a place for her, she might not come back."

Ellery heaved a deep sigh. "She's got your old spot on the couch."

"Warn her it comes with a hound's tongue bath in the morning."

"It's more fun when the guests figure that one out on their own."

Reed slid his gaze to the laptop screen. "Listen," he said, "wherever Chloe is and how she got there, I don't think she sent the threatening text to her mother."

"She sure seemed fed up with her to me."

"She is that. But Chloe modulates her texts based on her audience. She uses slang and text-speak with her friends but more or less proper grammar when corresponding with her mother. It's so ingrained that I doubt it would occur to her to switch now."

"Great. We're back to the probability that someone took her."

"Someone who doesn't care for Teresa Lockhart." He had a developing theory that the person might have used Chloe's exasperation with her mother as an opening, a shared bond: *Here, have a secret cell phone where we can trash your mom together.*

"Wait a sec, I've got Conroy on the other line."

Reed used the intervening time to kiss his daughter's warm head and tuck the covers securely around her. She mumbled something unintelligible into her pillow and clutched the pony around its neck. When Ellery returned to the phone, her tone was grim.

"The FBI is officially involved now."

"What happened?"

"Teresa got another text from a different burner phone. I'm sending you the screenshot."

Reed braced himself, the cords of his neck rigid, but the image still stole his breath away. Chloe Lockhart appeared in a close-up in front of what looked like a gray concrete wall. She had duct tape across her mouth, bruises on her face, and someone had chopped off her hair at the one-inch mark. Her blue eyes looked dazed, out of focus under the bright light from the camera. The accompanying text said: *WILL U CRY IF SHE DIES LIKE THE 1ST ONE?*

"There's no way a twelve-year-old girl did this to herself," Ellery said. "It's definitely an abduction."

It's worse than that, Reed thought as he sank down on the bed. *It's the prelude to a murder.*

13

Ellery stared out the floor-to-ceiling window of her loft at the city lights below her. Logically, she knew there was nothing more she could do for Chloe Lockhart at that precise moment. The tech team was doing their best to extract any information from the electronics. Every officer in the state remained on high alert, and Chloe's picture was all over the news, meaning that millions of eyeballs across New England were on the lookout for the girl. Ellery's eyes would simply be one more pair. She had no special knowledge, no obvious clue or place to start. Still, she felt restless, her skin crawling for need of something to do.

Behind her, Ashley took stock of her CD collection, which sat against one wall of the living room. Ellery had largely switched to digital music, but she'd built that collection with meager money saved over many years and she couldn't bring herself to part with it. "Springsteen, okay," the girl said. "The Smiths. Journey. The Cure. Joy Division?" She turned and wrinkled her nose at Ellery. "How old are you?"

"Hey, some of those are classics."

"I know what they are." Ashley replaced the albums one by one. "They're his music." She glanced at Ellery. "Dad's."

Ellery didn't need to be told this. Some of her few happy memories were riding around in her dad's truck with him, the music on blast and the wind in her ears. He took the truck with him when he left, but the music stayed with her. "You can't keep him away forever, you know," she said to Ashley. "He may have agreed to let you stay here a couple of days, but legally, he can have the cops come haul you out of here any time he wants, and there's nothing I can do to stop him."

"He can drag me back, but he can't keep me there."

Ellery suspected John Hathaway appreciated this truth better than most fathers. A wife and two kids hadn't tied him down one whit. She sighed and went to the kitchen. "I'm going to make tea. Would you like tea?"

"Sure." Ashley followed her and leaned against the counter to watch Ellery fill the red kettle. "Don't you hate him? You must hate him."

Ellery hated that she had to think about him at all. *He didn't give a shit about me,* she'd told her therapist last spring when the woman wanted to probe at her relationship with her errant father. *Why should I spend two seconds talking about him now?*

Maybe you could consider talking to him, Dr. Sunny Soon had suggested.

About what? About how he walked out and never looked back until the day his second daughter got sick . . . at which point he came crawling back to ask for a literal piece of me?

"He loves you," she told Ashley. "So maybe he's not all bad." She'd confined her father to a soundproof room in her head. He could scream all he wanted, but she would never hear him. She kept her back to the girl as she pulled down two mugs and fussed with the tea bags.

"He calls me Abby sometimes," Ashley confessed in a hushed voice.

Ellery jerked in surprise at the mention of her old name, knocking a mug to the floor, where it shattered on the tile.

"Shoot, I'm sorry." Ashley hurried to help her clean up.

"No, no, it's fine." *I'm fine. I'm always fine.* Ellery ignored the pounding in her ears as she struggled to hold the dustpan and broom in her shaking hands. "No one calls me that anymore," she told her sister without looking at her.

"I know." The girl's sympathetic tone made it worse. "I read all about you when Dad told me who you were. I read Reed's book and I watched one of the movies. I just meant . . . he didn't forget about you. When he'd slip up and call me the wrong name, he'd say that I reminded him of a girl he used to know named Abby, and that our names were similar. Abby, Ashley."

A girl I used to know. Ellery swallowed past the painful lump in her throat as she disposed of the broken mug. She got down a whole one, just the same, like nothing had ever happened. "I'm sorry," she muttered as she lifted the kettle. "That must have been confusing to you to be called the wrong name."

"I believed him at the time about why he got it wrong. Later, when I found out how much he'd lied—that was confusing." Her voice grew small. "You came and saved me after everything he did to you."

Ellery looked at her. "It's not your fault you got stuck with a crap dad."

The girl shrugged. "You didn't have to do it, but you did. You didn't stick around, though. You didn't let me say thank you."

"No thanks are necessary. Just—drink your tea."

"I want to help you." Ashley persisted, following Ellery back to the living room with her tea in hand. "I can clean your apartment if you want."

The dog-fur tumbleweeds under the furniture said she needed it, but Ellery winced at the idea of someone touching her stuff. "It's fine, really."

"I could walk the dog while you're at work."

"He's got a pet sitter, thanks."

"There must be something I can help you with," Ashley said, flopping back dramatically against the couch cushions.

In her head, Ellery saw the picture of Chloe, duct-taped and scared to death. "What do you know about video games?" she asked her sister.

Ashley perked up immediately and sat forward into Ellery's space. "Which one? Anya's Journey? StarKwest? World of Battle-craft?"

"I don't know," Ellery admitted. "The girl we're looking for, Chloe, she played online. We think she may have met a boy named Ty in the process."

"Sure, I've met tons of people gaming. When I was sick, it was one of the only things I was allowed to do, because I couldn't leave the house. Some of the kids I met turned into friends IRL, but others lived in, like, Japan. You can meet people from all over."

"IRL?"

"In real life."

"We think this girl did meet up with the boy in person."

"You think he, like, took her or something?" Ashley's eyes turned concerned.

"We don't know. The problem is that we don't know his name or where he lives. If we turned on her gaming system, do you think we could find a record of their interaction?"

"Mmm, not really. Most gamers use headsets or outside apps to communicate now. Like, to talk to each other while they play? I don't think anyone's recording that stuff." She brightened. "But if you know which game they met on, you could go in as her character and chat up her crew. If he's one of them, people might know who he is or where to find him."

"Would you know how to do that?" Ellery checked her phone and saw the time was nearing ten, but she would bet money the Lockharts weren't asleep.

"Sure, if you show me her stuff and the logins are preset."

"Get dressed," Ellery said as she sprang from the couch. Her tea sat neglected on the end table. The tech boys would have a better handle on the programming and the software, but they didn't speak teenage girl. If the Lockharts agreed to the plan, they wouldn't have to wait for warrants. While Ashley changed out of her pajamas, Ellery put back on her boots and her dark jeans. She wound her hair into a knot and shrugged into her leather jacket.

"Damn," Ashley said with admiration as Ellery holstered her weapon. "You could be starring in your own video game."

"No," replied Ellery as she grabbed up her keys and headed for the door. "This is IRL."

She called the Lockharts from the road and so she was not surprised to arrive to find the house ablaze with light. A pair of news vans remained parked outside in the shadows, just in case of any action. Ellery did her best to act casual as she ushered Ashley through the gate and up the front walk. Martin Lockhart opened the door before they had a chance to knock. He looked like he'd aged ten years since yesterday.

"I apologize for the lateness of the hour," Ellery said as he let them inside.

"Time has no meaning anymore," he told her.

Teresa appeared in the doorway to the living room, her pale eyes red rimmed and glazed. "Agent Markham isn't with you?"

"No, ma'am, not this time."

She sucked in her mouth, looking pained. "He's the profiler, right? I wanted to ask him. I wanted to know why, if this is about me and what a terrible mother I am, why they are torturing Chloe? Why not just take me instead?"

"For God's sake, you're not a bad mother!" Martin snapped, and

Teresa covered her face with both hands. "You're protective and you love Chloe. You have a job outside the home that saves people's lives daily. If that's terrible, I don't know what to say about the women who give birth and leave their babies in trash cans."

Ashley stiffened at her side and Ellery felt a stab of guilt at involving her in this whole mess. She wished she'd brought Reed along, because he was so much better at soothing people than she was. Teresa Lockhart wept into her hands as her husband glared at her from across the entryway. "Ma'am . . . if I may. I'm not a profiler and I'm not here to pass judgment on your parenting one way or the other. But I can promise you one thing for sure: whoever is doing this to Chloe, it's is about what's wrong with them and not about you."

"Exactly," Martin said, holding his arms out to Teresa in beseeching fashion.

She raised her face and fixed him with an accusing glare. "They didn't say anything about you. You work as many hours as me, if not more. Why is it always about the mother?" She looked to Ellery. "The school notices come to me, not him. It's the mothers who are expected to contribute to the bake sales and make the posters for the book fair and volunteer at the Halloween parade. If the homework is late, if the child isn't practicing her piano enough, the teachers go to the mother, not the father. Fathers can jet off to work for weeks at a time. They can be twenty-five or sixty-five and no one bats an eye. No one asks them to go on television to say what a shit parent they are!" Her voice, which had been steadily rising, reached a seething crescendo at the end.

Martin crossed to Teresa and took her in his arms. She fought him at first but then sagged against his chest when he held fast. "We're terribly worried," he told Ellery. "As you can see."

"I know. That's why I've brought Ashley to try out Chloe's video games. She might be able to learn something about this unknown boy Chloe was photographed with."

"Go ahead," Martin said over Teresa's soft weeping. "Her room is upstairs and down the hall on the right, as you know."

Relieved to have an escape hatch, Ellery nudged Ashley, and they hurried up the stairs to Chloe's suite. "Whoa, that was intense," Ashley whispered to her. "Now I feel kind of bad for running out on Mom and Dad like that. Mom, especially. It's not her fault he's a douchecanoe."

"Not weighing in on that one," Ellery said as they reached the room. She led Ashley to the large television and gaming devices. "Here it is. Does this make sense to you?"

Ashley pulled over a beanbag chair and put on a headset. "Yeah, I got it." She turned on the various devices and the screen filled up with options. "Which one of these do you want me to try first?"

"Is there a way to see which one she played last?"

"Hang on a sec. Yeah." Ashley moved the arrow around through various titles. "It was this one, World of Battlecraft."

"Do that one."

"Gotcha." She took up the controls, hit a button, and the screen changed to reveal a sweeping landscape with high mountains and a purple sky. To the right, a line of thick trees suggested the edge of a forest. Just visible at the base of the nearest mountain was a cluster of houses. A female figure with flowing black hair, chest armor, and a longsword at her side began to run through the field of white flowers toward the houses.

"Is that you?" Ellery asked.

Ashley nodded. "This is Chloe's avatar." She ran the figure up to the end of a rocky overhang and then jumped her down onto a somewhat more well-worn path toward the town. The woman on the screen huffed and puffed like an actual runner. She drew up short as a troll-like green figure materialized out of nowhere in front of her. His mouth moved and Ellery heard a voice through Ashley's headphones. She leaned in closer to hear.

". . . going to do a raid on Alavan's castle. Are you in?"

"Not now," Ashley said. "I'm looking for Ty. Have you seen him?"

"Not for a couple of days. We're gathering at Tu'laq Peak if you change your mind."

"Thanks." The Chloe figure on the screen continued onward toward the town. "If he's not logged on, we won't find him."

"Can you call him through the game?" Ellery had no idea how this worked.

"No, but if he's called Ty here, I can check to see if he's logged on." She called up a menu that appeared to list Chloe's contacts. Ellery saw a couple of the troll-like creatures, a muscular young man with brown skin and glowing eyes, a blond woman with a fancy silver collar, some sort of hairy beast with large teeth, a unicorn, a blue guy with long white hair . . . the list went on and on, and most of them had names like Lothar, Indigo, CreeXanthes, or Pulani. If they were logged on, the avatar was in color and alert, blinking out at the user. If the person was not logged on, the avatar was grayed out and unmoving.

"I don't see a Ty," Ellery said as Ashley scrolled on by.

"People don't name their characters after themselves. See? Chloe is Amara."

"Chloe!" The shout that came through the headphones knocked Ashley backward for a moment. "Where are you? What happened?"

Ashley exited the screen to find the blue man with white hair standing in front of Chloe's character. She shrugged silently at Ellery. "What do I say?" she whispered.

"Tell them you're not Chloe. You're a friend and you're looking for Ty."

"I'm not Chloe. Just using her setup. I'm a friend who's worried about her."

"God, man. Me, too."

"I want to find Ty."

The blue figure gesticulated wildly. "I'm Ty. What do you want with me?"

"Have you seen Chloe?"

"Naw, man. I ain't seen her in days. They're saying on the news she got kidnapped."

Ashley mouthed at Ellery, *What now?*

"Ask him when he saw her last."

"When did you last see Chloe?"

"Last Tuesday at the Y as usual. She was acting normal."

"Did he know Chloe had a bunch of money?" Ellery whispered.

Ashley relayed the question.

"I knew she had some bread, yeah. What's that got to do with anything?"

"The cops are interviewing all her friends," Ashley improvised. "They may want to talk to you, too."

"What? No way. I don't need no part of this."

"I don't mean you're a suspect. I mean to help with finding Chloe."

"I'd help if I could, but I don't know *nothing.*" He stressed that last word hard. "Ask me, the cops should be talking to her dad."

Ellery made a rolling motion with her hand. *Follow up. Come on.*

"Why her dad?" Ashley asked.

"He's got some pervy-ass friends, that's why. One of 'em been creeping on Chloe, asking her for pictures and shit."

Name, Ellery mouthed. *The man's name.*

"What guy? What's his name?"

"I don't know his name. I've gotta blast. I hope you find Chloe."

"Wait," she said, but the blue figure on the screen melted away.

14

Reed woke to the sound of his phone buzzing on the hotel nightstand and he craned his head up to look at it. Sarit again. He couldn't ignore her forever. "Hello?" he said, his voice still rough with sleep.

"Have you completely lost your mind?" she said by way of greeting. "You're supposed to be walking the Freedom Trail and showing her where the tea went into the harbor. Instead, I see her face on CNN. What the hell, Reed?"

"We're sightseeing today," he replied, sitting up and rubbing his eyes with one hand. He didn't mention it would be in Philadelphia.

"That doesn't explain why I saw our daughter at a crime scene."

"It wasn't a crime scene. It was a family home with a dozen law enforcement officers crawling all over it. Statistically, Tula was probably safer than she's ever been in her life."

"Don't give me that bullshit."

"She was fine, Sarit. She had some cookies and played with a dog while I had a conversation."

"You're working, then?"

"It was just a quick conversation," he replied.

"Oh my God, you are. You just can't stop, can you? Not even when you're on vacation. Not even when you're supposed to be caring for your daughter."

"I am caring for her." Reed glanced at the bed where Tula slept, limbs akimbo amid the chaos of sheets and blankets. "Just because my version doesn't precisely match yours doesn't mean it's wrong. Tula is safe and happy and you're just going to have to deal with the fact that she has two parents. You don't outrank me, Sarit."

"That's not what the custody arrangement says."

"Is that a threat?"

"More like a promise. To our child, Reed, that I will always put her first, whatever it takes."

"Daddy?" Tula stirred, her hair stuck to one side of her face as she blinked at him in the half-light.

"I've got to go," he told Sarit. "Tula's awake and I have to send her out to panhandle for our breakfast." He hung up before she could register her outrage.

"What's 'panhandle'?" Tula asked, bouncing from her bed to his.

"It means we're having breakfast on a train. Let's get ready."

They took the Acela speed rail train from Boston to Philadelphia. Tula had never ridden anything more than a kiddie train before, and she was entranced by the East Coast scenery rushing past. "Wait till I tell Ashley the train has a bathroom, too," she said to Reed as she stuffed part of a blueberry muffin into her face. "And a restaurant!" Reed smiled at her enthusiasm.

He gave Tula the tablet computer to use for drawing while he called up the Boston branch of the FBI to let them know he was crashing their case. Fortunately, the local guy assigned was someone he knew, Jeff Zuckerman. "You know we'd love your help," Jeff said when Reed reached him. "This one is seven kinds of weird so far."

"It doesn't follow any of the usual patterns," Reed agreed. Out of all the kinds of kidnapping, Chloe's abduction seemed to most closely parallel those with political motivations. The point wasn't to get money or to sexually abuse the victim but to force attention to a particular cause. However, the kidnappers were willing to harm the abductees to make a point or exact revenge against whatever entity they felt had wronged them. In this case, that seemed to be Teresa Lockhart. "I'm en route to Philadelphia at the moment. I plan to talk to Ethan Stone, Teresa's first husband. I'd like to go by the Stone house as well."

"You think the cases are related? We're talking two different geographic areas, one abduction versus a double homicide. I know the mother is a common element here, but she seems to be the only one."

"Yet she's the focus, or so it seems. I'm not saying the cases are definitely connected, but there are a few aspects that do concern me. First, did you notice the date? We are coming up on the fifteenth anniversary of the Stone incident in just a few weeks. Second, Trevor was twelve, the same age as Chloe. There are certain offenders who are attracted to a particular age group rather than one sex or the other. Finally, Ethan Stone was in the Boston area the past few days attending an economics conference at MIT."

Reed glanced at Tula, careful to keep the lurid details out of her earshot. She had headphones on, listening to music as she used her finger to draw rainbows on the tablet, but he never knew what she might pick up, as Sarit was going to discover regarding her supersecret move to Houston. "There is a case I know of," he said to Zuckerman, "in which a heavily pregnant woman was murdered in her home—stabbed by someone furious with her, it would seem. But she was well liked by everyone the investigators questioned. She had been divorced for more than ten years from her ex-husband and her new marriage reportedly was in good shape."

"Yeah, and?" Zuckerman said with a hint of impatience.

"The ex-husband was eventually arrested for the attack. He and the victim had shared a child together, a boy who died in a car accident five years earlier. The victim was behind the wheel at the time. Her new pregnancy five years after the fact triggered something in the ex-husband. He felt like she was replacing their son with a new baby.

"So you think . . . what? Stone went nutso because Chloe Lockhart reached the same age as his kid when he was murdered?"

"I'm just saying I want to talk to him."

"Okay, I agree he's a loose end that needs to be tied up. Let me know what you find out."

The train rolled into the 30th Street Station shortly before noon, and Kimmy met them in the vast lobby with its travertine façade. Tula tilted her head all the way back to exclaim over the high coffered ceiling, which was painted red and gold. "Like a castle!" she enthused.

Kimmy, in her designer sunglasses, aquamarine sundress, and matching heels, looked like she could be an extra in any one of the movies that had filmed in the stylish station. "Thanks so much for doing this," Reed said as he embraced his sister. "I owe you one."

"You owe me about three million by now," she retorted without rancor. "I'll forgive you because you come with this amazing girl right here. Hey there, sunshine. Are you up for some lunch?"

"She ate on the train."

"I'm starving," Tula replied with real feeling, and Kimmy laughed as she took her hand.

"Me, too. Say bye to Daddy and let's hit the market."

"I'll text you to meet up," Reed called, and Kimmy waved without a backward glance. He purchased a caprese sandwich for himself and wolfed it down while waiting for his ride share to show up. The driver was an affable white-whiskered man about sixty-five years old, round at the middle and with a lead foot on the gas. He recognized the Chestnut Hill address that Reed had entered when he summoned the car. "You're not the first person I drove out there. But the new owners, they don't let people on the property," he cautioned as he lurched them through city traffic. "There's a fence and security cameras up now. Too many lookie-loos coming by every time the story was on TV again."

"Does it get a lot of coverage?"

"Not so much these days. A few years ago, these guys did a pod-cast about it. Went on for weeks and got tons of attention. That's when we started seeing lots of folks showing up, wanting to see the house where that boy died. Pretty damn ghoulish if you ask me." He gave Reed a reproachful look in the rearview mirror.

"It is," Reed agreed. He had run across the podcast in his inter-net searches. The hosts' theory was that Trevor and Carol had been murdered by a man who was later found to have killed four people over a ten-year period, one of whom was a girl just a few years older than Trevor Stone. He had briefly been part of a landscaping crew that worked on a house several doors down from the Stones' place.

As they reached the Chestnut Hill region of the city, Reed recog-nized it as similar to the neighborhood where he grew up in Virginia. Formidable brick estate houses, dating back to the late 1800s, sat well back from the street and a good distance apart from one another considering they were still within city limits. A canopy of thick trees as least as old as the houses lined the road on either side. The front lawns were meticulously maintained with carpets of lush grass and blooming summer flowers. One of the multistory brick mansions strongly resembled the house from the movie *Home Alone,* except it had a spiked iron fence in front. The driver pulled to a stop in front of it. "Here you are," he said. "Enjoy." Reed noticed he didn't even glance at the place as he let Reed out and sped away.

Reed took a stroll down the street and back. He noticed the quiet more than anything. Not a single car passed him. Not one other person appeared from anywhere. It was the middle of a workday, yes, but the effect was rather like an expensive ghost town. Only the eerie sensation of distant eyes on him as he walked gave any indica-tion there might be someone watching. As he walked back to the old Stone house, he considered how an unusual car or pedestrian would be instantly out of place on this desolate street. Well off the main roads of the city, it was a destination unto itself. No one without a good reason to be here would ever cross its path.

He approached the intercom system at the locked gate and pressed the button. When no one replied, he hit it again. Eventually, an irritated male voice came through the transom: "Yes?"

"Hello," Reed said as he pulled out his FBI credentials and showed them to the camera. "My name is Reed Markham, and I'm an agent with the FBI. I'm in the middle of an active investigation and I wondered if I could talk to you for a few moments."

"Investigating what?"

Oh, come now, Reed thought. *You must know. A hundred amateurs have already shown up at your door.* "The murders of Trevor Stone and Carol Frick."

"We've got no part in that."

"I understand, sir. I just wanted to take a quick look around the property."

"This is not just my home; it's where I work. I'm at work now."

"I completely understand, and I am sorry for this intrusion. But I am also at work, and there are lives on the line here. If that isn't sufficient motivation for you, perhaps you can try this for size: if I can solve these murders, folks will quit coming around bothering you all the time."

"Solve them," the man replied with surprise. "After all these years?"

Reed felt the weight of his skepticism, but he answered with a quick nod. "I certainly aim to try," he said to the lens of the camera. A moment later, the gate clicked open. Reed was met at the front door by a tall African-American man. He wore a button-down shirt and tie but khaki shorts and sandals. "Amos Duncan," he said, shaking Reed's hand. "Please forgive my appearance. I had to videoconference into a meeting this morning."

"Please forgive my dropping by like this. I'm only in town for today."

"You have a hot new lead or something?"

"Or something," Reed replied grimly. "You may have heard on the news that Teresa Lockhart's daughter has been kidnapped."

"I did see a headline like that. Poor woman." He scratched the back of his head. "But, uh, do you really think it's the same guy who did it?"

"We're investigating all angles," Reed said, looking around him at the spacious entryway. The upstairs crossway from one end of the house to the other must be the place where Carol was overthrown. That would put her dead roughly where Reed stood on the checkerboard marble floor.

Mr. Duncan could read his thinking. "Yeah, that's where she fell, or so I hear. My wife and I didn't live in Philly at the time, but people have been happy to fill us in on all the details, whether we want to hear them or not."

"Did you know the history when you bought the place?"

"Of course. That's how we got it for a steal." He shrugged. "Tamara and I don't believe in ghosts, and our kids are grown and gone. Her sister down in Florida won't come visit, though. Says the place has bad juju, especially since they never caught the guy who did it. I've got to tell you, I figured at this point you never would."

"Never is a long time." Reed's mother's case went unsolved for more than forty years before he'd cracked it last spring. "Would you mind showing me to the room that was Trevor Stone's?"

"We use it as a guest room now. It's this way." He extended his hand to invite Reed to climb the steps. Reed ran his hand along the smooth, sturdy railing. He followed his host to the left; he noted that the positioning of the room was not unlike Chloe's in the Lockhart home. He paused at the spot where Carol Frick would have been thrown over and peered down below. The drop was probably about twenty-five feet. He patted the banister, which came up past his hip. "They say she died protecting the kid," Mr. Duncan said, reading his thoughts. "Tragic."

Reed tried to envision it. Had Carol pursued the intruder up the stairs as they tried to get to Trevor's room? Or did she encounter them on their way out, the deed already done? This of course presupposed that Trevor was the intended victim. The podcast that pushed the gardener as the perpetrator also believed that Carol was the target. Trevor was killed ostensibly because he would have recognized the man from the neighborhood. But Carol wasn't supposed to be there that day, Reed told himself. Possibly someone saw her come inside.

He followed Mr. Duncan deeper into the house while his mind worked to try to make the pieces fit. Trevor murdered and Chloe abducted. If there was a connection, who would want to target these children? "Here it is," Mr. Duncan said, swinging open a wooden door to reveal a sunny bedroom painted cheery yellow with white trim. A patchwork quilt decorated the queen-sized bed, and a vase full of daisies sat on the nightstand. Reed touched one and found it to be a realistic fake. The air smelled pleasant but stale, as though the door hadn't been opened in some time. He looked out the window into the big backyard. "Did you add the fence back there as well?" he asked.

"No, the privacy fence came with the home."

The fence and the bushes would give cover for anyone coming or going from the home from the south side. He knew from the police reports that the back door was unlocked at the time of the homicides, a usual habit for the Stones. "Could I please see the back door?" he asked.

Mr. Duncan obligingly showed him through a sprawling kitchen to the mudroom at the back of the house. "We keep it locked," he said pointedly. "I don't think that maniac is going to come back here, but why take chances?"

"Have you had any trouble at all? You or the neighbors?"

"Outside of the kooks with a murder fetish trying to climb my fence, it's pretty quiet down this way. It's the reason we bought the place."

"No burglaries? Break-ins? Nothing unusual at all?"

"No." He paused. "Well, unless you count the gun."

Reed's eyebrows shot up. "The gun," he repeated.

"Come out this way," Mr. Duncan said as he opened the door. He led Reed across a stone patio and down a garden path to a wooden shed near the back of the property. "There was a shed here when we moved in, but it was in poor condition. We had it torn down and re-placed. During the work, the crew found a gun that had been buried in a coffee can under the ground."

"I don't suppose you know what kind of gun it was."

"I suppose I do," he replied with satisfaction. "It was a Beretta 92."

"What did you do with it?"

"I called up Ethan Stone and asked him if he wanted it back. He said it didn't belong to him. I said what do you want me to do with it then, and he said to turn it over to the police. So, that's what I did." He shrugged. "They didn't seem too interested. Trevor and that housekeeper, neither one of them got shot, you know? The ser-geant who took it from me said people find guns in weird places all the time. I didn't think anything more of it." He peered at Reed intently. "Why? Do you think it's important?"

"I don't know right now what's important. That's why I'm here, to collect as much information as I can."

"Well," Mr. Duncan said with a deep breath. "I wish you luck, but these walls here don't talk." He turned and shaded his eyes, looking up at the hulking brick mansion. "Imagine the stories she'd have to tell if she could."

15

Reed took another car to Penn's Department of Economics. He quirked a half smile when he saw the building—tall, concrete gray with small windows, rather like a prison—compared to the modern glass political science home base right next door. He'd booked a two o'clock appointment with Ethan Stone, but he stopped in the main office to check in and determine where Stone was located. The office manager, a pleasant-faced woman with tight gray curls, was duly impressed by a visit from the FBI. Her nameplate read: NANCY POTTS. "Professor Stone isn't in any trouble?" she asked with a tiny frown from behind the counter.

"No, ma'am, not that I'm aware of, in any case."

She breathed a sigh of relief. "I didn't think so. He's the nicest man. Brings me flowers on Secretary's Day and pralines for my birthday." She leaned toward Reed confidentially. "They aren't all like that, you know. Some people think I'm just like those file cabinets over there—yank open and rustle around for what you need, then slam 'em shut again without so much as a by-your-leave."

Reed smiled at her old-fashioned idiom, which reminded him of his mother. "Have you known Ethan Stone a long time, then?"

"I was here before he was. Let's see, he came on about twenty-two years ago now. Gosh, the time really does fly." She took out a Baggie filled with baby carrots and began crunching her way through them. "Would you like some?"

"No, thank you."

"I don't blame you," she said, eyeing the bag with disgust.

"You knew Professor Stone before his son was killed, then," Reed said.

"Oh, dear, yes. That poor sweet boy. We were all just brokenhearted when we heard about it. What a completely terrifying thing to happen, having someone come into your home and murder your child. Professor Stone hasn't been the same since, really."

"What do you mean, he's not the same?"

"Oh, you know. He's quieter. There's a sadness to him. Sometimes I walk past his office and catch him looking at the picture of Trevor that he keeps on his bookshelf in there. It's not fair how bad things happen to good people. Professor Stone, he's had more than his share of bad luck."

Reed opened his mouth to ask about that, but Ethan Stone appeared in the office before he could get a chance.

"Speak of the devil," Ms. Potts said with a broad smile. "Professor, it seems you've got the FBI here to see you."

"Thank you, Nancy." Ethan Stone stood about six feet tall, with a trim frame and salt-and-pepper hair that just brushed the edges of his crisp white collar. He extended his hand to Reed and gave his arm a firm shake. "Ethan Stone."

"Reed Markham. Thank you for seeing me on short notice."

"Of course. Please join me in my office. Do you want anything—water, coffee, tea?"

Reed had long ago learned to take what his interview subjects offered him. "Coffee would be great, thank you."

"I have a machine at the ready."

In Stone's office, Reed immediately saw the framed photo of

Trevor that Nancy Potts had referenced. It had a place of honor on the shelf with an African violet sitting next to it. Trevor had been in the tween years—dark hair cut in a basic boy trim, a close-mouthed smile, possibly to hide braces, but no traces of acne yet or the teenage turmoil that would never come. Stone noticed him looking and turned the photo so Reed could have a better view. "His last school picture," he said to Reed. "His classmates have all graduated now, but Trevor never made it to junior high."

"I'm sorry. I really do appreciate you talking with me today. I know it must be painful to revisit."

"Yes. Well." Stone busied himself with the coffee. "The thing about losing a child is that nothing anyone does can make it any better, but nothing can make it any worse, either. It's a hole that never fills no matter how much dirt you throw on top of it." He glanced at Reed. "I know why you're here. I saw on the news about Teresa's daughter and I couldn't believe it. How horrible. I even picked up the phone to give Teresa a call, but I realized I don't have her number."

"You don't keep in touch?"

"No," he said. "It wasn't pretty at the end. That dirt you throw to fill the hole? Turns out you get messy in the process. I think we both needed to move on. Do you take milk or sugar?"

Teresa had moved on, Reed noted. New city, new family. Ethan had stayed where he was. "Black is fine."

They sat on the low-slung leather couch that took up a good part of one wall. "Teresa was young when she had Trevor," Reed said. "In the middle of her residency, yes?"

"Yes. He was a surprise." He paused to smile over the rim of his coffee cup. "The best kind."

"Were the two of you planning to have kids?"

"Actually, no, not at first. I already had a son, Justin, from my first marriage. Teresa was focused on her career. Once she turned up pregnant, though, we got used to the idea in a hurry. We hired someone to do the nursery, and they handled everything but Trevor's library. Teresa wanted to stock that herself. She loved to sit in the rocking chair and read with him."

"What kind of mother was she?"

"Busy," he replied without thought. "Her work is life-or-death, every day. Hard to walk away from that to watch a little boy play in the sandbox or fix grilled cheese sandwiches. But she loved him. Of course she did. We took vacations to the shore and they'd hold hands, jumping the waves in the surf. They liked to do jigsaw puzzles and riddles together. She would design elaborate scavenger hunts for him on his birthday and hide his presents at the end." He shook his head. "The last one was just a month before he died."

"The investigation looks to be thorough from what I've seen," Reed said. "What did you think of it?"

Stone set his coffee cup aside as he considered his answer. "At first, I thought it would be over quickly. I didn't have any experience with law enforcement, but I guess I'd absorbed the typical narrative from crime fiction—the perpetrator is caught, always, and usually in short order. I remember preparing myself mentally for the image of him. For what it would feel like when the police dragged him from his hole into the light of day. I'd always been against the death penalty, you see. If you think about it from a market perspective, it doesn't make any sense. The death sentence doesn't deter other criminals from committing their crimes, and it's not fairly adjudicated. But when it was my child—" His jaw unlocked briefly, quivered twice before he got control again. "I wanted the person responsible to be evaporated from the earth. I didn't want a molecule of him remaining, you understand me?"

"I do."

"I built up all this anger and then there was no target for it. The investigation went on, seemingly endless. They interviewed Teresa's patients. My fellow professors. My students. Our neighbors."

"Your son," Reed added, and Stone's face darkened, quick as an April sky.

"Yes," he said. "They had a particular focus on Justin, despite lacking any evidence. We had to engage an attorney to protect him from their bizarre fixation that he murdered his younger brother."

"One of his fingerprints was discovered on the plastic bag." Reed didn't have to specify which bag—the one used to smother Trevor.

"Yes, mine, too. And Teresa's, and Carol's, and even Trevor's. It was a disposable grocery bag. We kept them around in the kitchen pantry to reuse as necessary."

Reed had read the reports. Justin, at the time of the murders, had been unwelcome in the Stone home at Teresa's insistence. He'd left rehab after only six days and was crashing with fellow addicts in the city. The detectives wondered how he'd left fingerprints on a bag when he hadn't been around much prior to the homicides. "How did Justin get along with Trevor?"

"He loved him," Stone shot back. "Trevor worshiped the ground his big brother walked on. Who wouldn't enjoy that?"

"I read that Justin took your remarriage somewhat hard."

"He was five. Five-year-olds want their mommies and daddies to be together forever. Justin adjusted. We had a number of good years after Trevor was born. He—he was happy."

The spiral into addiction suggested otherwise, but Reed didn't challenge. "What's Justin doing today?"

"He's a sales manager for a home appliance company. He's good. He's clean. I don't want you bothering him with this, understand me? Imagine having your little brother murdered and the cops think you're the one who did it. He already hated himself so much that he tried to drown his own brain in a toxic miasma of drugs and booze. And then to be suspected of such a monstrous crime . . . Justin worked damn hard to carve out a life for himself, and I won't have you people destroying it."

"I'm not here to destroy anyone. Just trying to get a sense of the facts."

"Justin didn't do this. That's a fact."

"I'd still like to talk to him."

"You can't." Stone stood up abruptly and went to his window. "He's—he's traveling at the moment. Won't be back for several days yet."

Reed didn't have several days. He decided not to belabor the point and shifted gears. "You were in Boston recently for a conference. Is that correct?"

"Yes, at MIT." Stone turned around again, but he remained wary, on guard. His body posture was closed off and defensive. "I gave a talk last Friday, had dinner with colleagues Friday night, did a little sightseeing on Saturday, and returned home yesterday morning."

"You didn't see Teresa or Chloe at any point?"

"No, of course not." He pointed at Reed. "Wait. You don't think I took that girl?"

"I don't have any reason to think that. But I'm sure you appreciate we need to examine every possible angle right now."

"Did Teresa say something to you? Did she accuse me?"

"No one has accused you of anything," Reed said mildly.

"God, I would never. The thought is abhorrent." A stain of color appeared across his cheekbones. "I would never do anything to harm a child."

"Okay, I hear you. When did you last speak to Teresa?"

He didn't have to think about it. "Six years ago. We ran into each other at a café in Berlin, if you can believe it. I was there on business and she was vacationing with her family."

So he knew she had a daughter. "That's ironic," Reed said aloud. "How did it go?"

"It was awkward. I spotted her before she saw me, but they were standing between me and the door, so there was no way to make a quick exit. We had to say hello."

"Is that all you said?"

"More or less." He forced a tight smile. "One might even call it an achievement of sorts, after all the bitterness from before."

"What were you bitter about?"

"Losing Trevor, naturally. The police never caught anyone, so there was no one else to blame but each other. She was supposed to have been home that afternoon. She didn't get a sitter."

"Was that unusual?"

"Not completely, no. He had just turned twelve and was fine being home by himself for short periods of time. But Teresa's job at the hospital kept her away for hours. She might not have been back until midnight."

"But surely you would have been home by then."

"Too late," he said, hoarse with regret. "They'd been there a couple of hours already by the time I returned. I called nine-one-one right away, but there was nothing they could do for Trevor."

"I am sorry."

Stone's shoulders rose and fell. "Our lives were ripped to shreds. You're here to observe the tatters, to sift through the pieces one more time, as though that will change anything. I hope you find Teresa's daughter. Maybe, somehow, you'll even solve this case. But you'll understand, I hope, that I won't be waiting by the phone."

"I do understand. And I hope you understand that I'll need the names of the colleagues you had dinner with, just to follow up. The faster we eliminate you, the sooner we can move on."

Stone's mouth was a hard line. "That's what they said last time and yet here I am again, answering all the same questions." But he rose, went to his desk, and jotted down the names on a notepad. He ripped off the paper and handed it to Reed. "I trust you can see yourself out."

Reed left Stone's office but didn't head for the exit. He detoured past the main office, where Nancy Potts greeted him with a cheery wave. "Why, hello again. Did you and Professor Stone have a nice chat?"

"We did."

"Isn't he the sweetest man?"

"You mentioned earlier . . . something about him having an unfair burden of troubles."

"Some people," she said with a sympathetic sigh. "If it weren't for bad luck, they'd have no luck at all. Don't you think?"

"What sort of bad luck did Professor Stone have?"

"Oh, losing Trevor was the worst of it. No question there. But just last winter, he broke his arm skiing. The year before that, it was his ankle. Just plain stepped off the curb wrong—can you imagine?"

Reed nodded. This wasn't the boon he'd hoped for when he circled back to talk to her. "That is unfortunate."

"Yes, and then there was that awful student who accused him of groping her."

"Oh?" Reed perked up. "When was that?"

"Mmm. Five, maybe six years ago? The university investigated and it turned out she made the whole thing up because he gave her a failing grade. The students these days, they are the most spoiled, entitled—"

"Do you remember this student's name?"

"Kennedy," she replied, her mouth drawn in a sour moue. "Kennedy Harris. I remember thinking what a dishonor it was for her to have the same name as one of our greatest presidents. The school expelled her, and good riddance, I say. Professor Stone is so popular, I don't know why she ever thought she'd get away with it."

"That is quite the run of unfortunate incidents," Reed said.

"Tell me about it. There was also that one time someone set his car on fire."

"I beg your pardon?"

"I know! Unbelievable. Right here on university property, too. Probably some other student who didn't do the work but expected a four-point-oh average anyway."

"When was this?"

"Oh, a long time ago now." She tapped her chin, thinking back. "More than ten years for sure."

"Before or after what happened to Trevor?"

She lit up as he helped her remember the timing. "That's right. It was before Trevor."

"Right before?" Reed couldn't imagine so. He hadn't read anything about it in the reports.

"No, a while back before that. A month, maybe? Could be longer. Professor Stone would remember, I'm sure. You could ask him."

"Oh, I will. Thank you." Reed smiled and wished her well. He would no doubt have more questions for Ethan Stone, but first he had to find some better answers.

16

They had been partners only three months, but Ellery knew if she showed up at Dorie's condo before 7:00 A.M. then she had better bring coffee. She carried a Dunkin's cup in one hand, its lettering as pink as the new morning sky. Ellery knocked, and Dorie appeared a few minutes later, sleepy eyed and dressed in gray sweats, with a trio of wagging dog tails following behind her. "Has there been a break?" she asked, instantly alert when she saw Ellery.

"Nothing concrete." Ellery handed her the coffee and began greeting the dogs, who had lined up in turn to receive ear rubs. She explained about Ashley's attempt to ferret out "Ty" by playing Chloe's character in the video game. "He said he saw her at the Y."

"You dragged your little sister into this mess?" Dorie put a hand on her hip. "I thought we had covered Boundaries 101 back at the start. Maybe you need a refresher course. Lesson one: Don't bring civilian family members into active investigations. Especially if they're minors."

"She got us a real lead on this Ty kid, faster than the tech boys would've done it. I checked, and there's only around a dozen YMCAs

in the Boston area. I say we start with the ones closest to the Lockharts' house and work outward."

"Do the Lockharts look like Y people to you?"

Ellery blinked. "What do you mean?"

"I mean they probably swim at some fancy country club with
yachts in the pool. Which of those centers is closest to Margery's
house? If Chloe's spending time at a YMCA, it's probably with the
nanny. That's your better bet."

"I don't know which Y is closest to the nanny."

"Get your butt in here while we figure it out. Be quiet, though;
Shelly's still sleeping."

Ellery had left Ashley still sleeping as well. She'd ended up giving
her sister the bedroom while she camped out on the couch. Ashley had
protested, but Ellery didn't mind the sofa. She spent a lot of her nights
dozing in front of the gray light of the television, its soft droning en-
tertaining her brain long enough for it to find its way to sleep. Coben
had kept an old metal bed at the farmhouse, where he had tied her
to it when he didn't have her shut in the closet. The mattress stunk
from the blood and sweat of the girls who had suffered there before
her, a fetid stench that haunted her dreams. She ran her body to the
point of exhaustion some days but still couldn't sleep. The doctors
gave her pills. They asked her if she had nightmares. It was more
that she could never again see bed as a welcoming place. How was
she supposed to surrender herself each night in the space where she
had nearly died? The only way to manage it was to pretend it wasn't
happening, which was what she did when she was on the couch.

Dorie reappeared dressed in a formfitting suit and sensible loaf-
ers. "I didn't know you had a sister," she said.

"Neither did I." Dorie's eyebrows rose, but she didn't pester Ellery
for details. This was why their partnership worked. "According to
the almighty Google, the closest YMCA to Margery Brimwood is
one in Roxbury."

"Your call on whether we take Tremont or Warren," Dorie said as she grabbed a protein bar and her coffee. "This hour, they're equally jammed." Boston filled up with cars by 6:00 A.M. and the crush did not abate until almost 10:00. Ellery wished it were practical to take the subway for her job. It sure would be faster half the time.

As they sat idling in commuter traffic, Dorie called up Margery to ask about her possible attendance there. She put the call on speaker so Ellery could hear, too. "Yes, my granddaughter takes swimming lessons there on Tuesday afternoons," Margery said. "Sometimes when her mother has to work, I take Brianna for the lesson."

"And Chloe comes with you?"

"Yes. She sits and does her homework."

"Right next to you? The whole time?"

"Well, she's outside the pool area sitting on one of the benches, but I can see her through the windows, sure." She hesitated. "Except when I'm in the changing rooms with Brianna. She's just five, you know, so she needs help getting in and out of her bathing suit. Why?"

"We're following a lead on the young man pictured in the photo with Chloe on her phone. We think he might know her from the Y. Do you recall Chloe talking with anyone while you were there?"

"She's chatted with a few kids from time to time, I suppose. Nothing that stood out as unusual or improper. I mean, they're all just kids."

Dorie and Ellery exchanged a look. They'd both stood over a four-year-old boy shot in the head during a drive-by. The shooter turned out to be just sixteen years old. "Thank you, Mrs. Brimwood," Dorie said. "You've been very helpful."

Ellery parked her SUV in the first available space by the YMCA and Dorie dropped a couple of quarters in the meter. "You think they're ticketing this early?"

"City needs the money more than I do."

They located the manager, a brown-skinned woman with kinky hair and lots of freckles who introduced herself as Freida Maxwell. Her T-shirt had Electric Mayhem, the band from the Muppet show, pictured on the front and she had a smile as big as Dr. Teeth himself. "How can I help you, Detectives?" she asked from behind the high counter.

"We're trying to locate this boy," Ellery replied as she showed off the picture she had of Chloe and the mystery kid on her phone. "He may go by the name Ty."

Ms. Maxwell enlarged the photo with her fingers and studied it. "Oh, sure. Tyreek Cantrell. He's one of our junior basketball coaches. Sweet kid." Her brown eyes grew concerned as she handed the phone back to Ellery. "I hope he's not in any trouble."

"We're definitely not out to make trouble for him," Ellery said as a non-reply. "We just want to talk to him as a possible witness."

She sighed. "That no-good cousin of his got himself mixed up in something again?"

"I can't really get into it. Do you know where we can find Tyreek?"

"From two to five this afternoon, you should be able to find him here in the gym. Before that, he lives with his grandma over on Sycamore Street. She's a nurse up at the medical center, so Ty's on his own a lot."

"Has he been in trouble before?" Dorie asked.

"Here and there. Nothing too serious, I don't think, but he came to us originally as part of mandated community service about two years ago now. It's his cousin Darius who's the wild one. I always tell Ty he needs to think for himself and not just follow along with whatever his buddies are doing, but . . ." She shrugged. "Teenagers just want to belong."

Dorie smiled. "As do we all." She rapped the counter gently with her knuckles. "Thanks for your help."

Back in the car, Ellery called in and requested a background check on Tyreek Cantrell. "Let's see what 'nothing too serious' actually amounts to," she said to Dorie.

"See what you can find out about the cousin while you're at it. Darius?"

Ellery relayed the information that they had and then waited for a reply. She spotted a man in a suit wolfing down a breakfast sandwich and wished she'd grabbed more than a donut when she had picked up Dorie's coffee. "I don't know what this kid's story is, but he didn't seem from his exchange with Ashley like he knew where Chloe was. He was surprised to see her character turn up in the game."

"Maybe because he has her stashed in a basement somewhere and wondered how the hell she got access to a computer."

"If he does have her, he's got to be sweating bullets by now."

"Him and me both." She unbuttoned her collar and squinted out the window at the hazy summer sky. "It's supposed to be over ninety today. At least that's something, huh? We don't have to worry about Chloe out somewhere freezing to death."

Ellery hummed an acknowledgment and turned her face away. It had been hot as the devil's breath the night she was abducted, heat radiating back off the concrete even after dark. Coben had given her just enough water to survive and she'd had to beg him for every drop, her mouth open like a desperate baby bird's while he'd laughed as it sloshed all over her face. Her hands tightened around the steering wheel. "Let's not wait for background. Let's just head over there."

Dorie gave her a long look as Ellery started the engine. "You okay?"

"It's just the damn heat." She wiped her forehead and then fiddled with the vents to point the air at her face.

Dorie settled back with a snort. "I hate to tell you this, Hathaway, but it only gets hotter from here."

They drove a surprisingly long ten blocks to Sycamore Street. Records had already revealed Tyreek Cantrell's address, which turned out to be a double-decker apartment that had several shingles missing on the left side. The tiny yard was well trimmed, but the walkway had cracked and become noticeably uneven. A cheery wreath with purple and white flowers hung on the left-side door. Before they could exit the car, a call came through for Ellery with the results of the background check on Tyreek.

"Uh-huh," she said. "I see. He pled out? . . . What about the cousin? . . . Okay, great. If you could send me copies of those files, I'd appreciate it."

"Well?" Dorie asked when she hung up.

Ellery cast another look at the house, which appeared quiet. "Tyreek was arrested two years ago on charges of aggravated rape of a female minor. He pled down to lewd behavior. The cousin, Darius, got three to five years."

"Let me guess—he's already out."

"Released two months ago. Current address is in Hyde Park."

"Well, let's start rattling cages here," Dorie said. "We can progress as necessary."

They knocked sharply on the door of the lower unit, and when that did not produce a response, Ellery switched to pounding with the side of her fist. Eventually, the door cracked and a pair of hooded dark eyes peered out at them. "What do y'all want? It's early."

Ellery showed off her shield. "Detectives Hathaway and Bennett, Boston PD. Are you Tyreek Cantrell?"

He widened the door and Ellery saw his attire—boxers, bare feet, and a gray T-shirt. At least the kid wasn't packing. "This is about Chloe, isn't it?"

"We need to talk to you for a minute. Okay to come inside?"

"Yeah, all right," he replied grudgingly. He scrubbed his considerable amount of hair with both hands. "I got to warn you, though—I don't know nothing about where she's at."

Ellery stepped into the house, which was already warm. Drawn shades held back the worst of the heat in the living room, but the air felt like a wet blanket. Beads of sweat formed on the back of her neck as she surveyed the property. She did not see anything amiss, but the décor was an odd mix of old and new. The dated sofa showed worn patches on the arms, its pillows dented in each center. The coffee table had a slim paperback novel under it to hold it in place, and its wood veneer had a sizable chip on one side. Meanwhile, the 60-inch projection screen television practically gleamed. Ellery noted the gaming system similar to Chloe's, complete with expensive headphones. In the corner, she saw a pair of black Nike running shoes that she knew retailed for more than a hundred dollars. "When was the last time you saw Chloe?" she asked him.

"Last Tuesday at the Y." He flopped down onto the sofa. Dorie poked her nose around the corner, peering toward the kitchen. "We just said hi and stuff. She asked if I was going to be online later and I said I was."

"Did you talk to her online that night?"

"Yeah, we played for a couple of hours, like regular."

"How did she seem to you?"

"Like normal. She didn't say she was planning on being kidnapped."

"Those are nice kicks over there," she said, nodding at the sneakers. "Are you a runner?"

"Kinda." He shrugged one large shoulder. He was fit and strong—a man's body even if he was only seventeen. Legally, though, they were questioning a minor without his guardian present.

"Where's your grandmother?"

"She's at work. Left at six. She don't know where Chloe's at, either, in case you're wondering."

"Where do you think she is?"

"Man, if I knew, I'd go there myself and get her. Whoever took her, they'll catch these hands." He held up his fists.

"What's that you have on your knuckles?"

"Oh, that," he said, sounding embarrassed as he tucked his hands away. "I was just messing around." Ellery waited, expectant, and he reluctantly held them out to show her. One hand read: "DEATH," but the other said: "LIFE." "It's just Sharpie. See?"

"I see. Does it mean anything?"

He looked at her like she was an idiot. "Only everything. Every day, you got to choose."

"You make good choices, Tyreek?" Dorie asked as she rejoined him.

"I try to," he said, wary now.

"What would your PO say? Would they agree?"

"Hey, I'm so clean I squeak, man. You can ask my PO. You can ask anybody."

"You weren't so clean a couple of years ago," Ellery answered.

He huffed an angry breath and jumped off the couch. "I didn't do anything to that girl. I was just there, you understand? I didn't even know it was going down until she came out of the room with her clothes all ripped up. I thought she was into it, that she wanted to be with Darius."

"Why don't you tell us what happened?"

He took a deep breath and held out those enormous hands. "It was a party thrown by some dudes that Darius knew. Yeah, there was drugs there. No, I wasn't doing them. My grandma would shoot me herself if I started taking that stuff. This girl, Tre'ana, she was at the party too. People were drinking, smoking up. There was loud music playing. At one point, I look over, and Tre'ana's grinding on D. So when he took her upstairs, I figured it was probably her idea. But they didn't come back and it got late. I had to get home and D was my ride. I went up there to the bedroom and I knocked. I knocked a bunch of times 'fore the door opened. D had no clothes on. Tre'ana had no bottom. Her top was ripped. D laughed and asked if I wanted a turn. While he was talking to me, she grabbed her clothes and ran. She had a cut on her hand and the blood got on me when she ran by. So when the cops showed up, they thought I was in on it."

"The girl must've said otherwise, no?" Dorie asked.

"She was high. There was other dudes in the room off and on. She didn't know who all they were, but I was the only one with blood on him, so I'm the one who got busted. I swear to you, I didn't touch her."

"She was fourteen years old," Ellery said, looking at him steadily.

"She looked older." At her glare, he held up his palms. "She did! But you see, it don't matter how old she was because I didn't touch that girl. I'm not that kind of guy."

"What kind of guy are you?" Dorie asked.

"Nowadays? I'm the kind who minds his own business."

"Tell us about your relationship with Chloe," Ellery said.

"Man, what 'relationship'? We're friends, that's it. She's just a kid, like a little cousin or something."

"And you met her at the Y?"

"Yeah, about six months ago. Turns out she's a gamer, like me." He gestured toward the television. "That girl can shoot, let me tell you. Course I wanted her on my squad. Plus, I don't know . . ." He scratched the back of his head.

"What?" Ellery demanded.

He shrugged. "Around here, you want to mind your own business, you've got to stay off the streets. I didn't want no part of what Darius was doing—that's his road, not mine. His crew came around a few times while he was locked up, thinking maybe I'd want to take his spot. I told them no way. After a while, they believed me. They stopped coming round. It got awful quiet in here. That's when I got into gaming and other stuff—to keep busy, find someone to talk to, you know? I think maybe it was the same way for Chloe. Her parents are, like, insane strict. She doesn't get to hang out with her friends."

"Did she ever come hang out here with you?"

He cackled. "Yeah, that'll happen. I sneak in some little white rich girl to hang out. Her parents would have me in bracelets quicker than you can say statutory rape."

"I thought you weren't into her."

"I'm not," he said, belligerent. "But I know how the world works."

"You said she's rich," Dorie said as her gaze slid to the large television that Ellery had noticed. "How did you find that out? Ever been to her place?"

"No, I told you. We talked only at the Y and online. I know she's rich because of the stuff she says. Like, they got two laundry rooms in her house. Why the hell do they need two laundry rooms? There's only Chloe and her parents living there." He shook his head, baffled. "Meanwhile, Grandma and I have to haul our clothes to the Suds-o-mat three blocks away."

"So Chloe's never been here," Ellery said. "Not once?"

"She didn't so much as walk by outside."

"Good." She nodded with satisfaction now that she'd locked him into his story. "Then you wouldn't mind if we took a look around."

"You think I got her stashed in a closet or something?" He spread his arms and made an exasperated sound in the back of his throat. "Go ahead. Look all you want. There's nothing to see."

Ellery and Dorie walked the length of the stuffy apartment, the old wooden floor creaking beneath their feet. In her mind's eye, Ellery pictured Chloe as she was on the day of her abduction, in the pink T-shirt, jean shorts, and sandals. She had diamond stud earrings and a black-and-white beaded bracelet around her left wrist. Ellery didn't really believe Tyreek had stashed Chloe in a closet, but she held her breath each time they opened one. Their search turned up nothing but winter coats, a vacuum, and a bunch of boxes. Ty's grandmother's room held a Shaker-style bedroom set and another expensive television was mounted on the wall. A window fan spun lazily in the mild breeze. She had framed pictures on the dresser, including one of a young woman and a toddler who looked like he was probably Ty. The room smelled like perfume and felt heavy with memory.

Ty's room smelled like teenage hormones. His walls displayed posters of basketball stars like Steph Curry and Kyrie Irving. Ellery noticed a laptop computer on the bed, one that cost more money than hers did. Someone in this house had big-time disposable income. "Where did you get that?" she asked Tyreek, who had been following them around the place.

He didn't get a chance to answer. Dorie spoke instead.

"Hathaway."

"Yeah?"

Dorie jerked her head to indicate Ellery should join her by Tyreek's cluttered desk. It held a stack of graphic novels, dragon figurines, mismatched socks, a fork, and a bunch of takeout menus. "Look at that," Dorie murmured to her.

Ellery followed her gaze to a black-and-white item peeking out from beneath one of the paper menus. It looked like Chloe's bracelet.

17

When the caller ID read: "U Penn police," Reed ducked out from his sister's breakfast table to answer it. "Agent Markham? . . . It's Jed Bolden. I got a message here this morning that you wanted to talk to me about an incident with Professor Stone's car some years ago."

"That's right. I was told yesterday that you were the one who responded to the scene?"

"Yes, sir. It was just past ten at night. Professor Stone was working late in his office. A student out jogging saw the blaze and called it in. Someone had poured gasoline on that silver BMW Z20 and then tossed a lit match. No witnesses. At the time, we had cameras at the front of the building, but not at the back where the car was parked in the lot, so we didn't have much to go on."

"You never identified the perpetrator?"

"Professor Stone thought it might be one of his students angry about a bad grade. We do occasionally see that sort of thing. A few years ago, a failing student took a fire extinguisher and sprayed it under the door of his teacher's locked office. Destroyed four grand's worth of computer equipment."

"Did you interview the students?"

"We talked to them. They all denied it, of course. We didn't have anything to prove otherwise, and well . . ."

"Well, what?"

"Professor Stone didn't seem all that eager to continue the investigation. He kept saying his insurance would write it off, but of course, they were leaning on us for answers before they'd pay up. I wondered if Professor Stone might have known more about the fire than he wanted to say."

"You think he set it himself?"

"No, we ruled that possibility out right away. Computer data showed he was in his office working when the car went up. But he has a son, you know, and rumor had it that the kid was struggling with drug addiction at the time. I heard his parents had kicked him out, they were so fed up."

"Justin," Reed said, musing to himself. His name kept coming up.

"Right. That was his name. Justin Stone."

"Did you look into whether he'd set the fire?"

A heavy pause came through the other end. "You mind telling me why you're asking? I'm happy to cooperate, but it's a little strange to have the FBI poking around in a property crime fifteen years after the fact."

"I'm not at liberty to disclose any details. However, I do appreciate any help you can give me."

"Right. It's just—I work for the university. So does Professor Stone. He's got some AI grant about teaching computers to predict economic recession that got a write-up in the papers last year. *60 Minutes* came out and interviewed him."

"You don't want to make trouble for him."

"I don't want to make trouble for myself."

Ah, Reed thought. *There's something here.* "You did look into Justin Stone," he surmised. "What did you find?"

"A whole lot of nothing," Bolden admitted finally. "As in, he couldn't account for his whereabouts at all. But he had a McDonald's receipt from three blocks away just about three hours before the fire. I checked every gas station in the vicinity to see if he might've picked up a can. No one remembered seeing him. But no one could swear he wasn't there, either. Between you, me, and the lamppost, I figured he did it and his father was covering for him."

"Okay, thank you." Reed paused. "What, if anything, do you know about a possible complaint against Professor Stone a few years ago? One by a female student."

Another long pause. "I heard about it," Bolden replied at length. "I also heard she made it up."

"Did you do any investigation into her complaint at the time?"

"No, sir. The Dean of Students told me they'd handle it."

"What did you think about that request?"

"What did I think? I think Professor Stone's grant is more than a million dollars a year. That buys you your own personal investigation by the special committee."

"Does it also buy you a particular outcome?"

"I don't get to ask those questions," answered Bolden. "But you go right ahead."

Reed thanked the man for his time and candor and then hung up the phone. It rang again immediately in his hands. He braced himself when he saw Sarit's name on the screen. "Hello, Sarit," he said through gritted teeth as he answered.

"Hello. Just checking in to make sure you're not dragging our child into any other police investigations. How is Tula?"

"She's fine. Would you like to say hello?"

"Yes, please."

Reed found his daughter with her cousins, Renee and Callie, dancing in their pajamas and singing along to Taylor Swift. Reed was a tad alarmed to note his seven-year-old appeared to know all the lyrics. "It's Mama," he said over the din as he handed her the phone. He motioned for Renee to cut the music. "Come give me the phone when you're done," he told Tula.

"Mama, guess what? I'm at Auntie Kimmy's house!"

Reed winced as he left the room, knowing he would get an earful about this later. Sarit was an only child to older parents who had long ago passed on. She had cousins in India she had met a few times, but stateside he and Tula were her family. She had always been intimidated by Reed's ever-expanding brood of relatives and the way they were enmeshed in one another's lives, whereas Reed relished the sense of belonging he felt whenever they were together, even if it did get noisy or uncomfortable at times. He wanted to give that same grounding to his daughter, the knowledge that there was a small army of Markhams on her side, ready to pick her up should she ever fall. To Sarit, it seemed like he was passing off Tula to whoever was handy, as though he didn't value time with her, but Reed did not want his daughter to be a stranger to her extended family.

Kimmy was on her third cup of coffee from a mug that read: ALL MY PANTS ARE SASSY. She watched him as he lowered himself into the empty seat next to her. "Did you bring up Houston?" she asked.

"No, it didn't seem like a great idea to get into that over the phone."

She smiled and tousled his hair. "Look at that—my little brother is learning."

"Do you even own any pants?" he asked as he ducked away from her touch. Kimmy dressed in skirts and heels almost exclusively.

"Of course. I do yoga."

"With sass, I take it."

"Honey, I do everything with sass," she replied, putting on the Southern drawl for effect, and he grinned and shook his head. She sobered and regarded him with serious blue eyes. "I looked over that paperwork you forwarded me. It does say that the custody terms can be renegotiated if either party doesn't abide by the initial agreement."

"I have abided," Reed protested.

"You told me you didn't always stick to the schedule."

"My life doesn't happen on a strict schedule. Sarit damn well knows that."

"Yes, and that's probably the source of your problem," Kimmy told him. "You're still with the other woman."

"What? I didn't even start seeing Ellery until a few months ago. Sarit and I were long divorced by then."

"I am not talking about Ellery. I'm talking about your job. You remember—the thing that broke up your marriage. I'm sure in Sarit's view, your work took you away from her and now it's taking you away from Tula. She thinks she's protecting her."

"Tula is right in there, with me."

"So you're working a case with your seven-year-old daughter in tow? I don't think I'd bring that up, either. And, as long as we're laying all the cards on the table, then yes, there's Ellery, too. Sarit doesn't like her."

"Sarit doesn't know her."

Kimmy frowned. Sarit hadn't met Ellery, but she had. "All things being equal, that's probably a good thing. She's, um . . . well, she's a lot." Reed shot her a look and Kimmy held up her palms. "Hey, I like her. I do. Now. But you have to admit, Reed, she comes on like a freight train. She's got nails in her closets. She nearly lost her job because she shot a guy in cold blood."

"A man who nearly killed me."

"I know." She reached for his hand and squeezed it. "I know it all makes sense to you and her, and maybe that's how love is supposed to be, but a judge is going to look at the considerable number of hospital bills and wonder whether she's fit to be around kids."

Reed jerked his hand back at the word "love." He didn't say anything for a long time. "You're saying I have to choose, then. Is that right?" He gave Kimmy a hard look. "Tula or Ellery?"

Kimmy didn't get a chance to answer. Tula came bounding into the room with Reed's cell phone. "Here, Daddy. Mama says to tell you she'll deal with you later." She peered into his face, her eyes worried. "Are you in trouble? That's what she says to me when I'm getting punished."

"No, baby."

"Good." She slid into his lap and threw her arms around his neck. He hugged his daughter close, laying his cheek atop her shining hair, and he met Kimmy's gaze. She looked away with a sad smile and Reed closed his eyes. If he had to choose, there was no choice at all.

Reed had one additional stop to make before returning to Boston on the train. Fortunately, Kennedy Harris worked as a barista in a coffee shop just one mile from the station. "How would you like to buy some cookies to eat on the trip back to Boston?" he asked Tula, who was skipping along beside him, swinging his hand back and forth as they walked.

"Yeah, chocolate chip!"

"Let's see what they have." His phone buzzed as he pushed open the door to the coffee shop. "Ellery," the ID read. He took the call and prayed for good news. "How goes it?" he asked as he and Tula took their places at the end of the line.

"We found the guy from the picture, Tyreek Cantrell. We've brought him in for questioning."

"Sounds serious."

"He's got Chloe's bracelet. The one from the day she disappeared."

They shuffled forward in line. "You don't sound convinced he's the guy."

"We checked the apartment, even going down to the basement. There's no sign of her. He's not giving off the vibe of an angry kidnapper, though. We're letting him stew by himself for a few minutes before we hit him with the bracelet. Meanwhile, people here are divided on whether Teresa should do another televised plea."

"What does she want?"

"She wants to do it."

Reed glanced down at his daughter. Of course a parent would say anything, do anything. Pluck out all their eyelashes. Give away their savings. Stand naked in Times Square and scream for God Almighty to smite them for their sins. The kidnapper was using this natural desperation for their own pleasure. Whoever it was didn't care about Chloe. It was about making Teresa suffer, and Teresa would do so endlessly. Reed's concern was the end game—taking Chloe's life would be the final move. They had to hope the kidnapper hadn't made it yet.

"Reed? Are you there?"

"Yes, just thinking."

"What do you say? Should she do it?"

There were justifications either way from a tactical point of view. Conceding to the demand invited Chloe's abductor to make further contact, and each contact increased the data they could draw on to find her. Giving in could also embolden the kidnapper to up the ante, moving them all closer to the end. But as he stood there, Tula's warm hand in his, Reed answered like a parent, not an FBI agent. If this went bad, if the worst happened, he would want Teresa to know she had done all she could. "Do the TV appearance," he said finally.

"There's not much else new. Just some additional security camera footage from the T. Chloe got on the Green Line at Arlington headed inbound."

"Can I see the footage?"

"Sure, I'll send it. What about you? Anything from Philly that explains this case?"

"Nothing yet. I'm headed back to Boston shortly and I'll fill you in then."

He heard voices on her end. "I've got to go," she said.

"Ellery—" He almost said, *Love you,* but bit it back. "Be careful," he amended.

She hesitated, like she heard what he didn't say. "You, too."

At the counter, they ordered a milk for Tula, a coffee for Reed, and a pair of chocolate chip cookies to go. Reed set Tula up at a small table with her iPad and went to pick up his coffee. The barista had a nose stud and bright red hair pulled back into a bun. She prepared the coffee in no particular hurry, looking preoccupied with her thoughts. Her name tag read: KENNEDY, so he knew he had the right woman.

"Reed!" she called out as she brandished the paper cup.

"That's me," he said, but he didn't take the coffee from her. Instead, he showed off his FBI credentials. "Are you Kennedy Harris?"

She didn't look impressed. "You already know that I am or you wouldn't be asking."

"My name is Reed Markham. I was hoping to ask you a couple of questions."

She waved at the expresso machine. "I'm kinda busy here."

"It's important."

She rolled her eyes, but she hollered toward the back, "Hey, Max! Can you cover for me?"

"It's not your break yet!" a male voice yelled in return.

"Tell that to the Feds."

A young man with floppy hair and visible arm tattoos emerged to look at Reed. He held up his ID again. "Holy shit, Kennedy. What did you do?"

"Just cover for me, will you?" She pulled out a pack of cigarettes from her back pocket and headed for the door. "We can talk outside."

Reed took his coffee and brought Tula along to the sidewalk. Tula regarded their new companion with solemn eyes. "You shouldn't smoke. It's bad for you."

"I'll quit tomorrow," Kennedy said around the cigarette. She looked to Reed. "Talk fast. I've only got five minutes."

"I'm here about Professor Ethan Stone."

"Oh God, not this again." She spun in a circle, her gaze to the sky. "I haven't been anywhere near the guy. I swear."

"You filed a complaint against him with the university," Reed said. "For inappropriate behavior."

Her gaze flickered to Tula, who was sucking her milk through a striped paper straw. "Do you always take children around with you on your cases?"

"Never mind what I do. I want to hear about the complaint."

She blew out a frustrated breath along with a plume of smoke. "I made it up, okay? Is that what you want to hear?"

"If it's the truth."

"Ha, right. The truth. It's out there—isn't that, like your motto or something?"

"Or something. Why did you make that complaint about Ethan Stone?"

"Because he was an asshole who liked to stare at my breasts and then he flunked me. I studied for that exam, too."

"He stared at you. Did he do anything else?"

"No," she said, impatient again. "Not to me."

"What do you mean?"

"I made up the complaint, okay? He didn't corner me in his office and grab my ass. He did it to this other girl, Laurie Schofield. She told me what happened, and I saw the bruises he gave her. She didn't want to make a big stink about it, though. Her grade was already an A."

"I see. So then you used her story in your complaint."

"If she wasn't going to use it, sure. Someone should make the asshole pay, right?" She glanced at Tula. "Sorry." Tula shrugged.

Reed had to give Kennedy points for cunning. If the story was true, Ethan Stone would have recognized the details and known the true origin. It was a power play of epic proportions, but unfortunately for Kennedy, Ethan Stone didn't blink. "Laurie didn't come forward," Reed said. "Not even when the investigation let him off the hook."

She turned her head away to blow out smoke. "It's all fine when it's just a story," she said. "When it's real, you don't want to talk about it." She looked him up and down, assessing. "What's your angle here, anyway? Did some other girl get groped?"

This, Reed thought as he considered Professor Stone's grant, *was the million-dollar question.*

18

Conroy met with Dorie and Ellery in the hall outside the room where they were holding Tyreek Cantrell for questioning. He had the bracelet, which sat inside a plastic evidence bag. "The nanny has confirmed this is the bracelet Chloe was wearing the day she went missing," he said. "We need to lean on this kid hard."

Ellery chewed her bottom lip. "I don't think he's our kidnapper."

"I agree, Captain," Dorie said. "We found a kid who's clearly spent the last couple of days sitting around in his underwear playing video games."

"He got that bracelet somehow. The press is crawling up my ass for answers, and right now, we don't have any. So I'm telling you two as plainly as I can: go in there and get some." He shoved the bracelet into Ellery's hands. She looked to Dorie, who indicated with her eyes that they should just get this over with already.

Ellery took a breath and pushed open the door. Ty had been slumped over on the table, but he righted himself quickly at their appearance. "Do I need a lawyer or something?"

"You tell us," Ellery said as she pulled out a chair. "Did you do anything you'd need a lawyer for?"

"No," he said defensively.

"Then you don't need one."

"I told you everything I know."

"I don't think that's true. For starters, where'd you get this?" She tossed the bracelet on the table in front of him. He stared at it a moment.

"You took that from my room."

"Answer the question," Dorie cut in. "Where did you get it?"

"From Chloe," he said reasonably. "She made it for me a few months ago. It's, like, a friendship bracelet or something." Color heightened on his cheeks. "I took it, but there's no way I'm wearing some string of beads like that. I'd be laughed off the courts."

"Chloe was wearing a bracelet just like this the day she disappeared."

"She made two of them. One for me and one for her. Only I just told you, I don't wear mine. I made pretend like I did because I didn't want to hurt her feelings." He spread his hands. "Is that it? Can I go now?"

"Chloe had a second cell phone," Ellery said, ignoring him. "What do you know about that?"

He flopped back in his seat, deflated. "Man, I don't know nothing about that. We played games and cracked each other up—that's it. I don't know what kind of cell phones she had."

"You didn't buy her one? Maybe so you could keep in touch on a line not being monitored by her strict parents?"

He made an offended face. "No. I gave her a stuffed kitten I won at the arcade once. That's all."

"You seem to have a taste for expensive electronics," Ellery said. "TV, gaming systems. Those shoes you're wearing go for more than a hundred bucks. Where did you get them?"

"Nike."

Ellery repressed a sigh. "I mean how did you pay for them?"

"Nike." They stared at him, disbelieving. "They gave me the

shoes, man. I use them when I do my tricks, and it's like advertising for them."

"Tricks?" Ellery asked, arching an eyebrow.

"Yeah, on my YouTube channel—FlyGuy?" He got up lightning fast and seemed to walk sideways up the wall. Then he flipped over his head and landed on both feet. "See? I can show you." He took out his phone. "I have more than three hundred thousand subscribers. The companies pay me to wear their gear."

"You realize we can check this."

"Check all you want. I got receipts. Gran lets me spend a chunk of it, and the rest goes in my college savings."

"College," Ellery said.

"Yeah, college." He folded his arms across his chest. "You think I want to spend the rest of my life here? I got the grades. I just need the dough, and now I'm about sixty percent of the way there."

"That's great," Ellery said, meaning it. "Good for you." Ellery had had to pay her own way through school, too, through even more dubious means, so she admired the kid's ingenuity. She hoped like hell he wasn't guilty of anything that could pull him from the ladder he was stubbornly climbing, one stunt at a time. "Back to Chloe," she said, and he yanked the chair back out to take a seat with them. "You mentioned there was an older guy creeping on her. What do you know about that?"

"What? How'd you hear that?"

"The game last night," Ellery explained. "That was us you were talking to."

He slumped in his chair. "Figures," he muttered. He picked at his cuticles and his leg started to bounce under the table. "I don't know much. Just that some older guy, one of her parents' friends, was bugging her to send him pictures and stuff. He liked to hug her and once he grabbed her butt."

"Did she tell her parents?"

"Naw, she was scared to. This guy's been in the family for a long time. I think he's some kind of lawyer?"

"She never said his name?"

"Not to me. I told her she should knee him in the balls real hard and let him explain how he got that injury." He smiled to himself, remembering. "I didn't think he'd really try anything serious with her. I mean, a lawyer messing with a kid like that, he could get in major trouble if she told anyone."

Ellery looked to Dorie. "Wintour," she said softly.

Dorie nodded. "I'm on it." She left to run a background check on Martin Lockhart's attorney friend, while Ellery returned her attention to Ty. "You've been helpful so far, thank you," she said. "But I need you to think harder. Chloe needs you. Anything else you can tell us about her plans, her fears, her relationships—it could be the key to finding her."

He looked glumly at the bagged friendship bracelet on the table. "I wish I could help you. On TV, they're saying that the kidnapper chopped off all her hair. Is that true?"

"We're not sure. Maybe."

"I liked to yank her pigtails, just a little bit. It made her laugh."

"Anything else she may have told you," Ellery urged, leaning forward.

He searched himself. "She was always pissed at her parents, especially her mom. Her brother got killed, you know, before she was born, and that's why her mom didn't want Chloe to go anywhere. She said once, 'She didn't even want me. My dad had to make her.' Which, I dunno, man. How do you make someone have a kid? I told her that her mom was probably just scared after what happened before. Chloe said that didn't help her now."

Ellery tamped down her rising frustration. None of this was especially new information. "What about the second cell phone? Did you ever see one?"

"No, she had an iPhone in a Hello Kitty case. That's all I saw. Wait." He sat up with a jolt and pulled out his own phone. "She texted me once from a different number. She said it was a friend's phone, but maybe it wasn't. I can show you the number—would that help?"

Ellery tried not to grab the phone out of his hands too eagerly. A real break. Finally. "Yes," she said. "I believe it would."

Ellery cursed as she fed her dollar bill into the soda machine for the third time, only to have it spit the bill back out again with an electronic hum. Dorie appeared next to her, took the dollar, flapped it like a waiter might do with a linen napkin before placing it into a woman's lap, and then gently inserted it into the machine. It took. "Patience, grasshopper," she said to Ellery.

Ellery hit the button to dispense a Diet Coke. "What did you find out on Wintour?" she asked as she cracked the tab.

"His record is clean. Which may mean he's not our creeper."

"Or he's really good at getting away with it."

"Yeah, well, here's a piece of free advice from someone who's been there before: we don't want to rattle the cage of a six-hundred-dollar-per-hour lawyer without more evidence than hearsay from a teenager. We'll have to do a full background and hope something shakes loose."

"That takes days, often weeks." A complete background required tracing Wintour back through every address he had ever had, contacting law enforcement in those districts, as well as talking to former friends, relatives, and neighbors.

"We have no choice unless we find something much more incriminating than a rumor."

"We have her computer data."

"Just one month's worth. If there was anything substantive there about Wintour, it'd have been flagged already."

Ellery chewed her lip and worried the pop-top of her soda can back and forth. "We could tail him, see where he goes." This was how Reed had caught Coben all those years ago. The detectives had interviewed the serial killer and released him, deciding he was not their guy. Reed had seen Coben's weird obsession with hands and decided to follow him anyway. He'd been green at the time, barely on the job a few months. He was supposed to be aiding background checks, not surveilling suspects, but he'd played a hunch and it panned out. A few more hours in that hellhole and she would have died from her injuries and the infection that had set in. Chloe had been gone for almost three days now.

"Conroy isn't going to authorize surveillance based on what we've got so far. We need more."

Ellery's brain was still whirring. She drained her drink and tossed the can into the nearby recycling bin. "We don't need more. We just need Wintour to think we have more."

"Did you not just hear me about the dangers of bluffing a shark in an Armani suit?"

"We won't be the ones doing the bluffing." She checked the time on her phone. "Come on, we can meet Conroy at the Lockhart place and run it by him. Teresa's set to make her next public statement in less than an hour."

"What about Chloe's second phone? Did you find out anything from the number?"

"It's a burner phone purchased from a third-party distributor. He says he sold it at some farmers market in Providence back in May. The buyer paid cash and he doesn't remember who it was—not a big help."

Dorie halted in mid-stride. "Did you say Providence?"

Ellery stopped, too. "Yeah, why?"

"Stephen Wintour owns a second home in Narragansett."

Ellery turned on her heel and doubled her determined pace. This time, Dorie didn't try to slow her down or make her argue her position. She beat her to the front doors by a nose.

At the Lockhart mansion, Conroy gave them permission to discuss the idea of confronting Wintour with Martin Lockhart. Ellery reasoned that if anyone could con Wintour into making a slip at this stage, it would be his friend. "But tread lightly," Conroy said, directing the caution more to Dorie than to Ellery, as though she were the one who would actually heed it. "If he does have the girl, the absolute last thing we want to do is spook him. In the meantime, I'll put some people on the deep background check. Maybe we get lucky and they'll find an early hit."

Ellery and Dorie found Martin Lockhart at the back of the living room, watching as the cameras and microphones were set up around his wife. He gripped the back of an armchair so hard his fingers had turned completely white. "The FBI said she should do it alone this time," he said to them as they came to stand near his side. "It's supposed to make her look more vulnerable, which is apparently what this guy wants. He wants to see her fear, they said. I said, why does it have to be just her? Look at me." He jerked his hand free from the chair and held it out to show them. His fingers trembled as though they were leaves riffling in the breeze.

"I'm sorry," Ellery said. "I'm sure they have their reasons."

"It's my fault, you know." He snapped his mouth shut, his jaw tight.

"What's your fault?"

"All of it." He stared straight ahead as the white lights came up on his wife. "Teresa didn't want a child, not at first. I wore her down. Hell, I practically begged her. I promised her it would be different this time." He swallowed visibly. "She loves Chloe, with every cell of her being. I'm sure of it. But she was so afraid. And now look where we are."

"You didn't know this would happen," Dorie said.

"I didn't know it wouldn't," he shot back, his voice raw with pain. "That's what I didn't see, what I wouldn't admit. Teresa knew it." He made a fist and pounded it lightly on the chair. "This monster is punishing the wrong person."

"Mr. Lockhart," Ellery said. "We need to talk to you in private."

He turned hawklike eyes on her. "Is it Chloe? You know something?"

Ellery kept her tone neutral. "Is there someplace we can go?"

"My study." He led them down the hall to his private office, taking care to shut the heavy wooden door behind them. "What is it?" he asked, his expression anxious. "Please don't keep me in suspense here."

"What can you tell us about Stephen Wintour?" Ellery asked.

"Stephen? We work at the same firm. We've been friends for two decades now. He's as upset about Chloe as anyone."

"He and Chloe are close, then?"

"He was at her christening. He brings her little treats whenever he comes to dinner—costume jewelry, markers, that sort of thing. He plays piano, so they've done duets together for fun sometimes. He's like an uncle to her, I guess you could say."

A *funny uncle*, Ellery thought. "Does he have her cell phone number?"

"I wouldn't think so, but maybe. She might have called him at some point."

"What if he called her?" Dorie broke in pointedly. "Would that be a normal occurrence?"

"Why are you asking me all of this? I don't understand."

"Chloe told some of her friends that an older man was 'creeping on her,' to use their words about it. She said it was one of your friends. A lawyer." Ellery watched him for a reaction. His expression turned incredulous.

"That's impossible and frankly disgusting. Stephen dates

women—adult women. His interest in children is purely avuncular. He organizes charity drives for Boston Children's Hospital. He takes kids from the Boys and Girls Club to Red Sox and Celtics games."

"He spends a lot of time with kids, does he?" Ellery asked.

"You make it sound sick. Stephen helps these kids. He—he betters their lives."

"He may have asked your twelve-year-old for a nudie pic," Dorie said.

"Prove it," Lockhart said harshly. "Show me the text if you have it."

"It wasn't in the material covered by our warrant," Ellery said.

"I don't believe it then." He went to the window and peered out at the pink flowers. "Stephen would never hurt Chloe."

"That's good. That's what we're hoping for." Ellery took a step closer to him. In her pocket, her cell phone buzzed. She pulled it out and saw a text from Conroy: *Wintour was arrested in Cambridge in 1989 for kidnapping a minor female. No charges brought. Claimed misunderstanding, but he agreed to move out of the building. It was his landlady's daughter.* "Mr. Lockhart," she said as she tucked the phone away again, "Stephen Wintour was arrested once for kidnapping a girl. Did you know that?"

He whirled from the window. "What?"

"The charges were dropped. My guess is that she and her parents didn't want to endure a trial. They just wanted him gone, and he agreed to move."

"When was this?"

"Back in 1989."

"Stephen would have been in law school then. Lots of students move around."

"Mr. Lockhart," Dorie said, but he held up his hands.

"Stop! Enough. You can't be telling me it's Stephen. You can't be telling me I let the wolf through the gate."

"We don't know," Ellery replied steadily. "But we need to find out. You can help us."

He eyed her, wary. "How?"

"He's not going to let us through his front door, but he would let you in. You can look around and ask him about Chloe."

He let out a bitter laugh. "Right. I just ask my friend if he's been sexting my preteen daughter? Maybe I demand to check his closets to see if he's hiding her in there?"

The girl in the closet. Ellery's flesh rippled under her clothes. Her skin went clammy and her vision started to swim. "I . . . you?" Her throat tightened and she couldn't think. Her brain buzzed an alarm that told her to run. *Go, go, go.*

Dorie's hand appeared on her arm, gripping her. "We understand your skepticism," she said. "And maybe you're right. Maybe Stephen Wintour is a kindly man with the best intentions toward kids, including Chloe. But your wife is out there sweating bullets under the cameras, debasing herself on live TV in the hopes of getting your daughter back. I'd like to think you could at least ask your friend a few questions."

Ellery released a slow, shuddering breath. Lockhart squeezed his eyes shut for a long moment. "What is it you want me to do?" he asked finally.

"Ask to visit Wintour's home. We will equip you with a wire ahead of time to record your conversation. Ask him generally if he has any idea of where Chloe is or who might have taken her. His answers could be revealing. Then, we'd like you to bluff him a little bit."

Lockhart thinned his lips. "Stephen's the poker player. Not me."

"Good," Dorie said without missing a beat. "Then he'll believe you."

"What is the bluff?"

"We'd like you to say that you've found a diary of Chloe's, and that she wrote he asked her to send him photos of herself."

"You want me to lie."

"If he didn't do it, then it doesn't matter," Dorie replied.

"I don't understand," he said, holding out his hands in imploring fashion. "If you suspect him, can't you go in there and ask these questions yourselves?"

Ellery's thoughts snapped back like a rubber band. "We don't have enough evidence yet for a warrant," she said, righting herself. "If we go in hard, he's liable to clam up and refuse to speak to us. That doesn't help us get any closer to Chloe."

He bowed his head, his eyes on his smooth mahogany desk. "You really think he could have done this," he whispered.

"I think we need to find out, and fast." The room fell silent and nobody moved. An antique wall clock conveniently ticked out the passing seconds as Lockhart struggled with their request.

"Okay," he relented at last. "I'll do it."

19

Reed did not believe in a sixth sense, but he had studied enough about neuroscience function to know that the brain did not take in all of its surroundings at once or with the same conscious understanding. If someone were to toss an apple at his head, he knew that there was one brain area that noticed the shape (round), another that detected its color (red), while a third fired off the message that the object was approaching (fast), and, finally, some executive higher-level processing that put all this information together and told him he'd better duck. Sometimes these disparate areas detected important information that got mislaid or did not immediately make all the requisite connections for true comprehension. Your brain signaled an alarm before you consciously knew the threat. Reed had learned to trust that inner alarm that said *pay attention,* even when he wasn't sure yet why it mattered. He froze the video camera footage from the subway on a shot of Chloe that revealed the same male figure hovering twenty feet behind her, pretending not to watch. The man's face continued to be obscured by sunglasses and a ball cap, but he felt familiar to Reed in a way he couldn't yet articulate.

Faced with this urgent development, his brain made another choice, this one perhaps less rational: he'd left Tula in the care of Ellery's teenage sister. "I used to babysit all the time before I got sick," Ashley assured him as he once again stressed they were not to leave the apartment. He wrote down his cell number in three places. He left money to order in pizza. He stated specifically that they were not to take off on any cross-country trips. Ashley seemed horrified at the idea. "With a kid? Are you crazy?" She took Tula's hand. "Come on, we can paint our toes this time." Tula had pirouetted with joy.

Reed found Ellery huddled with her partner, her captain, and what looked like Martin Lockhart. The frisson of energy around them told him there had been a significant development. Ellery broke loose from the group when she spotted him, the relief on her face plain at the sight of him. "Oh, good, you're here."

"What's going on?" he asked, nodding in the direction of Martin Lockhart.

"Stephen Wintour is looking like our guy. Seems like he may have attempted to kidnap another girl years ago, but the charges were dropped." She gave him a brief outline of the situation, including the news that Wintour had a second home not too far from where Chloe's burner phone had been purchased. "We don't have quite enough for a warrant. Martin Lockhart has agreed to meet with Wintour while wearing a wire. If he can get Wintour to admit to additional contact with Chloe, that might be enough for a warrant."

Reed's alarm bells went off again. "You're sending in the father of a kidnap victim to confront her possible abductor?"

"He won't talk to us. Time is running out, Reed. It's day three."

Her staccato speech, the fevered look in her eyes—he wondered if she'd slept at all for the past two days. "I realize time is important," he said softly. "But this is a dangerous proposition. Need I remind you what happened the last time we paired up a victim and a perpetrator in an unregulated setting?" That meeting had ended in a shower of bullets.

"He won't be armed. We'll make sure of it." She rubbed her eyes as though they had grit in them. "It's one conversation. One that may lead us to Chloe."

Reed held his laptop under one arm. His half-formed hunch about the man in the baseball cap felt weak in light of the developments on Wintour. "It's just . . . I'm worried for you."

"I'm not the one trapped in the closet."

He blinked. Did she even hear herself? "No one said Chloe's in a closet. We don't know where she is."

"What we know is bad enough." She looked annoyed with him. "You have a kid. Wouldn't you want to do absolutely anything you could to bring her back?"

"Of course." He understood completely why Lockhart had agreed to this setup. "But my role here is to think like an agent, not like a father. What are you thinking as?"

"Like someone who wants Chloe back."

She tried to brush past him, but he stopped her by grabbing her arm. "You're projecting," he said softly. "It's understandable, Ellery, but it's also dangerous. It's okay to take a step back. It's okay to let someone else take the lead."

She yanked herself free. "That's a laugh, coming from you. Remind me why your marriage broke up again?"

He stiffened. "That's not the same thing at all."

"Isn't it? Where's your kid, Agent Markham? The one who is supposed to be on vacation with her father?"

"Hey, I didn't ask for this," he said, more loudly than he intended. "Neither did I."

Heads turned to watch as she stalked off to where the others surrounded Lockhart. Reed turned his back to them, unwilling even to look at her right at that moment. After several deep breaths, he opened his laptop and forwarded what he had to the local FBI office, with instructions to look for additional closed-circuit footage of the man in the baseball cap. *Go back in time before the point we see*

Chloe cross his path, he wrote. *We need to check if he went into any of the nearby shops that might have a better view of his face.*

That task done, he repacked his laptop into his briefcase and joined the war room that had sprung up around Martin Lockhart. Ellery greeted him with a level gaze, but Captain Conroy appeared relieved to see him. He didn't look like a man who had slept much in the past few days, either. "Agent Markham, please come in. We're about to head over to Stephen Wintour's apartment building, but perhaps you could give us some insights about the best approach."

He felt the weight of Ellery's stare and her silent message: *Don't fuck this up.* He licked his lips and chose his words carefully. "If Stephen Wintour is a predatory pedophile who is responsible for Chloe's disappearance, then this is likely something he has planned and fantasized about for a long time. He will not be easily dissuaded from his course."

"I still don't believe it," Lockhart said. "I asked him to pick her up from school one day last year when Mimi was on vacation. Why wouldn't he have run off with her then?"

"Again, if he's the guy, then my best guess is that either the situation did not come close enough to his fantasy or he had reason to figure he'd be discovered. If you had asked him to pick her up, then he would have been the prime suspect if she'd disappeared."

Lockhart frowned. "If he's the guy, then won't he just refuse to let me in?"

"Possibly," Reed agreed. "But he'd also wish to avoid drawing suspicion on himself. Pedophiles are adept at blending in and appearing normal in everyday interactions."

"Let's go over the rules again," Conroy said to Lockhart.

The man grunted. "Ask him if he has any theories about Chloe. Tell him she kept a diary and that it says he asked her for pictures."

"That's right. Don't confront him or accuse him. Don't push too hard. Just try to get him talking about Chloe, and we'll follow up later if it comes to that. We'll be listening outside the entire time, so please keep your hands away from the mic." He checked his watch. "It's go time."

They all piled into an unmarked white van and drove to Back Bay, where Wintour kept a condo in one of the old brownstones. They parked about one block away next to a similar building to Wintour's. Dorie looked out the window at the three-story brick structure with its iron railings and arched windows. "What do you think a place like this goes for? A million? Maybe two?"

"Five and a half," Lockhart said, his gaze trained on the floorboards.

Reed could almost feel Conroy's sphincter tighten at the thought of all that money coming down on BPD. The captain coughed and opened the back door of the van. "Remember, keep it casual. You're here to get comfort from an old friend."

"I don't feel at all friendly." Lockhart climbed out and walked down the street to Wintour's place. "I hope you can hear me," he said, glancing back as he mounted the steps to the front door. His voice crackled loudly through the speakers, and the officer at the wheel flashed his headlights once in acknowledgment. Lockhart rang the bell, and a few moments later Stephen Wintour appeared to let him in. He did not sound like a man with a terrible secret.

"Martin, good to see you. How are you holding up?"

"It's hard. Harder still on Teresa."

"I saw her on TV today, the poor thing. She said she'd been an awful, selfish mother, and I don't mind telling you, I yelled back at her on the screen that it's not true. She's wonderful to Chloe."

"You don't have to tell me."

Wintour became harder to hear as they moved into a larger room, someplace with high, echoing ceilings. "The police . . . no leads at all?" he asked. Their footsteps continued into a room with better acoustics. Reed heard the creak of a leather sofa as Martin took a seat.

"They have nothing so far. It's hell, the waiting. I feel useless, impotent. I want to go door-to-door searching for her."

Wintour gave an uneasy laugh. "Well, she's not here. You can cross this place straight off your list."

"I keep wondering, you know, where he's keeping her. The photo doesn't offer any clues."

"Someplace private, I guess. Jesus, Martin, I hate to say it, but she could be anywhere by now."

"Where, do you think?"

"Me? What I think?" Wintour was taken aback.

"Sure. If you were him, where would you go?"

"I don't know. I guess if I'd planned this, I'd have a room already arranged. Somewhere remote—a cabin, maybe. Or a hidden, sound-proof room."

"Like an escape room."

"Sure," Wintour replied, sounding uncomfortable. "Like that."

There was a moment of silence, and Reed could feel Lockhart thinking. "You have one of those, as I recall," he said at length.

"It came with the house. Thankfully, I haven't had cause to use it—knock on wood." Reed heard three quick raps on a wooden surface. "I damn sure haven't stored any kids in there."

Reed met Ellery's gaze, and she obviously heard the same odd tension in Wintour's voice. Goose pimples broke out over Reed's forearms, despite the hot conditions in the back of the van. He shifted closer to the speaker.

"Can I see it?" Lockhart must have detected something off in Wintour's reply as well. His tone had hardened.

"What, now?"

"Sure, why not?"

"Martin, I realize you must be going out of your mind, but you can't believe I've got Chloe here."

A pause. "No, no. Of course not. It's just, with everything, I wonder if maybe I should get one of those rooms myself, you know? For when Chloe comes back. Teresa would appreciate the extra se-curity, I'm sure."

Everyone in the van held their breath. Dorie cracked her knuckles in the silence.

"Maybe another time," Wintour said. "When Chloe's back. I'll have you all over for dinner and give you the grand tour."

"Sure, okay."

"You want anything? Coffee, tea—vodka? I'd be tempted to drink myself blind in your position."

"You have any of that scotch we drank for Allan's retirement?"

"Ah, now you're talking." The sounds of glasses clinking came over the transmission.

"Stephen, there's something I've got to tell you."

"Oh?"

"The police are probably going to want to talk to you about Chloe."

"Of course. Anything I can do to help." Wintour was trying for breezy, and he almost pulled it off.

"No, I mean we found out Chloe kept a diary. Your name is in it."

They heard the sound of a glass hitting the table. "My name? Why?"

"She said—I'm sure they've got this wrong, but she said you texted her and asked her to send you pictures."

"No, that can't be right." He paused. "I mean, maybe I asked her to send me a picture of a selfie we took together. That could be true."

"Sure, right." Lockhart cleared his throat. "Except this wasn't that kind of picture, if you understand what I'm saying."

"I think I do. And you're wrong."

"Look, I'm not saying anything about it. The police have their suspicions. You know how they can twist things, how they see ulterior motives everywhere. They think the worst of everyone."

"You'd have to, in that job. But Martin, I never—and I mean never—asked Chloe to do anything inappropriate. I remember now. I once asked her to send me a picture of her from our trip to the Cape last summer. She had that cute one on the rocks, remember?"

"The one in her bathing suit."

"Yes," Wintour replied with relief. "You see? Totally aboveboard."

"Right. I see." There was another stretch of silence. "I just wanted to ask one thing, though. How did you get her number?"

"I'm sorry?"

"Her cell number. Teresa's pretty strict about Chloe giving that out."

"I don't really recall. I'm sure she must have called me at some point. Maybe one of those times when you asked me to give her a ride? All these questions. Martin . . . I feel like you suspect me of something here."

"Hell, my kid is missing. My little girl. I suspect the mailman right now."

"I understand. You must be going crazy." They heard a ring tone followed by some rustling. Wintour spoke. "I'm sorry, Martin, but I have to take this call. I'll just be a few minutes. Help yourself to the scotch."

Reed heard retreating footsteps and the sound of a door opening and closing. After that, Lockhart rose from wherever he'd been sitting and started walking the room. His footsteps were fast, his breathing erratic. "What's he doing?" Reed whispered to the others.

They heard him opening and closing drawers and closets. "No, no," Conroy said. "Nothing out of plain sight. He can't be going through the house without permission."

"We should get him out of there," Reed replied.

"How?" Ellery asked. "Anything we do now tips off Wintour."

"He's already been tipped off by Lockhart. He practically told him we'd be coming."

Through the speaker, Lockhart's voice crackled on the line. "Chloe? Chloe, are you here, sweetheart?" He was climbing the stairs now, practically running. His harsh breathing filled the van. "Chloe?"

They heard more frantic searching, the sound of doors opening and slamming shut again. "Oh my God." The stunned horror in Lockhart's voice made the hair on the back of Reed's neck stand up. "Oh my God."

"Martin?"

"What did you do with her?"

"Martin, calm down."

"I said: What did you do with her? Show me what's in the room!"

"Put down the gun, Martin. You don't want to shoot me."

"I want to see the room!"

Gun. Reed lurched to his feet, nearly slamming his head against the top of the van. "I thought you said he wasn't armed!"

"He wasn't!"

"It must be Wintour's weapon," Conroy said tersely. "We're going in."

He pushed open the back doors, and they all piled out into the street. They ran down the block and up the steps to Wintour's front door. "It's locked," Ellery said, yanking on the handle. The large door was made of thick etched glass with a gold inlaid design at the top. "Back up," she ordered. The others moved off the steps and she shot through the glass toward the floor. It shattered and she kicked the shards loose with one foot and then reached inside to flip the lock. "Boston Police!" she hollered as she opened the door with her gun drawn. "We're coming in!"

They entered the front hall just in time to hear an anguished scream and a gunshot from the upper floors. Ellery reached the stairs first, taking them two at a time with the rest of the group fast on her heels. "Martin—Mr. Lockhart? Talk to me. What's going on?"

She slowed her pace in the hall, her gun still at the ready. Over the rush of the blood in his ears, Reed could hear the sound of weeping from the room at the end of the hallway. The dark wooden door stood partially open. "Mr. Lockhart? Mr. Wintour? It's Detective Hathaway." She pressed the flat of her hand on the door and slowly pushed it open. Reed saw her sharp intake of breath. She held up a hand to forestall their entrance into the room. "Mr. Lockhart, I need you to put down the gun."

"Look at this. Look what he did."

Reed's mouth went dry. He didn't want to look. *God, please no.*

"I see. Put down the gun, and we'll talk about it."

She disappeared from sight, inching slowly toward him. Reed braced himself for the sound of another shot, but it never came. Instead, Ellery called to them a few moments later. "Clear," she said. "We need EMTs—now."

"On it," Dorie replied.

Reed followed Conroy into the room, which appeared to be Wintour's master suite. It boasted a bed big enough to sleep six, draped in a velvet green covering. Matching damask drapes held back the blazing summer sun, but they allowed enough light through to show the carnage on the floor. Stephen Wintour lay bleeding and unmoving on the floor. His low moaning said he was still alive. Around him lay girls' panties with cartoon figures on them. "They were in the dresser," Lockhart said, his voice barely above a whisper. He swayed on his feet, a man clearly destroyed. "And just look there."

Reed stepped forward to peer into the unlocked escape room. He saw a lifelike doll made to be a girl of perhaps ten years old. Stacks of DVDs with girls' names on them, as well as a television and DVD player. The worst of it was the wall of pictures—candid shots of girls in short shorts and skirts, bikinis at the beach and halter tops that showed their bellies. He scanned them quickly, searching for Chloe. He did not see her.

Behind him, Wintour gave the tortured moan of a dying animal. Lockhart screamed at him again, a cri de coeur that pierced Reed's skull with its force. "Where the hell is my daughter?"

Reed heard someone put handcuffs on him. The sirens outside said the ambulance had arrived, and moments later the sound of heavy boots came trooping into the house. Ellery materialized at his side, her anxious gaze on the photos in front of Reed. "Anything?" she whispered.

Reed shook his head. "She isn't here."

20

The Homicide Unit in Boston contained few women, just 7 percent overall, a dismal statistic to which Ellery knew she owed her current job. Under pressure to up the estrogen content on the murder squad, the chief of D's had been willing to take on a re-hab project—someone with a lightning rod personality and at least one questionable shooting already under her belt. Her background as Coben's lone survivor made her a curiosity. Dorie had let it slip once that they'd had a division-wide meeting prior to her arrival, with orders not to ask her about the infamous serial killer. Instead, she had to endure stares and whispers, or conversations that suddenly ceased when she entered the room. She'd caught one officer from the canine unit reading a copy of Reed and Sarit's bestselling book about the case, *Little Girl Lost*. She'd been prepared to ignore him until the guy asked her if she could get Reed to sign it.

The wide gender gap meant she could usually find solitude in the ladies' restroom, but it was closed for cleaning when she emerged from her debriefing over the shooting of Stephen Wintour. Wintour remained in ICU at the hospital, an armed guard posted nearby. The hungry press outside had pitched Martin Lockhart as a hero, and

with word that Ellery had been involved in the case, they were waiting to talk to her. Reporters never missed an opportunity to shove
a microphone into her face. Wherever the questions started, they
always came back to Coben. *I'd recommend leaving through the
parking garage,* Conroy had advised her. She had been sitting on her
hands so he couldn't see them shaking. She had "yes, sir"-ed her way
out of there and dragged a chair between the wall and the vending
machine in the break room, carving out a hidden alcove in which to
breathe. She pressed a cold bottle of water against her neck while the
sound of the gunshot played on a continuous loop inside her head.
Loud male voices entering the room made her sit up with a jolt.

"So, after all that, he didn't even have the kid?"

"Maybe he's got her stashed somewhere."

"If the pervert dies, then what?"

"Maybe her father should've thought of that before he pulled the
trigger."

"Can you blame the guy? I'd have wanted to pop him straight
between the eyes."

They had sent search teams to all of Stephen Wintour's registered
properties. So far, there was no sign of Chloe. They had warrants for
all his electronics now. Ellery felt sorry for whoever got the job of
wading through Wintour's hard drive. The pictures on his walls were
sickening enough.

Ellery heard the whirring of the microwave as one of the men
heated up his dinner. "Of course, the almighty Ellery Hathaway was
right there in the middle of it, like usual. She's on the job five months
and she's running point on a case like this? Come on."

"Conroy's running it. He was there, too."

"Should've been Nickerson's case. He's done a kidnapping before."

"So has Hathaway," the other guy reminded him, and they both
chuckled.

"Send one kidnapped girl to find another? Sure, okay. By that logic, it's the FBI guy, what's his name, who should be running the whole investigation. He's the one who found her."

"He was here earlier. I saw him."

"Mr. Hotshot FBI himself? And they still haven't solved the case? Damn, there goes my faith in the Feds. What's his angle here, anyway? Don't we already have enough G-men up in our business?"

The microwave beeped and she heard the door pop open. "You said it yourself: the almighty Ellery Hathaway. Where she goes, he goes. She's, like, his pet project or something."

"Or something," said the other one, and they both laughed again. "You think he's nailing her?"

Ellery shrank back in her chair, her face aflame. She'd kept her relationship with Reed private to the point where they'd argued about it. *We can have dinner in a restaurant,* he'd said the last time he had visited. *It's not a crime.* He didn't appreciate how it felt to have his entire life chronicled for public consumption. She could only imagine how the tongues would wag if everyone found out they were dating.

"Think about it," continued the first guy. "Markham's got a thing for serial killers, right? She could be like a memento."

"You're disgusting, Callahan."

"Hey, those scars of hers are disgusting. Have you seen them? Who wants a woman who's been carved up like a piece of meat?"

Ellery leaped to her feet. She knew she'd get these comments no matter what, but it pained her to hear Reed dragged into it. The two men jumped when she materialized behind them, a move that would confirm her status as the division whack job, hiding as she'd been behind a vending machine in the break room. *Ha,* she thought when she saw their uniforms and their horrified faces. *I outrank you.*

"De—detective Hathaway," stammered Tommy Burris, the less offensive one of the pair. "We, uh, we didn't see you there."

"I'd hope not. Otherwise your little conversation would be straight-up actionable as opposed to just wildly inappropriate."

"Our apologies. Ma'am."

Callahan sucked in his lips, but he didn't back down from her stare. She took several steps, advancing on him slowly. "Something you'd like to ask me about, Callahan?"

"No, ma'am."

"Really." She closed in to the point where his dinner steamed up between them. His fingers tightened around the Tupperware, but he didn't flinch. "Because it sounded like you had a lot of questions about me." She deliberately pulled up each sleeve in turn, showing off the scars. He glanced down once and then quickly away. "There's nothing I can clear up for you right here, right now?"

"No," he said, his jaw clenched. He no longer met her gaze.

"Three days," she said softly, moving her body so he had to look at her. "That's how long I spent with him and his knife. How long do you think you would have lasted?"

He did not answer.

"That's what I thought." She backed off infinitesimally and glanced down with disdain at his congealed dinner. "If you'll excuse me, I'm leaving now. It smells in here."

She drove home, still stinging, and trudged to her front door. Upon opening it, she nearly turned around and left again. Ashley and Tula were playing keep-away with Bump's tennis ball while he raced back and forth between them, barking vociferously. At her arrival, he broke free and came bounding over to meet her, skidding to a halt on the hardwood floor and immediately flopping at her feet, his tail thumping all the while. She sank down and buried her face in his fur. "Hey there, good boy."

Reed appeared from the kitchen, a dish towel in his hands. "Hi. I saved a plate of chicken Marsala for you. Also a big glass of wine."

"I need to shower first." She could pretend it was the sticky summer heat and not the men's words that left her feeling dirty.

"Any word on Wintour?"

"No change."

Reed put his hands on his trim hips for a moment, assessing her.

"All right," he said to the girls, "who wants to go down to the park with me to exercise the hound?"

"Me, me!" Tula greeted the idea with enthusiasm, but Ashley hung back.

"Not me, thanks."

"Ellery? Can I bring you anything?"

She shook her head. The steady stream of hot water rushing over her was all she wanted. That, plus a little peace and quiet.

"Come on, Sir Sheds-a-lot," Reed said with a sigh as he took up Bump's leash. "Let's go ogle the neighborhood poodles." Bump woofed his approval and began heading for the door.

Ellery stood under the shower until the hard shell of the day melted away at her feet. She got out and dried herself without looking at herself in the mirror, as was her custom. She wished she could lock herself alone in the bedroom, but she knew Ashley was out there, waiting for her. Her stomach's feeble rumble reminded her she hadn't eaten much all day. She dressed in leggings and an old T-shirt of Reed's and went in search of the dinner he had left for her.

"Hey," Ashley said, brightening at the sight of her. She had a water glass and a line of pill bottles in front of her.

"Hey," Ellery said as she eyed the orange prescription bottles. "What's all that for? Aren't you in remission?"

"Yeah, but I still have to take this stuff to keep it that way. My body could reject your cells at any time."

"Oh." She felt deflated. The battle, it seemed, was never fully won. "I'd just have to give you more then," she assured the girl.

Ashley gave her a sad smile. "It doesn't work like that. You get one shot. If my body rejects your DNA, then there's no rebooting it. Maybe I could find a new donor . . ." She trailed off and Ellery got the grim picture of how likely this would be.

"Then you'd better take those," she told the girl.

"I did already." Ashley began tucking them into her bag. "I did some laundry earlier. I hope that's okay."

"It's fine." Ellery ate a bite of chicken, which was tender and flavorful. Reed knew his way around a kitchen. "But, uh, we're going to have to have your dad come get you pretty soon."

Ashley regarded her with gray eyes so like her own. "He's your dad, too."

Ellery laid down her fork. "No," she said. "He's not." A dad helped you with your homework when you got stuck. He taught you how to drive a stick shift. He brought you comic books when you were sick and put a cold cloth on your forehead. Ellery hadn't had a dad since she was around Tula's age, when John Hathaway walked out the door and into his new life.

"He is," Ashley insisted with sudden tears in her eyes. "We're—we're sisters."

Ellery didn't feel that part, either. She barely knew this girl. "Look," she said, "I think it's great that he pulled his act together for you. He learned from his mistakes. He did better the second time around."

"Who's to say he won't do it again?" Ashely swiped at her eyes with her fingers.

"He won't."

"You don't know that."

Ellery sighed. She suspected if John Hathaway was going to wimp out and disappear again, he wouldn't have stuck it out through Ashley's cancer. "It's true. I don't know it. We don't always know what any of the people in our lives are capable of. I doubt your parents figured you'd run off here to Boston."

"No." She mustered a smile. "I usually do what I'm told."

"Good," Ellery said as she took up her fork again. "You should keep doing that."

"You don't," Ashley said, taking the seat next to her. "Reed said you answer to no one but yourself."

"That's a character flaw," Ellery told her, trying to sound convincing. She waved her fork around. "I'm working on fixing it."

Ashley snorted with disbelief. "Yeah, I'll just bet." She rubbed one blue-painted nail along the granite counter. "Reed is your boyfriend, right?"

Ellery coughed and nearly choked. "I guess," she said as she reached for her water. At the last second, she grabbed the wine instead. This definitely felt like a conversation that required alcohol.

"I've never had a boyfriend. I've never even been kissed. That's pathetic, right? I'm sixteen."

"It's not pathetic. You're young. You've been busy kicking cancer's ass. Now you can concentrate on, um, other pursuits." God, she hoped like hell that Ashley's parents had already given her The Talk. There wasn't enough wine in the world for that conversation.

"No one is going to want me," Ashley mumbled to her lap. "They think of me as the sick girl. After my first round of treatment, I went back for a few weeks and no one would sit near me. I found out someone had started a rumor that I was radioactive. They even put one of those hazard stickers on my locker."

"Are you radioactive?"

Ashley scoffed. "No."

"Then it doesn't matter what they think."

"It does if you want someone to take you to prom. Or sit with you at lunch. I'm supposed to be so happy I got to survive, right? But I don't want to go back to that hellhole. All the other girls, they've been going to parties and wearing the right clothes and makeup and it's like they speak a different language. My hair is, like, two inches long." She held out a few strands to illustrate.

Ellery tried to remember being sixteen. She'd been the freak at her school, too. She hadn't cared. She did recall the feeling of being trapped in her tiny apartment with her damaged body, how hopeless it felt, how doomed. Your reality at sixteen was the only one you'd ever known. "It gets better," she told Ashley.

"Yeah, that's what they all say. Trust me. No boy is ever going to want to kiss me. I'm the lamest girl who ever lived." She put her head down on the counter, and Ellery frowned at her, debating internally whether to say anything more. She took a breath.

"Reed is my first boyfriend," she muttered.

Ashley whipped her head up. "What?"

Ellery's ears grew hot. She'd never even used the word before, let alone had an actual male companion to fill the role. "So, there you go. You're not even the lamest one at this counter, okay?"

"Oh my God. You mean you never had sex with anyone before? You're, like, thirty."

No need for The Talk then, Ellery thought with relief. "I didn't say that. I said I'd never had a boyfriend."

"Oh." Ashley contemplated this for a moment. "How is it?" she asked finally.

"Hello, we're back!" There was a burst of noise at the door, and Reed came in with Tula skipping beside him. Bump smiled the grin of a dog who'd gotten his own cone. "I know you said you didn't want anything," he said to Ellery. "But this double chocolate fudge brownie from the bakery seemed to be calling your name." He kissed the top of her head and placed the wrapped dessert next to her plate.

Ellery smiled in spite of everything. "You know what?" she said to Ashley. "It's pretty great."

That night in bed, she lay awake but exhausted. Her brain hummed even as her bones felt like they could sink into the mattress. Her apartment felt too people-y. Tula had the couch, Ashley slept on an air mattress on the living room floor, and Reed lay next to Ellery, giving off heat and an air of concern. "We could turn on some music," he said as she shifted restlessly under the sheets again.

"No." Her brain told her she should be at work, looking for Chloe. Her body couldn't get out of bed. She wished Reed would hold her, but she didn't know how to ask for this. She'd trained him to give her space and she didn't want to take it all back because she had a single night of weakness. "I'm surprised you haven't said, 'I told you so,'" she grumbled into the pillow. "You were right that we shouldn't have sent Lockhart into Wintour's house."

He rose up behind her. "I'm in no position to gloat. You caught a predator. Just maybe not the one who took Chloe."

"What are the odds?" She rolled onto her back and looked at the slowly rotating ceiling fan. The question was rhetorical. They both knew how many sex offenders walked the streets every day. "Lockhart's in jail while they figure out what all they want to charge him with."

"Not much, I would expect."

"For his sake, I hope Wintour lives." She faced him, tucking one arm beneath her head. "Are you ever going to tell me what the deal is with Houston?"

"There isn't much to tell. Sarit is apparently thinking of moving there, and she would of course be taking Tula with her."

"Can she do that?"

"She would need to file for full physical custody. Kimmy thinks she has a reasonable shot at getting it because some of her grievances are grounded in reality."

"Such as?"

"My work. Travel. It keeps me away, as you know."

"And now me." She knew Sarit was not her biggest fan.

Reed took her hand and kissed it. "Don't worry about it. This is my problem, not yours. I will find an answer."

Then why did his kiss feel so much like regret? She touched his face in the semi-darkness, stroking the sandpapery stubble along his jaw. "Your family has to come first," she whispered to him. "I know that."

"You are that," he answered gruffly, gathering her against him.

She wriggled in his embrace, relishing the feel of his lean body against hers. She lived all her life on borrowed time, but none was as sweet as this. When they were alone together, she and Reed made sense. Out in the world, they were a curiosity, a freak show, and no one would forget their origin story. She knew Reed's family thought he hung around her out of obligation or pity, and on her darkest days she thought it as well. In her dreams, when the closet door opened she only saw two faces on the other side. With Reed in her bed, Coben would always be there, too.

Gingerly, she laid her ear against Reed's chest, the place where his own scars lay. She could never guess from its strong, reassuring rhythm that Reed's heart had nearly ceased for good. Tonight, she didn't need to hide behind the noise of the television or radio. She listened to the steady drumming of his heartbeat and imagined she could hear it say her name.

21

Reed rolled over in the morning, expecting to find Ellery weighing down her side of the bed, but instead, a sixty-pound barrel-chested, hound-scented mound of fur stared back at him. Reed squinted and plopped his head back down on the pillow. "Good morning," he said to Bump with a sigh. The dog wagged and slurped Reed's elbow in return. Reed ran his palm down the sheets where Ellery wasn't, figuring she must have gone out for an early run. Unlike his previous lovers, Ellery did not linger in bed.

He'd been naïve, he supposed, a romantic sop who figured his love and tenderness could erase her years of PTSD. She'd survived Coben by divorcing herself from all physical sensation, by pretending it was some other body he'd tortured with his farm tools. Sex had always been mechanical, she had explained to Reed, whenever she'd bothered to attempt it at all. She never allowed herself to feel anything—not even, she'd confessed to him once in the darkness, when it was just herself alone in the privacy of her bedroom. It was hard not to feel fury when she said these things. He fantasized about walking into Coben's cell on death row with a gun and ending him forever. The knowledge that this wouldn't fix anything—that the damage was unending—only made Reed angrier somehow, and anger wasn't what she needed from him.

Figuring out what to do instead wasn't always easy. Ellery was playful and generous in bed as long as he was on the receiving end; when it was her turn, she had difficulty permitting him to take the lead, relaxing, and letting him make her body feel things. He'd learned to ease into lovemaking with her, gently retreating and advancing like the overlapping waves of a slowly rising tide. The tsunami of her pleasure when he got it right made his patience worth it every time. He stroked the bed again, missing her and the intimacy he'd hoped to be sharing with her on this trip.

Bump repositioned himself under Reed's hand, stretching his legs luxuriously as he settled in for a massage. "You are no substitute at all," Reed informed him, offering a last scratch or two before rising from the bed. He checked his messages and found two key developments. First, the Philadelphia PD had answered his inquiry about the gun recovered from the shed at the old Stone house. It was registered to someone named Dale Goodwin, who lived on East Lombard Street in Baltimore. They'd followed up at that address and found Dale's widow, who said she hadn't known the gun was missing. Her husband had kept it in a shoe box in the closet.

"Baltimore," Reed mused to himself. The deceased housekeeper, Carol Frick, had lived in Baltimore before moving to Philadelphia. He wondered about the timeline and whether there could be a connection.

The second message he had was from Sarit:

TULA NEEDS NEW SHOES FOR THE START OF SCHOOL. DO YOU THINK YOU COULD TAKE HER? THEY NEED TO HAVE STURDY RUBBER SOLES— SOMETHING BASIC LIKE GRAY OR NAVY THAT WILL GO WITH HER UNIFORM. BUCKLE PREFERRED OVER VELCRO, AND NOTHING THAT ROLLS, LIGHTS UP, OR MAKES NOISE.

He was aware, dimly, that Tula like most growing children had already burned through eleventy-billion pairs of shoes, but not one pair of these had been purchased by Reed. Sarit simply cared more, as evidenced by the detailed instructions in her email. This request then, he decided, must be a trap, a test designed for him to fail so Sarit could score points in the coming custody war. *Your Honor, her father can't even manage her a single pair of shoes for school. It's clear she should be in Houston with me.*

This was how he found himself later that morning, not at the station with Ellery mucking through Stephen Wintour's child pornography, but at the local mall with Tula and Ashley. Ashley had tagged along only when it became clear Tula wouldn't go without her. It was perfect, really—the girl kept Tula engaged picking out shoes while Reed sat in a chair with his laptop, trying to make a timeline of the events he'd uncovered so far:

The gun was stolen in Baltimore, exact date unknown.

One month prior to the murders of Trevor Stone and Carol Frick, someone set Ethan Stone's car on fire at the university where he works.

Trevor Stone and Carol Frick were murdered in the Stone home in Philly seventeen years ago.

Two years later, Teresa Stone married Martin Lockhart. Two years after that, Chloe was born.

Chloe was kidnapped not far from what would have been the anniversary of the murders at the Stone household.

Reed frowned at the bullet points on his list. Carol had a third child, he remembered. There was Lisa and Bobby and a teenage daughter who died in a car accident some weeks before Carol herself was killed. Reed made a note to find out the precise date.

"Daddy, look at these." Tula crashed into his lap, forcing him to put aside the computer. "Aren't they awesome?"

He regarded the pink sneakers on her feet. The had blue flames on the sides and blinking lights around the edges. "They are spectacular."

"Show him what they do," Ashley prompted.

Tula stomped her foot and a rocket noise came out of the shoe. "Blast off!" she cried, leaping into the air.

"Those are impressive," Reed said. "I don't think they will work for school." Sarit would have his head.

"Aw, I don't want boring old stupid shoes," Tula complained, kicking at the floor.

"Maybe we can find some in between," Ashley told her. "I'll help you look."

Reed opened his mouth to thank her when he noticed Ashley's ancient pair of Chuck Taylors. They were worn and dirty, and the sole had started to separate on the left one. "Why don't you find a pair for yourself?" he said, nodding at her feet. "You have school starting soon, too."

Ashley's face flushed the same shade as Ellery's did when she was embarrassed. "Thanks, but I didn't bring the money."

Didn't have the money, Reed guessed. He knew that cancer treatment sent many families into bankruptcy. "It's my treat."

The girl cast a longing glance at the rows of shiny sandals and bright white sneakers. "No, that's okay. The ones I have are still good."

"It's a thank-you," Reed clarified. "For looking after Tula."

Tula grabbed her hand and tugged. "Come on. I'll help you look," she said, and Ashley relented with a grin. Reed took out his computer again and began to search for any information on Carol Frick's daughter. What he found instead surprised him: Carol's husband, Vincent, had not been killed in an accident as described by Lisa. He had been shot to death in a mugging attempt on the streets of Baltimore several years prior to the murders at the Stone household. Reed added this to his timeline. He didn't know yet what to make of the disparate events, but the Frick family's recurring tragedy seemed like it had to be deeper than a run of bad luck. Dead father, dead mother, dead daughter. Trevor Stone was the odd one out in this pattern. Maybe Carol the housekeeper had been the target all along.

Reed fired off a note to an old friend he had in the Baltimore PD, asking for any insider information on the Vincent Frick homicide. The internet search he'd performed suggested it was unsolved.

Ashley and Tula appeared in front of him again with more shoes. "The sales guy said these are good to go with school uniforms," Ashley said, indicating the sensible pair of navy shoes on Tula's feet. They were buckled, not Velcro, so to Reed they seemed to pass muster.

"They don't jump as good," Tula said as she made a halfhearted attempt.

"What about for you?" Reed asked Ashley.

"I found some new Chuck Taylors. I can't decide whether to get the red or the black."

"Well then, both, obviously." His sisters at Ashley's age had rows upon rows of shoes in their closets. He suspected Kimmy still did.

"Oh, I can't."

"You can," Reed said as he put away his computer and scooped up the original pair of sneakers that Tula had selected. "In fact, you both can." Tula launched into a celebratory dance, and Reed reflected how easy it was to make her happy now with a single pair of rocket ship shoes. Sarit would be livid when she saw them, probably thinking he'd bought them just to spite her, but if she ever bothered to ask him he would tell her it had nothing to do with her. He'd cleaved his family at Sarit's request, leaving the home and agreeing to see his daughter on a fixed schedule, like she was a dentist's appointment. He'd willingly made himself smaller in her life because that's what Sarit had argued was best for Tula. Stability. Harmony. But, oh, how his heart ached whenever he had to send her off again, when the weekend was up and he had to watch her face in the backseat of Sarit's car, disappearing down the road. It seemed to him as though Tula grew two inches between visits. Gone was the chubby-cheeked toddler and the preschooler who always had paint on her nose. His daughter was growing up and away from him, eventually for good. At least now she'd be taking a piece of him with her when she left.

Reed paid for the shoes and then dropped both kids at his rented hotel suite. He gave the key card to Ashley. "Stay on the property, but feel free to use the pool or rent a movie. You can order room service for lunch and it will just go to my bill."

"What should we get?" She looked anxious again. "Like, what's the limit?"

He momentarily blanched, thinking of the six-dollar candy bars in the mini-fridge. Then he remembered he was leaving these girls to go in search of another one, a girl who had a fridge full of food at home but was perhaps starving nonetheless. Reed decided he would take whatever quick win the universe offered to him. He clamped a gentle hand on Ashely's thin shoulder. "Order whatever you want."

At headquarters, Reed checked in with Jeff Zuckerman to see if they had been able to identify the ball-capped figure from the security video he'd seen of Chloe. "We think we located him about an hour earlier, buying a bottle of water inside this convenience store. The hat's still on, but he took off the glasses, so you have a better view of his face." Jeff showed Reed a clip of what looked like the same man—white, trim build, mid-twenties, maybe early thirties—at the register paying for the bottle of water. The black Northeastern T-shirt appeared to be the same one from the earlier shots. Jeff drew up a still shot, zoomed in on the man's face. "This is the best we can do."

Reed leaned in to get a better look. The man had dark hair that curled out under the edges of his hat. No visible scars or tattoos that Reed could discern. Still, there was a familiarity to his eyes and nose that continued to bug Reed. "At the very least, he's a potential witness," he said to Jeff. "We should get it out to the media immediately. Try to ID him."

"We're already on it. Also checking with Northeastern to see if he could be a student there."

The door behind them burst open and Ellery came in, radiating a kind of tense excitement. "I heard you were in here," she said, looking to Reed with bright eyes.

"What is it?"

"We got a tip just now. Chloe's been sighted at a Target store."

Reed didn't feel similar elation. "We've had dozens of similar sightings so far," he reminded her. "None has panned out."

"This Target is in Providence," she replied. "Also, look at this."

She went to an open computer and called up an image that was clearly taken inside of Target's trademark red store. It showed a woman in shorts and a T-shirt, perhaps thirty years old, trailed by two children. One was a boy of about five or six. The girl was a blonde who matched Chloe Lockhart in build and coloring. "She's quite similar," Reed agreed.

"No, she's a dead ringer." Ellery showed him a still shot of the girl's face taken from a moment when she'd looked almost right into the camera. Reed felt her stare like a blow to his chest. Chloe's bright blue eyes bore right into him. "It's her, right? It's got to be."

"Chloe's hair was chopped off. This girl has her original shoulder-length hair."

"The video is two days old," she told him impatiently. "The manager just reported it this morning after a cashier saw Chloe's picture on the news and remembered the girl." She tugged on his arm. "Come on, let's go." He could feel his own excitement rising. He heard it in Ellery's voice. "Let's bring her home."

22

Ellery flew down I-95, the wheels of her SUV barely meeting the road as she wove her way around the slower traffic. Dorie rode shotgun while Reed sat in the back, swaying with the body of the car and periodically clutching the door. "Let's get there alive, okay?" Dorie said, looking up from her phone.

"Yes, please," Reed called from the backseat.

"What's the latest on this woman?" Ellery asked. "Jenna Desmond?"

"She's clean," Dorie replied as she checked her phone. "No record."

"Nothing on our end, either," Reed added.

"She's thirty-two years old, married to a guy named Nicholas Desmond, and works as a speech therapist for the Providence schools. Address is listed as Gray Street in Providence per her driver's license."

Ellery shook her head. "None of that makes any sense. What's her connection to Chloe? Could she have worked in the Brookline schools, too?"

"We're checking, but no sign of that so far."

"What about the Lockharts? Did anyone ask them about her?"

"Conroy ran the name Jenna Desmond past them and they deny knowing her."

Ellery looked to Reed in the rearview mirror. "Help me out here, Reed," she said. "What's her deal?"

"Your guess is as good as mine right now. Perhaps she is not your kidnapper. She may be covering for someone else." He hesitated. "Or perhaps it isn't Chloe on the video—though I'll admit, the likeness is impressive."

Ellery tightened her hands on the wheel. It wasn't just the likeness. Yes, the girl in the Target store had Chloe's aquamarine eyes, blond hair, and fine bone structure. But Ellery had spent hours by now looking at the video of Chloe Lockhart leaving the Public Garden on the day she went missing. The girl in the store moved like her, too. They had the same walk, the same body posture. "No," she said, more to herself than the others. "We're right about this."

Dorie's phone buzzed again and she took the call on speakerphone. It was Captain Conroy. "I'm with Teresa," he said. "There's been another text, which I will forward to you in a moment. The picture shows Chloe in a large cage—the kind you might use for a big dog. She's got on the same clothes from the day she went missing and there's duct tape across her mouth. Lighting is poor, so it's hard to tell if she is otherwise injured. No visible blood from the angle of the shot. The text says: 'If she dies, will you just get another one?'"

"We're ten minutes away from Providence now," Dorie told him.

"Good. There's one other thing. It looks like she's being held in a basement. The background of the photo shows a stone foundation—big rocks held in place with mortar. The FBI says that means the house is old, maybe 1880s. Possibly still intact or there may be a more modern house built on top of the old foundation."

For Ellery, the closet had been an upright coffin. Smothering in the summer heat, she'd been literally dying of thirst and bleeding out on the wooden floorboards around her. She could still feel the gouges from the desperate girls who had been there before her. The ones who never got free. She pressed the gas pedal all the way to the floor.

The large marble dome of the Providence State House came into view on the left side of the road, signaling their arrival at the city limits. It was too far away to see clearly the eleven-foot figure Ellery knew stood atop the dome, a golden statue of a semi-naked man crowned in a wreath of greenery and holding a spear. Her eyes sought him out anyway because of his name, The Independent Man, and the principle he stood for: freedom. As they headed for Jenna Desmond's address, Ellery had to slow the car or risk rolling the SUV around a sharp corner.

She knew she'd hit the right neighborhood when she saw a lineup of Providence PD black-and-white units parked all in a row. She slowed further, driving past them and around the corner onto Gray Street. "That's the place right there," Dorie said, leaning forward to peer out the front window. Ellery pulled off to the side and parked the car.

"We've got company," she said, nodding up the road to a parked sedan with a pair of men sitting in it. She flashed her headlights at them, and one of the men, a moustached but otherwise hairless guy, got out of the car. He wore mirrored sunglasses and walked like he'd been sitting for a while. She rolled down her window as he approached.

"Detective Jake Osborne," he said to her. "We've been watching the place for two and a half hours now, ever since that Target video set off all kinds of alarms."

"And?" Ellery asked him. She looked toward the house. It was a pinkish-beige color, two stories, with a neat row of bushes at the front. Colorful perennials added cheer and the metal railing on the porch appeared to be freshly painted. She spotted a kid's bicycle overturned on the front walk and, beyond it, an old stone foundation.

"Nothing. No one in or out. The Subaru in the driveway is

registered to Nicholas and Jenna Desmond, which suggests someone is home. We had someone walk by with a dog about an hour ago to glimpse the backyard. Nothing there but a kiddie pool and some lawn furniture. She confirmed the AC unit is on, which again points to the house being occupied. Mostly, though, we've been hanging back, waiting on your move."

Ellery looked around at the neighboring houses. All were well-kept historic homes. She spotted several other rock foundations. New Englanders had built these houses hundreds of years ago, and generations of frugal Yankees kept right on recycling them. Ellery wished she had X-ray vision to see inside. The thought of Chloe in a cage in the basement made her want to take a battering ram and knock down the door. Osborne seemed to read her thoughts.

"We've got backup parked one block over, if you need it. We can take the place whenever you want."

She clenched the wheel, tempted. Reed's suggestion that Jenna Desmond might have a partner gave her pause. They had no idea who or what might be on the other side of the door. "Maybe there's another way."

"What are you thinking?" Dorie asked.

Ellery squinted at Osborne. "You have a florist shop around here?"

He looked surprised but pointed westward. "Sure. There's a grocery about three blocks thataway."

Ten minutes later, Ellery had a vase full of purple flowers bound by a green bow. Osborne, his partner, Dorie, and Reed all suited up in protective gear emblazoned with law enforcement logos. Ellery demurred. "I'm the decoy, remember? I have to look like a civilian." She adjusted her windbreaker so it did not show her holster while Osborne had the backup teams come around the block on foot. He gave instructions for four men to go around to the rear of the house and wait. The rest of the teams flanked the front stairs, crouching under the windows as Ellery and her flowers mounted the steps.

Her heart beat erratically, the vase growing slick in her hands.

Lace curtains blocked her view in the front window. The front door was a solid brown with no way to see inside. She rang the bell and waited. A few moments later, she heard footsteps and the door cracked open partially. A young woman with a blond ponytail—the same woman from the Target video—peeked out at her. "Yes?"

"Jenna Desmond?"

"Yes, I'm Jenna."

"I have a flower delivery for you." Ellery forced herself to smile.

"Really, for me? How nice." She widened the door, relaxing somewhat as she started to reach for the flowers in Ellery's hands.

Ellery's gaze fixed behind her. She saw a shadowed hallway and a moving figure with the unmistakable shape of a gun. "Gun!" she hollered, dropping the vase to the concrete porch. It shattered at her feet as she grabbed Jenna and dragged her out and to the side. Behind her, men with their own guns streamed into the house. Someone was screaming and crying. *A child*, she realized.

"What are you doing?" Jenna cried, her face pressed down on her own porch. "Let me up!"

"Where's Chloe Lockhart?" Ellery demanded, pushing her harder into the wooden planks.

"I don't know. Please, you're hurting me."

Dorie appeared with a screaming and thrashing boy in her arms. "This one had the gun. It wasn't real."

"Mommy! Mommy!"

"I'm right here, baby." Jenna struggled to get free, but Ellery held her in place with a knee to her back. "Stop it; you're scaring my children. It's okay, Mikey. Mommy's right here."

Dorie carried the boy away from the house, which caused Jenna to fight harder.

"Where are you taking him? Michael! Let. Me. Up."

"Tell me where she is," Ellery replied harshly. "Where's Chloe?"

"Ellery," Reed said, but her name barely registered.

"Tell me! What have you done with her?"

"Ellery!"

She forced herself to look. She saw Reed standing on the far side of the porch. A blond girl stood next to him with tears in her striking blue eyes. "Stop it," she demanded of Ellery. "You're hurting her."

"Ellery, it's not her." Reed said the truth that was now apparent to everyone. "It's not Chloe."

Ellery eased off of Jenna in surprise as she stared at the girl from the top of her messy ponytail down to her grubby flip-flops, where her toes curled in distress. This girl was shorter than Chloe by two inches; she could see it now. She did not have pierced ears. Her tanned arms and legs said that she got to spend more time outside in the sun than Chloe Lockhart ever did. Otherwise, the resemblance between the girls was eerie. "I'm—sorry." She rose and let Jenna Desmond off the porch. Both of them trembled in the aftermath.

Jenna brushed bits of glass from her arms and legs. Blood trickled down the inside of her left forearm, but she reached for the girl anyway. "Izzy," she said, hugging her tight. She glared at Ellery. "Where is Michael? What have you done with Michael?"

"He's right here," Dorie called from across the lawn. She put the boy down and he raced to join his family in the group hug.

The crushing weight of disappointment hit Ellery like an anvil from the sky. *Not her.* They weren't bringing Chloe home. They weren't even close. The girl was still out there somewhere, caged in a stone basement.

"We're terribly sorry for the mix-up, ma'am," Reed said, stepping forward. "We're looking for a girl named Chloe Lockhart, and we had reason to suspect she was being held here."

Osborne appeared on the threshold as if to verify. "The place is clear," he reported. "No sign of Chloe. Just this pretty young thing here who happens to look just like her." He smiled at Izzy, who hid her face in her mother's chest. "We apologize sincerely for our mistake."

Jenna's face twisted in a mask of pain and she stroked her daughter's hair. "You've got it all wrong," she said in a watery voice, "I would never hurt Chloe."

The hairs on Ellery's arms rose. "You know her?"

Jenna swallowed. "I'm her mother."

23

A befuddled Nicholas Desmond had to come home from work to take custody of his children while his wife rode away in the back of a squad car all the way to Boston. Jenna Desmond wasn't under arrest—she had agreed to cooperate—but they had not cleared her of any wrongdoing as yet. Upon the return to Boston, Ellery and Dorie got first crack at questioning her, while Reed went to the Lockharts' place to brief Conroy and tackle the delicate task of bringing Martin and Teresa up to speed on this latest development.

Jenna sat with Ellery and Dorie in the close quarters of the beige interrogation room, turning a bottle of water around in her hands but not drinking from it. Mentally, Ellery urged her to take a sip. They would need the woman's DNA to verify her claim about Chloe. "Would you prefer something else?" Ellery asked. "Coffee? A soda?"

"I'm fine."

"Okay, then why don't you tell us about Chloe."

She blinked rapidly and clutched the bottle with both hands. "About fourteen years ago, I was in college, paid for with a bunch of student loans, and also working two part-time jobs to try to pay for books, rent, food—you name it," she said. "One of those jobs was as an after-school nanny for a couple of sweet little boys. But the dad got a job transfer to L.A. and the whole family up and moved in the middle of the school year. No one is looking to hire a nanny at the beginning of February. Believe me, I tried. A friend of a friend had done egg donation the previous summer. You know, selling your ova for money? She made ten grand that way and said I could do the same."

"You sold your eggs?" Ellery said.

Jenna winced. "You make it sound so cold. Transactional. I donated a few eggs so that someone else could have a child. The clinic harvests a bunch of them, but there are rules about how many times they can be used. You don't get to find out if your eggs are chosen, let alone whether they turn into an actual baby. I'd always wondered, especially when I got pregnant with Izzy, if I had other kids running around out there someplace. I didn't think about that part when I gave up the eggs. I just needed the money so bad, and I liked the idea that I'd be helping people who couldn't have a child of their own."

"And you believe Chloe is one of those children."

Her blue eyes, the same unusual shade as Chloe's, widened at Ellery. "Of course. Don't tell me you don't see it. You're the ones who practically broke my door down thinking Izzy was Chloe."

"There's a resemblance," Dorie acknowledged. "But a lot of girls look alike. We've had more than two dozen calls per day from people who think they've spotted Chloe somewhere."

"It's her. She's mine." Her chin lifted in defiance.

"How did you find her?" Ellery tried a different tack.

"Pure coincidence. She was on local TV about a year ago—part of a group of kids who won the right to play at Symphony Hall. They gave her name and the town where she lived, so I looked up her family. The Lockharts are older parents, just the kind who would've been using the clinic I went to. Teresa was in her forties when she gave birth to Chloe."

Ellery didn't challenge her logic for the moment. "Okay, you saw her on TV and looked her up. Then what?"

Jenna started picking at the label on the water bottle. "I told myself to let it go. I said this is what I'd wanted, to know my kid was happy and taken care of by parents who loved her. But—I don't know. I'd always wanted a big family. Four kids, maybe five. I started young, so I figured time was on my side. But I nearly bled out during birth with Michael. The doctors repaired the damage, but they said it would be dangerous to get pregnant again. I wondered if maybe God was punishing me somehow for giving away my kids early."

"You didn't give up your kids," Ellery said. "You gave up eggs."

"At least one of them turned into a kid. One who looks just like Izzy." Her eyes swam with tears, begging Ellery for understanding. "Once I knew she was out there, I thought about her all the time. I decided I would drive to Boston and get a better look. To satisfy myself that she was really okay."

"How did you find her?" Dorie asked gently.

"She goes to public school. It was easy enough to find out which one. I pretended to be a parent moving to the area and I asked for a tour. I knew it was crazy. I just wanted to be closer to her. We saw her in the art room. She was making a paper-mache parrot."

"Did you talk to her? Interact in any way?"

"Of course not. The guide was standing right there. The room was full of kids."

"Okay, so what did you do next?"

"I went home and tried to forget about her. But I just couldn't. I told myself I'd find a way to talk to her, just say hi, and that would be enough." Her rueful expression said she realized how her goals kept shifting, expanding into more contact with Chloe. "We don't have the same vacation breaks as the kids in Massachusetts, so I started using my free time to go wait outside her school. I saw that the nanny was sometimes late picking her up. Traffic, maybe. I don't know. Chloe would be waiting by the fence by herself, looking annoyed. One of the times I saw her standing there, I just did it. I got out of my car and went to talk to her."

"What did you say?" Ellery asked, genuinely curious.

"I told her I liked her shoes." She smiled. "They were red leather booties with black trim. I get my kids' stuff from Target. You could tell these weren't off some discount rack."

"What did Chloe say?"

"She said thanks. I told her I had a daughter who looked like her. She seemed interested, so I showed her a picture of Izzy on my phone. She was surprised. She said something like, 'That could've been me in fifth grade.' I recognized her nanny's car pulling up, so I said a quick good-bye and walked away."

"That wasn't your last contact with her, though, was it?" Dorie asked.

She shook her head slowly. "I know I should've left well enough alone. I know it. If I hadn't gotten involved with her, she might not be missing right now."

"What do you mean?" Ellery asked.

"I went back to see her again a few weeks later. I said I thought we could be related and I gave her a cell phone so that we could talk. She's smart, though. She didn't just take it without asking questions. She pushed me on how we could be related, so I had to tell her. I said I thought I could be her biological mother."

Ellery tried not to show any sort of shock or disapproval. This was Dorie's admonition to her from the start—show compassion even for the worst of sins if you want people to keep talking. Still, she imagined twelve-year-old Chloe faced with this adult woman claiming to be her mother and felt it had to come as a verbal assault. They tell kids not to take candy from strangers or get in a car with someone they don't know. No one gives you a road map for some kook who says she's your mom and, by the way, here's a free cell phone.

"How did Chloe react to that news?" Dorie asked.

"She said—she said it explained some things. Later, when we

were texting, I asked her what she meant by that. She said her mother treats her like she's a precious painting or artefact that should be locked away, like a possession and not a person. I realized that maybe Chloe's life hadn't turned out so perfect after all. She seemed . . . well, miserable. Her parents work all the time, but they won't let her get out of the house and do stuff."

"According to our notes, Chloe does piano, soccer, and dance."

"I mean to spend time with friends. Didn't you have friends as a kid? People you hung out with at the mall? Or, you know, went to the park with just to kick rocks around?"

"Do your kids kick rocks?" Ellery wanted to know.

"They have friends," she replied firmly. "I don't keep them prisoner in their own home."

"Maybe the Lockharts were concerned about strangers giving their daughter an unapproved cell phone," she said.

Jenna held up her hands. "Okay. Okay, I deserve that. I'm just saying—Chloe didn't seem all that happy at home. She complained about her mother all the time."

"I think that's in the thirteen-year-old's handbook," Dorie remarked dryly.

Ellery tried to remember her feelings for her mother at thirteen. Guilt. Pity. Disgust. Simmering with anger at the father who'd left them and the mother who'd stayed but couldn't fill that hole, emotionally or financially. Ellery had vowed to be nothing like Caroline Hathaway. She would have no philandering husband, no kids to work herself to the bone to feed and clothe. She was surprised how strong those feelings still were, how they came whooshing up like hot air from a sidewalk vent.

"This was different," Jenna insisted. "She was lonely."

"Okay, she was lonely," Ellery said. "What did you suggest to fix it?"

"I didn't plan to kidnap her, if that's what you're thinking. I tried to listen to her, to be a friend."

"The day she disappeared, Chloe left the Public Garden. She abandoned her usual cell phone and apparently took the one you gave her. CCTV footage shows she boarded the T heading into the city. Do you have any idea where she might have been going?"

Jenna bit her lip. "Was she coming to me, you mean?"

"I mean did she say anything to you that might indicate where she was headed that afternoon?"

"That morning, she said she had a surprise for me. I asked for a hint, but she wouldn't give me one." She swallowed with effort. "We had talked about how the commuter rail train on the T runs from Boston to Providence."

"Did you make plans to spend time together in person?"

"I said maybe one day." She bowed her head. "I wanted her to know my kids. I thought if I waited until she was older, she'd have more freedom. It would seem less like . . ."

"Like interfering with the custody of a minor?" Ellery couldn't keep the judgment out of her tone. This woman thought all about herself and nothing about how confusing it would be for Chloe to have this second-mother possibility foisted upon her.

"We just texted most of the time. That's all. I gave her some money." She bit her lip. "More than I should, probably. It's not like she needed more stuff. I just—I wanted her to like me."

"Why didn't she tell the Lockharts about you?"

Jenna flushed a deep red. "I said it should be our secret for now. That Teresa's feelings might get hurt if she knew we were in touch. I kept thinking, you know, that we should bring our relationship out into the open, but then it always seemed better just to wait."

"Better for whom?" Ellery asked pointedly.

Dorie stepped in again, her voice more soothing. "You wanted the chance to build a rapport with Chloe. I can understand that."

"Exactly." Jenna nodded vigorously at Dorie. "We were getting to know each other. Besides, it was easy enough for Chloe to keep it quiet from her parents. They were never home." She paused. "There was one thing, though, I did tell her to bring to her parents. She mentioned that one of her father's friends was asking her to send him pictures of her. I said she should tell them immediately, but she was afraid they wouldn't believe her."

"Right," Dorie said. "We heard about that."

Ellery shifted in her seat, impatient at the retread. Stephen Wintour remained in a medically induced coma, his prognosis uncertain. There would be a line of prosecutors, both state and federal, waiting to get to him if he recovered. The Feds were combing through his electronic records now, looking for other pedophiles they could oust based on their interactions with Wintour. They had evidence that he'd shared some snaps he'd taken of Chloe, apparently without her knowledge. The monsters on the receiving ends of those photos had to be dragged out into the light for questioning, as it was possible one of them had been moved to abduct Chloe. Ellery was glad that particular job did not fall to her.

"I think I saw him once," Jenna blurted. "Maybe."

"Saw who?"

"The guy who was creeping on Chloe. One time, I was sitting in my car outside her school, waiting to see if I could catch her alone. But the nanny was on time that day. While I was waiting, I saw this guy idling in his car not far from me. I thought maybe he was a dad coming to pick up his kids. When Chloe appeared, he started to get out of his car. I noticed because I thought, oh, crap, it's her father. But then the nanny appeared and the guy got back into his car. He didn't seem interested in any of the other kids. We were both watching Chloe."

"Did you get a good look at him?"

"He was on the other side of the street from me and wearing sunglasses. I don't know if I'd recognize him again."

Ellery used her phone to bring up a picture of Wintour. "Could it have been this man?"

Jenna took the phone and studied it. "I don't think so. The guy I saw was younger. He drove off the same time I did, when Chloe went home with the nanny."

"Did you get his license plate?"

"No. It was a dark-colored car. Blue, maybe black. I was busy watching for Chloe, so I wasn't paying too much attention. I only thought about it afterward, when she said some guy was harassing her." She placed her hands flat on the table. "Wait, are you saying this isn't the same guy? There was another man after her?"

Ellery and Dorie looked at each other. "We're going to need to see your text exchanges with Chloe," Ellery said finally.

"Sure, fine, anything you want. I've been over them and over them myself since she went missing." She swiped around until she found the correspondence with Chloe. "Here. It's all there."

Chloe's last words showed up first on the screen, time stamped from the period when she and Mimi would have been at the street fair, right before she disappeared.:

My mom believes every I is a secret killer, but it's not true. A woman with 2 little kids just tripped and dropped their lunch on the sidewalk. A guy helped her clean it up and bought new hot dogs for her. Ppl are way nicer than she thinks.

Also, I thought about sumthing last nite. If ur my bio mom then Trevor was never my bro. I mean, he wasn't anyway bcuz he was killed b4 I was born, but now it turns out we're not even related. I'm sorry for what happened 2 him. But it never had anything to do w/me.

24

Reed was met at the Lockharts' door by Margery Brimwood. The tender skin under her eyes looked bruised and tired. He wasn't certain, but he thought she might be wearing the same clothes she had on yesterday, and he wondered if she had been home, if the Lockharts had thought to dismiss her. Her young charge had vanished and now her "Mimi" spent hours drifting in this enormous house without purpose. "Martin is upstairs in the bedroom, but Teresa is in the living room with the captain and the others," she told him as she prepared to lead the way.

He touched her shoulder and she flinched. "Sorry," he murmured. "I'd actually like to speak with you for a few moments if I could. How are you holding up?"

She made a noise of disbelief. "Me? I'm fine. It's not my child who is missing."

"Yes, it is," Reed said gently, and she teared up.

"It's all my fault," she said as she wiped at her face with the sleeve of her sweater. "I shouldn't have let her go off like that. I keep waiting for Teresa to shout at me, to fire me. I deserve it. I thought her rules were insane, that they were stifling Chloe and making her unhappy. I thought I knew better than her own mother.

"When Chloe returns, she's going to need both of you."

She leaned against the wall and looked at the ceiling. "I tried to resign. Teresa wouldn't let me."

No, Teresa wouldn't let herself imagine a future when she didn't need Chloe's nanny. "I think that's wise."

She shook her head. "When the police came to my home, thinking Frank grabbed her, I got so angry. I thought the Lockharts sent them, because they'd called the cops out on me before. I didn't realize it was the dry cleaner who accused him. I got a lot of stuff wrong, I guess."

Ah, Reed realized. This was a confession of sorts. "It was you who phoned the tip line about Martin's affair."

She gathered the sweater around herself and shot him a guilty look. "I suppose you're going to tell me I'm wrong about that, too. All I can say is that I saw them kissing a few weeks ago. They didn't see me. No one here ever does, except for Chloe. It's like a one-way mirror in this place. I guess that's why I thought I had figured everything out."

"You may have more information than you realize. When you pick up Chloe from school, what is your routine?"

She drew a shuddering breath. "Well, school lets out at two fifteen. I pick her up out front and take her to her lessons or back here."

"Are you always on time?"

"I try to be." Reed waited in silence while she sat on that equivocation. "Traffic can be unpredictable," she added. Reed nodded but still didn't say anything in reply. She huffed out a breath. "Okay, sometimes I'm a little late on purpose, but it's because Chloe asked me to do it. She said it's embarrassing being picked up by a nanny in front of her friends, like she's some kindergarten baby. I figured what's the harm? There's teachers and parents and a ton of kids around. Nobody would be stupid enough to try anything right there in front of the school."

Reed had noticed a pattern with Mimi's care. "You let her go buy a pretzel by herself at the fair. You let her do her homework in another room at the YMCA."

"Yes." She blurted the painful word. "It's my mistake. I know that now. They told me not to take my eyes off her, not ever. I followed that rule when she was littler. I swear I did. But she started fighting me on it tooth and nail these past couple of years, and I felt like maybe she had a point. How can you be your own person if someone else's eyes are always on you?"

Reed thought back to his early childhood, when he'd wandered the fragrant, chattering woods at the back of his family's estate. His mother was usually home but busy with her affairs. Lulabelle cleaned the house and clucked at him if he tracked dirt on her shiny floors. Clark and Henry tended the grounds and the garden. Sometimes they'd let him have the leftover dirt for mud pies, but mostly they waved and ignored him. He'd spent his days climbing trees and using his pocketknife to slice open pinecones, nuts, and berries or whittle sticks into swords. He walked barefoot over the slippery stones in the creek and caught frogs for company. The adults were around but not watching him, an invisible safety net. He could have choked on a berry or fallen out of a tree with hours gone by before anyone found him. Instead, he'd lived a thousand private adventures.

"I see what you're saying," he told Margery. "Let me ask you something else. Do you recognize this woman at all?" He used his phone to show her a blown-up picture from Jenna Desmond's driver's license.

The nanny held the phone with both hands, moving it up close to her face and then far away. She wanted to say yes, Reed could see. But she shook her head. "She looks like Chloe, if you want to know the truth. But I don't know her. Who is she?"

"We're still figuring that out," Reed said as he tucked his phone away. "What about anyone else who might have been watching Chloe outside the school? Did you notice anyone paying special attention to her? Did she mention anything?"

"No. If she had, I would've told the Lockharts. You can be sure of that."

He pulled out his phone and showed her a still image of the man who'd been loitering nearby when Chloe disappeared from the Common. "What about this man? Do you know him?"

She grabbed the phone again and studied the picture, her brow furrowed in concentration. "He might be familiar, but I can't swear to it." She gave the phone back to him in defeat. "I'm not much help, am I?"

"You've been plenty helpful. I'd like to speak to Teresa now, if I may."

Reed knew the way by now. He walked briskly across the foyer but halted in the doorway, catching himself on the threshold because the living room gave off an otherworldly force of sadness. Teresa Lockhart sat unmoving on the sofa, staring at her hands. Conroy sat next to her, grim faced and not speaking. A handful of uniformed officers tried to blend into the furniture near the back. Reed stuck a tentative foot into the room and signaled for Conroy's attention.

The captain murmured something to Teresa, who didn't look up. He joined Reed near the door. "She took the news that it wasn't Chloe on that video really hard," he said. "I think everyone did."

"Have you told her about Jenna Desmond's claims?"

"Not yet." He rubbed a hand over his jaw. "I've had to give people awful news. Murdered kids. Deaths from a traffic accident. But this stuff bends my mind. Are you saying she gave birth to Chloe, but this Desmond woman is the biological mother?"

"Egg donation, yes. It's the same thing as a sperm donor, just from the female."

"Two mothers. I swear, the handbook doesn't prepare you for this."

Reed smiled for the first time in ages. His recent quest to discover who killed his birth mother had given him an unexpected second chance to know the woman, as well as surprising insight into Marianne Markham, the woman he still called Mama. "No, sir, it surely doesn't," he agreed. "You just muddle through as best you can."

"Are we sure this other woman is legit?"

"We're investigating her claims. Obviously, Mrs. Lockhart could confirm if Chloe was conceived via egg donation, but a DNA sample from Chloe would remove all doubt."

The big man's shoulders rose and fell with his heavy sigh. "Let's get on with it, then." He returned to his seat on the couch next to Teresa Lockhart, while Reed took the armchair to her right.

"Mrs. Lockhart," he said kindly, "how are you doing?"

She jerked her head up to look him in the eyes. "Better than Martin. That's all you can say right now. He's upstairs under a blanket of sedatives. Also, he shot his lawyer, so we have to find a new one. Not that I'm sorry he did it. I don't think anyone is sorry, which is why Martin's upstairs and not locked in a jail somewhere."

Reed had seen the headlines. Public opinion was divided between calling Martin a justified hero for shooting Stephen Wintour and feeling outrage that Martin hadn't been charged merely because he was rich and white. Privately, Reed felt both sides were correct in their assessment. "All the same, I'm sure it's an extra burden you didn't need right now."

"I need Chloe back, but I can't have that. I need to work, but I can't do that, either. Look at me." She held out her hand and Reed saw her fingers tremble. "The hospital is juggling the surgical calendar as best they can, but there are only a handful of doctors who perform the operations that I do. It's not like they can call up a temp agency. Someone has to help these patients or they will get sicker. They will die."

"The someone doesn't always have to be you." Reed heard the words come out of his mouth and realized they sounded familiar. Sarit had told him the same thing many times.

"It has to be someone. If not me, then who? I feel it all the time. When I'm here, I feel like I should be there. When I'm at the hospital, I feel like I am missing at home. No matter where I am or what I do, it's never enough." She held up her phone, clutching it so hard her knuckles turned white. "They're right—whoever is sending these messages. They're right. I've failed."

"You can't let those messages be the voice in your head. They're from a sick individual."

"That doesn't make them wrong."

Reed looked to Conroy, who looked away. "We need you to stay strong right now. Chloe needs it. You can help us right now by finding her hairbrush or toothbrush so that we can do some testing."

"Oh God." A deep, guttural moan wrenched from Teresa, and she doubled over as if in physical pain. "You've found her. You've found her body."

"No, no. That's not it at all." Reed rushed to reassure her.

"You want her DNA for identification purposes. Why else would you need it?"

Reed decided to be direct. "We have a woman claiming to be Chloe's biological mother."

Teresa sat up, her cheeks wet. "What?"

"The woman from the Target video, the one with the daughter who so looks like Chloe. She said she's Chloe's genetic mother through egg donation. We need to know from you: Is this possible?"

He saw on her face that it was. "I—I . . . Where did she come from?"

"She lives in Providence with her family. She saw Chloe on a news program last year and decided that they were related."

"I couldn't get pregnant on my own," Teresa murmured as if in a daze. "Martin desperately wanted a child, and he was willing to do anything. The doctors said egg donation was the only way. My eggs were too old. I imagined them dried up, like they all turned to ash the day Trevor died."

"So, this woman could be your egg donor."

"The information said she was a college student with no medical issues. She had blond hair like mine, and blue eyes, like mine and Martin's. But it's not the same blue. My eyes are blue but a washed-out faded-jeans kind of blue. You have to get close to see the color. Chloe's eyes are like the Caribbean Sea. Strangers used to ask sometimes when we pushed her in the carriage, where did she get those eyes? We'd say they came from my great-aunt Hope. Because that's what we called Chloe before she was born, when we barely believed she could be real—Hope. It's her middle name now."

"We'd like to have Chloe's DNA tested to see if she's a match."

"Why? Do you think this woman took her?"

"It doesn't look that way," Conroy interjected. "Obviously, we're still checking."

Teresa drew herself up and pursed her lips. "Then it shouldn't matter."

Reed had spent years wondering about his birth mother and his origins. Like Chloe, he had a talent for the piano. Had he inherited it from his mother? Did she have brown eyes like him or share his love of spicy food? Where did he get the shape of his hands or his funny toes or his allergy to strawberries? "If she's Chloe's mother," he began, but Teresa cut him off.

"I'm her mother! Me. You know how I know? Because I'm the one getting tormented with these messages. Not her. I'm the one who has to go on television and say I'm unfit, that I don't deserve my child." She hurled the phone at the wall, where it hit with a hard slap and landed facedown on the floor.

She covered her face with both hands. *Hear no evil, see no evil,* Reed thought.

He relented and sat back in his chair. Conroy shifted uncomfortably. "The thing is, Mrs. Lockhart," he said, "this woman has been in contact with Chloe already. They've exchanged text messages for months."

She dropped her hands, her mouth open in horror. "Months?"

"She bought Chloe a second phone so they could keep in touch."

"She's been planning this, then. Planning to take her from me."

"Like we said, we don't think so," Conroy replied. "But we are still investigating."

Teresa shook her head. "The paperwork specifically said she had no rights. We can sue her or get a restraining order or something, right? She can't just do this."

"We need to focus now on bringing Chloe home," Reed said, and the fight drained out of Teresa as she sagged into the cushions.

"Home," she repeated dully. "Home to what?"

They had no answer for her, so silence fell over the room.

After a few moments, Teresa rose stiffly. "I'll get you what you need," she whispered.

None of the men moved until she had exited the room, at which point Conroy released a long breath and the officers at the back began murmuring to one another over the spectacle. "We should interview the husband," Conroy said. "Nicholas Desmond. Maybe Jenna had help, stashing the kid somewhere. The abductor has shown they know to use burner phones, just like the kind Jenna gave to Chloe. And maybe this is the piece we've been missing, why the kidnapper seems so angry at Teresa Lockhart. She feels like Teresa's doing a lousy job raising her kid."

"The pictures show Chloe in a cage with her hair chopped off and tape over her mouth," Reed reminded him. "Do you see Jenna Desmond doing that to Chloe?"

"I don't understand anyone doing it," Conroy muttered. "That's the problem."

"Interview the husband, yes. But I don't think he'll have the answers we need."

Teresa reappeared holding a hairbrush, a toothbrush, and a worn, floppy-eared stuffed bunny. Chloe's dog, Snuffles, came running in alongside her. Teresa handed over the personal care items to Conroy and then sat with the bunny on her lap. Snuffles bounded up on the couch with her and put her tiny chin on Teresa's leg next to the stuffed animal. "It doesn't matter what the test shows. That woman isn't her mother in any way that matters. I don't care what she says. It's been all over the news what happened to Chloe, and where was she? Why didn't she come forward right away to explain about the cell phone and her contact with her? Why did you have to chase her down from some security camera footage?"

"My guess is that she was afraid," Reed said.

Teresa's pale eyes stared into him, naked to her soul. She had bared her desperation on national television for everyone to see. No kind of pretense remained in her. "Afraid for herself, yes. Afraid of what you could do to her, or what I could. But she doesn't know my fear. She doesn't picture Chloe in that cage, alone and terrified and crying for her mother. And I—" She broke off as she momentarily lost composure. "I'm not there."

The dog whined and pawed at her leg, and she patted the animal without seeing her. Conroy jerked a nod to Reed that they should have a private conversation in the hall. Reed excused himself and followed the captain to the grand foyer. The fresh flowers displayed in the vase against the wall were starting to droop, he noticed. Stray petals fell to the floor. "I can run those items back for you, if you like," Reed said, indicating the paper bag in Conroy's hands that held Chloe's effects.

"I'll have one of my guys do it. I wanted to talk to you because I got information back a little while ago. You had asked us to check on Ethan Stone's alibi for when he was in town for that conference."

"Right, yes."

"Well, he checks out as much as we can tell. He was at the conference every day, and he did have dinner with colleagues the night before Chloe disappeared. We can't account for his every second, but it seems doubtful he slipped off, came across the river, and snatched her during the coffee breaks."

"Okay, thank you."

"Wait, that's not all."

Reed raised his eyebrows. "Yes, go on."

"Stone didn't mention there was another member of the dinner party, not a colleague. His son Justin was there, too. See, it wasn't just any dinner. They were celebrating some career award given to Ethan Stone at this conference, and so his kid was along for the ride."

"Kid. He must be over thirty by now." Around the age of the mystery man seen near Chloe on the CCTV footage. "Interesting that Ethan Stone didn't mention his presence."

"Yeah, well, Justin Stone's got priors like my aunt Gwen has teacups. More than you can count."

"Ethan said he was clean now."

"Maybe he believes it. Maybe wishful thinking. I ran him through our system just for kicks, and what do you know, he was busted for soliciting a prostitute while he was in town last weekend. He pled out and took time served. They're kicking him loose from Suffolk Jail on Nashua Street." He checked his watch. "Should be any minute now."

Reed glanced back at the living room where the officers lingered. "Any chance I could have one of your squad give me a ride?"

"Take the one outside. He'll even run the siren for you."

The Suffolk County Jail sat right in the heart of Boston on the Charles River, with the modern Zakim bridge and the pointy Bunker Hill Monument nearby. The intense blue of the river and the greenery of the park across the street gave the immediate area some cheer, as the building itself was an imposing multistory mix of old bricks and concrete. The low, sloping front steps had been patched numerous times in recent years. Reed waited at their base for Justin Stone to emerge. Conroy had called ahead to ensure Reed hadn't missed the man, and indeed, Reed only had to loiter perhaps twenty minutes before a tall, thin man came through the glass front doors. He wore a burgundy leather jacket and black boots, and his dark hair hung lank, nearly brushing his shoulders. He paused to put a cigarette in his mouth. Reed checked his face against the photo he had of Justin Stone and decided it was a match.

"Justin Stone?" he said, walking up the steps.

Justin paused in the act of lighting his smoke. "Depends on who's asking."

"Special Agent Reed Markham." Reed showed off his ID and Justin rolled his eyes.

"The Feds care about soliciting now? What, you don't have some Mob boss or terrorist asshole you could be harassing instead?"

"I don't care one whit about whom you take to bed," Reed replied. "I want to talk to you about Chloe Lockhart."

Justin took a drag. "Who?"

"Teresa Lockhart's twelve-year-old daughter. She's been kidnapped."

"Yeah? I'm sorry for her." He started down the steps, walking past Reed. "I don't know anything about it."

Reed caught his arm and stopped him. "I'm asking for just a few minutes of your time."

"Yeah, well, I'd love to chat, but I'm behind schedule already due to my inconvenient stay here." He gestured back at the jail. "I've got to get home or my ass will be fired on top of everything else."

"Where are you going? I'll give you a ride." Reed nodded at the patrol car waiting for him down the block.

Justin scoffed a laugh. "Yeah, I don't think so. I can walk." He started off again, perhaps headed for the T, and Reed fell into step beside him.

"You were here with your father, to celebrate his achievement."

Justin gave a thin smile around his cigarette. "I was here because he paid for me to be. It's not real success unless you have a bunch of witnesses, people to clap for you and tell you how smart you are."

"Did you go to the conference?"

"I went to the part on the last day where they gave him his crystal trophy. Then I went to dinner with him and some of his snooty friends. I'll say this for them, though—they bought good wine."

"What did you do while your father was at the conference?"

"What do you mean, what did I do? I worked my usual job back home and then I caught the train up. You think he'd pay for me to spend more than one night here?"

"After the dinner, what did you do?"

Justin shook his head with a grin and then stuck his tongue out, waggling it in Reed's direction. "You can read about that part in the arrest report."

Reed ignored him. "At any point, did you go to the Public Garden?"

"Oh, yeah," Justin replied with caustic sarcasm. "I took high tea with the mayor and then we went to admire the lilies together. Later, we went to the symphony."

"What about Newbury Street?"

"Yeah, I bought a Birkin bag and a new pair of heels."

They paused for a traffic light. "Were you aware that Teresa had a daughter?"

"My dad told me years ago." He glanced at Reed. "Never met her. Didn't even know her name until now. Nice, though, that Teresa could just hit the restart button—presto, instant new family."

"You sound angry."

"Yeah, my shrink says that to me a lot. I tell him I've got lots of stuff to be angry about."

"Such as?"

The light changed and Justin set off across the street in long strides. Reed hustled to keep up. "The part where people think I murdered my little brother, that's for starters. Everyone else got to be sad. I got put in a windowless room with two cops who took turns verbally beating on me for twelve hours. 'Just tell us why you did it, Justin. You'll feel better if you tell us.'" He halted in the middle of the sidewalk. "They actually thought I would put a bag over his head and smother the life out of him. Murder a little kid like that. Over some money in his piggy bank."

"You were using drugs," Reed said, his voice neutral. "Marijuana, pills, cocaine—everything you could get your hands on back then. Your parents had banned you from the house."

His eyes narrowed. "Teresa kicked me out. My father never gave a shit what I did as long as I didn't make a mess on his front porch, so to speak. I think he kind of liked the cover, if you want to know the truth. Whatever trouble I made, it gave him space to make his own."

"What kind of trouble?"

He blew out a long smoke trail and then dropped the butt to the sidewalk, crushing it with his heel. "He ran around on my mom. That's why they broke up. Later, he did the same thing to Teresa."

"How do you know?"

"I caught him once. Showed up midday at the house when I was supposed to be at school—and so was he, by the way. I was looking for cash; he was looking at some red-haired girl sucking his dick in the living room."

"Did he see you?"

Justin looked almost amused. "He wasn't interested in much else at the time. I used the opportunity to take fifty bucks from the stash they kept in their bedroom."

"Do you think Teresa knew?"

"I don't know and I don't care." He resumed walking. "She tried to mother me, you know, when they first hooked up. 'Justin, let me take you shopping for new jeans. Justin, would you like some of these cookies I made?' She was so damn thirsty for my approval."

"You were young then."

"I was five." He looked sideways at Reed. "I ate those cookies and I hated myself. I felt like I betrayed my mom. My mom, she didn't go to college. Not like dad, and not like Teresa. She's worked in the same hair salon for the past forty years. Teresa was in medical school when she and my dad got together. My mom used to say he'd traded up. A doctor. She must be real smart. Not so smart if she couldn't see what my dad was when he married her."

Reed registered the contempt dripping from every word in Justin's analysis. He didn't think much of his father, and he hated Teresa for falling for Ethan Stone's act. "What about when Trevor was born?"

Justin stopped again, the hard set of his shoulders sagging. "He was a funny little dude. He used to run around naked after his bath, laughing hysterically while I'd chase him. I'd hold him upside down by the ankles sometimes, you know, like this? I'd swing him back and forth and make bonging noises like Big Ben. He loved that shit. Teresa would get on my case and tell me to stop roughhousing with him, but he couldn't get enough."

"What about later?" Reed probed gently.

Justin's face turned hard again. "I used him, okay? Is that what you want to hear? I stole his birthday money, his Christmas money, and even his bike. Yeah, they kicked me out and I deserved it. But I didn't . . . I would never . . ." He broke off, unable even to say the words. "He was my brother. My little bro. I wouldn't have done anything to hurt him."

"Teresa and your father seemed to support you."

He gave a bitter chuckle, starting to sweat under the hot summer sun. "Yeah, well. They knew the cops were full of shit. It wasn't me who was there that afternoon. You can tell because nothing got stolen."

"Who do you think did it?"

He dropped all pretenses, his face open and full of sorrow. "I don't know. I've asked myself that question so many times. It's the hardest part to live with, you know? The not knowing."

Reed's brain kept unwinding all the threads of this story and reweaving them again, trying to find a narrative that made sense. "Do you think it's possible your father could have been having an affair with Carol Frick?"

"The housekeeper?"

"You said he had trouble remaining faithful."

"Yeah, but she was like twenty years out of his target range. Old Pops likes 'em fresh off the vine."

"Like his students?"

Justin pointed at him, double-barreled finger guns. "A new crop each fall, ripe for picking."

25

"Y ou know, it would be understandable if this case has stirred up bad memories for you," Dorie said from behind her dark glasses as they drove westward through the streets of Boston, straight at the setting sun.

"I'm fine," Ellery declared without looking over at her partner.

"Okay. It's just—the turn for my place was two blocks back."

Ellery muttered a curse as she checked the rearview mirror to affirm Dorie was correct. In Boston, the joke said that if you missed your turn you had to go back home and start over. There were no right angles and every street was one-way. In the crush of traffic, her mistake added at least twenty minutes to their journey. "Sorry."

"Hey, it's your gas money. And that sunset is incredible."

The sky had turned the color of Mars, with the sun glinting lasers off the shiny buildings as it sank down to the horizon. Ellery said aloud the refrain she'd been telling herself since Chloe first turned up missing: "What happened to Chloe isn't the same as what happened to me."

"Sure. But she's about the same age, right? Frantic mother, news vans camped everywhere . . . the whole city crawling with cops who aren't getting anywhere fast. It would be natural for you to feel spooked."

"I'm not spooked." She felt hot and sparky, like a live wire twisting in the street.

"We've all got stuff is what I'm saying. This job, it'll get to you one way or another. No one is immune. You'll be cruising along like usual and then some weird case detail sends you down the rabbit hole. The feelings show up whether you want them or not."

Ellery did glance at her now, curious. "You don't have stuff." Dorie had an easy grin, a steady home life, and a stellar career behind her. Conroy hadn't been subtle when he'd paired them up: *Dorie Bennett's the best we got. If you want to stick around here, you're advised to follow so close you could be her shadow.*

Dorie wrinkled her nose and looked out the window. "Did I ever tell you why I joined up?"

"No."

"I got jumped coming out of a bar in Allston. I was twenty, my girlfriend Nicola at the time was twenty-six. I liked her wild, curly hair and the fact that she could order booze for both of us." She paused to give Ellery a crooked smile. "It was summer, probably right around this time. Humid nights with all the bugs chirping at you. The street seemed quiet when we left. Nicola looked gorgeous under the streetlamp, the light shining off her bare shoulder. I leaned over and kissed her cheek. We were usually pretty careful about that stuff in public, but it was one in the morning and I'd had a couple of beers. Plus . . . I don't know . . . I was crazy about her."

Ellery saw where the story was going. "But you weren't alone," she said.

Dorie shook her head slowly. "There were a couple of skinheads camped out, smoking behind the bar. They saw us go past and fell into step behind us. This was before everyone had cell phones. There was no one around. We had no way to call for help. The guys, they started taunting us. Calling us pussy lovers and faggots and whatever else slurs their pea-sized brains could dream up. We ignored them, walking faster toward the T, and that's when they jumped us. The one guy broke Nicola's jaw. I dislocated my shoulder and had finger-marks on my neck for a week."

"God, that's awful."

"A cop on patrol saw what was happening. He was on his usual rounds, cruising by the bar as it was getting ready to close down for the night. There was one of him and two of them—big guys hopped up on testosterone and God knows what else. The cop didn't blink. He jumped in and laid them out flat."

"Good." Ellery pictured the scene. The hard, mean place inside her hoped the cop cracked their skulls in the process.

"He knew immediately what had happened. Two women, coming from a gay bar. I half-expected him to say we'd asked for it, you know? The Boston PD didn't have a great rep back then in the queer community. But he helped us to a safe spot, called for a medic. He pulled out a damn handkerchief and gave it to Nicola to stop the bleeding over her eye. Then he called for backup to take in the ass-holes who'd attacked us so that he could go with us to the hospital and take our statements. I was scared shitless to call my folks. They didn't know I was out yet. The officer said he'd give me a ride home. 'I'll tell them you got mugged if you want,' he said. 'Your call.'"

Ellery pulled over by Dorie's condo and idled the SUV. "And did you tell them?"

Dorie looked dreamy, lost in memory. "No, not then. But that's the night I decided I wanted to be a cop."

"And we're all better for it."

Dorie snapped out of her reminiscences and yanked off her sunglasses. "I'm telling you this because six months into the job, I pulled a teenager out of a window. He was breaking in, a smash and grab. I had him on the ground so fast I think his eyes rolled back in his head. Then I put my gun in his face."

"What?"

"He was unarmed. I had no cause. But I'd been scared going into the scene and then he had dark eyes, pale skin, and a bald head just like the guy who jumped me. So, I went off on him."

"What happened?"

Dorie chuffed. "Nothing official. But my partner said I'd better get my shit together, because he didn't want to work with a hothead. He said, 'You pull your piece when you don't need it and I'll be the one getting shot.'" She looked pointedly at Ellery, who raised her hands from the wheel in defense.

"I haven't pulled my weapon once since I started."

"It's not about your gun." Dorie tapped the side of her own head. "It's about where you're at up here."

"I told you. I'm fine."

Dorie looked at her for a long time. "Okay, you're sticking with that for now. All right. We all walk our own path. Just try to get some sleep tonight, will you? You look like a raccoon on a three-day bender."

Three days. Ellery's nerves tightened in a coil. "I'm just frustrated. We don't know which dead-end alley to run down next."

"Whichever one gets us to the person who hates Teresa Lockhart. This is about her, not Chloe."

Ellery didn't agree. "Funny, then, that she's holed up in her mansion with a bunch of servants while her daughter's locked in a cage."

"You don't think she's suffering?"

"You know what Reed said. Teresa didn't want Chloe in the first place. It was Martin who insisted they keep going to the point of using a donor egg."

"That's not what I took away from her story. I see a woman who lost one child in the most horrific way possible and was terrified to try again. Can you blame her?"

"Hell, yes, I can blame her. She used that fear to make a prison for her daughter. Chloe was already living her life in a cage, just a much nicer one. And for what? It didn't keep her safe. Instead, Teresa forced Chloe to keep secrets and sneak around on her, which is how we ended up in this whole mess."

"Teresa deserves this. That's what you're saying? You sound like the kidnapper."

"I'm saying if this is her version of love, it's not good enough."

Dorie turned her face to the window. "Love never is."

Ellery looked at Dorie's wedding ring. "Michelle must love to hear you talk sweet like that."

"She's used to my style after twenty-two years together," Dorie replied with a wry smile. "And as a veteran, I can assure you—love rarely arrives in the precise form we wish it to. You get imperfect, or you get nothing." She reached over and patted Ellery's knee. "Go home and hug your kid sister."

"Wait," Ellery blurted as Dorie started to get out of the car.

Dorie turned around. "What is it?"

"What happened with you and Nicola?"

"Oh. Her." Dorie's voice became tinged with regret. "We broke up before the bruises healed. We tried, for a while. But we each looked at the other one and saw the skinheads. I heard she moved to New York City. Good night, Hathaway. I'll see you tomorrow morning and we'll do it all again."

Ellery watched as Dorie jogged up the steps to her condo and went inside to her wife and her dogs. She pulled the rearview mirror toward her so that she could evaluate her face the way that Dorie saw it, and the image showed gray skin, lips chapped from where she'd chewed on them, and wide, dark circles under her eyes. Almost like she'd looked after her time in the closet.

She shoved the mirror away. If she had any makeup, she could try to fix her appearance before Reed saw her. But then again, he'd seen her look worse. She swallowed with effort and dragged her hand up to put the SUV in gear. *Reed.* He felt destined for her because he'd been there at her origin. They'd been forged together. Only in the dark times did she remember who'd done the welding. If she was Reed's and he was hers, it was because a monster made it so.

Ellery parked her car and picked up Bump from his neighborhood sitter. The five-minute walk took fifteen with a hound who needed to sniff every inch of terrain, despite the fact that he'd run his nose over it numerous times in the past. "Let's go, I'm hungry," she grumbled at him as he examined a maple tree. She hoped Reed had beaten her home and started dinner, but the fact that he hadn't answered her latest texts suggested she would be doomed to disappointment. *Takeout it is,* she thought as she pulled open the door to the lobby.

Right away, a dark-haired woman in a navy business suit leaped up from the low couch by the windows and started striding toward her with great purpose. "Ellery Hathaway," she said.

Ellery halted with the leash in her hand. The energy radiating from the woman wasn't friendly. "Yes."

"Where is my daughter?"

Sarit, Ellery's brain supplied as the face clicked into her memory bank. *Oh, shit.* She'd never met Reed's ex-wife but had snooped around on her social media enough to recognize her. "Um, I don't know." Reed hadn't told her what his plans were for Tula today, and Ellery didn't consider it her business to ask.

"You don't know? Do you realize how ridiculous that sounds? She's staying here with you, is she not?"

Ellery vaguely remembered she wasn't supposed to admit to this. "You should call Reed."

"I have. Several times." She held up her cell phone to illustrate. "It goes straight to voice mail. I checked at the hotel and they rang the room, but no one answered. I decided to wait here until I could get information out of someone, and yet here you are with nothing."

"Sorry. I've been at work since seven." It was nearing eight now.

Ellery moved toward the elevator, and Sarit followed her, her low heels clicking on the tile floor.

"And you've received nothing from Reed about where they might be? No word all day?"

"She might be with my sister," Ellery said as she hit the button.

Sarit's brown eyes went wide with horror. "The teenage runaway?"

"She's not a runaway," Ellery replied, irritated both by this characterization of Ashley's behavior and by the fact that it wasn't entirely wrong. Sarit already thought Ellery was some sort of irresponsible psycho and now she was lumping Ashley in the same bin. "She's visiting me for a few days."

"After running off from her parents and riding a bus overnight. Tula has informed me of all the exciting details."

The elevator doors slid open and Ellery cast a beleaguered look at the empty car. She wouldn't even get one elevator ride's worth of solitude. "Would you like to come up?" she asked finally.

Sarit stepped around her into the elevator like she was bypassing hot lava. "Thank you."

They did not speak as the slow trip got underway. Ellery glanced at her companion and saw her staring at the scars on Ellery's arms. *She knows,* the voice in her head whispered. *She knows what he did to you.* Sarit had co-authored Reed's book. As a journalist, she was the writer, not him.

Ellery leveled a cool gaze at Sarit. "I read your book," she said pointedly. Neither of them had bothered to consult her first.

Sarit had the grace to look chagrined. To presume to write someone else's story without ever consulting them took a special type of arrogance. Reed had apologized and amended his behavior; Sarit, she knew, hoped for a sequel.

The elevator dinged its arrival and Sarit trailed Ellery down the hall to her apartment door. To her credit, she did not make the slightest face as Ellery opened all three locks. Bump bounded in ahead of them, making a beeline for his dish, as though some good fairy might have visited during their absence and left a T-bone in his bowl. Sarit took slow, cautious steps into the apartment, looking around at the framed posters on the wall and the high beams across the ceiling like she expected them to have spikes or nails coming out of them. The folded blankets on the couch and the air mattress on the floor told the story of who'd been bunking with her, so Ellery didn't bother to equivocate. Any chance that they might go unnoticed disappeared when Bump, finding his dish empty, used the air mattress as a doggie trampoline before collapsing, belly-up, and writhing around on it as he moaned his frustration at the bowl situation.

"He's, uh, very vocal," Sarit said over the din.

"He's hungry. So am I." She went to consult the takeout menus clipped to her refrigerator. "Do you want something? I can order pizza, Thai, burgers . . . ?"

"No, thank you."

Sarit probably served home-cooked meals full of green vegetables. Ellery phoned in an order for pizza and dumped some food into Bump's bowl. He let loose a joyful howl and came trotting over to eat it. Sarit stood near the windows in the living room as though she was afraid to touch anything.

Ellery took off her holster. "If you'll excuse me, I'm going to go change."

Sarit eyed the gun. "Do you have a lockbox for that? It's not safe around children."

"It's perfectly safe in my room." She retreated to the bedroom, her face flaming because she knew Sarit was right on this point. With a kid around, the gun should be under lock and key. Tula was never supposed to have set foot in the apartment. Ellery changed into casual clothes and put the gun in its holster on top of her high dresser. Then she locked the door behind her on the way out; she could get back in later with a bent paper clip. "There," she said to Sarit, "all locked up." Why she was trying to impress this woman, she did not know.

"That's an unusual way to keep your knives."

Ellery looked to the kitchen. The industrial-style loft came with a magnetic strip over the sink to use as a knife holder, and Ellery's displayed a carving knife, a butcher knife, and several paring knives. "I like to keep them handy," she said. "Easy reach in case I need them."

"Oh, do you cook?"

"Nope." She went to fill Bump's water bowl. As she stood at the sink, she saw her reflection distorted in the knives. She called back to Sarit, "Reed says you're moving to Houston."

Sarit's gasp was loud enough to make Bump tilt his head. "I'm sorry, what?"

"Houston," Ellery repeated as she turned around with the water. "You're job hunting there?" She set the bowl down on the floor.

"He said that—to you?"

"I believe Tula said it to him," Ellery replied, and Sarit stammered in response.

"I n—never—I didn't mean . . . nothing is settled yet. That's why I haven't brought it up to Reed."

"Yeah, I don't think Tula got that memo."

Her parenting under judgment, Sarit recomposed herself and folded her arms. "My partner, Randy, has a job offer in Houston, and he's asked us to join him there. If I can also find work, it could be a great opportunity for all of us."

"Not for Reed. He would be far away from Tula."

"I will never stop him from seeing his daughter. But it's funny that you're the one making this argument to me and not him."

"He loves her." She hesitated. "I would hate to see him punished because you have a problem with me."

Sarit sniffed. "It's not about you."

"Tula didn't get that memo, either," Ellery said steadily, and Sarit's expression turned guilty.

"Look, you have to understand—Reed has a bit of a savior complex. Yes, his instinct to help people is an admirable quality, but he takes it too far. He doesn't know when to say when."

"Meaning me," Ellery said, her voice hard.

Sarit shrugged in a *you said it; I didn't* kind of gesture. "You have to admit you met under difficult circumstances—historically dramatic, even. Adrenaline running high on all sides, I'm sure."

"You seem to know a lot for someone who wasn't even there. For your information, we barely exchanged any words back then. He wasn't my case manager. He wasn't my doctor or my shrink. He wasn't anything to me."

Sarit clucked at her. "Now who's kidding themselves? No normal woman could ever hope to compete with you where Reed is concerned. I used to wonder, you know, what it would take to keep him from running out the door after the next missing kid or suspected serial killer. You've found the formula, I guess. You are his obsessions brought to life."

"You don't know what you're talking about."

"I know him better than you do, apparently. Do you really think he'd be here with you if not for your shared history? Do you really think you'd pick him above all men—a workaholic who's twice your age and comes with a seven-year-old daughter?"

"He's not close to twice my age."

"Sure," Sarit said, now sweetly magnanimous. "Quibble about the margins. We both know I've drawn up the essence of it correctly."

Ellery slumped, exhausted from the long day and this conversation. "Think what you want," she muttered, walking away. "Hate me if it makes things easier for you."

"I don't hate you," Sarit blurted, and Ellery halted with her back to the woman. "I quite admire you, actually. I can't imagine what it would be like to live in the shadow of that monster. Whatever he did to you, whoever you've become as a result of that, it's not your fault."

Ellery clenched her fists. "Thanks so much for the absolution." She turned around and locked eyes with Sarit. "Just because your name is on a book about me doesn't mean you know who I am. You know the facts of the case. You don't know me."

"And you don't know where my daughter is."

"She's not my daughter."

"Exactly. She's not yours. You don't love her. And yet I'm supposed to let her come here where there are knives and guns and unsupervised teenagers, and that's just what I know about. She's my child, it's my responsibility to keep her safe, and I will do whatever it takes to uphold that duty."

"Even if it means taking her from her father."

"Even that, yes. If he's not looking out for what's best for her."

Ellery shook her head with sadness. "I would never do anything to hurt Tula."

"That's not enough for me," Sarit said in a clipped tone. Then her face softened. "It's not enough for Tula."

A ruckus at the front door caused Bump to leap up and bark. The doorbell rang three times in quick succession, and Ellery heard Reed's baritone reverberating in the hallway. "That's them," she said, going to open the door. She flipped the locks in turn and revealed Reed, Ashley, and Tula on the other side.

"Sorry we're late," he said. "We stopped for hamburgers."

"You haven't been answering your phone," she replied as the kids pushed past her into the apartment.

"No service on the T."

"Too bad. You could have had advance warning."

"Warning?" he said, his expression troubled. "Warning of what?"

Behind her, Tula shrieked with delight. "Mommy!"

The color drained from Reed's face as Ellery gave him a tight smile. "Your ex-wife is here."

26

Reed's first thought when Ellery unlocked her bedroom door and left him inside with Sarit was how long it had been since he'd been alone with her in an intimate space like this. After eleven years of sharing the same bed, they met in common areas now—kitchens and living rooms and occasionally Tula's bedroom with its menagerie of stuffed animals and their wide unblinking eyes. Sarit repeatedly tucked her hair behind her right ear, a gesture Reed recognized as nerves. *Good,* he thought. *She's not sure about this.* Aloud, he said, "You didn't tell me you were coming up to Boston."

"I called. You didn't answer."

He had already checked his phone and seen her messages. "You called four hours ago, already in town, I take it."

"I had a story in Connecticut, so it was just a quick trip from there."

"Ah," he said mildly. "To check up on me."

Her chin rose a notch in defiance. "The stories Tula's been telling are concerning, Reed. Sleeping on the floor? Spending time in the care of a teenage runaway? And this place—it's like a den of thieves designed it. Knives hanging on the wall in the kitchen. Look, there's her gun right over there where anyone could grab it." She pointed behind Reed at Ellery's holstered weapon sitting on the dresser.

"Ellery's used to living alone. I'll talk to her about the gun, okay?"

"It's not okay," she said, her face screwed up in frustration. "We have one job as parents, and that's to keep our kids safe. I get that she has no experience with . . . well, other human beings, apparently . . . but you're the father. You're supposed to see the loose gun before it becomes a problem."

"It hasn't been a problem. Tula hasn't been in a room with an unattended gun."

"Given your girlfriend's history with firearms, that doesn't make me feel a lot better."

"But moving to Houston would solve everything." He kept his tone as neutral as possible.

An emotion that might have been regret passed over Sarit's features. "I wanted to wait until I knew for sure it was happening before talking to you. I guess Tula must have overheard a conversation or two."

"You wanted to wait—why? So it could be a done deal and I'd have no way to fight it?"

"You don't have much standing to fight it. You don't abide by the agreement we have now."

"That's not fair. I see Tula the proscribed number of days per month, just not always on your schedule."

"It's not my schedule. It's the schedule we worked out with the courts and then you don't follow it, as usual. It's not about me, Reed. It's about Tula and giving her stability, constancy. She has to know she can depend on you."

"She knows that," he said testily. "I would do anything for her."

"Anything? You've pawned her off on some troubled teenager you barely know so that you and Ellery can play single, carefree lovers together."

"That's ridiculous. I've been working, not canoodling with Ellery."

Her mouth fell open. "Working. I suppose you think that's better."

"Sarit, my job requires—"

She held up both hands to forestall him. "I don't want to hear another word about your damn job. You were supposed to be on vacation with your daughter this week."

"I have been. She's had a blast. Just ask her."

"Just not with her father."

Reed glared at her and stalked to the window. He looked out at the dark, empty street, where the streetlamps cast angled shadows. A young woman on a bike went by. "Do you know why Ellery was abducted by Francis Coben all those years ago?" he asked without turning around.

"He liked her hands," Sarit replied, sounding tired. "It was the middle of the night and she was alone, so he just grabbed her. He was a murderous psychopath. Take whichever explanation you prefer."

"She was alone, yes," Reed said, turning around slowly. "Because her mother was at the hospital with her sick older brother. Her father had left the family."

"Yes, I recall. It's a sad story, Reed. What is the point?"

He spread his hands. "She had no one else. No aunts, uncles, cousins, or anyone else to step in when times got tough at the Hathaway household. If there had been someone . . . anyone to see that Ellery got fed supper that night. Someone, maybe, to bake her a birthday cake. Someone to keep her company in that apartment so she wasn't out riding her bike in the middle of the night all alone. If there had been just one extra person to care for Ellery, she wouldn't have been abducted."

"People from nice, whole families don't get victimized, then." Sarit wasn't buying it.

"They are less vulnerable. But it does happen, of course. However, then you have a family to help you heal from the trauma. You don't have to weather it alone and the damage is less durable."

Sarit rubbed her head as though it hurt. "Is there a point to this analysis, Mr. Profiler?"

"You want to protect Tula. I understand that desire because I share it." He put his hand to his heart. "But this move you are suggesting would take her away, not just from me, but from her grandparents, her aunts, uncles, and cousins. People who love her and whom she loves. They are not just family but her safety net, too."

"I'm trying to see that she doesn't need a safety net."

"You can't," Reed said with a tinge of sadness. "You can't keep her safe from all harm because it's not possible, not if you want her to have any kind of life at all. You are her mother. You were her first home, her first love. But you are not everything. Not now, and definitely not in the future, when she's crying about some hurt that you can't soothe either because you don't understand it or you aren't even there to see it."

Sarit blinked back tears. "That's a fatalistic vision."

Reed shook his head. "You worry about Ellery and her mental health. I don't think she's any threat to Tula at all, but I do see a lesson from her. You can't do it alone. You shouldn't want to. Kids need mothers, yes, but they also need fathers who will buy them rocket ship shoes and push the swing as high as it will go in the park. They need teenage babysitters with blue fingernails. They need aunts to take them to the art museum and uncles who will show them how to change a tire."

"I know how to change a tire," Sarit said, her tone grudging.

Reed smiled. "And who taught you?"

She met his eyes and their gaze held for a long moment. "You did."

When they left the bedroom, nothing was resolved as far as Houston, but Sarit had agreed to keep him in the loop on further discussions.

He found Ellery standing at the kitchen island over a pizza. She nibbled halfheartedly at one slice while Tula and Ashley, perched on stools across from her, devoured the rest. "Didn't you two just eat dinner?" Reed asked the girls.

"That was hours ago," Ashley replied.

"Yeah," Tula said, her mouth full. "Hours."

Reed nudged Ellery. "Can I talk to you a moment?"

She looked at Sarit and then back at him, obviously trying to guess the nature of his proposed conversation. "I don't know," she said. "Do you think she can be trusted here with the knives?"

Ashley tittered while Sarit shot her a dirty look. "I'll risk it," Reed said, tugging on her hand.

She allowed him to half-drag her to the bedroom, where he shut the door. "If you want to yell at me about the gun, Sarit already beat you to it."

"I don't wish to yell at you." He tugged some more until she stumbled into him, at which point he wrapped his arms around her. She was stiff and unyielding in his embrace. "I'm sorry she decided to parachute in behind enemy lines like this," he said against the side of her head.

"Is that what I am? The enemy?" Her voice was muffled against his shirt.

"No, of course not." He ran his palm down the smooth plane of her back. "Poor humor. I just meant that it wasn't fair of her, showing up like this out of the blue. One more person in your personal space, hmm?"

"One that hates me."

"She doesn't hate you." He paused with his chin atop her head, considering. "She's a brilliant woman who is suspicious of things she doesn't understand. This includes you."

Ellery pulled away with a sigh and sat down on the end of the bed. Reed joined her. "What did she say about Houston?"

"We've agreed to talk more about it when I get home."

Ellery flopped backward on the bed and looked at the ceiling. "Home," she repeated. "Yes, I suppose you'll have to get back there soon."

He lay back with her and studied the cracks in the painted ceiling. Old buildings wore their years like wrinkles on the body, each one a testament to survival.

"Reed?"

"Hmm?"

"Do you think we would be together if it weren't for how we met?"

His logical brain pounced on the inherent fallacy in the question. Of course they couldn't be together if they hadn't ever met. But he sensed what she really wanted to know. "If it wasn't for Coben, you mean."

She nodded, still looking at the ceiling. "It's macabre, right? He's the reason we're together."

His spine stiffened at the idea. "Did Sarit say that to you?"

"Not in those words. But I've wondered. You know how it looks from the outside, like I'm some unfinished project for you."

"I don't think that at all."

She didn't reply, and he had to wonder if maybe she believed it. He took her hand, the thing that Coben had most coveted, and kissed her knuckles. "I don't know if we would have met some other way. There is no way to know it. I do know that if we crossed paths otherwise my assessment of you would be the same. You are vexing and delightful in equal measure. I've interviewed a dozen Cobens, and I can promise you this much: I wouldn't be who I am now if it weren't for you."

She gave him a faint smile, as though she didn't quite believe him, but she didn't pull her hand from his. "What did you find out from Justin Stone?"

"He doesn't think much of his father, the esteemed professor. He confirms what I'd discovered in my trip to Philadelphia: the elder Stone has a penchant for young women. This got me thinking about a young woman who might have crossed Ethan Stone's radar some years ago, Beth Frick. She's the daughter who died in a car crash some weeks before her mother was murdered in the Stone house along with Trevor Stone."

"Right, I recall that."

"I called Baltimore today to speak to the accident investigator who looked into the crash. She said it was a single-vehicle incident, and the signs suggested Beth was driving more than a hundred miles per hour when she lost control of the car on the freeway and ran into a concrete barrier. She wasn't wearing a seat belt and was ruled dead at the scene. The investigator said there had been a long dry spell followed by patchy rain, which has the effect of bringing all the built-up oil out of the pavement and making the roads extra slick. There had been a number of fatal crashes the same weekend."

"Okay, so a teenager drives stupidly on the highway and pays the ultimate price. What's that got to do with Ethan Stone?"

"Part of the tragedy of Beth's death was that she was due to start college in the fall on full scholarship. At Penn."

Ellery yanked her hand away and sat up to look at him. "Where Ethan Stone teaches."

"Yes. Possibly a coincidence, but it's also probable she sought out his advice when applying. There's another thing. Her sister Lisa didn't mention it, so I am not sure if she even knows. She was quite young when Beth died. The autopsy revealed that Beth was pregnant."

"Just when you think this story can't get any sadder."

"I think it all fits together somehow—the crash, the gun in the Stones' backyard, the murders. I just can't make all the pieces come together."

"If Carol found out Ethan Stone was abusing her daughter, he might have killed her to shut her up."

"But killed his own son, too?" This was the piece Reed couldn't make fit with Ethan Stone as the killer. The man's grief over his dead child struck Reed as genuine, although he supposed the prominent picture displayed in Stone's office could also be considered performative. Still, it would take a skilled sociopath to pull off this level of deception.

"It does happen. Stone hasn't remarried, right? He's enjoyed playing the field. Maybe he saw Trevor as a barrier to his new life."

"Maybe." The best way to trap a sociopath was through repeated, probing interviews designed to allow them to spin grandiose lies and then to call them on the lies. Inconvenient truths had a way of slipping past the mask of sanity and revealing the lack of conscience underneath. Reed doubted he could make Ethan Stone sit for a second interview unless he had something concrete to force his hand.

"He has an alibi for the time of Chloe's disappearance. Whatever else Ethan Stone might be guilty of, he doesn't have Chloe."

"I don't think his son does, either. He's been in jail for the past few days."

Reed's cell phone buzzed in his pants, and he dug it out. The number was not one he recognized. "Agent Markham," he said as he answered.

"Agent Markham, it's Lisa Frick," came a distressed voice on the other end. "Do you remember me?"

"Yes, of course. What can I do for you?"

"I'm sorry if I'm bothering you. I didn't know who else to call. I saw on the news that you're looking for a man in connection with Chloe Lockhart's disappearance. They said to call right away if you recognized him because he might be a witness."

"That's right. Do you know the man?"

"I think—I think it's Bobby. My brother."

27

Sarit stayed with the girls while Reed and Ellery took off for Paw-tucket, Rhode Island, where Bobby Frick made his home. I-95 was clear of most civilian traffic at this time of night, leaving Ellery to zigzag around the dozens of big-rig trucks that hauled freight up and down the East Coast corridor. Reed hunched over his laptop, working his networks for any further information on Bobby Frick. "He has a record," he reported after a time. "Minor assault, public drunkenness, arrested with two other males at the scene. Looks like a bar fight from what I can discern from the aftermath. He was ar-rested again a year later, this time for assault against a girlfriend. She pressed charges and he did a couple of months before being released early. Most of these charges are old, though. The most recent is three years ago."

"Nothing with kids?" Ellery's stomach contracted in on itself like a sea urchin at the thought of what Bobby Frick could be doing to Chloe.

"Not that I see here."

"So, if he took her, it's not about sex."

"I don't think it ever was."

"What, then? Revenge?"

"Anger. Pain. His mother was murdered and no one ever paid for it."

"But then, why Chloe?" Ellery clenched the wheel, feeling trapped by her own futility. "She wasn't even born back then. If the answer is that he really wants to torture Teresa, that doesn't make much sense, either. Teresa Lockhart didn't do it. She was at the hospital at the time of the murders."

"According to Lisa Frick, Teresa asked her mother to be at the house that day, an afternoon that she wasn't originally scheduled to work," Reed reminded her. "But for Teresa's intervention, Carol wouldn't have been at the Stone house when the murderer arrived. Maybe Bobby holds her responsible."

"Unless Carol led him there. Unless she was the target all along."

"I'm betting Bobby doesn't see it that way."

They had pulled his driver's license photo and it was, as Lisa Frick had indicated, a good match to the man seen on the CCTV footage the day Chloe disappeared, but it was not yet proof he'd taken her. After the last painful dead end at the Desmond house, Ellery held slim hope they could be close to a rescue. That remnant of hope popped like a soap bubble when they arrived at Bobby's apartment building and she saw it was old but made of bricks with a solid concrete foundation. This wasn't the location where Chloe was being held.

A frantic-looking woman Ellery gathered must be Lisa Frick stood outside the apartment building's front door, clutching her cell phone. "Agent Markham, thank you for coming," she said as they walked over to her. "I've been calling him all day since I saw that picture, but the phone goes right to voice mail. I'm praying I'm wrong about this."

"We've checked and his phone is dead or turned off," Reed replied. "He's not taking anyone's calls, not just yours."

"Please. You have to help me find him."

"We're doing everything we can. This is his only known address?'

"For the past few years, yes. His place is on the third floor in the corner right there. Number Three-Oh-Two. I haven't been inside since he moved in, because he usually comes to Boston to see me."

Ellery tilted her head back to look at the darkened windows that Lisa had indicated. It was only nine thirty at night; most of the surrounding units still had lights on. "Do you have a key?"

"Yes." She pulled it out and closed her fingers around it. "I've been afraid to go inside."

"May I?" Reed held out his palm and she hesitated a moment before dropping the key in his hand.

"Bobby wouldn't do anything to hurt that girl. Maybe he saw the kidnapper. Maybe he's afraid and has been hiding out."

"Then we'll help him," Reed said as they went inside. He hit the button for the elevator.

"Has he mentioned Chloe Lockhart at all to you?" Ellery asked.

"I was trying to think about that while I was waiting. I can only remember him mentioning her one time, the first time he found out about her. I'd just started school up here and Bobby came to visit. He was hanging around the city during the afternoon while I went to class, and when we met up afterward he said he'd seen Teresa. He said she had a new husband and a new daughter, like nothing had ever happened. Poof—she just started over."

"Did he use those words exactly?" Reed wanted to know as they climbed into the elevator.

"Something close to that. I said I was happy for her. He said something like, 'I can't imagine being happy ever again, not after my kid got killed.' Then we ordered takeout and didn't talk about her anymore that I can remember. Bobby's always had a temper, but I can't believe he'd do anything to hurt that girl."

"He's hurt other people in the past," Ellery said, thinking of his assault record.

"He—he's been angry. Can you blame him? Our mom got killed

and we ended up in foster care. No one ever found out who did it. Bobby took it hard. But after his last arrest, he got into counseling. He's been taking medication. He's doing better, I swear."

The elevator stopped on the third floor and Ellery poked her head out to scan the hallway before letting the others out of the car. "It's clear."

Reed used the key to open the door to Bobby's apartment. "Wait here," he told Lisa.

Ellery entered first, her hand ready at her weapon. The place smelled like it had been baking in the summer sun for days, leaving hot dead air. She paused to listen, but the apartment was totally silent. "Bobby Frick? It's the Boston Police." She received no reply.

She felt along the wall with her left hand for a light switch, which she located and turned on. Reed and Lisa trailed behind her as she moved deeper into the apartment. It looked like a normal bachelor pad—inexpensive black leather sofa in front of a large-screen television. Big speakers. No plants or signs of anything alive. The kitchen was tidy, save for a single coffee mug sitting on the counter. Ellery glanced at the framed nature photographs on the wall, which depicted wet rocks up close so that their ridges and contrasting colors resembled abstract art.

"Bobby took those," Lisa said. "His hobby is photography."

"There's a card here," Reed called from the living area. He looked to Lisa. "It's addressed to you."

"That's Bobby's writing on it." Lisa grabbed the envelope from the end table and tore it open. There was a white folded piece of paper inside that had been wrapped around an old photo. "This picture was taken at our house in Baltimore," she said as Ellery came to look at it. It showed a boy and a girl, preschool age and dressed in finery, standing on some steps with a teenage girl behind them, one hand on each of their shoulders. A woman Ellery recognized as Carol Frick stood beside the steps. She wore a pink-colored skirt suit, a hat, and white gloves. "This was Easter Sunday in front of our old house. My dad took the picture. It was the last holiday before he died."

Ellery took the photo from Lisa as she opened the accompanying note. Carol Frick smiled in the picture, but her eyes didn't look to the cameraman. Instead, she seemed to be smiling beyond him, at someone or something far away.

Lisa read the note aloud: "'Dear Lisa, Do you remember Dad making quacking noises to get us to smile for this picture? Hard to believe it could ever end up like this. You were always the best of all of us—smarter, kinder, able to leave the past where it belongs. Maybe finally I can do the same. Love forever, Bobby.'"

She looked up with shining eyes. "We need to find him."

"We will." Ellery nodded at her and moved to the bedroom at the back of the apartment. The door was closed and she felt her heartbeat speeding up at the prospect of opening it, despite the fact that she was nearly certain there was no one on the other side. Her hand flinched as she reached for the knob. "Mr. Frick?" she called again.

The door swung open and Ellery gasped aloud. He had photographs, all right—hundreds of them tacked to his wall, and they all appeared to show Chloe Lockhart. "Reed? You're going to want to see this."

He materialized immediately at her side in the doorway. "Wow."

"What is it?" Behind them, Lisa hadn't yet glimpsed her brother's obsession. They parted so she could get a look. She gave a soft, horrified cry and her hands flew to her mouth. "No," she said mournfully. "No, it can't be true."

Ellery stepped into the room to get a closer look at the pictures. "He's been following her for weeks, if not months." The photos showed Chloe in her yard with her dog, Snuffles. Outside her school, chatting with friends or leaning up against the fence, looking bored as she stared at her phone. Getting into the car with Margery, her nanny. Walking along the streets of Boston with Margery. He had followed her into the YMCA, too, because there were multiple shots on different days of Chloe laughing and talking to Ty. At one point, he caught them shooting hoops together. Teresa and Martin Lockhart appeared incidentally in the photos, too. The entire family had been photographed leaving church together.

"I don't see a camera here anywhere," Reed said, peering in the closet. "He must have it with him."

"Look at this one," Ellery said. She pointed at the most disturbing photo, one that showed Chloe's face looking out her bedroom window. "He's been to her house."

"He's been everywhere she was," Reed replied, his gaze flicking over the wall of photos.

"Yes, but where are they now?"

Outside, the sound of approaching sirens signaled the arrival of backup. They would need a team to comb through the apartment for anything of evidentiary value. Reed pulled out his phone and turned as if to leave but stopped in his tracks. "Ellery. Look."

She turned around and saw the back wall. This one had printed-out newspaper headlines and articles from the murders of Trevor Stone and Carol Frick.

BOY, HOUSKEEPER SLAIN

STONE-COLD KILLER ON THE LOOSE

POLICE QUESTION BROTHER IN DOUBLE HOMICIDE

COULD THE HOUSEKEEPER HAVE BEEN A TARGET?

TREVOR STONE LAID TO REST

CITY MOURNS LOST SON

NEIGHBORHOOD PANIC GROWS AS KILLER REMAINS AT LARGE

TEN YEARS LATER, TREVOR STONE'S KILLER STILL UNKNOWN

"You see? Her name isn't anywhere," Lisa said, still sniffling as Ellery studied the headlines. "That's what bothered him. She was always just 'the housekeeper'—someone there by accident. Her death didn't matter at all."

"Did you know about this?" Ellery asked, indicating the paper trail.

"No. I mean, he talked about it whenever the case made the news again, how all the focus was on Trevor and not on our mom. But I had no clue he did . . . that." She gestured weakly at the clippings and printouts.

Ellery went to the bookshelf, scanning it for clues. Paperback techno thrillers, sci-fi, books on photography. He had a baseball signed by David Ortiz and a framed photograph of himself and Lisa against the backdrop of leafy trees and a textured wall of rock. Ellery picked up the picture and studied it. "If he's not here, where else might he go?"

"I have no idea."

"Think hard."

"I am. Bobby was always kind of a loner. He'd take his camera out into the woods to shoot pictures by himself. He was either doing that, visiting me, or at work."

"Where does he work?"

"At a stone quarry not far away."

"A stone quarry. Like where they process rocks for foundations and stuff?"

"I guess. I don't know the details."

"We have to get over there," Ellery said to Reed. "It could be where he's keeping her."

"I'll come with you," Lisa said, heading for the door.

"No," Reed and Ellery said at the same time.

She halted and turned around again. "I have to know what happened to him."

"We'll keep in touch," Reed said, touching her arm on the way by. "Right now, the arriving officers are going to need your help."

"But—"

Ellery didn't catch the rest of Lisa's protest. She heard only the sound of her boots on the stairs as she fled down the staircase.

Moments behind her, Reed caught up as she reached the exit. Ellery glanced up long enough to see Lisa's worried face in the window watching as they got into the car. "I don't blame her for wanting to tag along," she said. "It must be hell on her, too, the not knowing."

"She's afraid of what we're going to find," Reed said as she started the car.

"You mean Chloe."

"I mean Bobby. That letter he left her—it was a suicide note."

28

Reed worked the phones while Ellery drove. "The manager of the Stonewall Quarry is a man named Nga Nall," he explained to the Providence PD. "We need him to meet us there. Go pick him up immediately—there is a young girl's life at stake." His shoulder slammed into the car door as Ellery careened around a tight corner. "We'll also need a search team and medics on-site."

"You think we'll find her there," Ellery said when he hung up the phone.

"I hope we'll find her there." He'd been grasping for motive since Chloe's abduction, and now it was clear. Bobby Frick's psychological profile had never matched that of a typical kidnapper; he was more akin to a suicide bomber or a man who shot up a public place before turning the gun on himself. He was going down, but he aimed to inflict as much pain as possible on his way out.

They arrived at the quarry, which was surrounded by a high fence and blocked by a locked gate. Ellery left her headlights on for illumination as she grabbed the fence at the door and yanked with both hands. It swayed slightly, but the lock held fast. Reed checked his phone. "They have Nall. ETA is now fifteen minutes."

"We can't wait that long." Ellery started climbing the fence.

"What are you doing? There's barbed wire up there."

"So I'll get cut."

Reed looked up and down the deserted road, wishing for backup that wasn't yet close. Ellery reached the top and cursed as the wire caught her clothes. He heard a rip, followed by another string of cursing. "Are you okay?" he asked as she struggled over the barbs.

"Peachy," she muttered.

He shone his flashlight at her and saw blood on the palm of her left hand. "You're hurt."

"It's nothing," she said, slightly breathless as she jumped down on the other side. She found the lockbox and fished out a set of keys. She tried one, then another. "This is bullshit," she said. "They'll be here in another few minutes."

"Yes," he said reasonably. "They will."

"Aha," she said with satisfaction as the key fit and the lock sprang open. She yanked the gate open and Reed slipped inside. Mountains of rocks stood off to the right side. On the left was a long building with few windows, as well as smaller piles of daintier rocks. Reed sneezed as the dust tickled his nose.

Ellery had her flashlight out now and she began prowling the grounds. Reed followed at a distance, eyeing the hulking earthmovers that loomed like mechanical monsters in the dark. His phone buzzed with a message from their old friend Detective Jake Osborne, who was en route with the plant manager. *Nall says Bobby Frick hasn't been to work in a week,* the text message read. Reed relayed this news to Ellery as she stood on the edge of a dumpster-like container and peered inside. "He may not be here," he said to her. "We should be thinking of other possibilities."

Ellery shone her light on a pile of rough stones, each about the size of a small beach ball. "You see those fieldstones? They're the same kind we saw in the photo of Chloe. We're on the right track. Let's see if we can get into the building."

"Lead the way." Reed followed her to the doors, which were, not surprisingly, also locked. The keys she'd acquired didn't seem to work.

"Maybe we can use one of the rocks to break a window," she said, standing on tiptoe and cupping her hands around her eyes to try to see inside the building.

"Or we could have him do it." Reed gestured behind them at the arriving manager, who was accompanied by Detective Osborne and several uniformed officers. Osborne nodded at Reed and Ellery as they approached.

"Any sign of the girl?"

"Not yet," Ellery replied. She regarded Nga Nall, the manager. "Can you get us inside?"

"Yes, of course." He produced a completely different set of keys and used one to unlock the door. "But there's no girl inside here—just offices. I locked it up myself this evening."

Ellery didn't answer. She jogged through the open door and began combing the premises. Nall turned up the lights to aid her search. A couple of the uniformed officers joined her while Reed and Osborne hung back to question Nall. "What can you tell me about the operations here?" Reed asked.

"We're open eight to five, Mondays through Fridays. We're part of a larger corporation that hauls in stone from several more remote digs and we process it on-site here. There's a couple dozen people coming in and out of here all day long. If Bobby Frick tried to hide here, or to keep a young girl here, we'd know about it."

Reed looked at the crude floor. "What's under here?"

"Dirt."

"No basement?"

"No, sir. Just the slab cement foundation you're looking at and then more dirt."

"What about Bobby Frick? How has his behavior been lately?"

Nall shrugged one broad shoulder. "Who knows? He hasn't been here all week. Called in sick Monday and then we heard nothing since then. I told my guys, he'd better be in the hospital or something if he wants back to work after this. I never imagined he was mixed up in a kidnapping."

"Does he have a locker or a desk of some sort?"

"A locker, yes. This way."

Ellery rejoined them as they went past the break room with its vending machines and cheap plastic chairs. "I don't see any sign of her," she said to Reed.

Nall opened the locker and Reed stepped forward to examine the meager contents. He found a plaid shirt on a hook, a half-empty water bottle, a few toiletries, and a nature photograph tacked to the inside door. "Nothing of note here," he reported with dismay.

"He's keeping her somewhere that has a fieldstone foundation," Ellery said, grabbing the photograph for study. "Maybe an off-site job?"

"We provide materials for construction," Nall said. "Fieldstone foundations are not common anymore, but sometimes the older ones need repairs."

"Can you check your work logs?" Ellery asked as she put the photo back in the locker. "See if you have any recent jobs that involve fieldstone?"

"Yes, of course. I just need to boot up the computer." They followed him to his office and waited while he logged in and searched their records. "Nothing in the past two months," he told them with regret. "Our last completed job was repair of a fieldstone wall at an estate in Marblehead, Massachusetts. Before that, we did a new wall for one of the city parks."

"What about the unfinished jobs?" Reed asked.

"They would be ongoing," Nall explained. "Lots of people in and out. Except . . ." He stroked his chin, considering. He sat forward again and hit a few more keys. "We had a contract fall through in May. The buyer failed to make payments and the bank seized the property with construction half-finished. Nobody's been paid yet, so as far as I know, there's just half a house sitting there."

"Did Bobby Frick work on that job?" Ellery asked with renewed interest.

Nall turned the monitor around so they could read the address and crew list. "Yes, he did."

Ellery was in motion the moment the words left Nall's mouth, and Reed scrambled to keep up. "You want backup?" Osborne called from behind them.

"Yes, please!" Reed yelled back. The dirt kicked up under his feet as he ran.

Ellery started the car just as he reached it and clambered inside, her eyes bright on his. "This is it," she said. "I can feel it."

Reed sensed it, too, in the tightening of his gut and the zinging of adrenaline in his veins. "You need to prepare yourself for a potentially bad outcome." He said it for her benefit and for his own. He began every chase hoping to find the child alive but knowing the odds were not in his favor. The worst part of his job was showing up to meet parents with ashen faces streaked with tears, begging for the return of children Reed knew were already dead. *You have to keep hope,* he'd tell them, while mentally prepping himself for the opposite. No matter how many times he made this journey, he hadn't worked out how to harden himself enough. The end crushed him every time.

"She's alive," Ellery said with certainty.

He didn't argue with her. He couldn't. Sixteen years ago, he'd used a crowbar to open a closet he'd been sure would be a coffin. Every other girl Coben took had been dead by then. "It's a left up here," he said.

Ellery turned off the highway onto a more rural road that was framed by tall trees and dangling branches on either side. It reminded him of Woodbury and how quickly civilization could disappear in the rearview mirror. Occasional mailboxes popped up along the sidelines, indicating there were houses set far back behind the woods, hidden in the dark by long, winding driveways and the thick brush of the forest. Ellery turned on the high beams. "I can barely see a thing."

Movement triggered alarm in his peripheral vision. "Look out!" he hollered just as a deer darted out across the road in front of them. Ellery hit the brakes and swerved to the side, running the right-hand wheels into a ditch. They both breathed unsteadily as a stream of several more deer took a leisurely stroll from one side of the woods to the other. The windows of the SUV began to fog.

Behind them, blue lights appeared as Osborne and his team caught up. Ellery gunned the engine and pulled the car back out onto the road. "It should be up here on the left somewhere," she said, leaning forward and squinting.

Reed spotted an opening in the trees just as they were nearly past it. "There."

She turned at the last minute, sending him up against the door again. He righted himself as she took them through the tunnel of trees and down the pitch-black dirt road. The SUV rose and fell like a Martian rover over the bumpy terrain, rattling his brain inside his skull. He wanted to tell her to slow down but knew the words would be futile. At last, the trees parted to reveal the husk of a house—frame and walls in place, the roof partly done, but no front steps or windows. "This is it," Ellery said, eyeing the fieldstone foundation. She grabbed her flashlight and leaped from the car. Reed took his own light and followed close behind as the remaining cars rolled up the road.

Ellery climbed through the opening that would have been the front door. Reed shone his flashlight in and saw that there was a subfloor in place. He climbed up as well while Ellery pushed deeper into the house. He heard only the sounds of her moving up ahead of him. "Here!" she called out, and he followed her voice to the top of the basement stairs.

"Careful," he murmured as she started down the rickety temporary steps that were only half-formed. He tested the first one and the thin piece of wood bowed under his weight. When they reached the bottom, Ellery went left while he took the right.

"Chloe?" she called. Silence.

Reed shone his light around, picking up cobwebs and dead leaves accumulated in the corners. He saw a muddy boot print on the floor, but he couldn't say when it had been left there. At the back, he found an actual wooden door. It might have led to the furnace room. He tugged, but it held fast. Not locked, he realized, but swollen shut from the humidity. "I've got something," he said to Ellery. She appeared at his side to help him tug on the door. With both their weight, it lurched free, sending them stumbling backward.

The scent of urine coming from the room hit him hard. Ellery grabbed up her flashlight and he blurted, "Wait." Just a few more seconds and there would be no denying what was on the other side.

Ellery reached the threshold and let out a horrified gasp. He braced himself as he looked over her shoulder. There in the corner was the cage from the picture, the door hanging open. Inside on the floor lay a small figure with blond hair, curled up and motionless. She had a plastic bag over her head. "Chloe," Ellery called as she rushed over to her. "Oh God, no." She fell to her knees, the flashlight going off-kilter as she grabbed up the girl from the cage. "It's not real," she said with utter relief. "It's a mannequin."

"What?"

"It's a doll. Look." She hauled out the mannequin to show him and he could see the face was painted on.

"What's that?" Reed used his flashlight beam to point out another white card on the floor of the cage. Ellery pushed aside the doll to snatch it up. There was no name attached.

She opened the envelope to reveal a plain white index card inside. "'Tell Teresa she's too late.'"

Detective Osborne came thundering down the stairs with a pair of officers hot on his heels. "What've you got?"

"She's not here!" Reed called out.

Osborne stuck his head into the room and made a face at the smell. "What's that?" he asked, shining his light on the mannequin. Reed noticed for the first time that the doll was dressed in the pink shirt and denim shorts Chloe had been wearing when she disappeared.

"It's a doll made up to look like Chloe," Ellery said.

"Jeez, he's a crazy fucker, isn't he?"

"We're going to need another forensic team to go through this place," said Reed. "Maybe we can find something to indicate where he's taken her next."

"What, like a scavenger hunt?" Osborne asked, incredulous. "Follow the clues, find the prize?"

Ellery jumped to her feet at his words. "Yes," she said. "Exactly." She dashed out of the room without further explanation, so Reed had to chase after her.

"Where are you going?" he asked as she went back out of the house toward her SUV. It was still running with its lights on.

"I'm going to find Bobby Frick."

"He could be anywhere." Lisa had listed three usual locations for him: his home, his work, and the great outdoors. New England had thousands of acres of forest and mountain territory in which to disappear.

"That picture he had in his locker—I recognize the rock bridge. It's the same one that's visible in the shot he took with Lisa back at his apartment. That means the place must have special meaning for him, right?"

"Probable, yes," he said, admiring her insight. "We could ask Lisa where the picture was taken."

"We don't have to. I know it. It's Marble Arch Park out in western Massachusetts. Bump and I used to go hiking there sometimes when I lived in Woodbury." She climbed into the car and waved him along impatiently. "Are you coming?"

He glanced back at the house, torn. "We should take backup."

"Not them. Someone has to stay here for the forensic team. We can radio for more help on the road."

Convinced, he climbed in with her. "Then let's go."

29

Near midnight, the slow roll of Ellery's tires crunched over the grit and bits of gravel that comprised the parking lot for Marble Arch. Moonlight shone on the wet leaves, the air heavy with humidity. She felt the hair curling at the back of her neck as she got out of the car. "Look at that," she said, nodding in the direction of a white van at the end of the lot. It sported Rhode Island plates and was the only other vehicle nearby.

She and Reed approached from the rear, crouching to avoid being seen in the mirrors in case anyone was inside. Reed pulled out his phone to run the plates while Ellery slid alongside the van up to the driver's-side door. "Nothing visible here." She tried the handle and found it unlocked. The inside smelled like cigarettes and fried food. She found a cheeseburger wrapper on the floor and a soda bottle in the cupholder.

"The van is stolen," Reed reported from outside. "It was reported two days ago."

Ellery released the lock on the van's rear doors and went around to open them. "This is definitely him," she said, shining her flashlight into the cargo space. "There's the missing camera."

"Not to mention a half-dozen burner phones and a roll of duct tape." Reed trained his light on the inside of the door. "Is that blood?"

Ellery leaned in to inspect the red-brown smear. "Yes, I think so. Already dried."

Reed turned to look at the vast swath of trees behind them. "We're going to need a search team."

"Good, call them." She started for the path.

"Ellery, wait." He jogged after her. "There's ten thousand acres in there, with no light."

"I have a light." She waved her flashlight at him and continued heading for the head of the trail. "We can't wait. You said it yourself—he's suicidal, and from the looks of things, he wants to take Chloe with him."

"I know you want to find her, but—"

She halted and whirled on him, aiming the light right in his eyes. "When you found Coben's farmhouse, did you stop to call for backup?"

He shielded his face with one hand. "You know I didn't." A dozen movie and TV reenactments over the years had dramatized the pivotal moment when Reed broke into the old farmhouse and discovered Ellery nailed into a closet.

Satisfied, she turned again and strode toward the black maw of the trail. Behind her, she heard Reed on the phone relaying their location and the latest developments. The heady wet-earth scent of the forest enveloped her as the trees blocked out the moon from overhead. Bugs chattered at her, their electric hum giving the woods their own unique pulse. Lovesick frogs burped out a mating song in the darkness. She slapped at the mosquitos that thrilled to the arrival of fresh flesh, dive-bombing her bare arms with hungry, stinging tongues.

Quickening footsteps behind her made her heart miss a beat, and she whirled to find Reed hurrying up the trail after her. "It will take time to mobilize everyone in the middle of the night," he whispered to her. "But they're on the way."

Ellery reached a branching point in the trail—go higher toward the marble arch or lower down near the water. She cast her light on the ground for some indication of which way to go, but hundreds of hikers had probably passed this spot in the last few days. "We should split up."

"No."

"Yes. We can cover twice as much ground that way. You have your phone and I have mine. Contact me if you find anything."

"Ellery . . ." She set her shoulders against further argument, but he merely brushed her arm with his fingertips. "Be careful."

"You, too."

Light on the path shrank by half when Reed's flashlight disappeared onto the lower part of the trail. She could glimpse him at first, a flicker visible through the brush and branches, but then the light winked out for good. She stumbled over an exposed tree root, barely catching her balance. She couldn't see more than a few feet ahead of her. An owl screeched its disdain for human intrusion into the nighttime hours, the sound like nails down her spine. She pressed onward and upward, her calves starting to twinge at the unrelenting climb. She and Bump usually took the trail at a slow pace.

The humidity dampened her T-shirt into a second skin and perspiration condensed on her forehead and upper lip. She paused to listen but heard only her own heightened breathing and the distant sound of rushing water. She was nearing the stone dam, which was itself a work of art comprised of marble bricks stacked more than sixty feet high. A crack of a branch to her left made her freeze. She trained her light into the forest and saw the glowing eyes of a pair of foxes looking back at her. They watched silently, heads turning in unison as she continued onward toward the sound of the water. As she neared the river, the trees thinned and parted to reveal the gleaming water.

Ellery halted. There, in the middle of the river, standing on one of the dam's low columns, stood Bobby Frick. He was bare chested and staring down into the canyon below. Ellery knew the view was spectacular during the daylight hours—curved rocks carved out like honeycomb by the melting glaciers over thousands of years. The trickling of the river, slowed to a brook by the marble dam, bubbled over the rocks and highlighted their nooks and crannies. Bobby appeared to be unseeing, as if in a trance. Ellery took her phone out and texted Reed:

I FOUND BOBBY. HE'S ON TOP OF THE DAM. NO SIGN OF CHLOE.

She took a careful step from behind the protection of a tree so that she could get a better view of the surroundings. The fast-moving river stretched perhaps eighty feet wide and the other side of it was cast in deep shadow. She did not see any indication that Chloe was nearby, and she had a flash of terror that Bobby might be staring down at her in the ravine. She crept closer, moving in slow motion so as not to draw his attention. The roar of the water felt like it was inside her head. She held her breath as she reached the cliff's edge. Her vision swam, vertigo seizing her as she forced herself to look at the bottom. She exhaled in a rush when she saw the naked rocks and water below. No Chloe.

She eased backward in relief. "Bobby Frick," she called sharply, and his head whipped around to look at her. The square column he perched on was only about a foot above the waterline, just at the edge of where it went over the dam.

"Stay back!" He grabbed a gun from the waistband of his jeans and pointed it at her chest.

"Easy," she said, holding up her hands. "I'm not here to hurt you."

"Too late," he said. Then he screamed it, head back and shouting to the sky, "You're too fucking late!"

Ellery licked her lips and tried to remember Dorie's training.

Empathy first, no matter what horror they've committed. *Make them believe you are a friend.* "I'm sorry about your mother!" she yelled to him over the rush of the water. He stopped screaming and looked at her. "About Carol," she continued as she stepped forward. "It's awful what happened to her. What happened to you."

"She was the hero. Everyone just forgot about her."

"They focused on the boy," Ellery agreed, keeping her tone neutral. She advanced a step closer to the rocky dam. "It wasn't fair."

"She tried to save his life. He wasn't even her son. I was her son!"

"You were younger than him when it happened. Too young to lose a mother."

He wiped his face on his bare arm, his hand still clutching the gun. "They sent me and Lisa to different homes. Hers was nice, I guess. Mine didn't have enough food, and guess who got to eat last?"

"I'm sorry. I know how that goes. The empty feeling in your belly could swallow you whole. You can't think about anything else." She stepped up onto the edge where the water ran over the top, spreading her arms to keep her balance against the current. The cold river seeped into her boots, rising like the tide.

"What are you doing? I said stay away!" He pointed the gun at her again.

"I want to help you," she said, standing still.

He gave a bitter laugh. "No one wants to help me. Except maybe Lisa, and she has her own life to worry about. I just drag her down."

"That's not true. Lisa loves you. She's worried about you right now." She waded in closer to him, water up past her knees now. "I talked to her earlier tonight, and she very much wants to see you."

"You talked to her?" He sucked in his lower lip, considering. "Is she—is she mad at me?" His voice cracked at the end, like the hurt little boy he'd once been.

"She doesn't want you to get hurt. She loves you."

He shook his head resolutely. "No. It's too late. Why were you talking to her, anyway?"

"We were looking for you."

His expression darkened again. "No, you were looking for her. The girl. Don't lie to me and say it isn't true, because I know how you cops operate."

"I didn't say I was a cop."

"How many cops you think I've known? They came by the dozens at first, ripping up every inch of our little house, looking for some answer that they would never find. I heard the talk. They thought maybe my mother brought the murderer to the Stone place, that he was after her. Like they could pin it all on her."

"It wasn't her fault. It wasn't Teresa's fault, either."

He trembled at the words. "She called her! That was my mother's whole life, you know, living by someone else's schedule. It didn't matter if we had T-ball or felt sick or were on our way to the city pool. You know what my mother was doing when Teresa summoned her that afternoon? She was cleaning out Beth's room. She had to stop sorting her dead daughter's clothes to go polish silver for some dinner party. No one ever gave a damn about her and what she wanted. If one of her richie-rich clients called up with a hangnail, she had to go running over to help them. They never had to alter their perfect little lives."

"You think Teresa's life has been perfect?"

"She got herself a brand-new family, didn't she? A kid she barely sees. I know because I watched her for weeks. She was always at home or with the nanny, being trotted off to dance or swimming or piano. She looks happiest at the Y among the poor kids, if you can believe that. Teresa would probably shit a brick if she knew her precious daughter was mixing with the masses. My sister wanted to take dance, you know, back when she was a kid. Mom said too bad, we couldn't afford it, so Lisa used to twirl around in her bathing suit to the radio."

"You wanted to teach Teresa a lesson," Ellery said, wading in farther until she was just ten feet away from him.

"She got to start over. Her life wasn't ruined—it got better. She married an even richer asshole and got a fancy job at a big hospital. Her kid was running off on her. Did you know that? When I grabbed her, she'd ditched her regular phone in the garbage and was heading for the T. Her nanny didn't have a clue about it, either. No one gave a damn until I made them care."

"You were making a point. I think it worked."

"You're damn right it worked."

"But you don't want to hurt Chloe. It's not her fault who her mother is."

"She's better off this way."

A chill went through Ellery at the finality of his words. "Where is she now?"

Bobby looked down at the swirling water and rocks below. He did not answer.

"Bobby, where is Chloe?" she asked, her voice low and urgent.

A thrashing noise at the tree line jerked Bobby's attention from the water. Reed appeared, huffing and puffing from having run straight up the steep incline. "Cops are like friggin' rats," Bobby muttered. "Where there's one, there's dozens more you can't see." He turned his fevered gaze to the trees as if searching them out. "Go ahead!" he yelled into the forest, spreading his arms wide. "Shoot me."

He staggered forward, his bare toes at the precipice of the stone column. A few more millimeters and he'd tumble to the rocks below. "Bobby, listen to me. No one wants to shoot you. We want to help you."

"It's too late," he said, his tone turning mournful. His gun dangled from his right hand, maybe four feet now from Ellery. "Tell Lisa I'm sorry." The hand with the gun started to rise.

"No!" she shouted, and surged through the water at the same time, closing the gap between them with a single desperate lunge. She knocked the gun free and it sailed over the edge into the ravine. Bobby tried to leap after it. "No!" she cried again, clutching for him as he slipped on the wet rocks and slid down into the waterfall.

He grabbed her arm. She almost went with him. He sputtered as water poured into his face. "Ellery!" Reed screamed her name from the shoreline.

"Hang on. I've got you." Bobby had hold of her, really. She needed all her strength to keep from falling. She panted from the effort required to brace herself on the column, holding both their weight. Her arm felt like it would tear off. Dimly, she heard Reed crashing into the river after them. "Help is coming," she panted to Bobby. "Hang . . . on."

"No," he gasped around the water that splashed over his face.

The stone scraped her belly, her arm. They slipped farther over the edge. "Where is Chloe?" she said through gritted teeth. "Tell me."

"She's gone. In a better place. She'll be happy." His wide eyes bored into hers. "So will I."

He let go and fell straight down onto the rocks. Ellery sobbed and covered her ears instinctively as he hit the ravine. Reed reached her at that moment, pulling her from the edge as they fell backward together into the river. "I couldn't stop him!" she cried, completely drenched. She felt drowned, half-dead. She tried to sink back down, but Reed held her up.

"I know. I saw." He clutched her to his chest, and she heard his heart pounding like a hammer. Far overhead, a helicopter arrived with its searchlight. It found them easily and pinned them with the bright white light. "We need to get to shore," Reed said. "We need to get help."

Ellery looked to the edge of the dam and the water coursing over it. She didn't have to see the body below to know that Bobby was right: it was too late.

30

Reed sat in the waiting room of the E.R. where Ellery was being treated for minor scrapes, a twisted ankle, and a dislocated shoulder. The worst he'd endured was some uncomfortably damp clothes. He sat forward, his head in his hands, trying to stay awake. He had consumed three cups of black coffee already, but far from being energized, he felt smudged at the edges, like a sketch that had been drawn and erased several times. He sat up just in time to spot a familiar figure through the glass doors. Lisa Frick lingered near the rear exit as though she couldn't quite bring herself to leave. Reed forced himself to his feet so he could go make his condolences.

"Ms. Frick," he said, and she looked up in surprise. He saw she held the old family photo Bobby had left her at his apartment. "I'm so sorry for your loss."

She blinked back tears and showed him the photo. "Everyone in this picture is gone now, except me."

"I'm sorry," he repeated. He held out his arms in case she wanted a hug, and she almost fell into him.

"Why did he have to do it? Why did he leave me like this?"

"I don't know."

She pulled back, her chin wobbling. "Isn't that your job? To understand why people do these awful things?"

Reed considered. "Can I buy you a cup of coffee?"

Lisa looked at the exit and then back at him. "They have his body upstairs. I know he's gone, that he won't know if I leave, but I can't make myself go through the doors."

"Let's sit." He walked her to a quiet corner of the waiting room and then went back to the coffee stand once more.

"Just can't get enough, huh?" The guy behind the counter gave Reed yet another cup of coffee, and he stopped to scoop up a cream and a couple of packets of sugar just in case. Lisa Frick took them all without comment but didn't move to drink the coffee.

Reed lowered himself into the chair next to her. "People commit suicide because they're in terrible pain," he said softly.

"I didn't know it was this bad." Her head bowed, tears leaking from her eyes once more. She used the paper napkin Reed had brought to wipe them away and set the coffee on the floor by her feet. "He didn't tell me."

"He may not have had the words."

She took out the picture again and stared at it. "Dad getting killed in the accident was terrible at the time. I had no idea back then that it was just the start."

"You mentioned that before," Reed said. "That your father was killed in an accident."

"He was walking home from work in a storm and a tree fell over on him."

Reed had seen the police reports. Vincent Frick died from two gunshot wounds to the chest, not a fallen oak. "Who told you about the tree?"

"My mother, I guess. Maybe Beth. I was five at the time, so I don't really remember."

Perhaps the family had lied to the young kids to protect them, to help them feel safe after their father's death. Reed's family had lied to him for decades out of a misguided attempt to shield him from his origins. Love justified a multitude of sins. And yet. The tragedy that engulfed the Frick family felt like a house on fire, and Reed was not convinced the flames were out. "Beth had a scholarship to Penn," he said. "Do you know if Ethan Stone had any role in helping her attain it?"

"Maybe? She was so much older than me that she seemed more like a grown-up, another mom. We didn't talk about her scholarship. I remember Ethan Stone came to the house to pick her up once. He drove a red sports car and everyone came out to see it. Beth waved to us as they drove away." She leaned back in the seat with a sigh, the old photo on her knee. "You have all these memories, right? They make up the story of your childhood, the one you tell yourself you had. You remember your dad telling ghost stories inside the blanket fort you made. Or your mom making pancakes with curlers still in her hair. Your sister putting on makeup in the bathroom mirror with it all steamy from her shower. Sometimes you have photos, like this one, that line up with your memories. Other times . . ."

"Other times?" he prompted gently when she did not continue.

"Mom used to get bad headaches. She said it was from the cleansers she had to use when working, and she'd come home and lock herself in her bedroom. Beth made us dinner. Or we'd just have cereal. Dad would be angry when he found out. They would scream at each other in the bedroom while we hid in our closet and pretended not to hear."

"I think all families have good times and bad times."

"I always try to remember the good ones. Bobby kept the bad." She drew a shuddering breath and looked to the doors where the EMTs were bringing in a stretcher. "I guess I'm just wondering now which one of us was closer to the truth."

Reed pushed aside the curtain and poked his head into Ellery's room, where she lay dozing, propped up in the hospital bed. Her eyelids fluttered open at his approach. "Did you find Chloe?"

He shook his head and took her left hand, the one uninjured in her grappling with Bobby Frick. "Not yet. They have dogs and search teams combing the park. If she's there, we'll find her."

"You think she's dead."

Reed said nothing for a long moment. "The blood in the van is type B-negative, the same as Chloe's. Bobby Frick was type O."

"There wasn't much blood found. Certainly not enough to say she's dead." She pulled her hand from his and tried to sit up. The drugs made her unsteady and the pain made her wince. "I want to keep looking."

"Ellery, you're hurt and you're exhausted. There are plenty of people searching for Chloe."

"It's not that bad." She bit back a cry as her foot made contact with the floor. Reed stepped forward as she fell backward onto the bed. "Are you going to help me or not?"

"Not," he replied succinctly. "You need rest, not some foolhardy errand."

"It's not foolhardy," Ellery ground out. "Chloe is alive."

"Look, honey, I hope you're right, but I think you need to face the brutal facts here. Bobby Frick was clearly suicidal. He'd abducted a girl and treated her like an animal while she was in his captivity. He told you he wanted to punish Teresa Lockhart, who by his account didn't deserve Chloe, and then finally he said 'she's in a better place,' isn't that right?"

Ellery struggled to sit up using her one good arm. "He could have taken me with him."

Reed gaped at her. "I beg your pardon?"

"On the dam. He had a lock grip on my arm and there was no way I could get free of him. See?" She rotated it slightly to show off the deep fingermark bruises on her forearm. "I was slipping off the column. If he'd just held on, he would have taken us both over the edge. Or he could've just shot me when he had the chance. But he didn't."

"Thank God for that. But he didn't have the same obsession with you that he did for Chloe Lockhart."

"She's alive. I know it."

She rushed to get up, but the twisted ankle wouldn't support her weight. Reed caught her as she teetered and eased her back down to a sitting position on the bed. A choked sob escaped her at this defeat, and the small noise was like a bullet to his heart. Ellery already walked around with the ghosts of the sixteen girls who had died in Coben's closet. Gently, he tugged her head until he cradled her against his shoulder. She smelled like river water. "They're doing everything they can to find her," he whispered to her. "You need to go home and rest." His own face felt cracked and raw with sheer exhaustion.

Dumbly, she nodded and let him help her to her feet. She bit her lip hard as he put her injured arm in the sling provided by the doctors, but she did not make a sound. He collected the prescription painkillers and offered his elbow to her for support. She refused him, of course, limping toward the door on her own, and he managed a thin smile as he trailed behind her. Ellery rebounded like one of those boxing dummies at his gym; you hit her and she got right back up again.

He'd driven her car to the hospital and strategically parked it in the back lot away from the reporters and news vans waiting at the front. There was no way she could drive, so he climbed behind the wheel as Ellery winced her way into the passenger seat. He watched her struggle briefly for the seat belt before reaching over without a word and clicking it into place for her. "Thank you." She took his hand and kissed his palm once before holding his hand to her face. "Reed, I . . ." She looked at him and he thought she might finally say the words. His heart beat faster. He leaned in closer.

A camera lens appeared in the window next to Ellery. *Snap, snap, snap.* Ellery jerked away. A man's face peered in and he started shouting questions. "Agent Markham, Detective Hathaway . . . any leads on where Chloe Lockhart is now? Is Bobby Frick alive?"

Reed started the car and gunned the engine, narrowly missing the reporter's feet as he peeled out of the parking space. He took the speed bump faster than was advisable, jostling Ellery, who gripped the console with her good arm. "Sorry about that."

She leaned her head back and closed her eyes. "They never go away. They never will."

"I'll have you home soon."

"They know where I live. Everyone knows." She sounded dreamy, far away. The drugs were kicking in. "Do you think it will be like that for Chloe? Will they write her story and make a movie? Will they demand she comment every time some other girl goes missing?"

"I can't imagine Teresa will let them."

Ellery hunkered in deeper into the seat, half-asleep already. "She can't stop them," she mumbled. "Nobody can."

Reed drove the rest of the way back to Boston in silence, the sky brightening into brilliant sunshine around him. No matter how dark the night, dawn always arrived. He had stayed awake to see it many times in the course of his career, sometimes because the night's work was not finished, sometimes to remind himself he'd survived. Ellery roused as he hit the city limits, blinking like a mole rat. "Almost home," he told her as she frowned at her surroundings.

"No, I want to go to the Lockharts' house."

"Why?"

"I think I know where Chloe is. Where Bobby put her."

"She's not at home," Reed replied in what he hoped was a reasonable tone. Maybe she'd dreamed some crazy solution that had Chloe home safe and sound, but it was impossible. There had been police at the Lockharts' house round-the-clock for days now.

"I didn't say she was."

"Ellery . . ."

"Are you going to take me there or should I call an Uber?" She grimaced as she took out her cell phone.

"Only if you explain to me what you're thinking."

She outlined an incredible scenario that might as well have come from a dream for the infinitesimal probability that it was real. Reed sighed when she was finished and signaled a turn for the Lockharts' mansion. It was a dream worth believing in.

31

Improbably, Dorie Bennett opened the door of the Lockhart house. She looked Ellery over with a mixture of concern, compassion, and exasperation. "You look like death warmed over," she said as Ellery dragged herself over the threshold. "What are you doing here?" She asked the question of Ellery but looked to Reed for the answer.

"I tried to take her home," he replied. "She insisted on coming here."

"I see." Dorie looked at the car keys in his hand. "Did she also use psychokinesis on you to take the wheel?"

"You've met her, right? What gives you the idea that she's liable to take any advice that I offer her?"

"Hello. I, a person with verbal skills, also exist in this room," Ellery said.

"You probably have a head injury," Dorie told her. "Your vote doesn't count."

"My head is fine. It's everything else that hurts."

Dorie grimaced as she surveyed Ellery's bruises. Her touch was tender but her expression stern. "You know you broke about eleven different protocols by confronting the suspect on your own."

"Go ahead then," Ellery replied glumly. "Write me up."

"No." Dorie palmed her face briefly. "Not this time. You found Bobby by empathizing with him. You got into his head and figured out where to find him."

"For all the good it did."

"We don't get to pick the results, I'm afraid," Dorie replied with a sigh as she drew back. She looked to Reed. "You really ought to get your girlfriend home to bed. She looks about ready to keel over where she stands."

Ellery froze at the word *girlfriend*. She'd been careful not to hint of any personal relationship with Reed to anyone at work. Hell, she had put two feet of space between them right in the crowded entryway. "What did you say?"

"Yeah, sorry. Your story's out all over the news." Dorie took out her phone and showed Ellery the breaking news page. There was a picture of her holding Reed's hand to her face underneath the caption *"SERIAL" LOVE AFFAIR*. The subhead said: "FBI Profiler Reed Markham in Romance with Surviving Victim Ellery Hathaway." Dorie must have read the horror on her face, because she tucked the phone away. "I really am sorry," she said with genuine apology. "I thought you'd want to know the cat's out of the bag."

Ellery shook it off. "Speaking of cats, where is the dog?"

"The dog?" Dorie echoed.

"Chloe's dog, Snuffles. She's still here, isn't she?"

"I've got her." Teresa Lockhart appeared behind them holding the small white dog in her arms. "What do you want with Snuffles?"

Ellery glanced at Reed, who shook his head almost imperceptibly. They'd already discussed this on the way over, and she knew his position: don't tell Teresa. If Ellery was wrong, as was likely in Reed's estimation, it would crush Teresa. *You think Chloe is dead,* Ellery had replied. *At least I'm offering some hope.* To Teresa, she said, "I'd like to borrow Snuffles for a little while."

Teresa put her hand on the dog's head. "Tell me why."

Ellery had been terrified when Reed pried open the closet to set her free. The sound of nails coming loose meant Coben had returned for more torture. She'd heard the tinkle of the nails hitting the ground and prayed for death. When he'd identified himself as a federal agent and scooped her out of there, she hadn't yet believed him. She'd gone with him because she had no strength left to fight. "I think she might be able to help Chloe."

"You know where she is?"

"Not yet," Ellery hedged. "I have somewhere else I'd like to look."

"Fine, then I'll come with you."

"Dr. Lockhart, I know you want to help—"

"No," Teresa cut her off sharply. "I can't stay in this house doing nothing another minute. I'm going out of my mind. From what I know, you maybe understand more than anyone what Chloe is going through right now. So I am begging you to see it from my side. I need to help."

"You're doing that," Reed said. "Being here, supporting the search teams."

Ellery looked to him. He expected to find a body at the end. He didn't want Chloe's mother to see her like that, which Ellery could understand. But she saw the primal hunger in Teresa's eyes, the desperation and desire for any scrap of information on Chloe's condition. She wanted her baby, dead or alive. "You can come," Ellery said. "But you need to stay in the car."

"Okay, yes," the woman replied readily. The dog barked, sensing action.

Reed frowned his disapproval, but he didn't object, probably because he didn't expect to find anything of significance on this mission. "I'll drive."

"I'll come, too," Dorie said. She touched Ellery's good arm lightly. "You'll need both of us to scrape you off the floor when you collapse."

"I have such a supportive partner."

In the car, Ellery explained their destination, and while Teresa didn't seem especially convinced, she agreed to try. "I'd search every house, every quarry, every forest, if I could. I know how it works. I've been here before. Eventually everyone moves on. The helicopters and the dogs and the teams of people will go home, but I'll never stop looking." She held the dog on her lap, petting her absently as she stared out the window, her eyes checking every passing face.

Dorie studied her phone. "Conroy says there is no sign of Chloe so far at the state park. The dogs have been unable to pick up her scent beyond the stolen van."

To Ellery, this was good news. Teresa seemed less sure. "I've had to tell a lot of people that their loved one is gone," she said to the window. "People who die during surgery. Usually the family is expecting it, dreading it, but also hoping like hell it isn't true. You see the tightness around their mouth when you come through the doors and the tears already in their eyes because they know what you have to say to them. Sometimes they lash out. They blame you. Sometimes, maybe, it's even your fault." She looked down at her lap.

"You are not to blame for Bobby Frick's actions," Reed said from behind the wheel.

"Maybe not, but I do share blame." She looked up. "I've looked at Chloe her whole life the way those parents and children and spouses looked to me, just waiting for the bad news. Waiting for the shoe to drop. Dreading the worst will happen." She shook her head vaguely. "Now it has. I feel no better for having anticipated it. I feel no more prepared."

Ellery felt her first unease at bringing Teresa along on the trip, but it was too late to back out now. "We're almost there."

Reed made the last turn and pulled to a stop outside Tyreek Cantrell's duplex apartment building. The door was shut tight, all the window shades drawn as usual. "How do you want to play this?" he asked Ellery.

"Let me have the dog," she said to Teresa.

"Maybe I should come."

"No, not yet." She looked to Dorie. "Make sure she stays put, okay?"

Dorie held up her palms. "It's your play."

Snuffles, all of five pounds, was light enough for Ellery to hold with one arm. She panted eagerly and wagged as they walked up the steps. Ellery guessed the dog lived the same sheltered life as Chloe did. This probably counted as a big adventure for her. Reed rang the bell. They waited, and Ellery saw the nearest window shade move. No one came to the door. Reed rang again, longer this time. Eventually, the door cracked open and Tyreek's face appeared on the other side. His expression was guarded and he did not look pleased to see them. "What is it?"

"Can we come in?" Ellery said.

"It's not a great time. My grandma is sleeping. Late shift at the hospital, you know how it is."

"Yeah?" Ellery turned to look. "Her car isn't parked in the driveway."

Snuffles barked and wriggled, and Ty wrinkled his nose at her. "Is that Chloe's dog?"

"Yeah. She could use some water. Can we come in or what?"

Ty looked behind him for a moment before widening the door. "Okay, just for a second." They followed him to the kitchen, where he tripped over a chair and then fumbled the plastic dish he was using to get Snuffles some water. *Bingo,* Ellery thought.

"Did you see the news?" she asked.

"Yeah, that crazy dude grabbed Chloe. That's wack. I saw he's dead now. Is that true?" He folded his arms over his chest, leaning back against the counter in an attempt to seem casual.

"It's true. We haven't found Chloe, though."

"Yeah?" His voice cracked and he coughed to cover it. "That's, uh, that's too bad."

Ellery put the dog down near the water bowl. She took one lap at it and then took off sniffing around the kitchen. "You have any idea where she could be?"

"Me? Why would I know?" He jumped when Snuffles started vigorously sniffing at a crack under a door. "Hey, she's not going to pee in here, is she?"

"What's behind that door?" Ellery asked as Snuffles started to whine and paw at it.

He scratched the back of his head. "Uh, nothing. I mean, just the basement. There's storage and crap down there."

"I'd like to check it out."

"You guys already been down there," he protested. "Remember? You checked every inch of this place and I told you—I did not take Chloe."

"We believed you then," Ellery replied, limping for the door. She opened it and Snuffles took off like a cartoon animal, paws scrambling, practically leaving a vapor trail in her tracks. She barked excitedly as she hopped down the stairs. Ellery grimaced as she hobbled behind the dog with her bum ankle. Reed and Ty followed, too.

"Look, I can explain," Ty began as Snuffles found another door, this one apparently to the furnace room. She stood on her hind legs and did a dance in front of it. Ellery gave a crooked smile.

"Whatcha got there, girl?" She tugged the door open and Snuffles flew inside—right onto Chloe Lockhart's stomach.

The girl lay on a sleeping bag with a blanket over her. A half-eaten sandwich and a large cup of water sat nearby. She roused as Snuffles wriggled and pounced over her body. "Snuffy," she murmured, giving the dog a clumsy pat. "I missed you."

"She just showed up here on my porch in the middle of the night," Ty said. "You gotta believe me. She said the guy dropped her off and told her not to call the police or he'd kill her mother. I didn't know what to do, man. I've been waiting for Grams to get off shift so she could sort it out."

"It's okay," Ellery said, still smiling. "We believe you. Chloe . . . I'm Detective Hathaway, and this is Agent Reed Markham from the FBI. We're here to take you home now." She knelt next to Chloe and looked her over for any injuries, but the girl seemed to be in better shape than Ellery was. Ty had given her a bandage for the cut on her arm. She had visible bruises on her face and wrists and of course her hair had been shaved off, but otherwise, she appeared perfectly whole. "It's going to be okay. You're safe now."

Chloe cuddled the dog to her chest. Tears appeared in her eyes and her chin trembled. "I want my mom."

"She's right outside."

"Really?"

"She's been searching for you this whole time. Here, can you stand up or do you need help?" She held out a hand and Chloe took it as she got to her feet. She wore a giant T-shirt of Ty's and a pair of gym socks that slouched around her ankles.

"I didn't have nothing that fit her," Ty said with regret.

"You did fine," Reed assured him, clapping the kid on the shoulder.

Ellery led Chloe slowly up the stairs and out onto the front stoop. A second later, the back door of her SUV swung open and Teresa rushed out. "Chloe!"

"Mommy." Chloe sobbed as she fell into her mother's arms. "I'm so sorry. I'm so sorry I ran away."

"It's okay. It's okay. I love you so much." Teresa rained kisses down on her daughter's fuzzy head. "Oh God, thank you so much. Thank you, thank you, thank you."

Chloe sniffed. "He cut all my hair."

"I don't care."

"I threw away my phone."

"I don't care about that, either."

"Mommy." Chloe clung to her and buried her face in Teresa's chest. Her voice was muffled, mournful. "I did a terrible thing. I—I had a second phone. One that . . . that . . ."

Teresa took her daughter's face in her hands. "One that your other mother gave you. Yes, I know."

Chloe cried harder. "No, I didn't want another mother. I just wanted to know the truth. She seemed so nice."

"It's okay, my darling. We'll figure it out. If you want to talk to her, it's fine with me. If you don't want to talk to her, that's fine, too. Whatever you want, I will help you."

Chloe had a death grip on her. "I want to go home. I want to see Daddy. I don't ever want to go outside ever again."

Ellery looked away. That terror was too familiar, even now. Teresa stroked her daughter's back and held her close. "Yes, you will," she said fiercely. "You will grow up and go out into the world and live your life."

"No. He's out there."

"No, he's dead. He can't hurt you anymore, sweetheart."

The way Chloe shrank from the words told Ellery that the girl had already learned the hardest lesson. Bobby Frick was a threat she hadn't seen coming. What you can't see you can't protect yourself from. He might be gone, but there would be others. "He was crazy. He had a gun."

"I know he was scary. I know. I was afraid, too, the whole time you were gone." She rested her cheek on her daughter's head. "You know what else I saw, though? I saw these people—Detective Hathaway and Detective Bennett. Agent Markham. Captain Conroy. So many others, too. Your friends left messages for you. Your friends' parents dropped off food. Hundreds of people came out to look for you and to offer any help they could."

Chloe sniffed and wiped her cheeks with her hands. "What about Devon James? Did he leave a message?"

"Um, I'm not sure. Who is Devon James?"

"The most popular boy in school. He doesn't know I exist."

Teresa hugged her daughter tight. "Well, I'm sure he does now. Let's go home."

Dorie stepped forward with an apologetic cough. "She's going to need to be checked out by a doctor."

"I am a doctor."

"With all due respect, ma'am, you're her mother."

Teresa looked down at Chloe's face and brushed away the last of her tears. "Yes," she said with wonderment. "I'm her mother. Okay, a doctor. But one can come to our house to see her. I am not bringing her anywhere but home." She ushered Chloe to Ellery's SUV, and Ellery turned to see Tyreek watching the whole exchange from his stoop. She limped over to him and he gave her a wary look.

"I'm not busted?"

"You'll probably get a medal from the mayor before it's all done," Ellery said.

He waved her off with both hands. "No, thanks. I'm just glad she's okay."

Ellery looked at the tinted windows of her car, imagining the girl on the other side. "She's safe now. It may be some time before she's okay."

Ty looked uncomfortable. "How'd you know she was here with me?"

"Bobby Frick told me, in so many words. He said she looked happiest when she was with you." She smiled at him. "You've been a good friend to her."

He shrugged, embarrassed. "I don't know. I didn't do much, man. I have no idea what to say to her now."

Here Ellery had a hard-won answer. "Just be the same. Be the person who treats her the same. Because she's not going to get that anywhere else."

He nodded, sober. "Okay. Okay, I'll try."

She joined Teresa and Chloe in the SUV, and Reed drove them back toward the Lockhart house. Chloe promptly passed out in Teresa's lap, the dog curled up with her. As they neared their destination, he said, "You may wish to cover Chloe with a coat for added privacy," and Dorie produced a Boston PD windbreaker from the way back. Reed steered through the gathered throngs, into the Lockharts' driveway and around toward the back of the house. "There," he said with satisfaction as he cut the engine. "Home at last."

Teresa's eyes were wet. "Thank you." She didn't move to get out of the car. "You know the most ironic part of all of this? I didn't call Carol Frick to our house that day. I was in back-to-back surgeries that entire afternoon and well into the evening. It must have been Ethan who asked her to come. Of course, it's the mother who gets the blame, right?"

"Did you tell the police that at the time?" Reed turned in his seat to look at her.

"I don't know. I'm sure I didn't think it mattered." She stroked Chloe's shoulder. "I never dreamed we'd end up here." She nudged her daughter. "Wake up, darling. We're home."

Dorie followed them up the path, but Reed and Ellery remained in the car. "Where to now?" he asked her.

Ellery watched as Martin Lockhart emerged from the back entrance, his face crumbling at the sight of his wife and daughter. "Home sounds plenty good to me."

32

Reed awoke to a strange sensation of cognitive dissonance. He had been sleeping soundly, yet daylight streamed in around the edges of the window shade. Outside the room, the voices that had awoken him were achingly familiar: his wife and daughter, chatting happily about a topic he could not discern. The cadence of their words, their musical back-and-forth rhythm with Tula's giggle as a bubbly grace note, transported him instantly back to his old home. Meanwhile, he had Ellery asleep next to him, her body curled into his with her injured arm cradled protectively between them. He knew it was the drugs that had created this complete surrender in her, but he allowed himself a few minutes to enjoy the feel of her bony knees against his hairy leg and her warm breath fanning across his arm.

When his phone buzzed on the nightstand, he reached over to check it and found he had fifty-seven new messages. Time to get up. He eased out of the bed without waking Ellery from her dead sleep, took a quick shower, and went in search of the voices from the other side of the door. The smell of chocolate hit him the moment he opened it, and he discovered Tula and Ashley frosting a crooked cake at the kitchen island. Bump's long nose reared up to snuffle dangerously close to the edge, but no one else seemed to notice a giant hound on the prowl. "Down, boy," Reed ordered, and they all turned to look at him. The dog ambled over to lick his bare feet.

"It lives," Sarit remarked dryly.

"Sorry."

"It's no bother. The girls baked you and Ellery a cake as a congratulations on solving your case. Of course, they only had me and the internet for instruction, so there you have it." She waved at the lopsided confection.

Reed dropped a kiss on Tula's head. "I love it," he declared.

Ashley frowned at her attempt to make a pink rose. "Do you think Ellery will like it?"

"Ellery will devour it whole."

Pleased, the girls returned to finishing up their work while Reed and Sarit had a side conversation in the living room. "It's all over the news," she told him. "Chloe's parents made an appearance outside their home so the world knows the truth. It's an incredible story, Reed. You saved that girl."

"Ellery did. With maybe an assist from a seventeen-year-old acrobat."

"I beg your pardon?"

"Never mind." He shoved his hands in his pockets. "Thank you for staying with the girls."

"I see it now. It's the victories that keep you coming back, no? Chloe's home. She's okay. Her parents must think you all are miracle workers."

He wondered if this was a side dig at his relationship with Ellery. "It matters even when they don't come home alive." Coben likely had other victims they didn't know about, girls he'd disappeared and carved up and refused to say where they were now. As long as he kept them secret, the dead belonged to him.

"Speaking of home, I need to get back there. So does Tula, as her school starts up again next week."

"Yes, I know. We have tickets to fly back tomorrow."

She bit her lip, hesitant. "If you'd like, I can take her back with me tonight. This way you could stay here longer with Ellery. It seems like she might need someone to help her until her shoulder heals up."

Reed widened his eyes with surprise. "That would be kind of you—presuming you take Tula only as far as Virginia."

"God, Reed, I'm not planning to kidnap her." She gave a small shudder. "Don't even joke about such a thing."

"I'm sorry. You have to understand that it's not a joke to me, Sarit. I won't let you move her half a country away from me without a fight." He kept his voice low, but his intent was serious.

"Yes, yes, message received," she replied, her palms up, and he decided that would have to be good enough for now. He heard the bedroom door open and close and Ellery appeared from around the corner, her hair a hopeless tangle and the triangular imprint of a pillow corner on her flushed cheek.

"Do I smell cake?" she asked.

"Yes!" Tula cried, thrusting her butter knife in the air. "Now we can eat it!"

Reed served them each a piece, congratulating the girls on an admirable first effort. "It's not as good as the ones Daddy bakes," Tula confided to Ellery. "He made me one shaped like a volcano for my last birthday, with red lava running down the side and everything."

"Oh, yeah? He made me one for my birthday, too," Ellery replied, meeting Reed's gaze over Tula's head. He smiled at her in shared memory of the dark chocolate with lavender butter cream frosting concoction they'd shared at the end of an intimate dinner in this very kitchen. She had accused him once of being the man who caught the monster and then went home, never having to deal with the jagged holes the monster's claws left behind. Ellery bore those marks on her body and on her life, with the locks on her door and the scars on her skin and her usual refusal to celebrate her birthday, the day of her abduction. She was right that he would never fully understand. He couldn't climb into the darkness with her. But he could stand in the light and extend his hand and wait patiently to see if she would join him.

She smiled back at him and stuck the fork in her mouth, licking the frosting off with relish. Reed grinned and figured the odds of winning her over had to be in his favor.

His side had the cake.

Reed sat on the sofa, sorting through his messages. Tula and Sarit had left for Virginia, and Ellery and Ashley were headed out to the wharf. "She should see something besides the inside of my apartment," Ellery had said as she winced her way back into her sling.

"But your ankle," he'd protested.

"Also wants to get out of this apartment. We'll sit on a bench and look at the ocean."

She paused with her keys in hand on the way out the door and looked to where Speed Bump lay sprawled under Reed's feet. "You're using my dog as a footrest."

He didn't look up from his phone. "It was his idea. My feet were here first. I can't help it if he's wedged his way under them."

"Well, at least you can't make him smell any worse," she replied. "We'll be back in a couple of hours."

Reed might have said something in return, but he couldn't be sure. His attention diverted to an email message from the Baltimore PD in response to a ballistic test he had asked them to run. The bullet that was recovered from Carol's husband was too degraded to run any conclusive analysis to a specific weapon, but its caliber matched the Beretta recovered from the Stone house. Reed pondered if there might be another way to connect them while he continued through his email messages. He sat up in surprise as he reached one from *People* magazine.

Let us tell your love story, the subject line read. Inside he found a plea from an editor who wanted to interview him and Ellery about their romance. Their readers would be delighted to share in his happiness—it could even be a cover story. Reed snapped the window shut with nauseated horror. Just reading the note made him feel like he was at the end of a fish-eye lens. *My love story is none of your goddamn business.* Ellery wouldn't even say the words to him. They thought she'd somehow sit for an interview? This, he realized with guilty regret, was a mess partly of his own making. He'd written the book on Ellery. He'd sold her story to the masses years ago and still they hungered for more. Their appetite for her, for Coben, felt boundless, and he found himself on the receiving end of the bite. Furious, he opened his laptop and tapped out a heated reply: *Not interested. Don't contact me again.*

He sat back, still stewing. He wanted to punch someone but feared it was his own face that deserved the fist. Moreover, he had two murders that remained unsolved, contributing to the churn he felt in his gut. Bump jumped up and flopped on the couch next to him, his chin on Reed's arm. "I have a gun and a dead body, but I can't connect them with forensics," he told the dog. "What do you suggest?"

Bump rolled over, offering his belly.

"I don't think that will quite do it." Reed gave him an absent-minded scratch. When his fingers trailed off, Bump whined, got down from the couch, and trotted across the room. He stuck his head in a magazine rack and emerged with a half-chewed bone in his mouth, which he brought back and laid at Reed's feet. "That's disgusting," Reed told him, and Bump wagged with enthusiasm, accepting this as a compliment. "How long have you had that thing stashed over there?"

Bump nosed the bone, trying to get Reed to throw it. Reed complied with a sigh. As Bump raced after the skidding bone, Reed sat up ramrod straight. "Wait," he said. "You just might have something there."

Bump grumbled his displeasure when Reed declined to chase him for the bone. He flopped down with a noisy protest while Reed hunted down a phone number for the woman who had, until now, been a footnote in this whole complicated affair. He said a silent prayer that she could help him while the number rang through to Irma Goodwin of Baltimore, Maryland. "Yes, hello?" Her voice had the thin, creaky quality of the very aged.

"Mrs. Goodwin, my name is Reed Markham, and I am an agent with the FBI."

"The FBI? Has something happened?"

"Do you recall telling the Baltimore police about your husband's gun being stolen years ago?"

"Yes, it was a Beretta 92. But I don't know who took it or when. I explained all that to the nice young man from the police who came to ask me about it."

"Your husband kept it in the closet? In a shoe box, is that correct?"

"Yes, the bedroom closet. That's right."

"Ma'am, at any point have you engaged a cleaning service?"

She let out a gravelly chuckle. "A cleaning service? What do you think this is, Park Avenue? Mercy, no. I scrubbed all our floors and toilets myself. Still do, thank you very much."

Reed closed his eyes, his hopes fading. "I don't suppose you knew a Carol Frick socially then. Maybe through church or something like that?" The two women were different generations and lived in different parts of the city. If they'd crossed paths some other way, it would be hard to imagine where.

"Carol Frick, did you say?"

"That's right."

"A redhead, wasn't she? A little bitty thing. Yes, I remember now. We had a terrible ice storm—gosh, it must have been about twenty years ago—and I slipped on the back steps while taking out the garbage. I broke my left leg and was out of commission for six weeks.

The neighbors chipped in to hire a woman to come tidy up the place a few times while I was stuck on the couch, and her name was Carol Frick."

Reed made a fist of victory. Here was the last puzzle piece. He just had to fit them all together now. "Thank you, Mrs. Goodwin. It would be helpful to know the exact dates that Carol Frick came to your house. Do you think you can find that out?"

He heard her wooden chair slide out from the table. "I keep all the old calendars. Let me check them for you."

He waited, convinced this had to be it. He heard her footsteps and the clunk of the phone against the table as she picked it back up. "It was twenty-one years ago this winter," she said. "Does that help?"

Reed did some quick mental math. "Yes, I believe it does."

33

Perfect summer afternoons with a high blue sky and the salty ocean breeze almost made up for the brutal winters that held Boston hostage for nearly one-third of each year. Ellery sat on a shaded bench with Ashley, each of them in possession of a fresh-squeezed lemonade, near enough to see the boats on the harbor. Seagulls swooped in and out around them, patrolling for any piece of lost pretzel or hot dog that a wayward tourist might have dropped. Nearby at a playground, children laughed and chased each other around while tired parents chatted in the shade and called out periodic weak reprimands to stop throwing sand. The parents watched the children. Ellery watched the perimeter out of habit, just in case. Ashley saw her staring and turned her head.

"What are you looking at?"

"Nothing." There was no one. Not this time. "How's your lemonade?"

Ashley fiddled with her straw. "It's good. But we should probably head back soon."

Ellery gave her a questioning look. They hadn't been sitting long, and frankly, her bum ankle could use the rest. "There's no hurry."

"Yeah, there is." Ashley squinted out at the water. "I called Dad this morning. He's flying out to pick me up."

"Oh. That's good, I guess."

"I thought you'd be happy. I'll be out of your hair."

"No, I, uh, I'm glad you've patched things up with him."

Her sister snorted and kicked at the grass with one foot. "I didn't say that. He's still royally pissed at me for coming out here without asking. But I didn't have a choice. He wasn't going to say yes if I'd asked." She risked a quick look at Ellery and ducked her head. "Neither would you."

Ashley was right, but Ellery felt guilty that she knew it. "You don't know that."

"You didn't tell me. You came to see me when they did the transplant, but you didn't tell me anything about who you were. You just left after the procedure and didn't say a word."

Ellery pursed her lips. "I wrote to your father. He said you were doing well."

"Yeah, but you didn't say anything to me." Her voice was small and hurt.

"I'm sorry."

"Are you?" Ashley looked her over searchingly and then slumped back against the bench. "I know I probably seem like some dumb kid to you."

"No," Ellery said with feeling. "That's not true."

"I remind you of him. Dad. Of what he did to you."

"Maybe at first. A little. But now you remind me of you." She smiled at the girl. "And maybe a little bit of me."

Ashley smiled back almost shyly. "Really?" She hesitated. "Because I was thinking that I could apply to college out here. Mom says I have a good chance at some big scholarships on account of the cancer. Turns out you can write a kick-ass sympathy essay when you almost die and live to tell about it."

A laugh escaped Ellery. "Yeah, that's about how I did it." She hadn't considered this commonality with Ashley before. Odds said they should both be dead, and yet here they sat in the summer sun.

"And maybe, if I came out here for school, we could hang out sometime. Almost like real sisters."

"We're already real sisters."

"Yeah?" Ashley smiled, but it didn't reach her eyes. "You said Dad's not ever going to be your father again."

"That's different," Ellery replied with a sigh. "And it was his decision. He's the one who walked out and made no effort to contact me for years. Daniel died thinking his father didn't give a damn about him. Maybe it wasn't true, but that's how it felt from our end, and he did nothing to show us otherwise."

Ashley nodded, glum. "You can't forgive him. I understand."

"What he did to us doesn't matter for you. I'm glad he got his act together and that he's been a good dad to you. You deserve that. It's not your fault he settled down and stayed."

Ashley turned to her. "And it's not your fault he left."

Dammit, she was not going to cry in front of this girl. Ellery squeezed Ashley's hand as hard as she could. "That's right," she said, her throat tight. "It's not. So what do you say we head back and meet the old bastard?"

At the apartment, Ashley gathered her things while Ellery limped around tidying with Reed fussing behind her. "I can do this," he said as she attempted to fold a blanket with one arm. "Just tell me what you want me to do."

"By the time I tell you, I can do it myself."

He folded his arms. "Are you sure about that?"

She cursed as the blanket slipped through her fingers. "I don't even want him here," she said in a low voice.

"Then he waits downstairs," Reed declared flatly. "You don't have to let him in if you don't want to."

"Part of me does want to," she said, angry at the tinge of hysteria in her voice. "That's the crazy part. I want him to see this place and know I can afford it. I earned it. I decorated it. I live here by myself and I'm completely fine with it."

"I know you are," Reed said, trying to be soothing.

She let the blanket fall to her feet. "I hate that I even care what he thinks."

Reed stooped to pick up the blanket and he folded it in two seconds with his perfectly good arms. He handed it back to her with a tender smile and she held it against her chest like armor. "You won. He lost. He probably doesn't even realize how much he lost, and that's a shame. But it's his shame, not yours."

"Right." She took a deep breath just as the buzzer rang. "It's show time."

John Hathaway looked relieved that she opened the door for him. "Ellie." She still hadn't adjusted her mental image of him as the big strong man who walked out the door. He was older and grayer now, still tall but not as beefy. His brawn had moved to his gut and stayed there. "It's good to see you," he said, shoving his hands in his pockets.

She replied with a curt nod. "Come in. Ashley's about ready."

Bump read her body language and hung back behind her rather than giving his usual enthusiastic greeting. Her father tried. "Hey there, boy. Aren't you a handsome fella?"

Bump gave two perfunctory thumps of his tail and looked to Ellery for guidance. "Oh, go ahead," she muttered, and he went almost sheepishly, his tail between his legs, to collect his ear rubs and pats on the back. He returned immediately after to her side.

Her father looked around her loft apartment with naked curiosity. "This is a nice place you have here. Right downtown? Must cost some serious dough."

He had left them with no way to pay the rent. Her mother had worked two jobs just so they didn't get evicted. "I get by," she said evenly.

"Hi, Dad." Ashley appeared with her backpack in hand, and he broke into a wide grin at the sight of her.

"Ash, I missed you, kid. You about gave me a heart attack, running off like that." She let him hug her but did not return the embrace.

"Running off with no warning," she said. "It must be in my genes, huh, Pops?"

He became uneasy once more and let her go. "At the airport, all the TVs were playing some story about a kidnapped girl," he said to Ellery. "They say you found her." Ellery said nothing. Her father nodded at the sling. "Looks like you went about twenty rounds with the guy, eh? I always knew you were tough."

Ellery looked away. *Whatever you have to tell yourself to make it through the night,* she thought.

"Dad, shouldn't we be going?" Ashley said pointedly.

He looked to Ellery like he wanted to say more but didn't have the words. "Yeah, I guess so," he said at length. "Thanks for looking after my girl."

"She's part mine now," Ellery replied.

Ashley beamed and rocked on her toes with happiness. She bounced in front of Ellery and then sized up her injuries. "A half hug for a half sister?" she suggested, holding out one arm.

"Give me a second." Ellery grimaced as she slowly removed the sling. "There," she said, cautiously extending both arms. "The whole tamale."

Ashley teared up again as she moved in for a cautious embrace. "Thank you," she whispered against Ellery's uninjured shoulder. "For everything."

Ellery touched the back of the girl's head. "Text me when you get home."

She watched from the window as they climbed into a ride share and drove away. She turned to find Reed had disappeared into her bedroom again, and she dragged herself to collapse on the couch. Bump joined her and she closed her eyes, enjoying the quiet of her mostly empty apartment. Her father's remarks made her curious about the newscasts and what they might be saying about Bobby Frick. She located the remote and clicked around until she found the local news, where, to her horror, she found her own face. A woman with a frosted-blond bob and impossibly red lipstick was opining about her relationship with Reed.

"You have to remember, Cindy, they met under extremely emotional circumstances. Frightening circumstances. The moment of her rescue would be supercharged in their brain circuitry forever. Strong emotions like that can take on different emotional shading with time."

"I'm sorry. She was fourteen back then. A child. Are you saying he was attracted to her?"

"No, probably not then. I'm saying that because of their history they both get a brain buzz, so to speak, when they are in each other's presence. Over time, that buzzing may turn into attraction."

"I don't get it," said the anchorwoman. "Imagine having a serial killer for your matchmaker." An image of Francis Coben from his federal trial flashed on the screen and Ellery shrank back into the cushions. She grabbed the remote and clicked the television off, but her heart continued to pound even in the silence. She screwed her eyes shut and tried to breathe. She'd been an idiot to think it would ever work with Reed, that they could invent whatever relationship they wanted. Their story only ever went one place.

"Ellery?" Reed poked his head out from her bedroom.

She jerked up. "Yes?"

"Come see what I've done with your bedroom wall."

"I'm not sure I want to," she grumbled as she gingerly got up from the couch. "I like my wall the way it was."

"It's a temporary redesign."

She discovered he'd tacked up a bunch of yellow sticky notes. Each one had his handwriting on it, and she moved closer to inspect them. "'Irma Goodwin breaks her leg,'" she read off the first note. She turned to him. "Who is Irma Goodwin?"

"That's the start of it all," he said, a glint in his eye, the satisfaction of a man who had cracked the puzzle. He seemed to want her to play along now, but her head hurt.

"Reed, just tell me. What is all of this?"

"It's the answer to who killed Trevor Stone and Carol Frick," he replied, and she looked with fresh eyes across the long string of sticky notes. She limped along, barely reading them until she got to the end.

"Oh my God," she breathed as she pulled the square of paper free from the wall to stare at his conclusion. No wonder the cops had been running in circles for fifteen years. They had the theory of the crime wrong from the very beginning. Reed had discovered the answer to a question no one bothered to ask.

Reed put his hands on his hips and surveyed his handiwork. "Mind you, I can't actually prove any of this yet. I'm not sure it would ever rise to the level of a criminal prosecution."

"Who would you even prosecute? Bobby Frick was right about one thing—we're far too late."

He made a beleaguered gesture at the timeline. "Yeah, but if this is true, Bobby Frick was wrong about everything else."

34

The dean's office at Penn displayed several oil paintings of past men who had held the title. They wore dark robes and serious expressions, and Reed felt their eyes on him as he sat with his brief-case full of scant evidence at his feet. In the end, he had pinned his hopes on some old phone records, a piece of charred jewelry, and the only timeline of events that made coherent sense. His boss had demurred when Reed pitched the idea of this particular confrontation. *It's not the agency's purview,* she had said. *It's a university matter.*

The university failed to act, he had protested. *It set everything in motion.*

Even if I find that argument persuasive, and believe me, I'm inclined to find fault with them, it doesn't change the facts.

The facts are currently not on record, he'd replied. *We can change that.* This case had been a wrecking ball swinging loose through multiple families now. He could not repair the damage, but he could perhaps bring it to a halt.

He sat with the current dean, George Altman; the attorney representing the university, Ava Moss; and Ellery, who had insisted on coming even if she, too, was skeptical of what the outcome would be. *The actual murderer is beyond criminal prosecution at this point. All you have left is . . . I don't know . . . humiliation and public ruin,* she'd said.

Then public ruin it shall be, he'd replied.

He turned as the last person joined the meeting. Ethan Stone stopped with surprise by the open door, but he recovered quickly and forced his features into a welcoming smile. "George, good to see you. Agent Markham, I didn't realize you'd be back to visit us again so soon. Teresa's daughter is home safe and sound, I see. How wonderful."

"Thank you for coming, Ethan," the dean said. "Won't you have a seat?"

"Of course." His gaze slid to the lawyer, Moss. "It's Eva, isn't it?"

"Ava Moss," she said without a trace of warmth. Reed had given both the dean and the attorney a brief synopsis of the reason for this meeting.

"And this is my colleague who has assisted me in the investigation, Detective Ellery Hathaway," Reed said, indicating Ellery.

Ethan's eyes lingered on her. "I think we all know Ms. Hathaway. Not as well as you do, though, I'm sure." Reed took out his folders and put them on the table in front of him without opening the contents. Ethan regarded them with interest. "I thought you closed the case—Chloe's abductor killed himself. He was that boy of Carol's; at least that is what I read in the papers."

"You read correctly," Reed told him. "We're not here to discuss Chloe Lockhart's kidnapping. We're here because we finally know what happened to your son."

He sat back, his jaw going slack with shock. "Trevor? You know who killed him?"

"Yes, but we can't start with that day, not if we're to understand what happened. We have to go back some years. You're a world-renowned expert in economics, Professor Stone. What would you say that the basic principle of economics is?"

A furrow appeared in his brow. "Supply and demand, I suppose. Why?"

"Everything has a price. Is that right?"

"Yes. It varies according to relative scarcity of the goods or services in question and the size of the consumer audience."

"And there are trade-offs. You give up something to get something."

"Of course. I don't see what this has to do with Trevor."

"He was the price," Reed said, his voice taking on a hard edge. "The one you didn't see coming."

Stone turned to the dean in confusion. "George, help me out here. What is he talking about?"

"Shut up and listen," Altman replied.

"Carol Frick had been cleaning your house for about three years at the time of her death and that of your son," Reed said. "How did you come to hire her?"

Stone appeared incredulous. "That was twenty years ago. You expect me to remember a decades-old interview process for a housekeeper? Teresa and I both worked long hours. We had a small child who liked to track dirt into our house. We needed someone to help out. I don't recall how we found Carol. She may have been recommended by a friend or we may have called a service. Teresa handled most of our household affairs, so you'd do better to ask her."

"That's interesting you would mention Teresa's role as head of the household."

"I didn't say that. I said she managed the household."

Reed held his gaze. "Is there a difference? You just admitted you have no idea how Carol Frick came to be in your employ."

Irritated, Stone held up his hands in mock surrender. "Okay, Teresa wore the pants in the family. Is that what you want me to say?"

Reed took out the phone records from the folder in front of him. "So Teresa was the one who coordinated Carol Frick's schedule. She told her when to come and what you needed done on any particular week, is that right?"

"Yes. I didn't notice when the silver needed polishing." He said it like tracking this work was beneath him, but Reed would wager he'd notice if the flatware showed up tarnished on the dinner table.

"The day Trevor died," Reed said, sliding the phone records across to him, "Teresa didn't call Carol Frick. Neither did you, it seems. The records indicate that Carol called your office here at the university. Three times, in fact. Do you remember what you talked about?"

Stone did not immediately pick up the paper. He looked at Reed, his gaze assessing, trying to work out the correct answer. He cleared his throat and glanced at the phone records. "I'm afraid I don't re-call. Carol would phone me sometimes if she had a question—did we want her to change the bed linens or that sort of thing."

"You just said Teresa handled any instructions to Carol."

"My wife was busy with her surgeries. She wasn't always reach-able." He gave a thin smile. "My job is comparably more sedate."

"Carol phoned you three times that afternoon. That's a lot of questions."

"I don't know what to tell you. Maybe she got my secretary on her first couple of tries." He pushed the paper back at Reed. "You were going to tell me about Trevor."

"Yes, I promise it's all related." Reed took out a different piece of evidence, a photo of the gun retrieved from Ethan Stone's backyard. "Do you recognize this weapon?"

"No. Should I?"

"It was recovered from the shed behind your old house."

"I've never seen it before in my life. It certainly wasn't ours. Teresa saw too many gunshot wounds in her line of work. She would never abide a gun in the home, and I wasn't keen, either. Not with Trevor so young and Justin . . ." He trailed off and shifted uncomfortably in his seat. "Well, Justin had problems that could only be exacerbated by the presence of a weapon. Let's leave it at that."

"Would it surprise you to know it has been linked to a murder?"

He startled. "Murder. But . . . Trevor wasn't shot."

"No, it was used to shoot Vincent Frick."

"Vincent," he said, his eyes narrowing. "Carol's husband."

"Ah, so you know of him."

"Just by name. I heard he died, but I didn't know any details. I was under the impression it was some sort of accident."

"No, Carol murdered him with this gun. She stole it from one of her clients in Baltimore."

"What?" Shock colored his features. "She murdered her husband?"

"And collected fifty thousand dollars in life insurance money, which she used to relocate to Philadelphia and put the down payment on the house she shared with her children. You remember her children, don't you? Beth, the oldest, would have been about fifteen at the time Carol started working for you."

"I knew she had kids. I didn't know she'd killed anyone."

"Beth had a scholarship here. I understand you had a little something to do with that." He took out a copy of Beth Frick's senior year portrait, which he'd found in the school yearbook. It showed a young woman with chin-length auburn hair, a shy smile, and silver and mother-of-pearl earrings in the shape of seashells. He showed the portrait to Ethan Stone, who appeared reluctant to look at it.

"I probably helped her with her application—read it over, offered a word of advice here or there to enhance her chances. I do that with my friends' kids all the time, so I'm sure I would have helped this girl, too, if her mother had asked. But I'm not on the admissions committee." He pushed the picture back at Reed after barely glancing at it. "If she got a scholarship, she did it under her own merits."

"Her grades were top-notch," Reed agreed. "She was captain of the volleyball team."

Ellery took the picture and looked at it at length. "Those earrings look expensive," she said. "I know my mother never could have afforded anything like that when I was in high school."

"Maybe she had a rich boyfriend," Stone said. He made a show of checking his watch. "Can we skip ahead to the part about Trevor? I have a seminar to deliver."

"We've got your class covered," Dean Altman informed him, and Stone stopped short. He tapped his fingers on the table and regarded the lawyer as if seeing her for the first time.

"What's she doing here?" he asked.

"Observing," she replied, looking up from her notes.

"The thing is," Reed said to Ellery, "the earrings aren't that expensive. They look like they could be pricey, but these are mass-produced and probably retailed for around a hundred dollars." She knew this. They had already discussed the whole case in detail, so this conversation was for Ethan Stone's benefit. "They're essentially costume jewelry, well made as such—enough to fool someone young or without a lot of experience with fine jewels."

"That would be me," Ellery agreed. "I'm surprised you can tell so much just from this picture."

"Oh, I can't." Reed withdrew another piece of paper. "The insurance company had them appraised. See?"

Stone stretched his neck out like a turtle to see what Reed had handed to Ellery. "What's that?"

"It's the insurance assessment from a car fire," Ellery said as she read it over. "Your car fire, as it happens. There was a seashell earring found among the debris. You don't recall this?" She gave him the printout to read.

Stone took longer than necessary to examine the scant few lines that detailed the inventory from the fire. "No," he said finally. "What a coincidence. I guess Teresa must have owned a similar pair of earrings."

"We asked her," Ellery told him, her gaze turning steely. "She denies ever owning any earrings like these."

He snorted. "Of course she would. She'd deny ever knowing me if she thought she could get away with it. Look," he said, opening his body posture, trying to smile, "I remember now buying those earrings for Teresa. It was a little souvenir I picked up for her on a business trip to Quebec many years ago."

Reed saw his left eye twitch. "You buy a lot of jewelry." He pulled out more paper from his notes and put on his reading glasses to consult the list. "Two sets of earrings, a necklace, and a half-dozen bracelets in the past year alone. One of them contained actual diamonds." He peered over the top of his glasses and across the table at Stone. "You must have had a great deal to apologize for that time."

Twin spots of rage appeared on Stone's face. "You've been prying into my records? Is that legal? Can he do that?" he appealed to Ava Moss, who dismissed him coolly.

"I'm not here for you."

"Then I'm not here at all," Stone said, shoving back from the table.

"You don't want to know about Trevor?" Reed asked, and Stone halted with his hands balled into fists. "Or maybe you know already. Maybe you've always known, deep down."

"I don't know what you're talking about."

"You abuse your students," Reed replied. "You grope some and court others. We tracked down that diamond bracelet and found it in possession of a young woman named Shelby Colson. She was your teaching assistant last year. You seduced her, and when she tried to break it off you didn't take no for an answer. She ended up in the E.R. with a split lip and a broken collarbone."

"And she says I did it to her?"

"No, she's sticking to her story that she went over the handlebars on her bicycle." Reed paused for effect. "I talked to her roommate, though. It seems that Shelby doesn't own a bike."

"Beth Frick had next to nothing," Ellery added. "Her mom blew through the insurance money in under a year and the family was back to barely scraping by. Beth knew the only way out was to go to a good school, and her mother said she knew someone who could help her with that. She turned to you. You met with the girl, showed her around, maybe took her out to a fancy meal at the club on campus. You're a big man around here, right? She would have been wowed by you."

"They all are at first," Reed said. "Isn't that right? And then when it goes bad, when you push it too far and hurt them, they think it must be their fault. You're practically a god at this place."

"I don't have to stay here and listen to this bunch of lies." He tried to push past Altman to the door, but the dean stopped him with one raised hand.

"Actually, you do."

"George, you can't believe what he's saying. It's pure fantasy."

"Sit down."

Stone refused. He stood by the table with his arms folded. "You're wrong about everything, and if you breathe a word of it outside this room, I will sue you for defamation."

"You gave Beth Frick those earrings," Reed said calmly. "Whether it was before or after you slept with her, I don't know. It's been so long and too many players in this drama are not around to confirm the gaps."

"Gaps? Canyons, maybe. This is a bunch of horseshit you're shoveling. George, you can't be buying any of it."

"She threw the earrings back at you, probably when she turned up pregnant. I can imagine how terrified she must have been, how angry. Her future had been set and now suddenly everything went to ruin. She set your car on fire."

Stone's jaw worked back and forth. "So you say."

"You're right. I can't prove it. But I think you knew who it was even at the time, which is why you tried to prevent any real investigation. You wanted the whole mess to go away quietly, including Beth, and she obliged you by driving her car into a cement barrier."

Ava Moss stopped taking notes. "Are you saying the girl killed herself?"

"It's impossible to know for sure," Reed said. "What we do know is that the day Trevor Stone was murdered, Beth's mother, Carol Frick, was cleaning out Beth's room. Something she found in there triggered her to call Ethan Stone at his office. Repeatedly. When she couldn't reach him, she went to the house. Maybe she was looking for him. Or maybe she was already looking for Trevor."

He looked to Stone, whose face drained of color, his lips bloodless and waxy. "N—no," he stammered, shaking his head.

"You took her child," Reed told him. "So she took yours."

"No, it can't be. Someone broke in. A stranger. One of the land-scapers."

"No one broke in. Carol had a key, if she needed it, but the back door was open. She knew where you kept the recycled plastic bags because she often put them there herself. She didn't grapple with any murderer at the top of your staircase. She went to Trevor's room, surprised him from behind with the plastic bag, and smothered him to death. Then, in despair and fearing the consequences of her ac-tions, she threw herself off the upstairs walkway onto the marble floor below."

Reed laid out all the evidence end-to-end on the table. Ethan Stone's feverish gaze swept over it once and then again. "You're wrong," he whispered.

"It's the only explanation that fits."

"She killed him. My God, we sent flowers to her funeral."

"But you didn't attend," Reed said. "You probably couldn't bear to look at her surviving children, knowing what you'd done."

"She murdered my boy." He leaned heavily on the nearest chair. "He was innocent. He didn't ask for any of this."

"Neither did Beth," Ellery said.

"Or Shelby," Reed added. He nodded to the dean, who leaned over to the phone in the middle of the table.

Altman picked up the receiver and hit two buttons. After a brief pause he said, "Selene, could you please send them in? Thank you."

The door opened and four young women filed inside. Professor Stone looked up in horror as he recognized them. "Neither did Anita," Reed said, his voice rising. "Or Meredith. Or Isabelle. Or Laurie."

The women held up their pieces of jewelry as their names were called in turn. They looked on as Stone crumpled under the weight of their names, the strength of their presence. "Please," he said, tears coming at last, tears Reed knew were only for himself. "You have to understand. She's the killer. Not me. I never meant to hurt anyone."

Here Bobby Frick had the answer all along. Reed stretched across the table to speak softly in the professor's face. "Too late."

35

The high green trees of Rittenhouse Square stirred in the breeze, the faint rattle of their leaves the only sign of the arriving fall. The citizens of Philadelphia lay out in tank tops and sunglasses and strolled the cobblestones in flip-flops and summer sandals. A passing Corgi with its wide smile and panting tongue made Ellery smile and think of home. She walked with Reed in this city that did not lay claim to either of them, betwixt and between as they ever were when they were together. It felt like they were always saying good-bye.

"Do you really think it's fair to blame Ethan Stone for his son's death?" she asked Reed from behind her sunglasses. "Carol Frick was the murderer. She killed a twelve-year-old boy, and for what? Revenge? Nothing she did that day helped to avenge her daughter."

"She was a ticking time bomb," Reed agreed with a slight incline of his head. "Ethan Stone just pulled the pin. But you could argue he pulled a lot of pins with his gross misconduct over the years. He misused his power and his privilege over those young women, using and abusing them without a second thought to any consequences—a perversion of his office, both literally and figuratively."

Ellery watched a big-eyed toddler with crazy hair run pell-mell toward the fountain with his mother scrambling fast behind. She caught him just before he would have face-planted into the concrete rim. "Teresa is going to be horrified when she finds out she hired her son's murderer."

"It's not like she could have known. Baltimore PD had Vincent Frick's death listed as a mugging gone wrong. Carol wasn't even a suspect."

"So, what's the answer? Suspect everyone all the time? Trust no one?"

"Teresa has tried living like that once already. It almost cost her a daughter."

"Damned either way then," Ellery said with a sigh. "What about Lisa Frick? Have you told her yet that her mother was a murderer and not the hero they'd believed all along?"

"Not yet." Reed stopped and squinted into the distance. "I don't look forward to that conversation. She's the last one left. Her family destroyed itself around her."

"The sole survivor," Ellery murmured. "Not an easy way to live."

Reed looked sideways at her as they continued walking. "You don't have to worry that the press will come for her, not after the first wave, at least. There won't be any books or TV movies."

"You sound pretty sure of that."

"There's no happy ending here."

It was her turn to stop short. "There never is," she told him. "There's only what people want to believe when the credits roll or you turn the last page. In real life, there's only . . ." She searched herself for the words. "Enduring. Continuing on."

His brows knit together in concern. "You're saying you're not happy?"

"Right here? Now, with you? Yes. Or close enough to it for it to count." She tilted her head to the side and forced a smile. She would not cry. Not yet, not in front of him. This was more than she'd ever asked for, and she tried to tell herself it would be enough. Fall was coming, and winter after it. She had to hold tight to the warmth while she could.

Reed appeared to be turning over her words in his head, wondering if he could live with them. "Roll the credits now then," he said, reaching for her with a smile. She let him take her hand and pull her closer. "Let's be happy. I'm going to kiss you now and I don't care who sees it."

A shiver of anticipation battled with her usual flash of anxiety at being seen with him in public. *Let's be happy.* She decided to try, if only for a few hours. She didn't know when she would see him again after this. They kissed once and then again, more lingeringly. He held her tight against his body and she felt his smile on her neck. "We should go to the hotel," he murmured. "I want to kiss you again."

She ran her hand down his back, her nails lightly scratching. "It's okay. For today, I don't care."

"Well now, that's a lovely sentiment," he said, extending out his Southern drawl, "but I think the authorities might object to the kind of kissing I have in mind, should we attempt it here in public."

She threw back her head and laughed. "Lead the way then."

At the check-in desk, reality tried to prove her point to Reed. The young man with the gold name tag lit up when he recognized Reed's distinctive moniker. "You're that FBI profiler," he enthused, pointing at Reed. "The one who caught Francis Coben. I read your book."

"Thanks," Reed said flatly. "Is the room ready, then?"

The guy's gaze slid to Ellery and his eyes widened some more. "And you're that girl."

"Look here," Reed began, his temper rising, but she laid a hand on his arm to stop the protest. It wasn't worth it. He couldn't argue with every bellhop or waitress or gawker in a suit on the subway. She didn't want to spend her last precious hours with Reed fighting a battle they had already lost.

Inside the suite, he frowned when he saw there was a closet. He removed his necktie and knotted it around the double handle, tying it securely into place. "Will this suffice?" he asked.

She smiled and reached for the buttons on his shirt. "It's a start." She thought about all the rules she had for them, all the things she said she wouldn't do with him, and how she'd tossed every one of them by the wayside, the deeper in they got. Her body usually took convincing even now. It had been conditioned early against the weight of a man above her, trying to force her to feel something, and it didn't matter that Reed brought pleasure instead of pain. Her brain hushed it up this time as they fell into bed together, or maybe her skin recognized this would be its last taste of freedom for a good long while.

She closed her eyes and the lack of sight magnified all her other senses, filling her with the sounds of them, their breathing and murmurs, the soft rustle of clothing being eased aside, the scrape of his teeth against her plastic buttons as her shirt came undone in his mouth. The man had skills, and she tried not to think about where he honed them, not when his tongue was tracing the outline of her bra as his hands slipped down to her rear, urging her closer against him. Moments like this, she never wanted to be separate again.

In the aftermath, she lay curled on her arm and admired the fringe of his lashes as he slept next to her. She marveled that this beautiful man had somehow been hers to keep in these quiet hours, alone and away from prying eyes. If they could stay like this, just the two of them, she would never leave. He must have felt the weight of her contemplation, because he opened his eyes and looked at her. The slow, appreciative smile that graced his face made her heart hurt for what she had to do. He took her hand and kissed it. "Are you hungry?" he asked.

She shook her head. This small gesture was enough to put him on alert, because he sat up against the pillows.

"No? Are you okay?"

She took his hand this time and held it against her body. She couldn't look at him. "I love you," she confessed, and heard his answering intake of breath.

His thumb grazed her navel. "And I love you," he murmured.

She squeezed him hard and shut her eyes. "But I have to go."

"What? I thought we had until the morning at least."

"I'm sorry. I just can't do this anymore."

"Do what?" he asked, confusion evident in his voice.

Her throat closed up so tight she could barely get the words out. "Be with you." She dropped his hand and fled the bed, picking up her clothes as she went. "It's not you," she said with her back to him as she struggled into her jeans. "It's him. It's always, always him."

"Ellery, wait. Please. Let's talk about this." He got up naked and came to her.

"No." She swallowed and stepped back from his reach. "I'm stuck with him forever, but you're not. You—you don't belong with me. You have a daughter and a job who need you more than I do. You can have a life of your own."

"It's my life. I choose how I spend it, and I choose to be with you."

She blinked back hot tears. At least he got a choice. Coben was just one of a hundred monsters Reed chased down, another notch on his belt. If people talked to him about Coben, it was with admiration and awe. She was the girl he'd carved up, raped, and left for dead. The scars he'd left on her body marked her as his even as he sat rotting in prison halfway across the country.

"Is this about what happened downstairs?" Reed asked as he put on his clothes. "About the new movie coming out?"

She shuddered at the very mention. "No. And yes. There's always going to be another movie. That's the point."

"Screw the movie. It'll be fiction anyway, and you know it. It doesn't matter what story they make up. You and me, we know the truth. We *are* the truth." His voice was low and gruff, with a note of pleading that tore at her.

"But it's not just you and me, is it? It's the guys I work with and your ex-wife and the people on the street who never stop staring. When it's just you and me, I'm freer than I've ever been, but we can't stay here, Reed. This isn't your home and it's not mine, and neither of us can pack up and be where the other one is. Even if we could, it's not like we could hide from the outside world forever. Whenever we go out, it's always the same thing—you're the profiler and I'm 'that girl.' It's exhausting. It's terrifying. It's like I never got out of that closet."

"You make me sound like him."

"You're not," she said, her voice breaking. "But you're linked to him as surely as I am, and so he's there between us whether we want him there or not."

He sank down on the bed, defeated. She swiped at the tears on her face and tried to calm the erratic beating of her heart. She felt like she was bleeding on the inside. "When did you decide all this?" he asked finally.

"A while ago."

He nodded to himself. "What was all this, then? One last hurrah?" He gestured at the rumpled sheets around him.

Her chin trembled, emotion threatening to spill out of her again, and she clamped her jaw shut. "I—I wanted to see you," she said when she trusted herself to talk again. "I wanted to tell you that you're the best thing that ever happened to me, and that's not because of what happened with Coben when I was a kid. You saved me back then, yes, but it wasn't any kind of life. I was dead inside, numb to everything." She stumbled as the tears caught up to her. "Now I can feel, and I know that because my heart is in a million little pieces right now, and even though it hurts like hell I'm still grateful."

Reed surged upward and took her in his arms with a desperate force. "We can find a way to make it work. We can."

She let him hold her, this man who always believed the impossible, until she dried her tears against his hot skin. His faith had saved her once, but it wasn't enough now. "I'm so sorry," she murmured as she pulled away.

"So that's it?" he asked, his voice scratchy and raw. "You walk out like this and we never see each other again?"

Their story had been told a dozen times already and would surely be retold a dozen more. On some cable channel somewhere, a not-Reed would find a not-Ellery and pull her from that closet, setting in motion a series of events that would inevitably lead them right back to this moment. She almost laughed from the absurdity of it. "It depends," she said, giving him a watery smile, "on whether you think the credits have rolled yet. Until then . . ."

He got her reference. Nodded faintly. "Enduring," he said with resignation. "Carrying on."

She kissed his cheek fiercely in one last good-bye. "It's all there ever is."

Epilogue

A dismal January rain slashed at the windows while Reed watched from inside as Sarit unpacked Tula from the back of her Prius and hustled her up the steps to Reed's condo. He had the oven on to preheat, ostensibly because he intended to bake cookies with his daughter. The truth was he was cold. His most recent case had taken him to Aberdeen, South Dakota, which lay frozen under a foot of snow. That's where he'd found the missing young farmer, too, with a bullet in his head and a revolver in his hand.

"Daddy!" Tula gave him a wet hug around the waist and he returned it with a squeeze. The only time he felt real emotion these days was when he was with her.

"My sweet," he said. "I have everything ready for chocolate chip cookies."

"Yummy," she proclaimed as she bounded into the house and raced to her room to inspect that it was untouched since her last visit. To his surprise, Sarit lingered in the entryway, her boots dripping on the slate tile.

"I thought you would like to know," she said stiffly. "I won't be going to Houston. The job at the *Chronicle* fell through, so Randy and I are going to have to do long distance for a while. You'll have to give me some tips."

"I wish I could." He looked away. "Ellery and I broke up." He'd spent the past few months not saying the words, hoping she would change her mind. She hadn't.

"What? What happened?"

Francis Coben grabbed her off the streets and nearly killed her, Reed thought but did not say. He'd hoped he could be strong enough to outweigh the Coben legacy. He'd spent years looking at the story and seeing himself as the key figure, the hero. Hadn't the movies always turned on his dramatic rescue? Only now did he understand. His role was incidental; Coben was the reason the movies got made in the first place. As long as the fascination with his murders remained at a fever pitch among the general public, it didn't matter how many inches of concrete held Coben in his cell. He was everywhere all at once. Even, it seemed, between Reed and the woman he loved. "Long distance is hard," he said to Sarit. "I wish you luck with it."

"Thanks," she said glumly. She looked past him to the kitchen. "Cookies are a good way to drown your sorrows."

"Would you like to help make them?" he asked, surprising himself.

Sarit appeared downright flummoxed. "Me?"

"Sure." He shrugged. "Tula would love it."

"Well, if you don't mind . . ."

He held out his hand for her coat. "We can't eat them all ourselves."

Tula jumped in delight when she discovered her mother was staying to bake cookies, and her chatter helped fill the chasm left between her parents. Reed took the first sheet of finished cookies out of the oven just as the mail came through the slot at the front door. "I'll be right back," he said, wiping his hands and going to pick it up.

Junk, the water bill, and a white envelope with a postmark in Boston. Ellery. He tried not to look too eager as he tore it open.

He eschewed social media and so did she, so he'd been reduced to hoping her name would show up in the Boston papers. She and Dorie had solved a drive-by shooting a few weeks ago that made some headlines because it took the life of two teenage boys. He'd found news footage from the scene and glimpsed the familiar shape of her in the background. No quotes, no comments. Ellery didn't like the cameras.

A piece of plain white paper fell into his hands, along with a small clump of dark hair, and he realized instantly the handwriting wasn't Ellery's. It was Coben's.

Agent Markham—

It's been so long since you've been to see me that I've wondered if you'd forgotten about me. I decided I'd write you this letter to renew our acquaintance. It's quite dull here and I've had the opportunity to do some thinking. It occurs to me that we could collaborate on a new project. Wouldn't that be exciting? Mind you, I could have approached any number of law enforcement officials with this prospect, but I feel like you are the one who truly understands me.

You remember Tracy Trajan? Sweet girl, if a bit thick around the ankles. Lovely hands. I know her parents have been looking for her for almost twenty years now and I thought maybe you and I could help put their minds at ease. We could work together to find that girl. They keep my contacts here limited, but I do have a network that feeds me information. I believe I have a tidbit that could be useful in bringing poor Tracy home. I'd be happy to share it with you if you would be so kind as to bring me what I need.

Please let me know soon if you'll proceed. Tracy's parents shouldn't have to wait another day.

Yours,
FMC

Reed looked down in horror at the hair in his hands. Tracy Trajan had nearly jet-black hair, the same hue as the strands included in the letter. "I'll be right back," he called to Sarit and Tula. "I just need to make a phone call."

He went to his office and shut the door, his hand shaking so hard he could barely dial the number. His boss did not seem pleased to be bothered on a Saturday. "What is it?" she asked.

"It's Francis Coben. He sent me a letter at my house." How he got the address, how he was able to mail the thing from Boston when he was supposed to be locked up on death row in Indiana, was a terrifying mystery at this point.

Helen Fielding didn't have to have the urgency spelled out for her. "What does he want?"

"He wants to tell us what happened to Tracy Trajan." She'd been abducted from her neighborhood in the suburbs of Chicago in the late 1990s, around the time that Coben was active. They'd questioned him multiple times about her disappearance, but he'd always insisted he didn't know anything about her. None of the remains unearthed from Coben's farmhouse had belonged to Tracy.

"Finally," Helen replied. She, too, knew Coben and his hunger for the spotlight. "What's the catch? Does he want a national TV interview or something?"

"No, it's worse than that." Reed looked down at the letter, the one with a familiar zip code on the postmark. *Bring me what I need,* Coben had written, and Reed knew that meant only one thing. He sat back in his chair and closed his eyes. "He wants Ellery."

Acknowledgments

Four books in now, and I am more appreciative than ever of the terrific people who help me make this happen. I am fortunate to work with the great team at Minotaur, especially my intrepid editor, Daniela Rapp. Her instincts are never wrong, and this book is stronger for her input. Thanks also to Cassidy Graham, for her good humor and attention to detail in helping make this train run on time. If you've heard of this book and found it somewhere, that's probably due to the hard work of Kayla Janas and Danielle Prielipp. They are creative and amazing!

Thanks also to my terrific agent, Jill Marsal, who cheerfully answers all my annoying questions.

I am especially grateful to readers, many of whom I've heard from and whose comments, questions, and concerns are always a joy. I love that a shared passion for the written word connects us all.

As ever, this writer gig is way more fun if you are a member of #TeamBump. Thank you for your feedback and encouragement. I am blessed to have a crackerjack squad of betas that includes Katie Bradley, Stacie Brooks, Ethan Cusick, Rayshell Reddick Daniels, Jason Grenier, Suzanne Holliday, Shannon Howl, Robbie McGraw,

Michelle Kiefer, Rebecca Gullotti LeBlanc, Jill Svihovec, Dawn Volkart, Amanda Wilde and Paula Woolman.

Thanks as always to my wonderful family, especially Brian and Stephanie Schaffhausen and Larry and Cherry Rooney, for love and support.

Finally, if inspiration starts at home, I am the luckiest writer on the planet because I live with two inspirational human beings: my marvelous husband, Garrett, and our phenomenal daughter, Eleanor. They are the source of all my joy.